Lisa Brackman has worked as an executive at a major motion picture studio, an issues researcher in a presidential campaign, and as the singer-songwriter & bassist in an LA rock band. She's lived and travelled extensively in China. Brackman is a southern California native and lives in Venice, CA.

DAY OF THE DEAD

A holiday in Mexico is just what Michelle Mason needs after her husband dies, leaving behind a scandal and a pile of debt. On the beach, she meets a handsome American ex-pat — the margaritas have kicked in and she decides: why not? But their date ends horribly when Daniel is attacked by intruders in her hotel room. When Daniel disappears, Michelle is drawn into Mexico's dangerous underworld of corrupt policemen and powerful drug lords. What was a holiday romance suddenly becomes a matter of life or death. Can she trust Daniel — or is he responsible for the danger she is in?

LISA BRACKMAN

DAY OF THE DEAD

Complete and Unabridged

CHARNWOOD
Leicester

First published in Great Britain in 2012 by
HarperCollins*Publishers*
London

First Charnwood Edition
published 2013
by arrangement with
HarperCollins*Publishers*
London

The moral right of the author has been asserted

A catalogue record for this book is available
from the British Library.

ISBN 978–1–4448–1656–3

Published by
F. A. Thorpe (Publishing)
Anstey, Leicestershire

Set by Words & Graphics Ltd.
Anstey, Leicestershire
Printed and bound in Great Britain by
T. J. International Ltd., Padstow, Cornwall
This book is printed on acid-free paper

To my dad, who tried to be a good guy.

1

Michelle dropped the sarong she'd started to tie around her waist onto her lounge chair. Nobody cared what her thighs looked like.

Sand burned the soles of her feet as she walked down to the water. Look at these people, she thought. Foreigners, mostly. Like her. Older, a lot of them. Sagging, leathered skin, the ones who'd been here awhile. Pale tourists, big-bellied, pink-faced, glowing with sunburn. A family of locals — Mexicans anyway, who knew if they were really from here? Dark, short, and blocky, eating shrimp on a stick from the grill down the beach, giant bottles of Coke tucked in a Styrofoam cooler.

Out of shape. Lumpy. Flabby. Aging.

Nobody cares.

And her thighs weren't bad, anyway.

She stood at the water's edge, watching the rainbow parasail from the real-estate company lift a middle-aged woman into the soft blue sky, the motorboat gunning its engine and heading out into the bay, avoiding the banana boat undulating up and down as it hauled a load of college kids south toward Los Arcos. She watched them gripping the yellow tube with their knees, shrieking with laughter, several clutching beers, tanned and young and healthy.

They'd drink until they puked, screw each other till they passed out, go home and post about their awesome vacation on their Facebook pages.

She waded into the water until it was up to her hips. Warm as a bath, but the surf was pounding. She stood there trying to resist the pull as the receding waves sucked the sand out from under her feet.

After a while she'd had enough and went back to her lounger beneath the *palapa*.

She tried to read her book. It was about a woman whose marriage had broken up, and she'd learned to bake bread. Bread and muffins. After about thirty pages, Michelle was willing to bet that the heroine would end up with the overly educated woodworker and not the stressed-out options trader.

'Ma'am? Can I get you something? Something to drink?'

The hotel waiter, dressed in a white guayabera and smudged white pants, stood above her, round, sweating, tray in hand. Nutbrown, gray-haired, creases marking his face like wrinkles in a crumpled shirt.

She thought about it. 'A margarita, please.'

Why not? She didn't need to be sober to follow this plot.

They'd already paid for the vacation. It still seemed like an extravagance. She and Tom were going to go together. A getaway. A celebration, he'd said.

She wondered what it was that he'd wanted to celebrate.

★ ★ ★

She must have fallen asleep for a while. That was sort of the point with these vacations. You partied at night. Got up earlier than you'd like. Grabbed your *palapa* while the sun was still low behind the eastern mountains, spread out your towel on your blue canvas chair, put on your sunblock, found your place in your novel. First cocktail at lunch, to wash down the greasy quesadillas brought out to you on a paper plate. Try to ignore the vendors selling jewelry, blankets, offering to braid your hair, massage your feet. At some point you'd close your eyes, tired as they were from reading in the shaded sunlight, irritated from the sunscreen sweated into them.

When she opened her eyes, it was late afternoon. She'd been dreaming, about something. About being too hot. About . . . what was it about? About somebody breathing in her ear. Leaning over, touching her shoulder. A man, but not Tom. *Didn't you forget?* he'd asked. *Didn't you forget?*

A few clouds had come in, but it was still hot, and the sun glared in her eyes. She blinked a few times. Then something blotted out the light.

A parasail, between the beach and the sun.

It took a moment for her eyes to adjust. The parasail was its own small eclipse, dark against the sun. Now she could see it — the bloodred parachute, white letters glowing.

TOURISM KILLS! they spelled. In English.

Michelle blinked again and stood.

An atypical crowd had gathered on the beach. Elegantly dressed men and women — a wedding party, she thought at first. Waiters rushed to fill

3

shot glasses with tequila. Photographers ringed the group, pointing their cameras at the parasail, which was heading back from the bay.

Now she could see the person in the harness. Even at this distance, he appeared huge, roughly as spherical as a balloon. As he descended, she saw that he wore a three-piece brown tweed suit and a red plaid tie.

She wished she had her camera. But it was locked up in the hotel's safe . . . too valuable to risk leaving on the beach while she napped or waded.

The parasail crew — tattooed, in surfwear T-shirts and baggy trunks — kicked up sand as they staggered under the parasail rider's weight, trying to guide him to his landing, and for a moment Michelle thought they would all collapse in a heap. But at the last second a third man dressed in a crisp linen suit stepped forward, bracing his hands against the fat man's chest, pedaling backward until at last the body in motion came to rest.

The people in the crowd cheered and raised their glasses in a toast.

'That was different.'

Michelle turned.

The man next to her smiled.

'Yes,' she said. 'What was it, exactly?'

'Arts festival. It's running all this week.'

He was an American, or sounded like one. About her age. Tanned so dark that the creases around his eyes fanned out like tiger stripes.

'Should be interesting,' he said, 'if you like that kind of stuff.'

4

He wore a pair of baggy swim trunks and a faded batik shirt. Gray flecked his hair and the stubble of his beard, but he was rangy trim. A fit fortyish.

'Do you?' she asked.

'It's kind of fun,' he said with a shrug. 'I mean, art, you hang it on a wall or put it on a pedestal. I'm not sure what this is.'

'Performance,' Michelle murmured.

By now a procession had formed around the fat man: the well-dressed crowd, the photographers, and a group of young musicians wearing matching T-shirts, singing 'Paperback Writer' in perfect harmony. Together they set off down the beach, north toward the pier, laughing, drinking tequila. A brown dog followed in their wake.

'I was going to get a drink,' the man said. 'Would you like to join me?'

★ ★ ★

His name was Daniel. 'I live here part-time,' he explained. 'Got a condo in Amapas.'

'Are you retired?' she asked.

He drew back, mock offended. 'Wow. I hope I don't look old enough to be retired.'

'Not at all,' she said. 'But you never know what people's situations are.'

'Well, I'm not loaded either,' he said with a grin. 'I'm a pilot. The work is sort of freelance. So I have some flexibility about where I spend my time.'

They sat at a table under a *palapa*, on the sand. The sun wouldn't set for another few

5

hours; the restaurant staff had just begun to bring tables out to the beach for dinner. Michelle expected that the restaurant would not be full, even with the arts festival. Memorial Day weekend was the last gasp of tourist season in Puerto Vallarta, and it was still pretty quiet. Too hot this time of year. The crowds came earlier, for Easter and spring break, and later in the fall, after the rains.

'A pilot. For an airline?'

'No. Private company. We fly Gulfstreams and Citations mostly. Rentals.'

He scooped up guacamole with a chip, spooned salsa on top of that. 'You know, businessmen who can't afford their own but want to impress a client. Rich guys who want to get to a golf course or a football game in a hurry. That kind of thing.'

She nodded and sipped her margarita. They made good ones here. Not too sweet. You could taste the lime. 'Sounds fun,' she said.

He smiled. 'Works for me.'

The sun had moved behind a bank of clouds, illuminating them like a bright bulb in a shaded lamp.

'Check it out,' Daniel said.

She looked where he pointed. A pair of dolphins surfed at the crest of a wave. They leaped above its crest, plunged back into the water, caught the next swell, then shot up again, twisting in midair like a pair of dancers.

'Better than Sea World.'

She nodded. 'It's beautiful here.'

Daniel leaned back in his chair, took a final sip

of his drink. 'How long are you staying?'

'I'm not sure. My flight's on Sunday. I might change it.'

She wasn't sure why she said it. She had no real intention of changing her flight. It was just that when she thought about what was waiting for her in Los Angeles, it was easy to indulge in the fantasy of staying a little longer. Of never going back.

'Nothing pressing back home?'

He was looking at her in that way, sizing her up, what her intentions were, what she might be willing to do.

She shook her head.

'Are you retired?'

She laughed briefly. 'I'm between things.'

He didn't ask questions. Michelle wasn't sure how she felt about that. She wasn't ready to talk about any of it, certainly not to a stranger, but on the other hand one does like to be asked.

'This is a good place to be,' he said. 'When you just want to relax and figure things out.'

Maybe that wasn't such a bad answer.

He was a good-looking man, she thought, with sharp cheekbones and a firm jaw, sky-blue eyes that stood out against his black hair and dark tan. The gray in his hair, the crow's-feet around his eyes, made him more attractive. To her anyway.

Otherwise he would have been too perfect.

Men like that could have anyone.

'Another margarita, ma'am? Sir?'

Daniel grinned. 'I'm up for it if you are.'

She hesitated. This was her second of the day,

7

and she hadn't eaten much.

Losing control would be a bad idea.

'How would you feel about dinner?' she asked.

* * *

They had another drink so they could watch the sunset, ate some more guacamole to absorb the tequila. 'There's a restaurant not too far from here I like,' Daniel said.

'I'm not really dressed.' She'd only put on a gauzy white blouse over her bathing-suit top, wrapped the sarong around her hips.

'What you're wearing is fine,' he said, giving her a quick, appreciative look. 'It's a casual place. Lots of people go there after the beach.'

The restaurant was a few blocks away, on a street that ran up from the beach and bordered a small plaza, where there were a number of restaurants that catered to tourists. Farther up the street were shops, mostly clothing stores and handicrafts: Huichol beadwork, hand-tooled leather, embroidered blouses. Michelle had walked up there the day before.

'There's always lines out the door,' Daniel said. 'It's one of the only decent places to get Mexican food around here.'

They waited outside, by the open-air grill, where a woman made tortillas and a man tended meats.

'Really?'

He shrugged. 'Well, I'm sure there are some places the locals go to that I don't know about. Here in Zona Romántica — you can get better

Mexican food in Los Angeles.'

Michelle nodded. 'I'm from Los Angeles,' she mentioned.

'Oh, yeah? I love L.A. Where do you live?'

'Brentwood.'

Of course, that wasn't exactly true. The storage space with her things in it was in Torrance.

But she'd lived in Brentwood, before.

'Nice,' Daniel said. 'Good weather, right, that close to the ocean?'

It was hot inside the restaurant, even with the fans, even though the front was open to let in whatever breezes there were. There weren't any. The air was weighted down by heat and humidity, immobile.

Daniel recommended the tortilla soup. They both ordered a bowl. Had another round of margaritas. Mariachis played, whether anyone wanted them to or not.

'Hey, Danny!'

The man who approached their table was soft-featured, in his thirties, wearing Dockers and a polo shirt.

Daniel shifted in his chair. 'Ned, hey.' Something close to a frown creased his forehead.

'Man, I can't believe I ran into you here. I was just, you know, on my way to the restaurant, and I saw you.'

'Yeah, well, we're having dinner,' Daniel said.

Ned shuffled from one foot to the other, rubbed his hands together. 'I don't want to interrupt. But, look, I really need to talk to you. When you have a chance. Are you around, or . . . ?'

'Can you make it to the board meeting? We can talk then.'

'I guess . . . I'll try . . . It's just . . . kind of time-sensitive.' Ned looked around, eyes darting, still rubbing his hands. He reminded Michelle of the tweakers she used to know in high school. 'Hey, you could come by the restaurant tomorrow night. I'll hook you up. We're running some great specials. Surf and turf. Got some good wines in, too.' He finally focused on Michelle. 'You could bring your friend.'

'This is Michelle,' Daniel said. 'From Los Angeles.'

'Oh, cool.' He extended his hand to her. She took it. Sweaty, not surprisingly. 'My place is just down the street. The Lonely Bull.' He smiled at her for a moment and seemed to lose focus. 'Hope you can make it.'

'I don't know, man,' Daniel said. 'I've got some stuff going on. Look, just give me a call tomorrow, okay?'

Ned nodded like a bobblehead doll. 'Okay. Great. I'll call you.'

'The board meeting?' Michelle asked after he'd left. 'Are you in business together?'

Daniel snorted. 'With Ned? No.'

By now their carnitas had arrived, along with another round of margaritas.

I'm getting pretty buzzed, she thought. She no longer cared.

'The board meeting, it's just a bunch of us expats who get together on Fridays, at El Tiburón. We hang out, watch the sunset.' He stared at her. 'Think you'll be around?'

'Maybe,' she murmured. 'Tiburón. Like the town in California?'

'Maybe.' He grinned. 'It's Spanish for 'shark.''

★ ★ ★

By the time they finished eating, it was almost eleven. Not that late, but after all the drinks and a day in the sun Michelle had to step carefully off the high curbs onto the cobblestones. That was the thing here — the curbs were not a uniform height, you couldn't just assume you knew how to judge the distances.

'Whoa!' Daniel said, catching her elbow, steadying her.

Michelle giggled. 'Glad I'm not wearing heels.'

Now they had reached her hotel, bypassing the open-air lobby and entering through the arches that bordered on the wide, cobblestone drive.

'Which way is your room?'

Through the courtyard, to the right, in the tower overlooking the beach. Watch for the slick terracotta tiles, the sand gritting underfoot. Wait for the elevator, and when it doesn't come, climb the stairs to the fourth floor.

Michelle felt around in her sisal tote bag for her key, found the hard plastic wedge stamped with the room number, the key attached. Her hand closed around it.

She turned, her back to the door.

'Well,' she said.

'Well.'

He leaned down and kissed her. She tasted salt — from the drinks? From the ocean? She leaned

11

into him, let her hand rest above the small of his back. He pressed against her, hard. She wrapped her leg around his, felt his hands on her ass, lifting her up.

'Wait,' she said. She showed him the key.

He grinned. 'I was hoping you'd ask me in.'

The room was stifling. She'd turned the air conditioner off, out of habit. She switched it on, and the unit rattled to life. It smelled musty, like the spoiled damp of an old refrigerator. Still, with the sliding glass doors that led to the balcony left open, you could hear the ocean, catch a whiff of its brine.

Daniel stood and watched her, a dark silhouette.

'Come here,' he said.

By the time they'd made it to the bed, the air conditioner had chilled the room enough that Michelle was grateful for the warm breeze that blew in from the balcony.

'You have a beautiful body,' Daniel said, running a hand lightly over her belly.

'So do you.'

The words sounded stupid as soon as she said them. You don't tell men they're beautiful.

Daniel didn't seem to mind. He looked pleased. 'Gotta keep in shape for the things I enjoy.'

He had a nice body, he really did. Lean but not stringy. Energetic. She hadn't been with anybody like him in a long time. Certainly not Tom, and she'd stayed faithful to Tom.

Tom with his big belly, his barrel chest. Twelve years older than her and not exactly a stud.

'Hey.' Daniel said. 'Hey, what is it?'

She was crying, goddamn it. She rarely cried. She hated it.

'Hey.' He smoothed the hair around her face.

He was looking at her now, and she could tell what he was thinking: Great, I'm in bed with a crazy woman.

'Sorry,' she said. 'I'm sorry. Don't . . . It's stupid.'

'Listen, I mean, if you're not into this . . . '

He tried but could not quite keep the irritation from his voice.

'I am. I'm sorry. It's just . . . ' She tried to smile. 'I haven't dated in a while. My husband . . . '

'So . . . you're married?' Now the irritation seemed mixed with curiosity.

No disapproval at least. Perhaps a calculation about whether this was worth it.

'No. Not anymore.'

'Oh.' Daniel rolled over onto his side, propped himself up on his elbow. 'Yeah. It's tough getting back into things after you split from somebody you've been with for a long time.'

'My husband died, actually.'

She enjoyed it in a way, getting the reaction, seeing the look on his face, the shock, the embarrassment.

'I'm really sorry,' he said.

The way he said it, so simply, made her flush with guilt.

'No, don't be, I really . . . ' She wanted to reach out, wanting to touch him, to encourage him, but it felt so awkward, so phony.

'I want to,' she finally said. 'It's just a little hard.'

Daniel extended his hand, rested his palm on her cheek for a moment. 'Look. We both had a lot to drink. This is all kind of intense. Maybe I should just go.'

This time she did reach out. 'No. Stay. If you want.'

They tried again. But the energy that had gotten them into bed was gone now, dissipated, and after a few perfunctory thrusts Daniel stopped and mumbled, 'I'm sorry. I'm really tired.'

'Don't apologize.' She tried to smile. 'You've been great. I haven't.'

'Don't worry about it.'

His face was dark above hers, but she thought his expression was kind.

She kissed him, slowly.

'Mmmm. That was nice,' he said.

After that they both fell asleep, not spooning but close together, Daniel's hand resting on the hollow above her hip.

So many noises here. The familiar: unmuffled motorcycle, snatches of music, pounding surf. The unfamiliar: songbirds singing foreign tunes, parrots squawking, the *toc-toc* cry of geckos.

What woke her?

A muffled thud. A clatter. She blinked her eyes open. Two men, one entering from the balcony, the other crouched over the chair, Daniel's shorts in his hand, her totebag on the floor by his feet.

'Hey!' Daniel flung the sheet off, bolted out of bed.

Now Michelle saw they wore kerchiefs over the lower halves of their faces. The second pulled something from his pocket, something dark that he gripped in his fist. For a moment Daniel froze as the man took two quick strides to him, raised the hand that clutched the black pistol, and smashed it against his temple.

Daniel crumpled, as surely as if he'd been shot.

It happened so quickly that Michelle didn't scream; instead she gasped and clutched the sheet.

The man with the gun turned to her.

He was close to the bed. She could see that he wore dark clothes, a black T-shirt, jeans, and he took another step toward her. He had on a belt, woven brown and white leather; she could see it clearly in the light that leaked in from the balcony.

The buckle was a gun, and there were letters in the weave. She saw those as he tugged at the tongue of the belt to unbuckle it.

'¡Pendejo!' the other man spit, gesturing toward the balcony.

The man with the gun stared at her a moment longer before he turned and followed his companion out the sliding glass door, into the night.

2

There was a lot of blood.

Headwounds bleed a lot, Michelle thought vaguely. She'd read that somewhere. Or seen it on television.

It didn't mean that Daniel was dying.

But by this time the blood had covered one side of his face, was dripping onto the tiled floor, and he was unconscious, moaning now and again. Michelle couldn't decide what to do next.

Clothes, she thought, I have to put on some clothes. And I have to call someone. And get a towel, for the blood. Which first?

Phone.

She wasn't sure whom to call or how it worked, so she punched 'zero' on the room phone, and finally a woman's voice answered, asking a question. 'A sus órdenes,' Michelle made out.

'Help . . . I need help . . . in Room 452. I need a doctor.'

'You are having an emergency?'

'Yes. Someone's hurt. They came in, and . . . Please, just send help.'

She grabbed a T-shirt and a pair of shorts, thinking, I'm putting on clothes, and this naked man is bleeding on my floor. I should be doing something for him, but I need to get dressed, don't I? And it took only a minute or two, and by the time someone pounded on the door, she'd

16

crouched down by Daniel, had covered him with a sheet, was pressing a towel to the bleeding gash on his scalp. No one needed to know she'd gotten dressed first.

Two hotel workers had come, men who handled luggage, patrolled the grounds. Seeing Michelle at the door holding a bloody towel, Daniel lying on the floor behind her, one immediately reached for his walkie-talkie.

The first set of police arrived just before the ambulance did.

'He's not my husband,' Michelle tried to explain. 'He's a friend. *Un amigo.*' The blood had soaked the towel, had gotten all over her hand, and she wiped her hand on her shorts.

One of the policemen handed her a fresh towel. White, like the uniform he wore, white polo shirt and cargo shorts, black baseball cap.

The other policeman knelt down next to her. 'Let me help you, señorita,' he said, taking the towel. 'You can rest if you like.'

Suddenly she felt dizzy. 'Thank you,' she said. Somehow she made it to the bed, her hand reaching blindly for the solidity of the mattress. She sat on the edge of the bed, watched the ambulance attendants arrive and tend to Daniel with a minimum of fuss, bandage his head and lift him onto a gurney.

By now he was conscious, somewhat. 'Hey,' he said. 'What . . . ?'

'Where are they taking him?' Michelle asked the policeman.

'CMQ Hospital. Don't worry. It's a good place. He'll be fine.'

Two more men arrived. 'Judicial police,' the patrolman explained. 'They can take the statement from you.'

The new policemen wore plainclothes. Polo shirt again and khakis on one, a madras plaid and Dockers on the other, ID and badges hung on lanyards.

One of the ambulance attendants asked her a question. It took a couple of times for her to understand.

'*Su nombre*,' she heard. He pointed at Daniel. *His name*.

'Daniel.'

'The family name?'

Of course she didn't know.

The faces of the ambulance attendant and the policemen stayed studiously blank.

'So he is not your husband,' one of the new policemen stated, the one in khakis. 'Or a boyfriend.'

'No.' Her face flamed red. 'Just a friend.'

His partner lifted Daniel's shorts off the floor, patted the pockets, and retrieved his wallet. The policeman in the khakis gave a little wave to the ambulance attendants, who bundled Daniel out the door.

He was younger than she was, the policeman, in his early thirties, she thought: tall and well built, with a relaxed, loose way of carrying himself. Something about his accent, the cadence of his speech, was familiar, but she couldn't quite place what it was.

'Can you tell me what happened?' he asked.

There wasn't much to tell, really. She skipped

18

how she and Daniel had met. They'd had dinner.
Come back to the hotel. Were sleeping.

'So these men,' he said when she'd finished.
'Anything you can tell me, about how they
looked? Were they tall? Short? If we showed you
photos, could you identify them?'

'No.' She shook her head 'No. They wore
scarves across their faces. They were . . . I don't
know.' She tried to picture them, that moment
when she saw them entering from the balcony.
'One was skinny. Not very big at all. Short. The
other, he wasn't tall either, but he was stocky.
Like a wrestler.'

The one who'd approached her bed.

'He had on a belt,' she said suddenly. 'With a
buckle shaped like a gun. And there were letters
woven in it. ERO.'

'Guerrero?' the policeman asked.

'Maybe. Yes. I think so.'

He nodded. 'Okay,' he said, standing up.
'Sorry this has happened to you and your friend.
It's not so common in Vallarta, but it happens. If
you give me contact information, I'll let you
know if anything comes up.'

'What's Guerrero?' she asked.

'State next door. Lots of thieves come from
there.'

The other plainclothes policeman nodded.
'And *narcos*,' he said. 'Always causing problems.
Even now in Vallarta.'

After the policemen left, Michelle stayed
where she was, sitting on the edge of the bed.
Little piles of clothes lay scattered about, like the
aftermath of a freeway car wreck. She could see

19

the blood as well, the blood on the tiled floor. She'd gotten blood on her T-shirt and shorts, too.

What was she supposed to do now?

There was a knock on the door.

'Señorita?'

And naturally there was blood on her hands. She almost laughed at that. She hadn't done anything wrong, and she still felt guilty.

'Señorita Mason?' It was a woman's voice. 'Can we come in?'

'Who is it?'

'Claudia, from the front desk.'

She thought she remembered a Claudia, but she couldn't be sure. She got up, went to the door, put on the chain, and cracked it open.

A woman stood there, middle-aged and stout, wearing a blue shift that looked like a nurse's uniform. Michelle recognized her. Behind her was a man she'd seen sitting at a stand resembling a portable bar up at the entrance to the hotel driveway, where taxis dropped off guests.

'We are here to help you,' the woman said.

Michelle nodded. 'Okay.' She undid the chain. 'Thank you.' It made sense, she thought, that they'd send someone. To clean up.

They came in. The man spotted the bloody towel on the floor. He picked it up and put it in a trashbag. He wore latex gloves, like you'd use to do dishes.

Michelle sat back down on the bed. She didn't know what else to do.

The woman immediately squatted by Michelle

and covered her hand with her own, which was dry and a little rough.

'This is terrible,' she said, 'and we are so very sorry. These things should not happen in Vallarta.'

'Things like this happen everywhere,' Michelle murmured.

'I think we can move you to another room, right? A better room.'

Michelle thought about it. She stared at the heaps of clothing, the puddle of blood now drying in the refrigerated air.

'Yes,' she said. 'Yes. I don't want to stay in this room anymore.'

They moved her to a suite in a newer wing, one with a separate bedroom and a bar, a wide balcony with wrought-iron furniture. She checked the balcony first thing. It could not be reached through another suite; there was no way to climb up to it that she could see.

After the woman from the front desk and the man from reception moved all her things, hung the clothes that had been in the closet, arranged her toothbrush, cosmetics, and moisturizers on the bathroom counter — after all that had been done, the offer of tea by the hotel staff turned down, Michelle stepped into the shower. Stood under the spray for a very long time.

When she got out, she slipped into the silk pajamas she'd packed, the sleeveless top and shorts. She considered having a whiskey from the minibar, thinking it might relax her, might help her sleep, but she already had the beginnings of a headache, so instead she took an Ambien. Tom's prescription. Why let them go to waste?

She climbed into bed, closed her eyes. What replayed in her head was not the robbery, the assault, but Daniel's face, over hers.

Maybe I should have gone to the hospital, Michelle thought as the drug began to take hold. Would that have been the right thing to do? But she barely knew Daniel, after all. Couldn't even ask for him by name.

The breeze from the ocean billowed the gauzy curtains on the balcony. I should get up, she thought. I should close the door. But she was safe here, wasn't she? And she was so tired, and the air smelled good.

She watched the curtains expand and contract, as though they were breathing.

Eventually her breaths slowed down to match, and then she slept.

★ ★ ★

'We hope you can stay a little longer, Ms. Mason.'

The woman behind the front desk, a different woman from the one last night, briefly rubbed her hands before composing herself. She was trim, perhaps Michelle's age, carefully made up, with a gold necklace and gold earrings that looked to be a set. Even in the heat of the patio that served as the hotel lobby, only the faintest dewy perspiration dampened her forehead. Michelle was already dripping sweat.

'We are so sorry about what happened. We'd

like for you to stay as our guest and enjoy yourself.'

Everyone was being very kind, Michelle thought. Probably they were worried about lawsuits.

The robbers had somehow gained access to a vacant room next to her old room, climbed from that balcony onto hers. Obviously the security was not what it should have been. If she were in America, she could probably sue.

But in Mexico? How did things work here? Would it be worth it to try?

'Right now I'm scheduled to leave on Sunday,' she said.

'Of course, of course. We could make an arrangement for you to stay here in the future, if you'd like to return. Or if you decide you'd like to stay a little longer, we can do that as well.'

'Thank you,' Michelle said. 'I'll think about it.'

Even with what had happened, it was tempting. Spending time on the beach, drinking margaritas on the hotel's dime, sounded better than her current life in Los Angeles. Living in her sister's spare room. Listening to Maggie's fights with her boyfriend, to her son Ben's tantrums. It was why she'd come on this vacation in the first place, to get away from all that for a few days.

A giggle rose in her throat as she walked up the stairs from the reception area to her tower. Maybe she just wouldn't leave. See how long the hotel's free room was good for. They hadn't really said.

I'll live off room service and peanuts from the

minibar, she thought. Let my hair go gray, my thighs get fat, get a couple of cats and a Chihuahua. Fill the room with purchases from the beach vendors: loud serapes, wooden dolphin statuettes, flying Batman parachute toys, piled in stacks, all smelling vaguely of cat piss. Take her Chihuahua on walks down the Malecón. Maybe one of the cats, too.

She felt, for the first time in months, light. Unencumbered. Free.

The feeling wouldn't last long, probably, but why not enjoy it?

Maybe I'll take some pictures, she thought.

Get out the good camera. Wander around. See what caught her eye. She hadn't done that in ages, hadn't done it here at all, not even a few snapshots with her point-and-shoot, and she was a pretty decent photographer — or had been, once.

She decided to change out of the sundress and into some shorts and a tanktop. Better for taking photos, in case she needed to climb or crouch.

The hotel people hadn't arranged things the way she would, naturally, and she had to hunt inside the wardrobe to figure out where they'd put her clothes.

Underwear on one shelf. Blouses and skirts neatly hung. Sandals lined in a row.

Including one pair that didn't belong. A pair of Tevas, too big to fit her feet.

Hanging on the closet pole, a faded batik shirt.

Daniel's clothes.

She found the swim trunks on the shelf with her bathing suit and sarong.

Holding up the trunks, she felt a surge of irritation. How could they have forgotten his clothes? What was she supposed to do with them?

Maybe she'd give them to the beach vendors, to one of the Indian kids peddling garish magnets made in China.

It's not right for me to feel this way, she thought. She should care — shouldn't she? — about what had happened to him. Maybe he'd just needed stitches, maybe he was resting at home right now, or even back on the beach looking for some other tourist to fuck, but what if he'd been badly hurt? A skull fracture, bleeding in the brain, something like that.

But ever since Tom had died, she didn't seem to feel the things she was supposed to feel.

And maybe it wasn't so strange, not wanting to see Daniel, after what had happened. What did she know about him, really? Just that he was attractive, and after she'd taken him to her room, they'd been attacked.

It could have been a lot worse.

She shuddered thinking about it.

Just some clothes that he wasn't going to miss. Not her problem.

There was a sudden burst of music. She flinched, almost flinging Daniel's trunks in the air. What *was* that? Not the stereo from the beach bar, it was definitely inside the room. A rock song, something familiar. She finally recognized it as 'Pretty Fly,' by the Offspring. Coming from inside her tote bag.

It was her iPhone. I've never used that

ringtone, she thought. She grabbed it from her bag, hit ANSWER.

'Hey, Danny?' A male voice.

'No,' she said. 'Who's this?'

'Oh. Sorry. Wrong number.' The call ended.

She stared at the phone. The wallpaper on the screen was wrong — an ocean wave rather than the rows of mountains she used. A moment later it rang again. NED G came up as the caller. Same ringtone.

'Hey,' the same male voice said. 'This is Danny's phone, right?'

3

She hadn't thought it was Daniel's phone. It looked exactly like her phone. It was a black iPhone, for chrissakes; they all looked pretty much alike.

'Who's this?' she asked again.

'It's Ned. So is Danny around?'

'No. He isn't.'

'Oh.' A nervous chuckle. 'Well, sorry to bug you. But, um . . . is this Danny's number? Maybe my phone's screwed up somehow.'

She stared at the iPhone. 'I don't know,' she said. She didn't know what else to say.

'Okay,' the voice said. 'But you know him, right?'

She hit DISCONNECT before she could even think it through.

When she slid the bar to unlock the phone, ENTER PASSCODE appeared on the screen. She didn't use a passcode.

She had Daniel's phone. So where was hers?

She tossed his phone on the bed. Used the hotel phone to make an international call and dialed her own number, waited for the ringtone she used for unidentified callers, the default marimba.

Nothing.

The call went directly to voicemail, and then she remembered that she'd turned it off to avoid roaming charges. To avoid calls from her attorney. From the creditor who'd somehow found the number.

'Oh, fuck,' she said.

'*Leave a message*,' her own voice said.

Beep. She hung up.

She tried to remember where she'd put the phone last night. It had been in her tote at the beach, she remembered that.

Where she'd found Daniel's phone.

She checked the tote. Her phone wasn't there.

Then she remembered: the tote, knocked over, its contents spilling out onto the floor. The man, going through Daniel's shorts.

If she had Daniel's phone, maybe Daniel had hers.

The phone rang again, and she lunged for it. 'Hello?'

'Look, I'm really sorry to keep bugging you.' It was the man who'd called before — Ned. 'But if Danny doesn't want to talk to me, could I, like, leave a message or something? It's kind of important.'

Ned. That was the man who'd come up to Daniel in the restaurant the previous night. Tweaker Ned. Daniel didn't seem particularly happy to see him, but that didn't mean they weren't close, close enough at least for Ned to maybe know where Daniel lived.

'Is this Ned?'

'Yeah, it is.' He sounded relieved, like he was happy to have been recognized. 'Who's this?'

'Michelle. We met last night at the restaurant. I'm Daniel's . . . Danny's friend.'

'Great. So can you give Danny a message for me?'

'No, he . . . ' How to put it? 'He had a little accident last night. They took him to the hospital . . . He . . . '

'Fuck. Shit. Really? What kind of accident?' It was more than concern in his voice, she thought. There was a distinct note of panic.

'A robbery. I mean, he's okay,' she said, even though she didn't know that for sure, 'but he probably needed some stitches. And I ended up with his phone, and I think he has mine.'

'Oh, man,' Ned said. 'Oh, man.'

'So I was wondering . . . do you know where he lives? Because I'd like to get this back to him.'

'No. No, I don't know. I always just . . . you know, call him.'

'Great,' Michelle muttered. 'Okay, thanks.'

Well, that was useless, she thought, hitting the red 'disconnect' bar.

She couldn't call Daniel's contacts. Couldn't access any information he might have on the phone.

Maybe she'd try the hospital.

★ ★ ★

'Discharged,' the woman at the hotel front desk said.

Michelle had asked her if she would make the call, in case the hospital receptionist didn't speak good English.

'So it must not have been serious?'

The woman gave the suggestion of a shrug. 'I

29

think probably not.'

'Did they tell you . . . is there any way I can get a hold of him?'

As soon as she'd said it, she knew it was a waste of time. Hospitals weren't going to give out that kind of information.

'They say if you want, you can leave a note with them. That he must come back in a week or so for removal of the stitches.'

A week. She couldn't wait that long, could she? That would mean staying here till next weekend, at least.

Today was Friday.

Friday was when Daniel's friends met. At El Tiburón. The Shark.

★ ★ ★

El Tiburón was one of a string of bars just north of the small cement pier at Los Muertos Beach, where people caught fishing charters and the water taxi south to villages like Yelapa. Like most of the beach bars, it had a palm-thatched roof, wood floors, and a wooden rail running along the front, where a few vendors quickly draped their serapes and blouses and sarongs to display to customers before a waiter shooed them away.

We hang out, watch the sunset, Daniel had told her.

One of his friends would know how to find him.

She'd brought his things, on the off chance that he'd be there. Stopped at one of the little stores by the pier to buy a tote bag to put them in. Her choices were Frida Kahlo and Che Guevara, their faces outlined in black against fluorescent shades of green, red, and yellow, stamped on woven plastic. She chose Che.

Now Michelle stood on the beach boardwalk a few yards from the rail, squinting into the darker bar. That group at the long table, was that the board meeting?

She climbed the three steps that led into the bar, stood there a moment. It must be that table, she thought. There were about a dozen people there, and she thought they mostly looked like Americans, or maybe Canadians. White people, mostly. One black woman, an Asian man, and a guy who might have been Mexican.

Mostly middle-aged or older. Ordinary.

Certainly not dangerous.

Stupid, she told herself, it was stupid to even think that way. What had happened in the hotel room, that was just a robbery. Not Daniel's fault. Nothing involving any of these people.

'Miss? Would you like a table?'

'I . . . I'm looking for . . . There's a group that meets here?'

The waiter, a young man tanned as dark as strong coffee, gestured at the long table she'd already noted.

She took a tentative step forward, toward the table. Stopped.

This is silly, she thought. Just get it over with.

'Here for the board meeting?'

The man who spoke was hollow-cheeked thin, with a white-stubbled beard. He wore a Clash T-shirt, collarbones protruding above where the

31

neck had been cut out. A blurred tattoo ran down his shoulder, below the ripped-off sleeves.

'I'm . . . a friend of Daniel's. Michelle.'

He might have been in his sixties, but he looked like he'd lived hard. 'I'm Charlie.' He smiled, revealing yellow, channeled teeth, an obvious hole where a tooth should have been and a bridge wasn't. 'Danny's coming tonight?'

'I'm not sure I . . . ' She felt herself flush. 'He got hurt last night, and I was wondering if . . . '

'Danny got hurt?' He sounded concerned.

'Is he okay?' a blonde woman sitting across from him asked.

'I think so,' Michelle said, and then Charlie patted the empty chair next to him.

'Sorry, my dear, I didn't mean to make you just stand there. You want something to drink?'

She sat. He seemed nice. Harmless at least. And he knew Daniel.

'Thanks. Yes, I would.'

'I wouldn't have the margies here,' he confided. 'They use Sprite.'

'Have the piña colada,' the blonde woman said. 'Two for one during happy hour.' She was large, on the far side of middle age, the blonde an obvious dye job, wearing a Hawaiian shirt patterned with orange and white hibiscuses.

'Piña colada, I guess.'

'I'm Vicky.'

Her smile, unlike Charlie's, showed gleaming white teeth.

'Smoke?' Charlie asked.

'No, thank you.' Not surprising that he smoked. She could smell the cigarettes on him, layer upon layer of smoke on his T-shirt and shorts that no amount of washing would vanquish, on his index finger and thumb as well, browned and baked by burning tobacco.

Their drinks arrived, Michelle's piña coladas coming in two large plastic cups. She sipped one. The rum cut through the sugar with a tang of kerosene.

'What happened to Danny?' Charlie asked.

'It was a robbery.'

'Oh, my God,' Vicky said with a gasp. 'That's terrible!'

'He's okay,' Michelle said quickly. The more Vicky reacted, the less she wanted to talk about it. 'But I have some of his things.'

Both Charlie and Vicky had Daniel's cell number, but no landline. No address.

'You know who I bet does?' Vicky said suddenly. 'Gary. He told me he was stopping by tonight, and if he doesn't, I can call him.'

'Great,' Michelle said. Maybe she'd get her phone back. That would make the evening worth it.

'Oh, Gary. He's delightful,' Charlie muttered.

Vicky grabbed her wadded-up napkin and tossed it at him. 'Now, come on,' she said. 'Gary's . . . a good person. He really likes to help people.'

'He's not my sort,' Charlie said in an exaggerated whisper. 'He *golfs*.'

Michelle smiled, for a moment forgetting that she didn't want to be here.

★   ★   ★

She'd waited for almost an hour, listening to the blur of small talk around her and sipping her piña colada, when Vicky said, 'Oh, here's Gary.' She waved in the direction of a man who'd just come in. He wore a neat, expensive Lacoste shirt and khaki shorts, Ray-Bans pushed up onto his forehead.

'Well, hey there, Vicky,' Gary said. He made his way up to the table, next to Michelle, and gave her a long, thorough look. 'I don't believe we've met.'

Michelle wasn't sure how old he was. He had a face that seemed out of balance, his cheeks and lips plump like a baby's, the knowing eyes above peering out from wrinkled, puffy lids, all framed by blond curls.

'Michelle.'

He took her hand, gave it a little squeeze. 'Can I get you a drink, Michelle? You look practically empty.'

He signaled to the waiter before she could say yes or no.

'Michelle's a friend of Danny's,' Vicky said. 'Did you hear . . . ?'

Gary found a chair and pulled it next to Michelle. 'Oh, man, I sure did. So that was you in the hotel with him?'

She'd thought she was beyond embarrassment by now, but she wasn't. She kept her voice level. 'It was.'

'I'll tell you, this town . . . ' He shook his head, his bow lips curved in a little smile. 'It's getting kind of crazy here.'

'What happened to Danny?' an older woman a

few seats away asked. Karen, or was it Kathy? Michelle had been introduced to too many people to keep track. She was thin, tanned almost as dark as the waiter, her hair in a long gray braid.

'Oh, well, the way I heard it, some narcos tried to rob him, cracked him on the head.' Gary spoke loudly, so that others sitting at the table could hear him, even over the blare of Steely Dan playing on the bar's speakers.

'How do you know they were narcos?' the older woman asked, but no one paid attention.

'The narcos are out of control,' said a middle-aged man sitting two seats over. 'Did you hear about what happened by Bucerías yesterday?'

Everyone started talking at once. A battle with machine guns and grenades, between drug gangs and police. Narcos incinerated in cars. Police ambushed at a crossroads in retaliation.

Michelle felt dizzy. She closed her eyes. Clutched her drink. Took another long sip through the plastic straw. Like a pineapple milkshake.

'Fucking Sinaloa cowboys,' someone said. 'They ought to put an electric fence around that whole shithole state. Save us all a lot of trouble.'

'Guerrero,' Michelle said. 'They were from Guerrero.'

'It's just really sad.' Vicky's eyes glistened. 'I hate seeing this kind of thing happen in Vallarta.'

'If this were St. Louis, or New Orleans, no one would even blink,' Charlie said. 'But here in paradise we expect everything to be perfect.'

'Oh, come on,' the Asian man said — American, Michelle amended, from his accent. 'Machine guns? Grenade launchers?'

'I'm talking about a few robberies, not *narcos* killing each other.'

'This town depends on tourists and foreign residents. If crime gets out of control and people stop coming here, everyone is fucked. Right down to your favorite Babaloo on the beach selling shrimp on a stick.'

Michelle's head hurt. Probably from all the cheap rum and sugar. She really wanted to go back to the hotel and sleep, even though the sun had barely set.

'Gary, Vicky tells me you might have Danny's address,' she said.

'I might.'

Gary smiled, pushing his pillowy cheeks up to meet his puffy eyes. Like a debauched cherub, Michelle thought. 'You want to check up on him? See how he's doing?'

'No.' She pushed down the urge to snap off some hostile response. 'I mean yes, but mainly I have some of his things. His phone. And I think he has mine.'

'Ah.' From his little smirk, she wondered if he believed her. He appeared to consider. 'Well, I think I can help you out,' he finally said. 'Anybody have a pen?'

Vicky did.

He extracted a business card from his wallet and scribbled on its back. 'This isn't the exact address, but any cabdriver will be able to find it.' He held it out to her, fingertips brushing hers when she took it. 'I wouldn't go there tonight, though. I don't think he's home right now. Try him tomorrow.' The smirk again. 'Not too early.'

She glanced at the front of the card. Plain black letters on white linen — nice design and good-quality paper.

Gary Wallace. Trinity Consulting. A cell-phone number. An e-mail address.

'Thanks.' She stood up, unsteady from the rum. 'I'd better get going,' she said. 'Thanks for the drinks.'

Vicky rose with her and gave her a hug. 'This is a good place,' she said in Michelle's ear. 'Don't let what happened spoil Vallarta for you.'

4

'I think you will want to take a cab,' the woman at the front desk told her after looking at the address written on Gary's card. 'It is a ways from here, and up the hill.'

'But close enough to walk?'

'If you like walking.'

Between last night's drinks and the margarita she'd just had at lunch, she could use the walk. 'I do.'

'Maybe two miles.'

I could take some pictures, she thought. Like she'd set out to do yesterday, before Daniel's phone rang.

She went back to her room, grabbed the Che bag with Daniel's clothes, retrieved her Olympus E-3 from the hotel safe, and set off, heading south from the hotel, up a road that curved around the hill.

The heat made it hard to keep walking. It felt like being smothered in a steaming-hot blanket. Sweat dripped into her eyes, smeared her sunglasses when she pushed them onto her head. And trying to take pictures while juggling her purse and the Che bag was awkward. The camera, which usually fit so comfortably in her hand, slipped in her grip.

Nothing was going to go right today.

She tried. Shot a few images. Nothing very interesting. Wrought iron and bougainvillea.

Superhero piñatas. She'd seen these photos before, she was certain, and seen them better executed.

Michelle put the camera back in its bag and slung it over her shoulder.

The road ahead was cobblestoned, the banks lining it tangled with browning vegetation that would not green until after the summer rains, with plastic bags and food wrappers caught up in the branches. A lot of the houses looked expensive. New construction clung tenuously to the hillside, as though the flesh of the land had wasted away, leaving skeletal frames stacked unsteadily on top of one another, foundations undermined before they'd even been laid. With enough rain saturating the hill, she could just see one of these buildings giving up, letting go, the cheap rebar popping out of the ground like a rotten tooth.

Halfway up the hill was a little street that branched off the main road at an impossibly steep angle. She followed it, per Gary's directions. The street led to a cluster of small, multistory buildings — apartments or condominiums.

The one on the right, Gary's note said, light brown with a dark roof.

She looked. She thought the description fit, but blue tarps covered most of the roof, and there was other evidence of ongoing construction or repairs: a small cement mixer and a pile of gravel, a dug-up walkway, a boarded window. No workers. The place looked abandoned.

Daniel's unit was the one on the upper right, according to Gary's note. The tarps extended halfway across what would have been his roof.

Michelle stood there for a moment. She was absurdly sweaty, drenched; her blouse was actually wet, her hair separated into salty tendrils. Really, she wasn't in any condition to see Daniel if he *was* there.

Did she want to see him? She wasn't sure.

Stupid, she told herself. You need your phone. You've come all this way. Say hello, how are you, and good-bye.

She shifted the tote bag on her shoulder and approached the building.

An external staircase with a wrought-iron banister led up to Daniel's unit, crossing the side of the building and leading to a balcony facing the ocean, wide enough to accommodate two chairs and a small glass table.

When she reached the balcony, she could see only a sliver of water above the roof of the building below. Still a nice view, she supposed.

There was no name on the door, no number, no mailbox. She'd have to take Gary's word that this was the right unit. If it wasn't . . . well, this was a small building. Someone would have to know where Daniel lived.

If no one answers, she thought, I'll leave the bag by the door with a note. Take his phone back to the hotel, and he can pick it up there.

Heart pounding, she knocked on the door.

Which swung open. About six inches before the rusting hinges slowed it to a halt.

Michelle hesitated at the threshold.

'Daniel?' she called out.

She heard something from within. Not a

person. She couldn't make it out at first. A sort of hum.

A fly flew out the door, bumping into her shoulder.

I have to look, she told herself. I have to look.

She pushed the door further open.

It was dim inside, the curtains drawn, and hot. The smell, the flies — for that was the hum she'd heard, the buzzing of flies — hit her at once, and she couldn't entirely sort out one thing from the other — the darkness, the closed heat, the smell: a sweetish rot. She fumbled for a light switch, thinking there must be one, but there wasn't, not by the door at least.

Her eyes adjusted. It wasn't really dark. There was enough light seeping through the curtains, from the open door.

The living room. This was the living room. It was simple, hardly anything in it. A couch. A chair. A television. A coffee table.

On the coffee table was something dark, an oval shape with protrusions she couldn't make out. The thing almost seemed to shimmer, as though its lines were mutable, fluid, shifting ever so slightly.

She approached the table, and a cloud of flies rose from the object.

A head.

She shrieked, batting away the flies, one of them hitting her lip, another, her eyelid, her ear. She thought she might have inhaled them, and she swatted at them and retched a little, then finally stood still. She looked again.

It was a pig's head. A pig's head, sitting on the

coffee table. On top of a *Time* magazine, next to an empty beer bottle. Covered with flies. Maggots, too, little white filaments that pulsed and contracted as they burrowed into the rotting flesh.

For a moment she could only stand there. She felt nothing at first. How was one supposed to regard this? It didn't make sense.

Something prickled the skin of her forearm. She looked down.

A fly, rubbing its legs together.

Get out, she thought. Just get out.

She took a few steps back, toward the door, toward air and light, stumbling a bit, the back of her hand striking the doorknob. She clutched at it to steady herself. Leaned there against the wall, hand on doorknob, until her heart slowed and she could think again.

What did it mean? Why would someone do this?

Maybe she should call the police. She wondered how you did that here. Was it 911? Or something else?

But what would she tell them? That she'd found a pig's head in an empty apartment?

There was no one in the apartment. She was certain. How could you stand to be in there with a rotting carcass on the table? There was no movement, no sound other than the flies.

Then she thought maybe there *was* someone, unconscious or dead.

Don't be stupid, she told herself, but the idea burrowed itself into her head, and she had to be sure.

42

The apartment had a kitchenette, separated from the living room by a bar counter, and a short hall with three doors opening off it. A bathroom — blue tiles, plastic shower curtain. A toothbrush, some toothpaste, and a few sundries. Nothing much. Some curly dark hair in the sink.

The door next to that opened onto an odd little room — a bonus room, she supposed you'd call it — with a small barred window high up a whitewashed wall. You could put a daybed in here if you had guests, Michelle thought, but there was no furniture, just a workout bench, some barbells, a bag of golf clubs, and what looked like snorkeling equipment in a couple of crates beneath the window.

On the other side of the hall was the main bedroom.

No body on the bed. Michelle almost laughed. Of course there wouldn't be. The bed was big, a king. Well, Daniel probably had his share of overnight guests, judging from her encounter with him — though anyone who didn't know her well could say the same of her based on that night, and that wasn't how she was, not how she'd been for a long time, anyway.

Don't be so quick to judge, she told herself.

But it was hard not to wonder. The apartment — the condominium — was modest. Anonymous, almost. No paintings on the walls. Hardly any books. Nothing personal at all. Not much different from her room at the hotel.

This must just be a vacation home for Daniel, Michelle thought. Not the place where he actually *lived*.

Back in the living room, the flies had regrouped on the pig head.

Just leave, she told herself. It's not your problem, and you have a plane to catch tomorrow.

But if it was something criminal . . . People knew she planned to come here. Gary knew, and Vicky and Charlie. If she just left, would that implicate her somehow?

She felt the camera tucked against her side as the thought occurred to her.

I should take pictures.

Just to document it. She could decide later whether she needed to show the photos to anyone. But at least she'd have proof of what she saw. Just in case there were any questions.

She hadn't intended to get artsy, only snap off a few clear shots, but as she focused on the pig's snout, a part of her noted that it was a compelling image, with the flies around its eye sockets, the beer bottle next to it, the television in the background. As bland as the room was, the pig's head was the only thing that really drew your eye.

Still Life with Pig Head and Beer Bottle, Michelle thought, adjusting the depth of field, taking another shot, then the angle, shooting again. She almost laughed. All this time in Puerto Vallarta, and she'd finally found a good picture.

'What . . . ?'

She dropped the camera against her chest.

'What the *fuck?*'

Daniel stood there in the doorway.

44

'I . . . '

In two strides he'd crossed to the coffee table. 'What the *fuck* is this?'

His fingers dug into her arm, just beneath her bicep. 'You . . . Who told you to do this?'

'What are you talking about?'

She stared at his face: rigid and white with anger.

'I have some of your things,' she said. 'I just came here and saw this. I thought . . . '

'Who told you where I live?'

'Gary,' she said. 'Please let go of me.'

'Gary?' He released her arm with a jerk. 'How do you know Gary?'

'I met him at the Tiburón,' Michelle said. 'I didn't know how to get a hold of you. Gary gave me your address.'

'Why didn't you just call?' The anger had not diminished, only retreated.

'I have your phone.' She started to reach into her purse, and instantly he tensed again, not with anger this time but something cold and predatory.

She froze. God, did he think she had a gun?

'Check yours,' she said. 'I think it's mine.'

He reached into the pocket of his cargo shorts and pulled out an iPhone. Black. He powered it up. 'Shit,' he said after a moment. 'It . . . it was off. I just left it that way.'

'For two days?'

'I wanted to get some rest and not have people fucking calling me.'

'So can we trade phones now?' She felt a rush of anger. 'You're not going to . . . to attack me?'

45

'Sorry. I'm . . . ' He lifted his hand to his forehead, winced. His head was shaved where he'd been cut, a patch between crown and temple covered with a square of gauze. 'Fucking Gary.' He attempted a smile. 'This is probably his idea of a joke.'

'A joke?' The buzzing of the flies, the smell of rot, the close, shut-in heat of the apartment made her suddenly dizzy. 'I need some air.'

She pushed past Daniel and sat down on one of the chairs on the balcony, let her head fall into her hands.

'You okay?'

'Fine.' She raised her head. 'What kind of joke is that?'

'A stupid one.' Daniel sat down in the chair next to her. 'He knew I checked into a hotel for a few days. Air conditioner's busted here, and I felt pretty lousy. Figured I'd let somebody bring me food and make my bed.'

There was something he wasn't saying, something that didn't fit, but Michelle couldn't think of what it was.

'You want a beer? I think there's a couple cold ones in the fridge.'

He sounded friendly enough, but the way he looked at her, studying her face — was that concern or something else?

'That's okay. I think I'd better go.'

'No, listen, stay a minute. You had a shock. Let me get you a beer.'

He got up before she could object.

By the time Daniel had returned with the beers, bottles already sweating in the heat, she'd

46

figured it out. 'Why me?'

'Huh?' Daniel handed her a bottle. Bohemia. She'd had that a few times in Los Angeles.

'If he was playing a joke on you, why did he send *me* up here to find it?'

'He's an asshole.'

'He doesn't even know me.'

'Guess he thought it would be funny,' Daniel muttered.

The sun was striking the balcony now, the light glaring. He squinted for a moment and put on his sunglasses, which had been propped up on his head. Serengetis, she thought.

Michelle rested the beer on her cheek for a moment. The chill felt even better than drinking it.

'So the pictures,' Daniel said. He was smiling, trying to keep his voice friendly. 'Why were you taking pictures of that thing?'

'I thought there should be a record of it. In case someone threw it away.'

'Are you a photographer or something?'

She shook her head. 'It's just a hobby.'

They sat in silence for a while. What else was there to say?

'I should go,' Michelle said. She reached into her purse and got out his phone. He retrieved hers from his pocket.

'Let me get you a cab.'

'You don't need to.'

'I want to.' He smiled again. Maybe it was genuine this time. 'Look, I'm really sorry about how I acted just now. It was just . . . kind of a shock, finding you and *that* in my place, and

47

. . . I'm still a little jumpy over everything. You know?'

She supposed she did. 'Don't worry about it.'

He walked her through the apartment, past the pig's head.

'Let me buy you dinner,' he said suddenly. 'You went to a lot of trouble, and I didn't exactly thank you for it.'

'Thanks, but . . . I'm leaving tomorrow, and I need some time to pack.'

It was a lame excuse, and he had to know it, but he couldn't really want to have dinner with her after everything that had happened, could he? It was probably just a belated courtesy on his part, and she wasn't interested.

He was a nice-looking man, and maybe none of this was his fault, but she'd had enough. Enough of him, enough of his creepy friends and their sick jokes. Enough of this place.

It was time to go home.

'Well, if you change your mind . . . ' He stared at her, eyes hidden by his sunglasses.

'I have your number,' she said.

She didn't, but he didn't need to know that.

He still looked pale, she thought. Behind him the pig's head pulsed with flies. 'Do you . . . need some help with that?' she asked reluctantly.

'Thanks. That's . . . Thanks.' He smiled again, a real one. 'If you could, maybe just hold the bag?'

Daniel put on a pair of rubber gloves he had stashed under the kitchen sink, and Michelle held the garbage bag. He picked up the pig's head, holding it as far away from his body as

48

possible. Michelle did the same with the garbage bag.

Even after they twisted the bag shut, she could hear the buzzing of trapped flies.

5

'I'm all packed,' she told the woman behind the front desk the next morning. 'If I could leave my bags in the room, I'd like to go down to the beach for a while.'

'Certainly. Please, enjoy the rest of your time here.'

Though it was already 11:00 A.M., there were still plenty of empty *palapas*. The tourist season was over. 'This time of year, no business,' the waiter said, the nut-brown man who had served her before. 'Very hard on the family.' He shrugged. 'Maybe I take the job down the beach at this new restaurant. Make Caesar salads. The money is a little better.'

'I'm sorry you're having a tough time,' she said, and she was. Maybe she wasn't a Mexican waiter hustling for tips on the beach, but the idea that she might not have enough, might not be able to make enough to support herself, seemed all too relatable.

She'd gotten an e-mail from her lawyer saying that things weren't looking good, that Tom had been behind in the life insurance payments and he hadn't been able to get it reinstated. She'd been counting on the life insurance. The house was gone, foreclosed, and she'd had no clue until Tom wasn't around anymore to intercept the communications. His kids laid claim to every-thing else that was left. Whatever that might be.

She had nothing.

I have to accept it, she told herself.

'Something to drink?' the waiter asked. 'Something special? Since this is your last day here.'

She'd had far too much to drink on this trip already. But it was her last day. Quite possibly the last time she'd ever be here, on this beach.

'Just a margarita, I think.'

He brought her a double, and later he came by and topped it off.

I'll have to get a job, Michelle thought. But it had been years since she'd worked. She'd stopped shortly after marrying Tom, not that the photo gallery had paid much in any case. 'Look, I'm making plenty for both of us,' he'd said. 'Why don't you spend your time doing things you enjoy?'

Funny, that.

He'd meant it kindly, for the most part. But not working meant she ran the house. Chose the furniture, the appliances. Hung the right paintings on the walls. Made sure the gifts Tom sent were personalized and appropriate. Picked their charities and arranged for their attendance at the banquets.

And she'd kept herself in shape for all that. Yoga, Pilates, spin classes. She looked good, and not like one of those Brentwood plastic-surgery victims either.

'Michelle, you're so creative! Love the way you dress! Love your house!'

That was what everyone said about her.

How much had she actually enjoyed it?

She'd almost reached the end of the book about the woman who found redemption through baked goods. She thumbed through to the last pages. Sure enough, the heroine ended up with the cultured, overeducated woodworker. Why did people even read things like this, she wondered, where you know how it will end almost as soon as it starts?

Maybe they liked the certainty. The reassurance that things worked out all right in the end.

At three-fifteen she went upstairs, showered, changed, and finished her packing. At four she retrieved her valuables from the hotel safe and said good-bye to the woman behind the front counter.

'Alejandra,' the woman said, extending a slender hand. 'I hope you come back to see us again. It isn't right, what happened to you and your friend. We hope we can make it up to you.'

The cab arrived a few minutes later; the driver took her wheeled bag and put it in the trunk. Michelle climbed into the back, and as the cab pulled away, Alejandra and one of the hotel workers waved good-bye. Michelle returned the wave. She supposed it was simply good business, that after the attack the hotel workers wanted to do whatever they could to mitigate the bad publicity by being extra attentive.

Still, they were nice people.

The taxi chugged up the hill, heading in the opposite direction of the airport at first, then around a tight curve that straightened into a road heading north, condos at the crest of the hill, morphing into *colonias* as they descended.

The road widened, dirt shoulders on either side, concrete shoring up the hillsides, covered with graffiti and political posters, mostly for PRI and PAN. Michelle couldn't remember what the parties stood for here, though she thought that *pan* might be Spanish for 'bread.'

She leaned against the backseat, eyes half closed. She had the beginnings of a headache. I shouldn't have had those drinks, she thought. Soon as I get home, it's back to the regimen: the workout routine, the yoga, the raw food and greens. Definitely no margaritas. The calories in one were staggering.

The taxi driver muttered something under his breath that sounded like a curse, put his foot on the brake, and pulled over onto the dirt shoulder.

'What's wrong?'

The driver jerked his thumb behind them. '*Policía.*'

She turned and looked out the rear window. A squad car, black and white, compact, a little battered, light bar flashing blue and red.

Great, Michelle thought. Had the driver been speeding? Was a taillight out? She'd tried to leave plenty of time to get to the airport, but she'd heard that things with the police could turn complicated here.

Well, there was no point in panicking.

The policeman approached the driver's-side door. Best not to get involved, Michelle decided. She stared out the passenger window.

They'd parked at the edge of a lot that looked like an ad hoc body shop, with cars in various states of assembly, stacked sidepanels, bumpers, and doors. A tin roof propped up on poles was the only indication of any permanency. Odd, she thought. What would stop someone from coming in at night and stealing parts? Maybe the workers slept here. Maybe the whole operation was somehow magically packed up at dusk and reassembled the next day.

She could hear the policeman and the driver exchange a few low words. '*Aeropuerto*' was one she caught.

The policeman rapped his knuckles on the backseat window. '*Señora.*'

'What? Excuse me?'

The policeman gestured for her to open the door. She did.

'*Su bolsa.*'

'My . . . ?'

'Purse.'

She could feel her heart pound in her throat. Was this some kind of shakedown? A robbery in the guise of a traffic stop? What was she supposed to do?

She handed him her purse.

The policeman opened it, rifling through the main compartment, opening the interior zip, then moving to the exterior pockets. It was a Marc Jacobs hobo, and there were a lot of them.

The policeman extracted a brown paper packet. Folded. A square the size of a lopped-off business card. He opened it.

'Come out of the car.'

'What?'

'Out of the car.'

54

'What *is* that?' Michelle asked. 'I don't know what that is.'

'Now.'

'That's not mine!'

He grabbed her wrist and pulled her toward him.

6

Lawyer. How did you say 'lawyer'? The only word Michelle could come up with was *albóndigas*, and that, she was fairly sure, meant 'meatballs.'

Sitting in the back of the squad car seemed so unreal that she couldn't process it. The seat smelled like beer-scented puke. The policeman had *cuffed* her, hands behind her back and tight enough to hurt. Taken her luggage out of the taxi and thrown it next to her. Was he even a real policeman? He looked like one, she thought — a big man with a big belly and a mustache and aviator sunglasses. His uniform looked real. The squad car looked credible too. Now and again the radio squawked and broadcast chatter.

'*¿Dónde vamos?*' she managed.

'*A la cárcel.*'

'What?'

'Jail.' The policeman barked out a laugh. '*Tienes drogas,* go to jail.'

'Drugs? I don't have any drugs.'

He shrugged fractionally, shoulders tense, hands gripping the wheel.

A setup, she thought, it was some kind of setup. A con, a way to extort money. 'Look,' she said. 'This is a misunderstanding. Can't we work this out?'

As soon as she said it, she knew she'd made a mistake.

'What do you think, lady? You want to give me something?'

'No, I, just . . . '

'Money, maybe? Something else?' He laughed again, all the while staring straight ahead.

'It's a misunderstanding,' she repeated. 'I'm not trying to insult you.'

'You want to give me something, you want to stop right here?'

The squad car slowed.

On one side of the road, there were cinder-block buildings: apartments mostly, a few downtrodden businesses, peeling hand-painted signs, rusting cars, broken-down fences. On the other a steep hill, dirt roads, shacks interspersed among browning vines and palms.

'No,' she said. 'No.'

The car sped up again.

The jail was in a neighborhood like the ones she'd seen from the road, cement-slab and cinder-block apartments, unpaved streets in places, hardly distinguishable from the surrounding buildings except for its iron bars and guards with machine guns.

There was paperwork to fill out. They searched her and had her take off her jewelry and empty her pockets — the pants she wore, thin linen, had only a rear patch pocket anyway.

'I want to make a phone call,' she said, but no one listened.

Then a guard took her back to a cell. Cement floors, a cement bench, and a toilet that looked as if it hadn't been flushed in a week. There was a woman passed out on the bench, one stilettoed foot dangling off the edge at a wobbling right angle.

'When can I make a phone call?' Michelle asked the guard again. '¿Cuándo . . . teléfono?'

The guard raised a finger. 'Espérate,' he said.

Maybe that meant he'd come back.

She couldn't sit on the bench because of the passed-out woman (a hooker? Michelle thought she looked like one anyway), so she leaned against the wall opposite the barred front of the cell.

From here she could see into the cell across the way. It was filled with men, five or six of them, who milled around and muttered things she couldn't understand. One of them, a young guy, came over to the bars of his cell and pressed his face against them. 'Hello!' he said. 'Hello!'

Michelle ignored him. She hugged her knees to her chest and rested her head on them. It was stifling hot in the cell. No breeze came in from the small barred window above her.

This couldn't go on, could it? She couldn't stay here.

But she'd never make her flight, even if they let her out right now. And they weren't going to do that. Weren't going to suddenly decide it was all a mistake, that she was free to go.

They'd taken her watch along with her necklace and bracelets, so she had no way of marking the time beyond the square of darkening sky visible through the window. After it grew black, there was no way to tell at all.

Her head pounded; her body ached from

58

sitting on concrete. I shouldn't have had those drinks, she thought. There was a barrel of water, a sort of Sparkletts bottle in a wrought-iron stand that tipped to fill a solitary plastic cup, in one corner of the cell.

One cup? Michelle thought. One cup for everyone who's come in and out of here? And how clean was the water?

The woman on the bench stirred, moaned, and turned onto her side. She gagged a few times and threw up on the floor.

I should get up, Michelle thought, I should do something. Call for a guard. Make sure she doesn't choke.

She stayed where she was. The woman rolled onto her back, one arm flung over her eyes, and was mumbling to herself. Obviously she could breathe.

Not my problem, Michelle thought, and her own problems at the moment were nearly too long to list.

How had the drugs gotten in her purse? The policeman, most probably, but why? He hadn't seemed interested in a bribe.

Of course she hadn't checked in all of those pockets when she'd packed. There were several she rarely opened. It could have happened before that.

What were the penalties for drug possession in Mexico? Weren't they more serious than in the United States? And without a good lawyer . . . How would she find a lawyer? How would she pay for one?

Tears welled up without her even realizing.

This was too much, too much to take in, too much to handle.

A fight broke out in one of the other cells. That was what it sounded like anyway: sudden shouts, grunts, thuds.

Michelle stopped crying and wiped her nose on her gauzy sleeve. I have to keep it together, she told herself. There's no one to look out for me but me. Not anymore.

She'd get to make a phone call eventually, wouldn't she? The American consulate, that was who you called in situations like this. I'll call the consulate, she thought. They'll help me. This will all work out somehow.

Guards came to break up the fight, barking commands, slapping truncheons against the iron bars. The woman on the bench stirred again, spoke a few words seemingly in her sleep, and turned over to face the wall.

I have to drink something, Michelle thought. Her mouth felt as if the surfaces had been coated with glue. She stood up, tried to stretch out the cramps in her legs and back, and approached the water bottle.

Don't think about it, she told herself as she tilted the bottle and filled the communal cup. I'll just have to get a gamma globulin shot after I get out of here. Better that than passing out from dehydration.

After that she thought she might as well pee. Don't even look, she thought. Just go and get it over with. She squatted over the toilet, the backs of her thighs skimming the seat, willing her bladder to let go while she held the pose.

In the cell across the way, the young man had come back to press his face against the bars, watching her.

'Fuck off!' she spit, surprising herself.

★   ★   ★

The young man laughed and kept watching.

Whatever, she thought. What difference did it make at this point?

When she finished, she went back to her place against the wall, as far from the toilet as possible. She lay on the concrete floor on her side, head resting on her arm, and closed her eyes.

She didn't sleep — that was impossible. But she dozed, on and off. The murmurs of the woman on the bench, the laughs and cursing of the men in the cell across the way, all combined into a dream-narrative soundtrack that could not be precisely translated to waking life.

By midmorning even that poor half sleep was out of the question. The temperature in the cell rose steadily, the stink from the vomit and the toilet given fresh potency by the heat.

They took the other woman out of the cell around lunch, whatever time that was. Lunch was beans and tortillas and a Coke.

'When can I use the telephone?' Michelle asked. '*Teléfono*. I want to talk to the American consulate.'

'*Ahora no. Espérate.*'

'I have been in this cell for an entire day — '

She stopped herself.

Don't scream. Don't yell. Don't cry.

She took a few deep breaths, like she'd do in yoga class. 'When do I get to make a phone call?'

'Sorry, señora. Soon.'

A few more hours went by. They brought a couple of women into the cell, a beach vendor who'd gotten busted for selling trinkets without a license and a college student from Canada.

'Oh, my God,' the college student kept saying. 'Oh, my God. It was just a fender bender. I mean, that was all it was. And they put me in *jail*?'

Obviously yes, Michelle thought, but she didn't say that, just shook her head and made sympathetic noises. 'Things are a little different here.'

'Oh, my God, I can't believe this.' The student started sobbing. 'What . . . what happens next?'

A very good question as well.

Around sunset a guard called Michelle's name.

Finally, she thought, following him down the corridor. And then, *Great*. It had to be nearly 8:00 P.M. Would anyone even be at the consulate? What was she supposed to do, leave a voicemail?

The guard led her out of the cells, past the iron bars that separated them from the administration area, to the small green-and-beige lobby that was the gateway to the outside world.

Gary sat on a wooden bench against the wall, texting on his BlackBerry. Seeing her, he rose.

'Michelle, hey.' He crossed the room and rested his hands on her shoulders. 'How're you doing?'

She flinched. She didn't know Gary, but she didn't think she wanted his hands on her. 'I'm okay. Why — '

'First things first. Let's get you out of here.'

He cupped her elbow, fingers pressing against the back of her arm, guiding her toward the door.

'I don't understand.'

'I'll explain in the car.' He grinned at her. 'First things first.'

7

'The consulate called me.'

'I don't understand,' Michelle repeated. 'I didn't call them.'

They rode in Gary's car, a black Land Cruiser with tinted windows, looping around the airport on the highway, heading north. Leather seats. Gary seemed to do pretty well with his consulting, whatever it was.

'Mexican authorities are supposed to contact the consulate when they take an American citizen into custody,' Gary explained. 'That doesn't happen a lot of places, but Puerto Vallarta's better than most.'

'And the consulate called you?'

'I help them out now and again. I've got some experience with Mexican law.'

'I see.'

She must have sounded skeptical. Hell, she *was* skeptical.

'Well, their staffing's not what it should be,' Gary said. 'Not always enough to help out Americans in trouble. And when they mentioned your name, of course I wanted to do what I could.'

The sign on the two-lane highway said they were heading toward Tepic, wherever that was. The surrounding landscape was flat, green splotched with brown, broken up by the occasional gas station, cinder-block building and

64

cluster of scrubby palms. There was a lot of traffic, and the Land Cruiser's air-conditioning could not entirely filter out the raw diesel fumes from the buses in front of them.

'Where are we going?'

'Thought you might want to shower and change your clothes.' He tilted his head over his shoulder. 'Your stuff's in the trunk.'

They drove awhile in silence, the air conditioner drying the sweat on her skin to salt. Dirt from the jail powdered her arms and legs. Probably the rest of her as well.

'What's my situation?' she finally asked. 'Am I out on bail or . . . or what?'

'Looks like they won't be filing charges. At least not yet.'

'What does that mean, 'not yet'? Do I need to get a lawyer?'

'Well, you got me,' he said, turning to smile at her. 'And right now that's enough to keep you out of jail.'

'I don't understand.'

He turned back to watch the road, left hand on the wheel, right arm resting on the center console, hand drifting close to her thigh. 'You know, in Mexico you're guilty till proven innocent. If they'd charged you, the bail would've been pretty substantial. Or maybe they wouldn't have granted bail at all. Depends on the charges and the judge. Then the trial . . . well, it can take a while for the trial to even begin. A year's not unusual. You know the percentage of folks in Mexican prisons who haven't been convicted of anything? Then the sentences . . . ' His plump lips parted slightly as his smile broadened. 'Not a nice situation, especially not for a woman like you.'

'As opposed to a woman like someone else?' The words came out of her mouth before she could stop them.

Gary chuckled. 'You're a cool customer, Michelle. I sussed that out about you right away.'

They turned off the main highway and took a sudden turn to the left, toward the coast. Now they traveled on a two-lane road landscaped with evenly spaced palm trees. Michelle glimpsed tennis courts, swimming pools, brightly painted townhouses shaped like honeycombs.

'Here's what I don't understand: What was someone like you doing with cocaine? I'd of thought you'd know better.'

'It wasn't mine.' She didn't know if Gary would believe her or not, and she honestly didn't care. 'Somebody planted it. Probably the policeman.'

'A shakedown? Then how'd you end up in jail?' He shook his head. 'Maybe you ought to think about how else those drugs might've gotten into your purse.'

Michelle remained silent. She didn't have an explanation. Nothing made sense, no matter how she looked at it.

Gary sighed. 'You gotta be careful, hanging out with guys like Danny. Not that you had any way of knowing that.'

Daniel could have done it.

She felt like she'd swallowed an ice cube.

That night at the hotel, maybe. Or when she'd

gone to return his clothes. Or he could have hired someone else to do it. Maybe even the policeman.

But why?

She wasn't going to ask Gary. Not yet. She didn't trust Gary at all. But there was something else she could ask him.

'Why are you helping me?'

'You're a suspicious person, aren't you?' His grin broadened. 'Well, the way I see it, we're helping each other.'

★ ★ ★

Michelle took a long, hot shower. She was truly filthy, for one, and sore. Being in the shower also gave her time away from Gary. Time to think.

He'd taken her to a condo in a gated complex on the bay, a series of ten-story towers flanked by a golf course. On one side of the complex, the towers were only half built, still bare concrete and rebar, and even the completed towers had an unfinished look to them, uncluttered by any signs of occupancy. 'Yep, these just came on the market,' Gary had said. 'I practically have the whole floor to myself.' His unit, on the seventh floor, overlooked the golf course. 'It's a great course. You like to golf, Michelle? Maybe you and I could play a few rounds sometime.'

I should have just asked him to take me to the airport, she thought. I could have cleaned up in the restroom or something, gotten on a plane to somewhere, anywhere in the United States. But she'd been so tired, so out of her own element, that she hadn't thought of that soon enough. She'd just sat in Gary's expensive car, on Gary's expensive leather seats, and let him take her here.

There was something very wrong with this situation.

The attack in the hotel room. The pig's head. Two acts aimed against Daniel. And her. But it couldn't really be about her, could it? She was just a tourist who'd hooked up with a good-looking man she'd known nothing about.

So it had to be about Daniel. Until the drugs planted in her purse.

Maybe Daniel blamed her for what had happened to him, for the break-in and his injury. Maybe he thought that she'd set him up somehow, and this was some sick form of revenge.

The way Gary had shown up at the jail, playing her rescuer, everything suddenly fixed — she didn't believe that performance at all.

She felt dizzy and sick, like she was going to throw up. Which could have been from the jailhouse burrito and not just her nerves. Keep it together, she told herself. Get dressed and figure out some way to get out of here. Just get to the airport.

Figuring out what she'd landed in wasn't nearly as important as getting out of it.

She toweled off quickly, put on a clean blouse and knee-length shorts — because a dress felt too vulnerable — unlocked the bathroom door, and stepped out into the hall.

She could hear the TV blaring from the living

room — a comedy, she thought, because suddenly Gary laughed out loud.

Heart thumping, she stepped into the bedroom where her things were.

First things first. Make sure there were no more surprises in her luggage.

She searched her suitcase as quickly and thoroughly as she could. Nothing there, at least that she could find. She could tell that the suitcase had been unloaded and hastily repacked, but there was nothing unfamiliar here.

She checked her purse next. Opened every pocket. Dumped the contents out on the bed.

Nothing.

But something was different.

Her passport was gone.

★   ★   ★

Michelle decided to put on a little makeup. She didn't know what she'd gotten herself into with Gary, but she did know the advantages of looking good.

'Well, don't you look nice,' Gary said.

He'd turned the TV off. He sat at the table by the open kitchen, a setup not unlike the one at Daniel's place, though done on a larger, more expensive scale. It still had that same anonymous look. The art on the walls — Banderas Bay at sunset, with whales; donkeys by the cathedral, vaguely mystical; pseudo-Mayan corn maidens — she'd seen paintings like this countless times in the downtown Vallarta tourist galleries.

On the table was a pizza in a box, a salad in a plastic take-out container, and an open bottle of wine.

'Thought you might be hungry,' Gary said. 'I know this isn't exactly haute cuisine, but these guys do a pretty good job on short notice.'

'Thanks,' Michelle said, sitting down at the table. Pizza wasn't generally her thing, but she really was hungry. She helped herself to a slice and a scoop of salad. Gary poured her a glass of wine.

The pizza was good, and so was the salad. The wine was drinkable, which was good enough under the circumstances.

'You know, I can't find my passport,' she finally said.

'Anything else missing? Oh — ' He made a show of patting his chest, as if he'd stashed something in a nonexistent pocket. 'I have your phone and your jewelry. Almost forgot about it.'

'What about my passport?'

'Well, that's a little complicated.'

'Complicated how?'

He took a slow, deliberate sip of wine. 'They're dropping the charges, for now. But they don't quite trust you, Michelle. They want to keep their eye on you a little bit longer.'

That doesn't make sense! she wanted to scream, but she didn't.

'I guess I don't understand,' she said. 'Somebody planted a little bit of — what was it, coke? — in my purse. Not enough for anyone to really even care about. Otherwise you wouldn't have gotten me out so easily. Right? But you're

70

telling me they care enough to hold on to my passport?'

Gary smiled and served himself another slice of pizza, cutting the dangling strings of cheese with his knife. 'I knew you were smart. It's always a pleasure, finding someone like you. A diamond in the rough.'

'Look, Gary . . . ' How was she going to get herself out of this when she didn't even know what she'd gotten into? 'I'm really grateful for the help. But right now what I need to know is, when do I get my passport back? I have a lot on my plate, and I've got to get home.'

'Oh, yeah.' He seemed to find this doubly amusing. 'I imagine you do. I did a little checking into your situation — no place to live, a pile of debt, a lawsuit or two hanging over your head — I'm sure you can't wait to get back to all that.'

Michelle felt her cheeks burn red. 'I have obligations to deal with,' she managed.

'Husband dies, leaves you holding the bag . . . ' Gary shook his head. 'And all this time you spent . . . well, what is it you've been doing the last ten years, Michelle? Entertaining? You're capable of so much more.'

How the fuck did he know all this?

'Thanks for the compliment.'

Gary reached over to grasp the wine bottle, ready to refill her glass. Michelle put her hand on his and gave him a little squeeze. 'What about my passport?'

She wanted to see if the gesture would rattle him at all. It didn't.

71

'Like I said before, this is about us helping each other. Here's your chance to help me back.'

'What if I just went to the consulate, told them I lost my passport?'

'Oh, I wouldn't do that, Michelle.' His eyes widened ever so slightly, bloodshot beneath the puffy lids. 'I really wouldn't.'

8

He made It sound so simple.

'All you have to do is keep an eye on Danny for me a couple weeks. Let me know what he's up to, who he sees.'

'Why?'

'Danny's involved in some sketchy stuff,' he said. 'And it'd be real helpful to us to have a better idea of the specifics.'

' 'Us' being . . . ?'

'Well, it's really better if I don't say.'

Great, Michelle thought. 'You can't ask me to get involved with something when I don't even know who you are,' she said.

'Actually, I can.' He laughed, his cheeks rounded like a baby's. 'I just did.'

She almost got up from the table. What would happen if she just walked out the door?

'Now, come on, don't be mad. I'm a consultant, just like I told you.'

Cleansing breaths, she thought. 'And if I don't agree, you'll have me arrested again?'

'Now, where'd you get an idea like that?' Gary wiped the back of his hand across his wine-reddened lips. 'It's the Mexican authorities who'll have you arrested. I'm the one who'll keep them off you. So long as you do me this little favor.'

She watched him tuck a stray gold curl behind his ear. He was vain about his hair, she'd bet.

That color? Highlights.

'You want me to spy on him?'

'You make it sound so *formal*. Just spend some time with him, that's all.'

'And how am I supposed to do that?'

'We'll set you up someplace in Old Town, get you some walking-around money — I know things are kind of tight for you right now, so don't worry about any of that. In fact . . . '

Gary studied her for a moment. He put his elbows on the table, leaned forward, reminding her of a time-share salesman about to make his pitch.

'Michelle, instead of thinking of this as an inconvenience, why don't you think of it as an opportunity?'

'An opportunity?'

'This is important to us. We'll make it worth your while. Those financial problems you're having? I'm not gonna promise I can make them all go away. But I can help.'

She opened her mouth, then closed it. She'd very nearly asked him what kind of money he had in mind.

Don't get sucked into this, she told herself. There was no reason to believe a word Gary said.

'Gary, look . . . ' She let out a sharp sigh and poured herself some more wine. This man is crazy, she thought, watching his eyes light up, his cheeks flare red, as he spun this ridiculous scheme.

He'd better not be some sort of government agent, because she hated to think that her tax

74

money went to guys like this.

'I barely know Danny,' she said. 'What makes you think he's going to want to spend time with me?'

Gary chortled at that. 'Come on, Michelle. You know Danny likes spending time with you.'

'For one night.' Now she laughed. 'Look, it's nice that you think I'm some kind of . . . I don't know, femme fatale, but I have no idea if he wants to see me again. Especially after what happened.'

'What, the robbery? Well, that was hardly your fault.'

'Not just the robbery. When I went to his place to give him back his stuff . . . '

She thought about the pig's head. The flies.

Gary's idea of a joke.

That is, if Daniel had told her the truth.

'He didn't seem that happy to see me,' she said.

'Trust me, you play it right, he'll want to see you.' Gary leaned back in his chair, took a big swallow of wine. 'See, guys like Danny, they can have their little brown girls whenever they want them, but someone like you doesn't come along every day. Classy. Polished. Someone he can take to parties. Probably have celebrity stories to tell, living the life you did in L.A. He'll love all that shit.'

'Okay,' she said, just to shut him up. 'You want me to spend time with Danny. Say I do that. I'll tell you what we do and who we see. What if all we do is go to the beach and El Tiburón? Is that enough for you?'

'Just make a good-faith effort. That's all I'm asking.' He reached across the table and patted her hand. 'And trust me. I'll know if you don't.'

She wasn't sure what to say after that.

'You should tell me what he's involved with,' she finally said. 'That night in the hotel . . . Those men who came in — they had guns. You can't expect me to . . . to . . . '

Gary smiled at her. 'I wouldn't worry about anything like that happening again.'

She shivered a little in the overly chilled air.

He might not have had anything to do with the attack. Maybe he was just using it. Using her fear.

Don't let him see it, she told herself.

He stretched in his chair, wincing as he did. 'I can open another bottle of wine if you'd like, but I bet you're pretty tired. You should probably get some sleep. Start tomorrow fresh.'

Michelle nodded. 'I am kind of tired.'

'All right, then. See you in the morning.' He rose slowly, with a little groan, hand on his back. 'I'm gonna have to schedule a massage. You want a massage, Michelle? I know a great gal.'

Oh, I bet you do, she thought.

Gary started toward his bedroom. Then stopped. 'You take good photos,' he said suddenly. 'That a particular hobby of yours?'

Michelle didn't bother to ask him how he knew that. He'd had her stuff; he could easily have looked at the images on her cameras.

'I enjoy taking pictures,' she said.

'Like those ones of the pig's head. Sounds sort of funny to say, but those were artistic almost.

Like I could hang 'em up on my wall.' He gestured toward the kitchen. 'What do you think? Maybe do a . . . what do you call it? A trio? A triptych? Print up a few of those and hang them in the kitchen. I think that would look pretty cool.'

'If you'd like,' Michelle said. What else *could* she say?

Sipping the remains of her wine, she watched him go into the master bedroom and close the door. Finally, when there were no more sounds from Gary's bedroom, she stood and walked as silently as she could to the front door of the condominium. Jiggled the doorknob.

Locked. A double-keyed deadbolt, and no key in sight.

No phone. No neighbors. No way out.

* * *

She'd gone beyond exhaustion. Lying in bed, she felt wrung out, nerves exposed, like they'd been rubbed with sandpaper.

Who was Gary, and what did he want?

He wanted her to think he had government connections, that he was some sort of spook — that seemed pretty obvious, with all his remarks about 'helping' the consulate, his insinuations about her situation in Los Angeles, his claims that he would know whether she did what he wanted.

But she couldn't be certain — Gary didn't want her to be, for one thing. For another, it was easy to get information about people nowadays, wasn't it? There were plenty of public records, plenty of ways to get at things that were supposed to be private as well.

She hadn't called the consulate herself. She had only Gary's word that the consulate had called him. He could have set the whole thing up, with the policeman, with the coke, somehow manipulated the situation to get her out of jail, all so she would agree to 'keep an eye' on Daniel.

How did she even know if the charges had actually been dropped?

The only thing she knew was that Gary had some pull. Some power. And right now he had power over her.

Thinking of this, thinking of him sleeping in the room next door — he *was* sleeping, she thought; she could hear his gentle snoring through the wall — she got up, grabbed the little chair by the writing desk, and propped it under the doorknob, like she'd seen in the movies.

She still couldn't sleep.

What was the smart thing to do in this situation?

Maybe the whole business with the consulate was a bluff, and she should just go to them. Tell them her passport had been stolen, tell them she'd been kidnapped, tell them . . . well, maybe just that her passport had been stolen.

But what if Gary really *was* some kind of government agent? In the CIA or some other alphabet-soup agency? If he could set her up as easily as he had — as someone had — if the consulate was in on it . . .

This is crazy, she thought.

She tried a few cleansing breaths, but they didn't seem to help much.

Maybe an Ambien.

* * *

A driver would take her to her new hotel, 'a cute little place off Olas Altas,' Gary informed her the next morning as they sat at the table in his breakfast nook, drinking coffee. 'Not that Danny's likely to spot me if I took you, but PV's a small town. No point in taking chances.'

She'd harbored a vague hope that when she woke up this morning, things would have somehow gone back to normal. Gary would give her the passport, say it was all a mistake, and she'd head to the airport and home to Los Angeles.

And while she was fantasizing, she'd have a house again, preferably on the Westside. A condominium would do.

He gave her back her jewelry and her iPhone, everything but her passport. 'Oh, don't want to forget this.' He went into his bedroom and returned carrying an envelope.

Michelle took the envelope. It felt thick. 'Split it up,' Gary said with an offhand wave. 'Put some in your wallet and stash the rest.'

She opened it. There had to be at least five thousand dollars. Well, four thousand dollars and fifteen thousand pesos. Mouth dry, she counted out three thousand pesos and tucked the envelope into her sundries bag.

'Buy yourself an outfit or something,' Gary

said. 'And if you run out, just give me a call. I programmed a contact number into your phone. Speed-dial number eighty-six. Like *Get Smart*, right?' He snickered. Obviously he cracked himself up. 'The name that comes up for that is Ted Banks. It's an L.A. number. You can say it's your attorney or your cousin or your trainer — whatever you like. Just make it something you can sell. You know, in general, a good principle with this stuff? It's easier to keep track of the truth than a lie. So if you're gonna lie, keep it simple.'

'All right,' Michelle said, nodding like this was all completely normal and sane.

'I put Danny's number in there, too. You can tell him I gave it to you when I gave you his address, if he asks.'

Gary's phone rang. The ringtone was 'Ring of Fire.'

'Driver's here,' he said. 'Let me give you a hand with your bags.'

Outside the condo a white minivan idled by the driveway. Gary rattled off a few sentences in rapid Spanish to the driver, handed over some money.

'Okay, Michelle, looks like we're good to go.' He pointed to the driver. 'Gustavo here's a friend of mine. Make sure you get his card so you'll have someone reliable to drive you around town.' He opened the back door for her. 'Now, anything comes up, you don't hesitate to call me, okay?'

'Okay,' she said.

Gary held the door, waited for her to climb

into the backseat and buckle her seatbelt. 'Oh,' he said, like it was an afterthought. 'What was that about last night, putting a chair in front of the door?' He wagged a finger at her. 'What kinda guy do you think I am?'

For a moment she felt like she was a kid playing dodgeball back in elementary school — the ball catching her just under the ribs, knocking the wind out of her. How could he have known about that?

'I don't really know what kind of guy you are, Gary,' she said.

He smiled. 'No. I suppose you don't.'

9

Five thousand dollars. Gary threw around five grand like it was nothing.

Granted, there was a time when Michelle hadn't thought of five thousand dollars as a particularly large sum, from shortly after her marriage to Tom (she'd needed a while to get used to the idea) until shortly before his death (when some intuition had warned her that the way they'd been living was, on some level, not precisely real). But even then, five thousand dollars in cash stuffed casually into an envelope was not the way she was used to seeing money. Money was a concept, something represented by plastic, encoded in electronic transactions — abstract numbers to be moved from one account to another.

Five thousand dollars in cash, and more if I want it, she thought.

This just could not be good.

She briefly thought about asking Gustavo to take her someplace other than the hotel, maybe not to the airport but to the bus station, maybe. But though he seemed friendly enough — asking her where she was from, if this was her first time in Vallarta — he was Gary's friend.

Gustavo dropped her off at a small hotel tucked in a steep, cobbled street off Los Muertos Beach, not too far from the hotel where she'd stayed before. The entrance was easy to miss: a wrought-iron gate between two whitewashed walls, a narrow drive that dipped sharply and then rose up to meet a pink-tiled courtyard with a fountain in the middle. The rooms were grouped around it in two-story wings. A few mangy-looking dogs lay by the fountain, and a calico cat stretched out on a second-floor balcony, twined between two terracotta planters. About a half dozen guests — she assumed they were tourists, mostly older women and several older men — reclined in lounge chairs around the fountain, chatting with one another, reading books, sipping iced drinks.

The office was in a lower unit immediately to the right of the entrance. The side that faced the courtyard was almost entirely open to the air, with a low wall about waist high where abandoned drinks and ashtrays sat, waiting to be cleared. Inside was a counter, a round table with a grimy computer and several shelves of books, most of which were English-language paperbacks.

It shouldn't look so normal, she thought. It didn't feel real; it was like she'd arrived here in a state of jet lag.

'You're in Number Thirty-two,' the woman behind the counter said in lightly accented English. 'Do you need help to your room?'

'No. No, I don't think so.'

'We serve continental breakfast in the courtyard from seven to ten A.M.,' the woman explained. She was in her thirties, solidly built, with tanned olive skin, streaked hair, and above her breast a rose tattoo that peeked out from her embroidered tank top. 'And we have happy hour every night, from five until seven.'

'Great,' Michelle said. 'You know, I can't exactly remember. What's the last date of my reservation?'

The woman consulted her computer. 'You're paid through the fifteenth,' she said. 'But if you want to extend, just let me know. It's not so busy this time of year.'

Nearly two weeks. Was that how long she was expected to play this game?

At least the room was cute, almost a suite, with a mini-fridge, a microwave, a wardrobe that had a luggage stand and a small safe inside. Painted tiles formed borders along the walls; there were a few framed *molas* hung up as well, and the bed featured an elaborately carved headboard.

She put her suitcase down on top of the open cabinet by the wardrobe and stood there for a moment. The room was hot. It would take a while before the air conditioner cooled it down.

I have to get out of here, she thought.

She grabbed her purse and her good camera and bolted out the door.

In the courtyard the guests still sat, drinking, chatting, reading books. A dog trotted slowly past the fountain. It was as hot as her room and utterly still.

She slowed her steps so it wouldn't look like she was running, managed a smile and a half wave at the woman behind the counter, and pulled open the wrought-iron gate.

Free.

84

Up the hill, she thought. She was pretty sure that if she walked up the hill, she'd come to a broad avenue running north and south, where there were buses that went downtown, maybe even to the airport. What was stopping her from just getting on one? She had five thousand dollars in her purse. She could go pretty far with that, all the way to the border, certainly. Just walk across and tell the customs people she'd lost her passport. They wouldn't throw her in jail for that.

Behind her a car started with a misfire that sounded like a hammer on a tin can. She could smell the unburned gas. They probably didn't have strict emissions standards here, she thought, not like California. She kept walking, past a gay bar, a *lavandería*, which she knew meant 'laundry.' If I stay here, I'll need to wash my clothes, she thought; most of them were filthy. But it was crazy to think about staying here, wasn't it? This whole thing with Gary, whatever the money was, it couldn't be worth the risk.

It took a moment before she realized that the car she'd heard start matched her progress up the hill. It floated next to her, idling roughly, a presence she felt before she really took it in.

A police car. Not the Vallarta police, who drove white pickups with cheerful green geckos painted on them. A black-and-white sedan, with a shield on the door.

In the car just one officer: a big man with a mustache and aviator sunglasses. The man who'd arrested her.

When he saw that she'd noticed him, he

leaned his head toward the window. Stared at her, eyes obscured behind the sunglasses.

Her heart hammered. She almost bolted and ran, but she stopped herself. Instead she turned away and continued to walk up the hill. Act like there's nothing wrong, she told herself. Don't try to run. Don't give him an excuse.

The police car followed, cruising slowly up the hill, keeping even with her progress, past the Oxxo mart, past the yoga/Pilates studio.

The street dead-ended into a road that hugged the hill, curving out of sight a short distance ahead. At the junction were a sex shop and a tiny newsstand/Internet café.

She was aware of the police car turning left, toward downtown, though she wouldn't look directly. She kept walking another half a block, toward the junction, and then she stopped and turned around. The police car was gone.

The adrenaline drained out of her, leaving her trembling after it had gone, and she stumbled a little on the uneven pavement.

The policeman had staked out her hotel. He'd waited for her. Followed her. He'd wanted her to know about it.

Her phone rang. The soothing classical tone she used for known callers.

For a moment she didn't want to look. What if it was Gary, calling to threaten? To gloat?

It was her sister, Maggie.

Her hand shook, her finger slipped, and she almost missed the ANSWER key.

'Hello? Michelle? Is that you?' Maggie sounded frantic.

'It's me, listen . . . I'm fine . . . '

'What the fuck happened to you? We've been going crazy here! I mean, when you weren't home on Sunday, I thought, okay, maybe I got that wrong, but it's *Tuesday*, and — '

'I'm really sorry,' she said in a low voice. 'I'm still in Puerto Vallarta. It's been — '

'Jesus, Michelle! I mean, you could at least *think* about — '

'I'm sorry,' she repeated. 'But it's been complicated. Look . . . I'm in a weird situation. There's this guy named Gary, and . . . '

'Oh, you *met* someone?' Maggie's tone suddenly lightened. A new man — the big Get Out of Jail Free card.

'I wish. No, that's not it at all. This guy, Gary. Gary Wallace. Write that down. But maybe that's not even his real name. I . . . '

She took in a deep breath.

'Michelle? What . . . ? What's going on?'

She almost laughed. 'I wish I knew. They planted drugs in my purse and — '

'Are you in *jail*?'

'No. No. I mean, I was, but not anymore.'

'Jesus, what happened?'

Maybe I should write it all down, Michelle thought. Send Maggie an e-mail. But was that safe? Wasn't somebody, some government agency, reading everyone's e-mails?

If Gary was even part of the government.

'I don't know where to start. But write down Gary Wallace. And Daniel. Daniel . . . '

Christ, was it possible? Did she still not know Daniel's last name?

87

'Fuck,' she muttered. 'I . . . I have their cell-phone numbers. And some other information. I'll get it to you.'

'Michelle, can't you just . . . can't you just tell me — '

'No. I mean . . . '

If Daniel was involved with drugs . . . or if Gary was . . .

Could they do something to Maggie? To Ben?

She couldn't think right now.

'I'm fine,' she finally said. 'I'm probably here for another two weeks. I'll let you know what's happening. I . . . '

She didn't know what to say. She watched an older Mexican woman walk her Chihuahua down the street, stopping to scoop the dog into her arms before she stepped down off the tall curb.

'I'll let you know when I book the flight.'

I'll write a letter, she thought. A real letter, and I'll send it through the mail. Maybe to Maggie's office. Just in case . . .

She couldn't finish that thought. She stood there, hot and sweaty and unable to think at all.

Internet.

There were things she should look up. Things she should know. How the legal system worked here. What kind of trouble she might be in.

The chairs in the café were plastic and uncomfortable, the computers old and set to Spanish-language keyboards, but it still felt like a refuge, a place where she could sit and think and try to understand what had happened to her.

From what she could find out online in an

hour, Gary had told her the truth. At least about how the legal system worked. And the prisons — not that the prisons in the United States were much better, but someone in her position could probably avoid prison there. Here not so likely. Not while the case dragged on and on, waiting for trial.

The Mexican president had proposed decriminalizing small amounts of street drugs, but she didn't even know how much she was accused of possessing.

Before, she'd heard of a crackdown on drug smugglers by the Mexican federal government; she'd read stories about border massacres, headless bodies, corruption at every level of society, stories that had formed part of the fuzzy background to what little she'd known about Mexico. But she'd never associated any of that with resorts like Puerto Vallarta. Things like that didn't happen here, or so she'd thought.

Not often anyway.

Sinaloa cowboys. *Narcos*. Assassinations. Street battles with grenade launchers.

The cartels had infiltrated everything here. Police forces, judicial offices, even American embassies. There were former presidents whose relatives were awash in drug money from one cartel. A current president whose top officials were in the service of the another. The cartels slaughtered cops, politicians, journalists, and mostly, each other.

Maybe she was jumping to conclusions. She didn't know that the conflict between Gary and Daniel was about drugs.

But the money. The coke in her purse. And Daniel. He'd said he was a private pilot. Flying Gulfstreams. Wasn't that how you smuggled large amounts of drugs? In planes?

The air-conditioning chilled the sweat on her skin.

When she went outside, the police car was still nowhere in sight.

She started walking back to the hotel. The streets were quiet. A few tourists wandered in and out of the storefronts. An older gay couple stood on the corner, accompanied by a little dog straining at its leash. She passed a tiny stall, tucked between a money-changing window and a condominium building, that sold fresh juices, a youngish woman in a tight T-shirt grinding oranges, a small boy bouncing a soccer ball on his knee by the scoured wooden table where she worked. Then a boutique, with cocktail dresses and hand-tooled and beaded bags displayed in the window.

Michelle thought about the five thousand dollars Gary had given her. Maybe I should buy an outfit, she thought. Something nice, in case Daniel wants to go out with me again.

Crazy. She was getting as crazy as fucking Gary.

'Michelle?'

She flinched, and Vicky quickly said, 'Oh, sorry, didn't mean to scare you!'

Vicky, the American woman she'd met in El Tiburón. Gary's friend.

'Sorry,' Michelle said. 'I wasn't expecting anyone here to know me.'

Vicky wore another Hawaiian shirt, blue hibiscuses this time, a pair of khaki shorts that came just above her dimpled knees, and the Teva-style sandals that every American expat here who didn't wear Crocs seemed to favor.

'Well, it's a small town,' Vicky said. 'It's nice to see you again.'

For a moment Michelle had some strange thoughts — fragments of them, more accurately — like Vicky was actually an international drug smuggler, or a hit woman, or who knows what, a procurer of children for sex tourists. And then she took another look at Vicky, this stout, middle-aged American woman with dyed-blonde hair and a Hawaiian shirt and told herself she really needed to get a grip.

Even if Vicky *was* a friend of Gary's. One who just happened to be in the neighborhood.

Was Puerto Vallarta really that small a town?

'Nice to see you, too.'

Vicky frowned, wrinkling up her sunburned forehead. 'I'm not sure why, but I guess I thought you'd gone back to the States.'

'Well, I was planning to. But, you know, the craziest thing happened.'

She hesitated. She felt like she was about to step off a cliff.

'I was on my way to the airport, and my taxi . . . well, he hit a police car who pulled out in front of us. And the officer claimed his neck got hurt, and it turned into this whole drama. You wouldn't believe it.'

'Oh, my!' Vicky gasped. 'That kind of thing can get really nasty. What happened?'

'Like I said, it was crazy! They took me to jail, can you believe that? I mean, what did any of it have to do with me? And by the time they let me go, I'd missed my flight.'

Stick as close to the truth as you can. It's easier to remember the truth than a lie.

'Oh, honey, you've just had terrible luck.' Vicky gave her shoulder a quick squeeze. 'Yeah, that kind of thing happens when you get in car accidents here. It's because it's all the Napoleonic Code, you know? Guilty until proven innocent. But so long as you weren't driving, it's not really your problem.'

Michelle mimed a shudder, which wasn't hard to do. 'I can't imagine driving here,' she said. 'Especially after that.'

'So did they give you a credit for your ticket? Will you be able to get home okay?'

Her heart thudded hard in her chest. She hadn't thought to check on the status of her ticket.

You have five grand in cash, she told herself. Make something up.

'Sure, getting home's not really a problem. I just thought . . . ' Michelle smiled. 'You know, it's starting to feel like something doesn't want me to leave. I got a room down the street for the next week or so. Just so I could, you know, give this place a chance. See what I think about being here.'

She gave a little half shrug. 'It's kind of embarrassing for me to say this, but I don't have a lot going on at home right now.'

'I understand. I really do.' Vicky stared at her

with an almost enthralled expression, as if she'd found a fellow traveler. 'This is a nice place, Michelle. I'm so glad that you're giving Vallarta a chance. Not everybody would, if they'd had stuff like that happen to them.'

'Well, bad things happen everywhere. I mean, I'm from Los Angeles.' She spread her hands wide, palms to the heavens. 'I'm used to stuff happening.'

Vicky hesitated. 'You know, when you're an expat, it's easy to get isolated,' she said, a little shyly. 'Just sort of hang out with other Americans and stay in our routines. But there's a whole other side of life here. If you're interested.'

'Thanks,' Michelle said. 'That's really nice of you.'

Vicky rummaged around in her fannypack (a fannypack? people still used fannypacks?) and drew out a silver business-card case.

'Here,' she said, extracting a card. 'This is my contact information. If you ever feel like getting together, if you need anything, just give me a call or drop me an e-mail.'

★ ★ ★

A part of Michelle couldn't believe that she'd done it. She'd stood there and lied. Sticking close to the truth, as Gary had recommended.

Just like he'd wanted her to do.

It hadn't been that hard.

She felt as though she'd crossed some sort of line, but it wasn't irrevocable. It had only been with Vicky.

Trying it with Daniel wouldn't be the same.

Michelle sat on the edge of the bed in her room at Hacienda Carmen and weighed her options.

Play along and call Daniel or try to run. Trust someone to help her.

Not the local authorities, that was for sure.

The consulate? Would they believe her? Protect her if she got hauled off to jail again?

Was there someone back home who could help?

Her own lawyer specialized in finance. Bankruptcy. Civil lawsuits. He'd know a good criminal attorney, certainly, but she couldn't afford to pay the lawyer she already had, let alone a new one.

Not her sister. It seemed to her that Maggie barely coped with her life as it was — and besides, what could Maggie really do?

Tom's friends?

The ones caught up in the scandal weren't in a position to help. His acquaintances who'd ridden out the storm, how many of them wanted to be associated with Tom? With Tom's widow? They were *his* friends anyway, not hers, and a lot of them weren't terribly good friends when it came down to it.

The people in their social circle, the charity friends, entertainment-industry lawyers, doctors, entrepreneurs — any of them?

Her own friends, her real friends, she could count them on her fingers. Friends from college. One was a costumer for TV and film. Another a Web editor. Her husband was a lawyer, albeit

94

one who dealt with corporate mergers. Could he help?

Office manager. City planner. Interior designer.

What could she even say to them?

How had she ended up like this?

You can't think about that now, she told herself.

Just go along with it, then.

She tested that option, gingerly, as if she were putting weight on an injury, seeing how it felt.

It felt like giving up.

But was there a better choice?

It wasn't like Gary was asking her to be a drug mule or anything like that, she told herself. Just to hang out with Daniel, tell him what they did and who they saw — that is, if Daniel wanted to see her.

Danny's involved in some sketchy stuff.

If it starts feeling dangerous, if I think I'm not safe, I'll have to take my chances with the consulate, she thought. Or, better, get out of town somehow.

If she could, with the policeman watching.

★   ★   ★

She didn't think the story she'd used for Vicky would work on Daniel.

Vicky wanted to believe, loved Vallarta so much that she wouldn't question Michelle's decision to stay longer, even after all that had happened.

Daniel, however, had been there for some of the worst of it. Had caught Michelle in his

95

apartment taking pictures of a rotting pig head. Even if he'd believed her explanation, what must he think of her, finding her doing something like that? She could hardly explain it to herself.

Say one thing for Gary: At least he liked her photos.

Add the disastrous first date (if she could even call it that), with her weeping in bed followed by masked gunmen and concussions — why would Daniel even consider spending time with her at this point?

Why had he asked her out to dinner?

She could hardly believe he was still interested. Maybe he was just being polite.

Or he was suspicious of her and had wanted a chance to find out more.

She stared at her phone, her heart pounding, thinking, He might be dangerous. He doesn't trust me. He's into sketchy stuff.

He might still want to know more.

That was how to play it.

Great, Michelle thought. I'm thinking like Gary. And it's James Bond as told by *Cosmo*.

★　★　★

He didn't seem to recognize her when she called.

'It's Michelle,' she said. 'From Los Angeles.'

'Hey.' He sounded surprised. She couldn't tell if he was pleased. 'You back in L.A.?'

She laughed a little. 'No. I missed my flight.'

She made the call from the bedroom, pacing out onto the balcony from pent-up nerves.

'Oh, yeah? What happened? You get caught in

96

cruise-ship traffic or something?'

'It's . . . it's complicated.' She stood on the balcony staring into the courtyard, looking down at the guests sitting in their loungechairs, drinking margaritas, reading paperbacks.

This is a bad idea, she thought.

'I'm here for a couple more days,' she said. 'I was wondering if that dinner invitation was still open.'

There was a silence on the other end of the line. The calico cat stirred from its position between the terracotta pots, stretched, and padded over to sniff at her ankle.

Maybe he'd turn her down. If he did, then what? She'd tell Gary she tried? Would that be enough?

Yes or no. She wasn't sure which option was worse.

'Yeah,' he said. 'Yeah, it is. You free tonight?'

10

'It's a great place,' Daniel told her. 'The view's amazing, and the chef's from California.'

'Sounds wonderful,' Michelle said. She hoped she sounded enthusiastic.

Daniel picked her up at Hacienda Carmen in a black Jeep, a tricked-out Wrangler with the slogan RUBICON painted above the front fender. Great, Michelle thought.

'Something funny?'

She must have smiled. She was going to have to watch herself. 'No, I . . . This looks like a nice Jeep.'

'Yeah, it's really good for around here.'

He wore a white shirt and khaki pants, and she had to admit he looked good, with his tan and a shadow of beard. The bandage on his forehead was actually kind of rakish.

This is not your beach book, she reminded herself.

'How's your head?' she asked.

'It's okay. No big deal. I'll get the stitches out in a few days.'

'Have you heard anything? Did they catch the guys, or . . . ?'

'No,' he said shortly. 'They probably won't. The police here . . . ' He shrugged. 'Some of them try.'

They drove most of the way in silence, across the river, toward downtown and the cathedral.

What am I supposed to do? she thought. *Spend some time with him* — and do what?

'So what happened with your flight?' he finally asked.

'My taxi hit a cop car.'

Daniel winced. 'Oh, man. Seriously?'

'Yep.'

'Jesus, did somebody put a curse on you or something?'

He was smiling, acting like it was a joke, but she couldn't tell if he believed her.

'Maybe.' She smiled back. 'But the pig's head? That one's on you.'

'Hah.' He focused on the road. 'Yeah. I just need to find out who cursed me.' He glanced at her, smiling again, eyes hidden behind his sunglasses. 'Maybe we'll figure it out over drinks.'

★ ★ ★

Daniel was right. The view from the restaurant was amazing. The two of them sat at a table by the railing of a large balcony, sipping a decent Mexican chardonnay and watching the sun sink behind the cathedral tower.

'There's the pirate ship,' Daniel said, pointing.

It looked like a pirate ship, Michelle thought, a Disneyland reproduction of one anyway, a Spanish galleon that ferried tourists around the bay.

'Cannon'll start going off in about a half an hour,' Daniel said. 'Then there's fireworks. I went on one of those pirate cruises once.' He poured them both more wine, not waiting for the server. 'They make the women help raise the sails, but they'll give you a massage first. Then you sit around and learn about Mexican culture. And you can drink as much as you want.'

'Sounds like fun,' Michelle said, though in fact she did not think that it did.

Daniel shrugged. 'It's okay. Except after the big battle, the pirates all sing 'We Are the World.'' He grinned. 'Man, I hate that song.'

'Especially sung by pirates.'

'How about this?'

He meant the restaurant. It was a nice place, built around a series of terraces, simply but elegantly decorated. The menu reminded her more of Wolfgang Puck than Mexican; the service was attentive and professional.

'I like it,' she said, which was the truth.

Daniel ordered another bottle of wine for the meal, a red this time, also from Baja. Surprisingly good. Who knew they made good wine in Baja?

Their main courses had just arrived when Daniel leaned back in his chair and stared at her, smiling slightly, sizing her up, the way he had when they'd first met.

'So the thing with the cop . . . Did they want you to testify in court or anything like that?'

She flinched, thinking of the policeman who'd arrested her, of sitting in the back of the squad car with her hands cuffed, the pressure on her wrists, the smell of sour beer and vomit.

That wasn't what Daniel had meant, was it? He was asking about the lie she'd told him.

'I hope not,' she said. 'Basically we all went to the jail, and I told them what happened. They wanted my name and my number and contact information, and I gave it to them. I didn't really understand what was going on half the time, to be honest.'

'Man, if I were you, I would've thought about getting out of town.' He was watching her carefully over the brim of his wine-glass. 'You don't want to get tangled up with the police here. There's a lot of corruption.'

'Oh. I didn't even think about that. I thought . . . well, I wasn't driving, so it wasn't really my problem.'

She looked at him. Met his eyes. Pretend you mean it, she told herself. 'Should I worry?'

'Probably not,' he said, giving her that sidelong grin. 'Sometimes I'm a little paranoid. But you don't always know who they're working for.'

She hesitated. 'You mean they work for the *narcos*?'

She stumbled on the word.

Maybe he hadn't noticed.

'Sometimes,' he said, almost casually. 'Police don't get paid too well, for one thing. And sometimes they don't have much choice about it. *Plata o plomo*,' he pronounced.

'What does that mean?'

'Silver or lead. Get on the payroll or die.'

He poured her some wine, letting the wine splash against the side of her glass, deliberately casual, like he was a little drunk.

'How long were you thinking about staying?' he asked.

She managed a chuckle. 'After what you said, I'm really not sure.'

'The last time I saw you, you seemed like you were in a hurry to get back.'

'I was.' She toyed with her epazote-marinated shrimp. How to answer him? 'I have a lot to deal with. My husband, when he died . . . he left me with some loose ends. None of them very pleasant. When I missed the plane, I just . . . ' She put on a small smile. A properly tremulous one, she hoped. 'Decided I'd rather stay on vacation a little longer.'

'Yeah, I can see how that makes sense.'

The way he said it, his voice flat, she could tell that he didn't trust her. Why would he? The explanation sounded ridiculous to her own ears.

Fine, she thought. He doesn't trust me, we get the check, I go back to Hacienda Carmen, and tomorrow I tell Gary the whole thing was a bust.

And then what would Gary do?

I can't go back to that jail, she thought. I can't.

It was easy to let her eyes fill up with tears. It was hardly even acting.

'Tom was in finance,' she said. 'Real estate. He made some questionable deals. A lot of them, actually. I didn't know. I guess I should have paid more attention, but it was Tom's business. I thought it was okay. Or if it wasn't, he'd tell me. But he didn't. Then, when he died . . . '

'You were sandbagged,' Daniel said, watching her.

'Well, it was unexpected. Not like cancer, he just . . . It was his car. Totaled. They think he had a heart attack. He hadn't planned for it. I'm sure he didn't think that he'd . . . '

Hardly acting at all.

'It wasn't his fault,' she managed.

Even though she knew that it was.

'I should have paid more attention,' she repeated. Because that was true as well.

Daniel shook his head. 'Man . . . ' Then he did something unexpected — he reached out his hand and rested it on hers. His hand felt warm. Strong.

'You've had a really rough time. It sucks you've had to go through all that on your own.'

'I have friends. People have helped. It's just . . . ' She had to stop for a moment. 'Anyway, it is what it is. I just figured it could all wait a little longer.'

His thumb gently rubbed the back of her hand. 'Sounds like a good plan.'

★　★　★

When they got back to Hacienda Carmen, Daniel parked the Jeep outside the gate, climbed down from the driver's seat, and opened the door for her.

'Thanks for the dinner,' she said. 'I really enjoyed it.'

'Thanks for giving me another chance. I didn't think you would.'

She laughed. 'Well, I could say the same thing. I haven't been a lot of fun to be around.'

He grinned. 'I bet you're a lot of fun.'

They paused for a moment in the shadow of

the wrought-iron gate. He leaned down and kissed her.

She kissed him back, tasting the tang of wine on his tongue, the slight saltiness of his lips. He responded, circling his arms around her, bringing her to him, and she could feel herself wanting to let go, wanting to lose herself in him.

You can't, she thought. It isn't safe.

'So what do you think?' he asked, his breath warm against her ear.

It was what Gary wanted her to do, wasn't it? *Spend some time with him* — this was really what he had in mind.

'Look, no pressure,' Daniel said. 'I know things got off to a really bad start, and if you, you know . . . ' He shrugged a little. 'Whatever you want to do.'

Here was her out. She could say good-bye to him now, and that would be the end of it. There wouldn't be another date. You couldn't go backward, in her experience. It never worked.

What would happen if she ended it here?

She felt his body against hers, the stubble of his beard brush her cheek, the scent of him that filled her intake of breath.

She thought about the jail. The airless heat, the hard cement, the reeking toilet.

Silver or lead?

'Do you want to come up?' she asked. 'Just for a while?'

It wasn't really dangerous, she told herself. He couldn't actually hurt her, not here, in her own hotel. People would see him. People would know.

'Yeah,' he said. 'That sounds good.'

The lights were off in the little office behind the counter, the courtyard was deserted. There has to be someone up, she thought. It's only . . . What time was it?

A sudden blur of movement at her feet — the cat, racing up the stairs that led to her room.

'Cute place,' he said in a low voice.

'Yes.' Her voice caught. 'It's . . . it's quiet, mostly.'

I shouldn't have said that, she thought. He'll think we're alone here. That he can do what he wants and no one will know.

'There's usually people in the courtyard. It's not the most private. You can hear people in the next room.'

'I'll be vewwwwy quiet,' he said with a grin.

They climbed up the stairs. The cat waited there, on the low wall. Arched its back and then stretched down like it was doing yoga. Downward-Facing Cat.

'Hey, cat,' Daniel said, holding out his hand for it to sniff.

Her hand shook as she fumbled for the key.

It was hot inside.

She turned on the fans, the air conditioner that didn't exactly work. 'There's wine in the fridge,' she said. 'A white. Do you want some? Or . . . ?'

He crossed the room in a few steps, put his hands on her shoulders, and pressed up against her back. She flinched.

'Hey,' he said, stepping away. His hands guided her, gently, to face him. 'Are you okay?'

'I . . . ' She swallowed hard. 'Yeah. I'm just . . . '

'Look.' He stood there, hands at his sides. 'We don't have to do this.'

Was that true? Did she still have a choice?

She'd thought she'd already crossed that line.

She had to get a hold of herself, right now. Take control. Or . . . or what?

She didn't know.

Fake it, she thought. You know how to do that.

'Sorry,' she said. 'I just had, you know . . . ' She touched her forehead and tried to smile. 'I thought about that night we met, and those guys, and . . . ' She shuddered. 'It's stupid.'

He stared at her, his eyes narrowed, and then he seemed to relax. She could see the change in his face.

'It's not stupid. That was pretty messed up.'

He went over to the fridge and retrieved the bottle of wine. 'So how do we open this?'

'There's a corkscrew by the sink. In the drawer.'

'Sit,' he said.

She did, on the side of the bed, her legs trembling.

He came back with a couple of tumblers and the open bottle, and sat down next to her.

'Not like I need any more wine,' he said, pouring them each a glass.

'Me neither.' She clutched the tumbler he gave her and smiled shakily.

He lifted up his glass, and after a moment she raised hers.

'What are we toasting?' she asked.

'I don't know.' He gave her that half a grin, the one where she wasn't sure what he was really thinking, that crinkled the crow's-feet around his blue eyes and sharpened the lines of his cheekbones. 'Why don't you tell me?'

Her move, then.

'I'm not good at toasts.' You can do this, she told herself. She clinked her glass against his, took a swallow, and then put her tumbler down on the nightstand, her mouth dry, her heart pounding.

He took a sip of his wine and watched her.

She leaned in, her lips grazing his. Softly. A taste. He held back, still holding his glass, still watching her. Looking for something, some sign of her real intentions, maybe.

Fuck it, she thought. So show him. Pretend you mean it.

He let her kiss him. Let her straddle him. Her heart was still racing, but that could be from desire, couldn't it? That's what he'd think, probably. She wasn't sure herself by now.

'Guess I'd better put this down,' he said, stretching out his arm, setting the tumbler on the nightstand. He slid his other hand up her thigh.

It wasn't so hard to pretend.

11

Daniel slept for a while. She lay there listening to his deep, even breaths. At least he didn't snore.

Not that she'd been able to sleep.

Though it really had been okay. If she'd been able to forget the circumstances, it might even have been fun. She'd almost forgotten, once or twice.

Even so, she wasn't about to fall asleep with him in her bed.

I just need to find out who cursed me.

She lay there — muscles knotting in her shoulders, acid in her gut like a weight — and watched him sleep.

Shortly after dawn Daniel yawned, stretched, and sat up.

The rooster that had started up around 3:00 A.M. began another round of crowing. And was that a donkey?

'Hey,' Daniel said. He leaned over and kissed her cheek.

'Hey.'

'I should go. Got some stuff I got to do today.'

She watched him find his clothes, put them on, check his pockets for his keys, like it was all some jerky, stop-motion movie, her eyes closing now and then despite her best intentions to stay awake.

He came back to the bed and kissed her again, on the lips this time.

'I'll call you,' he said.

'I'd like that.'

She smiled at him, lifted a hand and wiggled her fingers as he paused by the door and gave her a mock salute.

Maybe he didn't mean it any more than she did — maybe it was just something to say after a one-night stand that he had no intention of repeating. Well, two nights, she amended, but the first night had hardly counted. This was just finishing what they'd started.

She managed to sleep for a little while after that, until her phone rang. The default tone for known callers. She fumbled around on the nightstand for the phone. By the time she found it, the ringing had stopped.

Two minutes later it started again.

She grabbed the iPhone and hit ANSWER.

'Hey, Michelle. Ted Banks.' A chuckle. 'You have a nice night?'

She stared at the phone. How could he know?

'You know, *Ted*, if you were really in Los Angeles, it'd be six A.M. Kind of early for office hours.'

Gary wheezed out another chuckle. 'Oh, I knew you were good, Michelle. Look, let's meet for lunch. I got a little something for you. And we can talk about your date. Call me when you wake up, and I'll let you know where.'

He disconnected.

Did he still have people spying on her? Was that how he knew? She thought about that night in his condo, how he'd known the next morning that she'd put a chair in front of the door.

109

Some kind of hidden camera? A bug?

What if he'd been watching?

She bolted out of bed.

She tried to remember movies and TV shows she'd seen where rooms had been bugged. Radios, she thought, they put bugs in radios, but there wasn't a radio here. In the television? She crouched down in front of the blank gray picture tube and saw only her dim reflection. She unplugged the television anyway. Jiggled the remote, opened it, plucked out the double-A batteries.

In the overhead light? She climbed up on top of her bed. Stretched out her arm to try to touch the dusty fixture. No use.

Electrical outlets, she thought. She'd seen some show where they planted bugs behind the switch plates.

She crouched down in front of the outlet by her bed, examined the screws, ran her finger over the heads to see if they stuck out, before it occurred to her that this was pointless.

If there *was* a bug in here, how would she even recognize it?

★ ★ ★

She fell back onto the bed, pulled the sheet over her head. She felt like shit. She hadn't had a decent night's sleep in days. Don't think about anything, she told herself. Try to sleep.

She tried. But there were the donkeys. The rooster. The kids, laughing, on their way to school.

110

When the gas truck rumbled up the street, with its recorded racing fanfare and distorted shout of *'Global Gas!'* broadcast through a bullhorn (and she heard it three times while the truck apparently waited in traffic), Michelle gave up.

She decided to do some yoga. Nothing complicated; the tile floor wasn't ideal. I could buy a mat, she thought, if I'm going to be here awhile. Use some of Gary's money. There was a Walmart here, and a Costco; they'd have things like yoga mats.

It was another one of those thoughts that, even as she had it, seemed like further evidence that Gary's insanity was contagious and she'd been infected. How can I even be thinking this way? she wondered. I need to come up with a plan. What I'm going to do. How I'm going to get out of this. Not think about what to buy with Gary's money.

But she had no idea what to do, none at all.

Yoga first. Quiet the monkey mind, the constant chatter of normal human concerns. Wasn't that what the instructors always said? She did fine with that as long as she was moving, doing poses. But at the end, Savasana, the Corpse Pose, when you're supposed to just let go, do nothing — that's when her monkey mind would come roaring back, the second the instructor started telling the class to relax, to think of nothing.

Stop it, she told herself. She went through the poses, lost herself for a while in the familiar movements, working up a sweat before she'd even started. It was already hot, so humid she couldn't tell if she was sweating or just taking on the water in the air.

After that she showered, dressed, and went down to the courtyard for coffee.

It was early yet, the sunlight still diffuse behind the hills east of town. Only two other guests were out, a heavy woman some years older than Michelle who sat in one of the loungers reading a novel, and an even older man puttering around the yard, his bony pelvis jutting against the waist of his shorts.

Michelle took her cup of coffee to a chair by the fountain and sipped, watching the cat chase leaves around the courtyard.

★　★　★

Gary wanted to meet for lunch at the Outback Steakhouse. 'In the Zona Hotelera — that's the Hotel Zone.'

'Okay,' Michelle said. 'I got the 'hotel' part, but where is it?'

'North of downtown, just before the marina. In front of the Krystal hotel. Ask any cab driver, he'll get you there.'

An Outback Steakhouse, Michelle thought. Great. She wouldn't think of going to a chain like that at home — hardly ever anyway. Now here she was in *Mexico*, where she should be eating . . . well, *Mexican* food, heading to the home of Bloomin' Onions and giant hot-fudge pecan brownies.

To meet with a crazy man.

I really should just leave, she thought, sitting in the back of the cab. Get out now. Go to Tijuana, seriously, and figure out a way home from there. All she had to do was get across the border; then she could take the trolley to downtown San Diego.

A story she'd read in the Internet café flashed into her mind unbidden. Something about headless bodies, in oil barrels, in Tijuana. Kids on their way to school finding them. Was that right? Or was she confusing two stories?

Corpses in vats of lye. A hit man called 'The Soup Maker.' Because that's how his victims ended up. Stewed in barrels of chemical soup.

If Gary was connected with people like that . . .

Staring out the window at the condominiums and Sheratons and Starbucks that populated the Hotel Zone, she thought, It seems so normal. So safe.

Things like that don't happen here.

She felt better physically at least. The yoga had helped, and that had been a pretty good workout last night, she thought, feeling the pleasant soreness between her thighs. She hadn't felt that in a while.

She caught herself smiling.

Don't make this into something it isn't, she told herself. Just because he's good in bed, that doesn't make him a good guy.

She thought of how he'd treated her at dinner. With real understanding, or a very good impression of it. How he'd been patient with her when they'd gone back to her room. Had let her decide what she wanted to do.

He *seemed* like a good guy.

If he found out the truth . . .

Maybe I should tell him, she thought.

She already knew that she couldn't trust Gary. He'd set her up, hadn't he? Had blackmailed her into this. Whoever he was, whomever he worked for, she had only his word that Daniel was some kind of criminal.

I'll see what Gary wants, she thought. Have the lunch. Decide after that.

*　　*　　*

Gary waited for her at a booth in the back of the restaurant. 'Hey there, Michelle,' he called out, patting the banquette next to him. 'I ordered us a Bloomin' Onion.'

She sat. 'Do you know how many calories are in one of those?'

'Well, that's why you look the way you do and I look how I do,' he said, grinning. 'I don't think enough about things like that. What can I get you to drink?'

'Just an iced tea.'

For lunch she ordered the steak salad, with olive oil and vinegar instead of the Danish blue cheese dressing and without the Aussie Crunch, whatever that was. After some hesitation she kept the cinnamon pecans. Fattening, but she liked pecans.

Gary ordered the prime rib.

'So tell me about your date,' he said after their drinks arrived.

'There's not much to tell. We went out to dinner.'

'What did you talk about?'

'Small talk mostly.'

'The whole night?'

'Well, no.'

She told him about the lie she'd made up to explain why she was still in Vallarta.

'And he went for it?'

'I wasn't sure at first. But he seemed to, after I . . . explained a little bit about my personal situation.'

'Danny to the rescue, huh? He felt sorry for you, right? You give him a few tears?'

It must have shown on her face, her surprise that he'd read the situation so accurately.

Gary chuckled. 'Trust me, Danny's a predictable guy in a lot of ways. A damsel in distress — I knew he couldn't resist.'

'You might have given me a hint about that. What if I hadn't come up with the right thing to say?'

'I had a feeling you would. And I guess I was kind of curious to see what you'd come up with on your own.' He lifted his drink. Scotch, it looked like. 'Good job, Michelle.'

'Thanks.' She didn't raise hers.

'So after dinner . . . what happened?'

The way he sat there, that little smile lifting the corners of his cherub lips, he knew what had happened.

He had someone watching her — he had to. The woman at the front desk. The policeman. Someone she didn't even know.

'We went back to Hacienda Carmen.' She kept her voice flat. Don't respond to him, she told herself. That was what he wanted, a reaction. To rattle her.

'How was it?'

Michelle felt her cheeks redden. 'What do you want me to tell you, Gary? You want a blow-by-blow?'

'Hey, don't be mad! I think you really have a talent for this sort of thing.'

'You mean sleeping with men I don't care about?'

'Now, come on, I didn't say that.' He patted her hand. 'You're good. You really are. Adaptable. That's important.'

She supposed there was some truth to that. She'd been adaptable enough in Los Angeles, hadn't she? Good at pretending she was interested in things and people she didn't care about.

Good at playing a role.

'So do I get a prize?' She knew she sounded angry. She supposed that she was. She didn't like thinking of her life this way.

Gary appeared to consider.

'Well, I told you we might be able to help with some of your financial problems.'

'Okay,' she said. 'So I fucked Danny. What's that worth to you? You'll pay off one of my credit cards?'

I'm done, she thought. Fuck this. I'm going to get up and walk out the door. Just leave. Let him stop me.

'Why, sure,' Gary said, sipping his scotch.

'Why don't we start with the Working Assets Visa? You use that one a lot.'

She froze. 'How . . . ?'

'Is that the card where every time you charge something at Fred Segal or Barneys or what have you, they throw a couple pennies at saving the whales? Or I don't know, maybe it's stopping global warming.'

Maybe he'd had access to her wallet when she was in the jail. That might be how he knew.

Have some ice tea, she told herself. Don't show him anything.

'We vote where the money goes, once a year,' she said.

She actually had no idea where the contributions went. She'd never paid much attention.

'Consider it done.'

Except . . . she hadn't brought that card with her. It was close to maxed, and she'd left it in Los Angeles.

I should say something, she thought. Tell him that she didn't want his money.

Maybe he didn't mean it.

Their food arrived.

'So here's what I'm thinking,' Gary said after a few mouthfuls of prime rib and potato. 'You know, I really am impressed with that photography you're doing. So my thought is, we should put that in play.'

Michelle took a bite of her steak. She didn't have much appetite, but eating slowed things down, gave her a chance to think before she responded.

What was he going to do, set her up as some

117

sort of photographer? Have her take wedding photos on the beach?

'What do you mean?' she asked.

'See, it would be real useful to us to get some pictures of Danny's associates.'

'You want me to take pictures of Danny's friends?' *Like I'm some kind of paparazzi*, she almost said but didn't. 'You don't think that would look a little odd?'

'We've got that covered.'

Gary reached for something next to him on the banquette. A small brown paper bag. He put it on the table, next to Michelle's iced tea.

'Take a look.'

She set down her fork and opened the paper bag.

Inside was what looked like a jewelry box — black flocking, hinged on one side. In that was . . .

A watch?

It was oversize, clunky, stainless steel, with a linked stainless-steel band, a sort of sporty look to it. Not the sort of thing she'd wear at all.

Oh, please, she thought. Tell me this isn't a hidden camera.

But it must be. Underneath the insert on which the watch sat was a small USB cable.

This was too much. The whole thing was too much, but this really was too much.

'Pretty neat, huh?' Gary said. 'You can do videos, too. Sound and everything. And when you're done, you can upload 'em to your phone and send them to me.'

Like a little kid. Playing spy.

118

'You can't be serious.' She took in a deep breath. 'This is out of control. I'm not . . . I can't do this.'

'Sure you can! Lemme tell you how it works. It's easy.'

She listened in disbelief as Gary babbled on about the pinhole lens, the Bluetooth connection, the USB port, and battery life.

'Gary,' she finally said, 'it's just not my style.'

'Well, yeah, I know you'd usually wear something classier. Cartier or whatnot. If I'd had a little more time, maybe I could've managed something more designer. But this one's not bad. We spent some money on it, you know?'

'I mean, taking pictures of somebody with a watch!' Cleansing breathes, she told herself. 'I wouldn't be comfortable.'

'Now, come on, Michelle, don't go all soft on me.' Gary's voice suddenly was far from soft. 'You can do this. When are you seeing him? Got any plans set?'

'Maybe . . . I mean . . . ' Get a grip. 'I'm not sure. He said he'd call.'

'He'll call. Trust me on that. I know Danny. I know what he likes to do when he's stressed.' He smiled at her. 'You play your cards right, maybe we'll pay another one of them off.'

Don't take the bait, she told herself. She drew in a deep breath. 'Is this about drugs?'

'Drugs? Now, what makes you say that?'

'Because I've heard about those people,' she went on, 'and they're not just violent, they're crazy. They cut peoples' heads off. And you want me to . . . to do . . . I don't even know what I'm doing here.'

'I told you not to worry about any of that.' He stared at her, his eyes hard, and for a moment he frightened her. 'All you have to do is exactly what I tell you to, and you won't have any problems.'

You can't let him intimidate you, she told herself. You have to stand up to him. 'You keep telling me Danny's dangerous, but you won't tell me what he does. How do I know? How do I know you're telling me the truth?' She stared back. 'Maybe you're the one who's into the sketchy stuff, Gary.'

He chuckled at that. 'I like your spirit, you know?' He took a long sip of his drink. 'Well, let's say you're right, then. Maybe you should be worried about what *I'll* do. I know an awful lot about you, Michelle. I know about your family, too.' He reached out and patted her hand again. 'And there are just so many ways I could cause you trouble, if I were that kind of guy.'

For a moment she couldn't say anything.

'But why?' she finally managed. 'I mean, what if Danny and I just go out to dinner a few more times? What can I tell you that's even useful?'

Gary leaned back against the red leatherette booth, taking a moment to intertwine his fingers and then stretch them.

'Here's the thing,' he said. 'Sometimes we just wanna keep tabs on somebody. Maybe you'll see something useful, maybe you won't. But you're there, just in case.' He smiled again. 'Keeps everyone on their toes.'

12

The credit cards had been her first clue.

'Tom, what's going on with the AmEx?' she'd asked. 'And the United card?'

Balances had appeared on both of them, high balances, seemingly out of nowhere.

'Oh,' he'd said. 'Yeah, I know. It's this new accountant. He's been moving money around. I keep telling him to leave the cards alone, but — I don't know — he keeps looking for the best deal.'

'On credit cards? Don't we have the money to pay them off?'

'Sure,' he'd said. 'Sure. It's just a fuckup. I'll get on it.'

She should have pressed him then. But the balances went down to zero, just like he'd promised they would.

He'd never given her a reason not to trust him before that. Though now she wondered if she just hadn't been paying attention.

⋆   ⋆   ⋆

'How'd you feel about going to a cocktail party with me?'

After the lunch with Gary, she'd gone to Costco and picked up a yoga mat. Stopped at a Starbucks and had a cup of coffee. Then she'd hailed a taxi and asked the driver to drop her off at the north end of the Malecón, so she could walk by the ocean and think.

It hadn't been the restful experience she'd hoped for. Several cruise ships had come into town, and tourists mobbed the boardwalk, moving together in tight packs like single, ponderous organisms.

She wanted to cut through them all. Get them out of her way. Enjoy the fucking scenery without hordes of Americans wearing loud shirts and graceless shorts.

As she crossed the bridge that led over the river into Old Town, Daniel called.

Just like Gary'd said he would.

'It's this charity thing,' he told her. 'We don't have to stay long. We can go someplace after.'

'Sounds great,' Michelle said, looking up the river, watching a pair of ducks paddle among the rushes. 'Is it the Tiburón crowd?'

'Not really. More some local people I know. Pick you up at seven?'

I'd better go shop for a dress, she thought.

Crazy.

★ ★ ★

She found a nice black dress at one of the shops on Basilio Badillo. Nothing fancy, but the cut worked for her. She'd found sandals there and a cute little leather purse at the purse store down the block, too.

After she changed for the party, she tried on Gary's watch. Wasn't this just the sort of occasion for it — a chance to capture Daniel's

122

associates? She stood in front of the mirror in the wardrobe of her room at Hacienda Carmen, in her new dress and sandals, holding the purse, the watch dangling on her wrist.

It looked ridiculous. Like she was a kid who'd tried on her daddy's watch.

She took it off. Put it in her new purse, thinking maybe she'd wear it later. Maybe people would be drinking and wouldn't notice how out of place the watch looked.

Maybe she'd take a chance and talk to Daniel.

* * *

'You look fantastic.'

Michelle smiled and climbed into the passenger side of the Jeep. 'You clean up pretty well yourself,' she told him.

He grinned and closed the car door behind her.

They drove across the river, into downtown Vallarta, then up the hill above the cathedral. 'We'd better park here,' Daniel said. 'You don't mind walking a block or two, do you?'

'No, it's fine. I like to walk.' Which was true, but she hated the idea of arriving in a sweat, and it was still hot. The sun hung over the ocean, full and ripe to the point of bursting.

'Where we're going's a great place to catch the sunset,' Daniel mentioned.

They walked down a narrow street that paralleled the ocean, the cobblestones so rounded in places that it was like walking on embedded baseballs. She could see why they'd had to park and walk, though — there was hardly any room for cars here, just occasional gaps in the raised concrete sidewalks where one or two small ones could maybe shoehorn in.

'This is it.'

It didn't look like a bar or restaurant; there were no signs, no valets, just heavy wooden doors, splintering in places, worn smooth in others, bound with darkened iron. A private club, maybe, or a very big house.

By the doors stood several bulky men with the thick-necked look of bouncers.

Daniel produced a card printed on creamy linen and showed it to one of the men, who glanced at it and nodded.

'After you,' Daniel said, holding the door for her.

She took a deep breath and went inside.

The doors opened onto a wide foyer — more of a patio, really. A bar was set up to one side, under an awning. A young man served drinks there, dressed in black and white — catering staff, Michelle thought. They were the same everywhere. He was slight, with drooping black hair and a gold earring, and she thought he might be wearing eyeliner.

'What can I get you?' Daniel asked.

'I'd love a glass of white wine.'

No margaritas, she thought. She needed to stay focused.

To do what, she wasn't sure. Take pictures with Gary's watch? It was still in her purse. She couldn't imagine actually taking it out, putting it on.

Confide in Daniel?

A few other couples stood around the bar, on the patio that overlooked downtown Vallarta and then the ocean. Expensively dressed. Lots of jewelry on the women.

'It's lovely,' Michelle said.

'Wait'll you see the main room.'

He led her through an arched entrance into a spacious gallery. It looked like a church, Michelle thought, domed vaulted ceiling painted with murals of robed saints, pink cherubs, spires piercing storm clouds, and overflowing bowls of fruit. Heavy wood and wrought iron framed the walls and entries; Talavera tile formed borders around terracotta flooring. The space opened up onto a large balcony that she glimpsed between thick pillars. A quartet of musicians played: guitars, marimba, guitarrón. Long tables bearing platters of food were set up along the open wall; small, round tables, chairs, and benches were placed here and there for guests to pause and eat and rest their drinks. There was a banner hung on one wall with a silk-screened design of children, palms, waves, and dolphins, and the legend PARA LOS NIÑOS. More thick-necked men were spaced at intervals against the wall.

Someone had spent some money.

'Whose party is this?' she asked.

'This woman I know, María, put it together. She's got this charity thing she runs. They're kicking off a fundraising campaign for the summer.' He shrugged a little. 'It can be tough around here during the summers, after the tourists go home.'

125

'I've heard that.'

'You wanna go catch the sunset?'

'Sure.'

They went out to the balcony, where a few tables had been set up, found seats at one end. The table had a small centerpiece with a card on a metal stand that featured the same graphic as on the banner inside. PARA LOS NIÑOS. By now the sun lit the surrounding clouds in great streaks of pink and orange, purpling above like a deepening bruise.

'I thought this was going to be a good one,' Daniel said with satisfaction. He lifted his glass — he'd also gotten white wine.

She raised hers in return.

'Thanks for coming with me,' he said.

'It's not exactly a chore. This seems like a nice party.'

He shrugged. 'Not really my kind of thing.'

'So why come?' And why ask me? she thought.

He gave her his half smile, his eyes holding steady on hers. 'Rich people, private jets, you know, they go together. I've got some clients here. I have to show face sometimes.'

Rich people and private jets might go together, but in her experience that didn't mean the pilots came to their parties.

You don't know that for sure, she told herself. You don't know how things work here.

'So how long are you staying in town?' he asked, still watching her.

'Maybe two weeks. Probably not longer than that. I can do some of the estate stuff from here, but I'm going to have to figure out the

126

rest of it at some point.'

Like where she was going to live. And how.

Daniel let out a brief, quiet laugh. 'Yeah, I hear that. I need to make some changes myself.'

They finished their wine as the sun dipped into the ocean.

He reached over and gently squeezed her hand. 'Let me take care of business, and we'll get out of here.'

They went inside.

The party had picked up some while they'd been on the balcony. Chatter, laughter, and the clatter of plates nearly drowned out the musicians.

She tried the red wine this time. It tasted corked. Daniel had a beer.

The two of them made their way through the main room, Daniel stopping now and then to greet people, men in short-sleeved shirts and linen slacks, women in silk and gold and Jimmy Choos, introducing her as 'my friend Michelle, from Los Angeles.'

She couldn't keep track of the names, the professions. There were too many of them. Developers, city officials, charter-boat operators, real-estate investors, restaurateurs, gallery owners, introduced and quickly dispensed with.

She felt on the edge of panic, as if she were in one of those dreams where she'd walked into a final exam unprepared. What would she tell Gary when she called him? That she'd been to a party, met a bunch of people, and couldn't remember any of their names?

If she called Gary.

Call Gary or tell Daniel?

Leave here and go someplace the two of them could talk, in private.

Not Hacienda Carmen.

They'd reached a tile fountain set in a cement nook on one side of the gallery. A woman standing there looked up and saw them.

'Danny, how nice of you to come.'

'María.' There was a peculiar weight to the way he said her name. 'Michelle, this is the woman who put this all together. María Aguilar. María, this is my friend Michelle, from Los Angeles.'

'*Encantada.*'

They air-kissed, something that Michelle had thankfully had much opportunity to practice in Brentwood.

María was in her fifties, at the point where the skin on her face had started to thin, conforming to the bones of her skull like soft, moist putty. She was still striking, her eyebrows slashes of dark ink, her eyes a luminous topaz.

'This is a lovely party,' Michelle said.

'Thank you. It is an important one. For the children. I'm glad to see that so many in Vallarta are willing to help, in spite of the difficult economic times.'

María turned to Daniel. 'I think Carlos is looking for you.' She glanced toward the balcony. 'I see him over there. My husband,' she said to Michelle.

Daniel lifted a hand, and a man standing beside one of the columns by the balcony returned the wave. Wide, fleshy face, well-cut silk shirt worn untucked.

'Hey,' Daniel said. 'Do you mind if I — This won't take long.'

'Don't worry,' Michelle said. 'Take your time.'

After he left, María tilted her head and studied Michelle. Michelle thought she recognized the evaluation: Her clothes. Her shoes. Her purse. How she did her makeup.

What kind of woman all this added up to.

'So you're a friend of Danny's,' María said. 'He hasn't introduced many friends to us before.'

What did that mean? Michelle wondered. 'Friends' as in 'dates'? 'Oh. Really. I would have thought . . . He's a social sort of person.'

'Perhaps he likes to keep his business separate from his pleasure,' María said.

Over María's shoulder Michelle could see Carlos and Daniel by the balcony, Carlos saying something, laying a thick hand on Daniel's shoulder.

'How do you know Daniel?' Michelle asked.

'He does some work for my family. Private charters. Transportation and . . . logistical arrangements.' María gave her another measuring look. 'But surely you know something about his business.'

'Only a little,' Michelle said, meeting her eyes. 'We haven't known each other long.'

'I see.' María smiled. 'Are you staying in Vallarta for a while?'

'Just for a few weeks.'

'Probably for the best,' María said. 'It is much too hot this time of year.'

129

There was a restroom at the back of the hall, between two pillars. Michelle made her way there. She felt dizzy. Maybe it was the heat. Maybe it was the encounter with María.

Surely you know something about his business.

Once inside the stall, she sat on the toilet for a minute or two, staring at the weathered wooden door. Her head throbbed.

It's just a party, she thought. Wasn't it? All kinds of parties had bouncers, or bodyguards, or whatever they were. Daniel just wanted a date to come with him so they could go out afterward. Have some fun.

Perhaps he likes to keep his business separate from his pleasure.

Which one am I? Michelle wondered.

Maybe I should take some notes, she thought. Write down some of the names. In case she needed something to tell Gary.

She found a scrap of paper in her purse — the receipt for the purse, actually — and made a few quick notes. Tucked it into her wallet, behind her driver's license.

When she came out of the restroom, she didn't see Daniel or Carlos. They must have gone somewhere more private to talk.

She'd abandoned her wine; it hadn't been very good. Maybe I'll get another glass of white, she thought. Open as the space was, the heat was still oppressive. She was sweating — she could feel her dress sticking to her back and thighs.

'You're Danny's friend.'

It was a woman who spoke. American, from her accent. She leaned against the wall close to the bathroom, a margarita in hand.

'I'm sorry?' Michelle said. 'I don't . . . '

'I saw you two come in.' She extended her hand, in a way that suggested she almost expected Michelle to kiss it.

Michelle didn't. She clasped the hand briefly.

'Michelle.'

'I'm Emma.'

In her late twenties, Michelle thought. She had a voluptuous look, almost as if she were imitating a 1940s pinup — round cheeks, thick black hair worn loose in spite of the heat, bright red lipstick. The neckline of her off-the-shoulder blouse gathered just above her breasts. The dark line of a tattoo peeked out above the right shoulder.

'Enjoying the party?' she asked.

'Oh, yes. It's a . . . a nice setting.'

Emma snorted. 'I saw you talking to María. Is she a friend of yours?'

'No. We just met.'

'She's a pretentious bitch, isn't she?'

Either she was drunk or she liked to play the provocateur. Looking at the way she leaned against the wall, one stiletto-clad foot pressed against it, Michelle thought maybe both.

'Well, I don't really know her,' she said.

'I guess you have to give her credit — it's a ballsy way to launder the family money. For the children!' Emma laughed.

Michelle took a quick look around. That

couple standing close by, the man staring at them — had he overheard?

If María and her family actually were some kind of criminals, maybe it wasn't a great idea to have this conversation surrounded by their friends and business associates.

'Do you want to go out on the balcony?' Michelle asked. 'Get some air?'

Emma peeled herself off the wall. 'If we can stop for drinks first.'

It was still hot out on the balcony, but at least there were breezes. Michelle led Emma to a corner table, away from other guests.

'So you're seeing Danny,' Emma said. 'That's interesting.'

'It is? I'm not sure why you say that.'

Emma laughed. 'It's just something to say.'

'He's a nice guy,' Michelle said. 'A lot of fun.'

Emma laughed again. 'Our Danny always brings the fun.'

'How do you know him?'

'He works for my father,' Emma said, sipping her fresh margarita.

'Oh.'

Who's your daddy? Michelle thought, but of course she wasn't going to say that. 'Private charters?' she asked.

Emma laughed again. 'That's right,' she said. 'He's Daddy's little bagman.'

Great, Michelle thought. How am I supposed to respond to that?

'I don't know that much about Danny's business,' she said. 'We just started seeing each other.'

'Really?' Emma leaned over the small table. 'I could tell you a few things about Danny.' She fumbled with the clasp of her tiny beaded purse and got out a cellphone. 'Why don't you give me your number?'

Michelle hesitated. Was this some kind of setup?

'Well, I'm not sure how long I'll be in town,' she said. 'But maybe we can meet for drinks.'

'I know some fun places,' Emma said with a sly smile. She slid the phone across the table. 'Here. You can put the number in for me.'

Michelle thought about entering a wrong number. Emma was trouble, she was pretty sure. But she was also information.

She punched in her number.

'You should call me,' Michelle said, handing the phone back. 'That way I'll have yours.'

'Hey.'

It was Daniel. He stood there frowning. 'Emma, what are you doing here?'

'Hi, Danny,' Emma said, straightening up. 'I heard it was gonna be a good party.'

'It's not your kind of thing.' He turned to Michelle. 'Sorry that took so long.'

'That's okay. It's a nice night.'

'It sure is,' Emma said, giggling. She hopped off the stool.

'Emma, you should get home,' Daniel said.

She stood toe to toe with him.

'And if I don't, what? You'll call my father?'

'You want me to?'

Emma hesitated. 'No need,' she finally said. 'It's boring here anyway.' She leaned over and kissed Michelle on the cheek. 'I'll see you.'

'Sorry about that,' Daniel said after Emma tottered off.

'That's okay.' Michelle smiled at him. Keep it light. 'She was kind of entertaining.'

'She's not somebody you want to get involved with.' Daniel stared off into the main room, where Emma had gone. 'What did she tell you?'

There was an edge to his voice, and she thought of the day he'd caught her in his apartment, his hand gripping her arm.

She thought about lying. But she was afraid to risk it. She didn't know what the relationships were between these people, what they might hide, what they might share.

It's easier to keep track of the truth than a lie.

'Mmm, let's see. That our hostess is pretentious, and she's involved in some sketchy business activities.' She smiled, like it was all a joke.

'Oh, man.' Now Daniel grinned back, and she wondered if his smile was any more sincere than hers. 'Emma is such a drama queen.'

'So it's not true?'

He shrugged. 'You know, this isn't the U.S. Some of the business practices here *are* kind of sketchy. *Mordidas* and all. That's just how it is.'

'She also said that you work for her father.'

'Yeah. True.' He sighed a little. 'He's kind of high-maintenance, too.'

He put down his beer.

'Let's get out of here.'

★ ★ ★

They walked through the main room of the party, Daniel nodding now and then at people he knew, and when they were in sight of the door, he circled his arm around her waist, let his hand rest just above her hip. For a moment she leaned against him, her own hand sliding down the curve of his butt, and she thought about when she was in high school, walking through the quad with her boyfriend, slipping her hand into the back pocket of his jeans.

'I never bring anyone to these things,' he whispered in her ear. 'Everyone's looking at you. Wondering who you are.'

★   ★   ★

She almost said something on the ride back. Opened her mouth at one point to ask the question, except she couldn't decide what the question should even be.

Maybe, what exactly does a bagman *do* anyway?

As they crossed the river, heading back into Old Town, Daniel sighed through gritted teeth. 'I'm going to have to call this early,' he said.

'Oh?'

'Yeah. Something's come up. Work.'

'Oh.' She hesitated. 'That's . . . that's too bad.'

'Yeah. It is.'

He fell silent.

They'd almost reached Hacienda Carmen when he said, 'I'm sorry how things worked out tonight.'

'Me, too,' she said. And she meant it. She was

sorry that the party had raised more questions about him than it answered. Sorry that she couldn't trust him. Sorry that for whatever reason she had the distinct impression she was getting dumped.

What the fuck was she going to say to Gary?

'Do you want to have drinks Friday night?' he asked abruptly. 'Maybe meet at El Tiburón?'

It was stupid, the relief that washed over her like cool water.

'I'd like that,' she said.

13

She'd turned off her phone.

More than anything else, she'd needed to sleep. That was the best thing about having her night with Daniel end early — she could just brush her teeth, wash her face, change into her night-clothes, and go to sleep.

She didn't need Gary waking her up at the crack of dawn playing one of his games, and the iPhone needed to be recharged anyway. She wasn't getting the battery life out of it that she should.

She still woke up earlier than she would have liked. It was the donkeys again, and an old woman, one of the hotel guests, yelling out to someone that she'd take her coffee in the patio, should she bring up a Danish?

Michelle sighed and lay in bed a while longer. Eventually she would have to get up. Do something.

Turn on her phone. Call Gary.

She didn't know what she was going to say to him.

Maybe things weren't the way they seemed to be at the party. Maybe Daniel's business was completely legitimate.

It sure didn't look like it.

Even so, she wondered if it still might not have been better to take the risk, to tell him what was going on.

I need more time with him, she thought. More time to decide.

She wasn't seeing Daniel until tomorrow night. What was she supposed to do in the meantime? Play tourist? Or, more accurately, play 'woman who was trying to figure out her next step in life,' since that seemed to be the role she'd adopted now.

'Oh, fuck,' she muttered. She could feel the pull of despair, like a physical weight dragging her down, and she just wanted to surrender to it.

Not an option, she told herself.

Maybe go to the beach. Call Gary from there. The beach felt more private than Hacienda Carmen.

She did some yoga. Took a shower. Put on a pair of shorts and a blouse over her bathing suit and went downstairs. Paused at the gate, looking up and down the street, in case the policeman was waiting for her there.

No police car in sight.

★　★　★

She went to a restaurant on the beach, one that was unattached to a hotel. The Beach Club, it was called. You could have a drink and a snack and sit there all day if you wanted.

She had her choice of the beige beach chairs. She picked a lounger under an umbrella that sat at the edge of the rise of soft sand, so she could look at the ocean unimpeded.

She ordered a coffee, some yogurt and fruit,

and a bottle of water, then got out her book and pretended to read. She'd swapped her bread-baking book at the front desk of Hacienda Carmen for this one, a British mystery set in Cornwall. Better that than the romance novel featuring vampires.

She couldn't read it. There was no point even pretending to try.

You have to call him, she told herself.

Finally she powered up her phone.

Three messages from 'Ted Banks,' her fake attorney. One from her actual attorney. A couple from friends. And a string of messages from her sister.

Call Gary, she told herself. Get it over with.

Instead she watched the waves and sipped her coffee.

Five minutes later her phone rang.

Ted Banks. Of course.

'Hey there, Michelle! I was getting a little worried.'

'Sorry,' she said. 'I forgot to charge my phone.'

'Look, it's real important that you stay in close contact. Guys like Danny, I told you, you don't want to take any chances.'

'I thought you told me I didn't have anything to worry about. That it was safe.'

'That's right. If you do exactly what I tell you to do.' A pause. 'Have you been doing what I told you to do, Michelle?'

'I . . . ' She closed her eyes. 'I'm trying. I'm spending time with him. Isn't that what you want?'

'So tell me about it.'

'We went to a cocktail party downtown. I met a bunch of people.'

'Did you get pictures?'

'No, it wasn't — '

'You have some problem with the camera?'

She swallowed. 'No, I just didn't . . . I didn't have a chance to use it.'

She heard him sigh. Once. Then again.

'I think we need to have a talk.'

⋆ ⋆ ⋆

A talk. What did that mean? He'd just hung up after he said it. Hadn't set a time or a place to meet.

She stayed at the beach a while longer. The beach felt safe. Away from Hacienda Carmen, where Gary had installed her, where there might be people watching her. Away from the streets, where the police car was.

'Señorita? Jewelry?'

A vendor had approached her chair — a young man a with a wooden display case.

'No,' she said, 'no, thank you.'

'You sure? I have silver. Turquoise. Good price.'

'Sorry. I'm not interested.'

He squatted down next to her. He wore an oversize white T-shirt and a Dodgers cap and a thick gold chain around his neck. 'Something else maybe?' He grinned, keeping his voice low. 'Something for maybe to party?'

Drugs. He wanted to sell her drugs.

'I'm really not interested.'

'You sure?'

'I'm sure.' She fought to keep her voice steady. 'Why do you think I'd be interested in something like that?'

He lifted up his hands. 'Hey, you just look like you like to have fun, that's all.' He rose to leave. 'You change your mind, I am on this beach all the time.'

After that the beach didn't feel so safe. She settled the bill, gathered up her things, put on her blouse and shorts, and headed up the beach, to where the street, Púlpito, ran into the sand.

Waiting there at the curb, next to the entrance of El Dorado restaurant, was a white minivan. Gustavo, Gary's driver, leaned against it reading a paper.

'Hello, señora,' he said with a friendly grin. 'I'm here to take you to Gary.'

14

He'd already opened the back door of the van for her when she said, 'This isn't a good time.'

'Oh, but Gary says it's very important.'

'I've been at the beach — I'm not even really dressed.'

'I think that's okay.'

'Well, it's not okay with me,' she said, and she was glad that she sounded more angry than afraid.

'Look, señora . . . I think maybe it's better if you do what Gary says.' His smile faltered. 'Because if he sends someone else to pick you up, maybe that won't be so good. You know?'

Just like that. The anger was gone, and she was afraid again.

She thought about running, but how far could she get?

'Don't worry,' he said. 'Gary just wants to talk to you.'

* * *

'Vallarta, It's too hot now,' Gustavo said. 'Too hot for the beach. Too hot at home. So for me, driving is the best thing right now. With the air-conditioning.' He patted the dash. 'Nice and cool in here, no matter what it's like outside.'

Michelle nodded, though he probably couldn't

142

see that. She sat in the backseat clutching the armrest.

'Where are we going?' she'd asked when they'd first started driving.

'Just to see Gary.' And then he'd smiled and continued talking about the weather, about various tourist destinations, about his cousins who lived in Los Angeles.

They headed north and east, away from the ocean. The neighborhoods they drove through reminded Michelle a little of the place where the jail was. She couldn't be sure if the jail was actually around here; there were no landmarks she recognized, just the sense that these were not the tourist districts, no sushi bars or Senior Frog's or Starbucks, just local businesses run down at the heels — appliance-repair stores, printers, a Mexican version of a 99¢ store called Todo de 25.

He just wants to talk, she told herself, that's all.

'You don't look so good,' Gustavo said, glancing at her in the rearview mirror. 'You want a Coke? I have one in the cooler, on the floor.'

Now the streets were unpaved, the buildings whitewashed brick and gray cinderblock. Newer cinder-block buildings competed with older wood and tin-roofed structures on the verge of collapse, seemingly held together by tarps and vegetation.

They drove on a broader dirt road, following a large truck kicking up clouds of dust, its bed piled high with garbage bags and mattresses and a doorless refrigerator. The truck pulled up to a guard shack at some kind of compound that was surrounded by a cinder-block wall. Big, whatever it was. Not a prison; the security hardly seemed adequate for that — no armed guards with machine guns, and the gate was wide and unbarricaded. Leading up to it and clustered by the wall were shacks, adhoc shelters made from whatever materials were at hand — cardboard, plastic sheeting, wooden pallets.

Gustavo stopped at the gate and climbed out of the minivan. 'Just a moment, señora,' he said before he slammed the door shut.

Michelle sat in the backseat and waited while Gustavo talked to the guards. I could get out of the car, she thought. I could run. Instead she sat. It didn't make sense to run, did it? Not really. Running would make things worse.

Gary just wanted to talk.

After a few minutes, Gustavo returned. 'Okay,' he said. 'No problem.' He started the car.

'Where are we?' Michelle asked.

'*El basurero.*' He smiled. 'The dump.'

At the base of what looked like a mountain, workers sprayed brown liquid from huge green hoses into a black-rubber-lined pit. Gustavo steered the minivan on a path that circled the hill. The lower levels were covered with grass, but as they wound their way up, the grass yielded to endless mounds of plastic bags, faded and bleached by the sun, the path at times partially blocked by baby carriages and cracked tires and rusting hunks of old appliances.

Headless bodies in oil barrels. Heads in garbage bags. If a body were dumped here,

144

would anyone ever find it?

Finally they reached the summit — a flat, man-made mesa.

Gustavo parked the van by a shack someone had set up, under a salvaged beach umbrella. A few workers, older women, sat beneath it taking a break. A slightly battered 4Runner was parked close by.

Gary stood in the shade of the 4Runner's open hatchback, red-faced and sweating, drinking from a bottle of water.

Michelle got out of the minivan.

When he saw her, he smiled. 'Well, Michelle. Glad you could make it.'

'Did I have a choice?'

'Now, come on. I figured you'd find this interesting.' He rummaged around in a cooler and retrieved another bottle of water. 'You look a little pale,' he said, holding it out to her. 'Better drink something. You don't want to get dehydrated up here.'

She took the water. She wanted to throw it at him.

'How about you give me a hand with these?'

Inside the hatchback was a crate of oranges. Gary slung a canvas shopping bag half full with them over his shoulder. 'Maybe put some in your tote?'

'What for?'

'I'm helping out a friend. She's part of a charity comes up here. Brings things to the workers. The *jóvenes*.' He chuckled. 'Don't know why they call them that. Most of them aren't very young.'

He gestured for her to follow. 'Watch your step. There's some nasty stuff around.'

She followed him. All the intimidation, the threats, hauling her off the beach in a near kidnapping, and he wanted her to hand out oranges, like he was some kind of demented social worker?

Crazy.

The surface of the mountain felt spongy. Michelle could feel it tremble through the soles of her feet as a bulldozer pushed a pile of trash from one place to another. The smell . . . it wasn't what she expected. It was nothing she could describe. Rancid meat, rotting fruit, spoiled baby food, shit — it was all of that and none of it.

'Used to be kids working up here. Can you imagine that?'

The top was a broad plateau, a plain of trash, heaped with garbage bags and stacks of cardboard. Workers sorted through the piles by hand. And there were birds everywhere. Michelle had never seen so many birds in one place. Flocks of buzzards and white herons, countless gulls, all come to feast on the dump's riches.

'They've found bodies up here before,' Gary said. 'Stuffed inside some garbage bags and dumped in the pile with everything else. Not the kind of thing you want to find when you're looking for soda cans.'

They approached a knot of workers dismantling a refrigerator. Gary greeted them, tossed out oranges, rattling off Spanish that she couldn't understand. The men and women

146

smiled, nodded, took the fruit. Two stopped what they were doing to peel theirs and eat.

She continued to follow Gary as they picked their way among the refuse. Here were cow parts. Skulls. Lips and noses. Random hooves. A vulture perched on a withered cow's head, tearing at the hide.

'Look at that,' Gary said. 'Too bad you don't have your camera.'

Fucking Gary, she thought, hearing Daniel's voice in her head. He was trying to freak her out, she guessed. To shock the privileged lady from Los Angeles — well, the formerly privileged lady anyway. And okay, she'd been pretty scared on the ride over.

But now? She was giving oranges to workers. To people who'd seen her with Gary — to witnesses.

Here was a donkey hitched to a splintered wooden cart heaped with flattened cardboard boxes, a dog dozing in the shade beneath it. Next to it an old man wearing a tall straw cowboy hat and a young man in a grimy Dodgers cap broke down the boxes.

'Well, come on, Michelle.' Gary's voice was loud in her ear. 'Give the boys some oranges.'

She went over to the two men. '*Hola*,' she said, trying to smile. '*Quieren*, um . . . oranges?'

They smiled back and nodded, the younger of the two springing up to take an orange, giving it a celebratory toss before digging into the skin.

The old man moved more slowly, extending a hand for an orange. She gave him one, felt the

147

hard, cracked surface of his palm. 'Take another,' she said.

They had reached the edge of the mesa. 'Check this out,' Gary said, gesturing ahead of him.

Below them was Vallarta, the old city to the left, the marina and the ocean, then newer developments, the new university, condos, creeping toward the mountain's northern flank.

'Some view, isn't it?'

Michelle nodded. It really was.

Was he done with his little show? she wondered. It was a horrible place, but it was a place where people worked, did their jobs, and here the two of them were, playing at charity like some sort of poverty tourists.

'I really should've had you bring your camera. I bet you could take some great photos up here. Of the workers and the trash and whatnot.'

'It's been done,' she said.

'Yeah, but I think you have a terrific eye, Michelle. You've got some talent. Which is why I'm really disappointed you didn't do what I asked you to do last night.'

'I told you I didn't feel comfortable — '

'And I told you to suck it up. What do you think this is anyway? You think you can blow me off? Is that what you think?'

'No, I — '

'People end up in trouble here when they don't do what they're told.' He took an orange out of the bag, tossed it at a flock of birds that had gathered close by. They rose up, screeching, then quickly settled back in place, a few gulls stabbing at the fruit.

'One time they didn't find a body till the next day,' Gary said. 'Guess it was at the bottom of the pile. You should've seen that after the buzzards got after it. Between that and the heat — '

'I get it, Gary.' You asshole, she added silently.

'I don't think you do.' He rested his hand flat between her shoulder blades. 'You think there's plenty of people around. Nothing's gonna happen to you in broad daylight. You think you're someplace safe.'

He pressed harder. Not exactly a shove. Just pressure. Urging her forward, toward the edge of the mountain. 'But what you don't get is, everything's for sale here. And everybody. And if somebody wants something bad to happen to you, it will.'

She could feel his palm's moist heat through the thin gauze of her blouse.

'All kinds of people end up dead. People with money. People with power. You? Nobody'd even blink.'

She stared over the edge, down the slope of bleaching plastic and cracked rubber, at the flocks of resting birds.

'Look — ' Her voice caught, and she swallowed hard. But maybe it was better to sound afraid. That was what he wanted, right? 'It was a cocktail party. I wore a little black dress. The watch would've looked ridiculous.'

She took in a deep breath and regretted it.

'You want me to do this, and I'm trying. You want me to . . . to play this part, and I'm trying to do it right.'

A long silence. She didn't try to fill it. Instead she stood there and stared at the view, at the birds, listened to the rumble of the bulldozers, to the thudding of her heart, the solid pressure of Gary's hand on her back.

'Michelle, what am I going to do with you?' he said at last.

He gave her back a little pat. Then he grabbed her wrist with his other hand and shoved her hard, where his hand had been.

She stumbled forward, started to fall, over the edge, and he hauled her up with a vicious twist, wrenching her wrist and shoulder.

She cried out, but no one could hear them here, where any sound would be masked by the birds and the bulldozers.

'See how easy?' he said in her ear.

He let go of her wrist.

She stood there shaking.

Gary guided her away from the edge, his hands resting lightly on her shoulders. 'I know you think I'm pretty much an asshole, but I'm doing this for your own good. You're around people who won't hesitate, and you need to understand that. They'll throw you over the side without a second thought.'

He got a bottle of water from his bag, opened it, and held it out to her. She took it, trying to control the trembling in her hands.

'Tell me about the party.'

She told him everything she could remember, the names she'd written down, the faces she could recall. She told him about Daniel going off with Carlos. About her conversation with María.

And then about Emma and how Daniel had reacted to her.

Gary listened. Nodded occasionally.

Was he taking any of this seriously? Was any of it important? Michelle couldn't tell.

'And Danny, how'd he seem?' Gary asked when she'd finished.

She thought about it. 'Tired. Kind of disgusted. He said he wanted to make some changes.'

'Oh, did he? He say anything else along those lines? Anything specific?'

'No. Just that it wasn't his kind of thing. The party. That he needed to show face and then we could leave.'

'So you left. After that what did you do?'

She hesitated.

'Now, come on, Michelle. Tell me what happened.'

'Nothing,' she said. 'Nothing happened. He said something had come up. Some work. He dropped me off, and that was that.'

Gary sighed. 'Well, that's disappointing. I'd've thought you could hold his interest a little longer.'

She felt a flush of anger. 'He wants to get together on Friday,' she said. 'Is that enough interest for you?'

He chuckled and gave her shoulder a quick rub. 'You're a hoot, you know that?'

★ ★ ★

A stocky blonde woman waited for them back at the 4Runner. Vicky. Wearing another Hawaiian shirt. This one featured palm trees and pink flamingos.

'Oh, Michelle, hi!' she said, beaming. 'I'm so glad you made it!'

'I wouldn't have missed it,' Michelle said.

'I told Michelle all about your charitable work,' Gary said. 'And of course she wanted to come and see it for herself.'

'Next time you'll have to visit the school. That's where you can really see the difference we're making in the neighborhood. This . . . ' Vicky spread her hands. 'Well, it's a tough environment. We just try to make things a little nicer for the workers when we can.'

'I loved coming up here to help,' Gary said. 'And I knew that Michelle would really appreciate it.'

He gave her a little smile, like they were sharing a joke, and though she didn't want to share anything with him, she knew that she was in on it.

'Well, I'm ready to go get a drink,' Vicky said. 'We have plenty of time to catch the sunset. What do you think? Maybe Daiquiri Dick's?'

'As much as I'd love to, I've got another appointment,' Gary said. 'Michelle, why don't you go with Vicky? I'll get a ride with Gustavo.'

'I can take a cab — ' Michelle began.

'Oh, honey, that'll cost, what? A hundred fifty pesos? If you don't feel like getting a drink, I can drop you off in Old Town. I live down there anyway.'

★　★　★

'You okay, hon? You look . . . I don't know, a little shaky.'

Sometimes we just want to keep tabs on somebody . . . Just in case.

'Just the heat. And . . . that place.'

Vicky turned up the 4Runner's air conditioner.

'Yeah. It's pretty awful, isn't it? It's hard to understand why people have to live that way.'

This was the third time she'd encountered Vicky. Twice when Vicky had been in the company of Gary. Once when she'd just happened to be in Michelle's neighborhood.

'Things have been really tough for the workers lately — nobody's paying good prices for recyclables with the economy in such bad shape. And they're closing that dump soon. Moving to a new state-of-the-art facility outside the city. I don't know what will happen to everyone then. There's just no work.'

She said she lives down there, Michelle reminded herself. And this is a small town. Wasn't that more plausible than, say, Vicky as a CIA assassin? In a Hawaiian shirt and fanny pack?

Bad enough she had to accept Gary as some sort of spy.

'So you know Gary pretty well,' Michelle said as they approached Old Town.

'Oh, just the way that you tend to know other expats here,' Vicky said. 'He's really been great, though. Just rolled up his sleeves and got involved with the community, and, you know, he's pretty new.'

'Oh, really? How long has he been here?'

'Well, let's see. I think I met him about five months ago. He comes and goes, like a lot of the expats.'

'I see.'

'So . . . ' Vicky hesitated. 'How is it the two of you . . . ? I mean, I don't want to pry.'

Great, Michelle thought. The last thing she wanted was a rumor spread around that she and Gary had hooked up.

What would Daniel think, if he heard it?

That would not be good.

If you're gonna lie, keep it simple.

'You know that problem I told you I had, with the police? Gary helped me out.'

'Oh, right,' Vicky said with a little gasp. 'Gary's great about things like that, isn't he? He really knows his way around.'

'He really does.' Michelle forced a smile. 'It's just that . . . well, the whole thing is pretty embarrassing for me. I wouldn't want people here to think . . . you know . . . that I'm the kind of person who gets into trouble with the police.'

'Oh, sweetie, everybody would understand! Sometimes the legal system here is just awful.' Vicky gave her shoulder a little pat. 'But don't worry, I'll keep it to myself.'

★ ★ ★

Daiquiri Dick's was more upscale than most of the restaurants on the sand south of the river, stuccoed cement painted the color of a ripened peach. They found a table next to the wall that bordered the beach.

'The margaritas are really good here,' Vicky said.

'I think I'll just have a glass of white wine.'

Vicky raised her hand to flag down the waiter, then studied Michelle, her expression concerned and slightly puzzled.

'Did you hurt your arm?' she asked.

Michelle flinched. She'd been rubbing her wrist, she realized, and it did hurt, and there were bruises coming up where Gary had grabbed her.

'Oh. I . . . I just tweaked it doing yoga.'

'Maybe you should put some ice on it.'

'Good idea,' she said.

'So did you ever get Danny's things back to him?' Vicky asked, a little tentatively, after their drinks arrived.

'I did.'

'And he's doing okay?'

'He's fine. Just some stitches.'

'I'm really glad to hear that. I like Danny, I really do.'

The unspoken 'but' hung in the air.

'I mean, he's just . . . exciting!' Vicky nearly giggled. 'And so cute. Not the kind of American you usually see living here. Mostly it's, you know, people like me and Keith — Keith's my husband. Pretty boring.'

'Come on, you're not boring,' Michelle said, because that was what was expected.

'Oh, you know what I mean.' Vicky leaned back in her chair, and the look she gave Michelle was unexpectedly shrewd. 'You're a little unusual, too.'

'I'm really not.' Michelle managed a smile. 'I'm just a housewife from Los Angeles.'

Stupid, she told herself as soon as she'd said it. Now she sounded like a married woman screwing around on her husband, having a fling on a Mexican beach.

'I mean, I *was*,' she amended. 'Now I'm . . . at loose ends, I guess.'

'I don't mean to pry,' Vicky said.

Sure you do, Michelle thought.

'I'm a widow,' she said. 'My husband passed away a few months ago. We were supposed to take this vacation together. I decided to come on my own. To just . . . I don't know, figure out my next step. I wasn't expecting to meet anyone.' She shrugged. 'I know that a lot of people would probably think it's too soon.'

Now I'm making it sound like the thing with Daniel is something real, she thought. Well, probably better to pretend that with a person like Vicky than to pass it off as some meaningless drunken fuck.

'Oh, I had no idea. I'm so sorry.'

Vicky seemed genuinely embarrassed. She probably was, Michelle thought. Most people weren't very good actors when it came right down to it. They might put on a show, but it was rarely convincing.

Vicky ducked her head, sipped her margarita, and then looked up, her cheeks pink. 'You know, I just want to say . . . I don't think it's up to me or anyone else to judge what's too soon.'

'Thanks. I appreciate that.'

Michelle stared out over the beach. The

156

parasails and banana boats had finished for the day. She wondered how much business they would do now that tourist season was over, in the coming summer's heat and rain.

'I'm really glad you came out today, Michelle,' Vicky said. 'If you're interested, you're welcome to visit anytime. I find that volunteering helps take my mind off things,' she added, almost shyly. 'And we have services on Sunday if you're interested in attending, close to the marina.'

'Oh, is your group a church group?'

She must not have hidden her skepticism well enough. Vicky hesitated. 'It's a part of our ministry. But we don't focus on that. Jesus said you give them something to eat. So that's what we do.'

'Sarong, señoras? Dresses? ¿Vestidos?' A beach vendor, a stocky Indian woman, with dresses and bolts of batik-dyed fabric draped over her arms, came up to the low, peach-painted wall.

'Ahora no,' Vicky said. 'Gracias.'

'Look,' the vendor said, holding up a tiny tie-dyed dress. 'For a little girl.'

'No, thank you.'

The vendor kept the same expression — the polite smile, the neutral eyes — and continued down the beach, in search of nonexistent customers.

'It's sad,' Vicky said, staring after her.

There was a chime from Michelle's iPhone — a text. She retrieved it from her Fred Segal tote.

chck yr cc accounts tomorrow. ted.

Michelle stared at it.

She felt a number of things at once. Violated that he knew these things about her, that he had access to her private life. Ashamed that she hadn't objected when he'd made the offer at lunch, that she'd just acquiesced. She could tell herself that she hadn't taken him seriously then, but that wasn't really true.

And curious.

What had he paid for?

'I heard they found bodies,' Michelle said. 'I mean, up at the dump.'

Vicky frowned. 'Bodies? Not that I know of. I guess it's possible, though.' She rolled her eyes and raised her glass. 'Honey, they find all kinds of things up at that dump!'

15

The next morning she checked her credit-card accounts on the iPhone. The roaming charges would be a fortune, but she didn't trust the Net bar.

The Working Assets was paid off. Her American Airlines AAdvantage Visa was, too. The United Mileage Plus, the AmEx Blue, and the Chase Visa were still close to maxed.

Two dates, two credit cards.

She was supposed to meet Daniel tonight at El Tiburón.

Did that mean Gary would pay off another one?

'Oh, fuck,' she whispered. This was not a good way to be thinking.

But how was she *supposed* to think about it?

She made a list in her head of what she knew.

She knew that Gary had power over her. That he could help her, or hurt her, and that he didn't particularly seem to care which.

She knew that she had no money, that she had nothing but debt and no real prospects to change that.

God, the things she'd seen and read lately. About all kinds of people who had more qualifications than she could ever dream of having, who'd still lost their jobs, their homes, their entire lives.

A few of her friends kept telling her it would

all be okay, but they had no real way of knowing that. It was just something to say when you didn't know what else to say, when there was nothing you could really do to help.

And then there was Daniel. Who might be a criminal. Whom she found attractive and thought she might even like but hardly knew.

Of course, in some ways knowing a person was overrated. She'd thought she'd known Tom pretty well. They'd been married for ten years; you'd think you'd know a person after that. She never would have imagined that he'd have done what he did, that he would have lied to her, repeatedly, about everything.

She was just now beginning to think that she understood what had happened. She guessed that it had started with a minor transgression, a small lie, and those little wrongs had fed each other until they'd turned into a monster engorged on its own deceptions, too huge to confess, or to bear.

Dying had been easier for Tom.

★   ★   ★

Around 5:00 P.M. she got dressed to go to El Tiburón. She decided on a casual sundress, Kenneth Cole flip-flops, and a Scala raffia hat.

Finally she put on the watch.

She stood in front of the long mirror in her bathroom at Hacienda Carmen and considered.

With this outfit it didn't look bad.

★   ★   ★

'Hey — Michelle, right?'

'Right. And you're . . . Ned?'

'Right!'

Ned, whom she'd met that first night with Daniel. 'Tweaker Ned,' she'd dubbed him. The guy who'd called her on Daniel's iPhone.

She'd arrived at El Tiburón only a minute before he did, had just climbed the three steps off the sand to enter the bar. She hadn't even located the group's table yet before Ned had tugged on her sleeve.

Ned looked at Michelle again, then around the bar. 'So . . . uh, you with Danny tonight?'

Sweat plastered his hair to his scalp, formed huge, ragged ovals under his arms. Nothing unusual about that; it was as stifling hot as it had been every day since she'd arrived in Vallarta.

But he'd been wanting to talk to Daniel since the night she'd met him, the night when everything started.

'He said he might be coming by later,' she said.

'Did he say when?'

'He wasn't sure. Have you tried calling?'

'Yeah, yeah, I called. Kept going straight to voicemail. He's hard to get a hold of sometimes.'

'Look, I just walked in,' Michelle said. 'I'm going to get something to drink. Do you want anything, or . . . ?'

'Sure. A beer. Thanks!'

'Okay. Be right back.'

She'd buy Ned his beer. Maybe he'd talk to her. Tell her something about Daniel's actual business. Maybe knowing wouldn't really matter

161

in the end, but it was still better to know, she supposed.

It would be something to tell Gary anyway.

She headed to the bar.

There was Charlie, she remembered him: the wizened survivor with yellowed nicotine fingers and rock-band T-shirt, sitting at the long table that stretched across one side of El Tiburón, facing the beach for the sunset, the same table as last week. Today his T-shirt was Thai, advertising Singha beer.

She bought a Corona for Ned and for herself a glass of white wine, which was sour.

When she returned from the bar, Ned had straddled an empty chair next to Charlie. He reminded Michelle of an elementary-school kid, like he'd just learned how to sit in a classroom but not how to sit still — hands clasped, torso unnaturally stiff, one leg jiggling up and down.

'Danny's friend,' Charlie said, lifting his hand. 'And how are you on this lovely evening?'

'I'm fine, thank you. Michelle,' she reminded him.

'I actually think I knew that,' Charlie said.

She sat down next to Ned. 'Corona okay?'

'Great. Yeah. Thanks.'

He grasped the beer with one hand. Patted his pants pocket with the other.

'Oh, don't worry about it,' Michelle said.

'I'll get you next round, then, okay? I'll put it on my tab.' Now he patted his other pants pocket. 'Thought I heard my phone.'

Michelle rested her elbow on the table, her chin on her hand, the watch pointed at Ned. It was easy to press the button by the stem. Easy to turn and face Charlie and press the button again.

There. She'd done it. She felt a shudder in the pit of her stomach. The kind of fear you felt at the top of a roller coaster. A rush.

'So how's business?' Charlie asked Ned.

'Oh, you know, slow this time of year, like everyplace else. But I'm running some great specials. Hey, you should come by. I'm doing two-for-one dinners.'

'You going to close for the summer?'

'Yeah. Maybe. I'm not sure.'

Charlie focused on Michelle, squinting a bit into the sunset. 'So how is Danny? He get out of the hospital all right?'

'He's fine. Just a couple stitches.'

'Did they catch those guys?'

'Not that I know of.'

'Ah, well. Unfortunately, they hardly ever do.' Charlie paused to light a cigarette, sucking in smoke until he started coughing, and drowned that with a swallow of beer. 'Thankfully, most of the time you run into trouble here, you have to go looking for it.'

'I wasn't,' she said. 'Looking for it.'

Charlie had lifted his beer bottle halfway to his mouth. It paused there, his arm in mid-arc. He put the bottle down.

'Sorry, my dear, I didn't mean to imply that you were. I just meant that you can't expect too much from the police here. But in the normal course of things, you don't have to. This really is a pretty safe place for foreigners, as long as you're sensible. You've just had a run of bad luck.'

Ned laughed nervously. 'Yeah. Lady Luck's a bitch, you know?' He sucked down a few more slugs of beer. 'So do you think Danny's going to come tonight?' he asked Michelle.

He really is a wreck, she thought, watching his leg bounce up and down. He seemed in much worse shape than he had a week before.

What was it that he hoped Daniel could do for him?

'I think so.'

'I guess I can wait a little longer,' Ned said, checking his watch.

'Robberies aside, I hope you're enjoying the town,' Charlie said. 'I'm guessing you must be, or you wouldn't still be here.'

Oh, yes, I had a lovely visit to the scenic dump yesterday.

Probably not the best answer.

'Parts of it I'm enjoying a lot,' she said.

'Danny's an entertaining guy.'

Did everyone know everybody else's business here?

She didn't hide her irritation well, apparently, because Charlie suddenly grimaced. 'Sorry,' he said. 'I guess I should've warned you, gossip is the town sport.'

'You must be a mindreader.'

'No, just an aging drunk with a tactless streak.'

Michelle laughed. She was starting to like him, nicotine stains and all.

'We've only been out on a couple of dates,' she said, 'but aside from, you know, the armed

164

robbery, it's been fun.'

'He really is an interesting fellow,' Charlie said. 'Seems to have his fingers in a lot of things.'

His tone was deliberately noncommittal, she thought, or was she reading too much into it?

'I don't know him that well, actually,' she said, leaning forward a little. Act like you're confiding in him, she told herself. If gossip was the town sport, Charlie had to be a player. 'I don't really know that much about what he does.'

'Ned knows him better than I do,' Charlie said. 'Right, Ned?'

'We hang out sometimes.' Ned sounded proud saying that. Like the high-school loser who every once in a while got to sit at the lunch table with the quarterback.

'What is it you need to talk to him about?' she asked. 'Is there something I can tell him for you? In case you miss each other tonight?'

He flinched, like a startled cat. 'It's just some . . . some business stuff. You know.'

Charlie wheezed out a chuckle. 'Hiring a private jet, Neddy? You're moving up in the world.'

'Hah. No. But he . . . you know, does some consulting and stuff.'

What was it María had said?

Transportation and . . . logistical arrangements.

'I'm going to get another beer,' Ned said. 'You guys want anything?'

She'd barely touched her wine. 'Not yet, thanks.'

'Ah, Ned,' Charlie said with an exaggerated

sigh, watching him make his way to the bar.

'He seems a little nervous.'

Charlie snorted. 'It's his nature. He's perpetually in over his head.' He took another long pull on his beer. He had startlingly blue eyes, Michelle noticed. He must have been attractive once. She could still see it when he smiled.

'A restaurant's a hard business to make work,' she said.

'That it is.'

'Hopefully, Danny can help him out,' she said, watching him.

Charlie lifted an eyebrow. 'Let's hope.'

She waited for him to say something else.

'Speaking of,' he said, glancing toward the beach.

She could just make out Daniel coming up from the shoreline, silhouetted against the last rays of the sun.

* * *

'Hey,' he said, sliding into the chair next to her.

'Hey yourself.' They stared at each other a moment. She found herself smiling.

He leaned in, and they kissed briefly, just long enough for her to want more.

Okay, so you're attracted to him, she thought. She already knew that. She had been since she'd met him.

Just don't turn it into anything else.

'How was the sunset?' he asked Charlie.

'Oh, fair to middling,' Charlie said. 'I'd give it a seven.'

'Sorry I missed it.'

'There'll be another one tomorrow, most likely. You're feeling all right, I take it?'

Daniel touched the square of bandage on his forehead. 'Oh, yeah. No big. Already got the stitches out.'

'Hey, Danny!'

Ned had returned from the bar, a beer in hand.

She could feel the weight of the watch on her wrist.

'Man, I'm so glad I caught you.'

I have to, she thought. This was the kind of thing Gary would want to know about. Wasn't it?

'Hey, Ned,' Daniel said. He didn't try to keep the irritation from his voice.

'You want a drink? I'm buying.'

Daniel made a show of checking his watch. 'Wow, and happy hour's even over. Sure. I'll take a beer.'

Ned handed him the one he'd just bought. 'Here. Take this one. Get you caught up.' He laughed, and it sounded desperate. Michelle was starting to feel sorry for him.

'Thanks.'

Ned pulled the chair that he'd vacated over to Daniel's side and sat.

She pushed the button. This time the rush was definitely nausea.

'So there's this deal I was wondering if I could talk to you about.'

Daniel let out a hard sigh. 'Ned, I'm pretty busy right now, and I'm not looking to get involved in anything else.'

'No, that's not . . . ' Ned perched on the edge of his chair, leg jumping. 'I mean, I just need some advice. Because, you know, I've got this thing going on, this little sort of side thing, you know? And the situation is, these new guys — '

'This isn't a good time.'

'But the thing is — '

'Do you not get English?'

Ned froze. Just like a scared little animal in the middle of the road, Michelle thought.

Then Daniel smiled. 'Okay, look, we can talk about it. How about I call you tomorrow after lunch? All right?'

'Yeah.' Ned nodded so hard that Michelle thought he'd give himself whiplash. 'Yeah, that would be great.'

She leaned over, opened her tote, pretended to hunt for something. Switched off the watch.

She couldn't wait to take the fucking thing off.

'Sorry about that,' Daniel said after Ned had left.

'It's okay.'

She'd seen that side of him before, when he'd caught her in his apartment.

'Ned's just kind of high-maintenance.' Daniel grinned and rested his hand on her knee. 'And I don't like having my date night interrupted.'

The way he could turn it on and off so easily, she hadn't seen that until now.

All the while Charlie had leaned back in his chair, watching them. The kind of 'aging drunk' who didn't miss much, Michelle guessed.

'You up for some dinner?' Daniel asked her.

168

'I am.'

'Good. I'm starving.' He drained his beer in a few gulps. 'I'll catch you next week, probably,' he said to Charlie.

'You two have a lovely evening,' Charlie said, lifting his shot glass.

★ ★ ★

They went to El Dorado, sat under a *palapa* on the beach with their feet trailing in the sand, had grilled fish and vegetables, watched the anchored boats bobbing up and down in the moonlight. A part of her made small talk while the other part of her sat back and monitored the results. She thought she'd done pretty well. He'd grinned and laughed and at one point stretched his hand across the table to twine his fingers in hers.

She'd laughed, too. He was fun to be around.

As long as she pretended, everything was fine.

'Where to?' he asked after he paid the bill.

'Maybe a nightcap?'

'Let's go to my place. I've got drinks.' He leaned over. His lips brushed against her ear. 'I even have a blender.'

She hesitated. 'I don't know . . . '

'Come on, I got the flies out. Promise!'

'My place is closer.'

'When we're at your place, I feel like if we make any noise, we're gonna give some old lady a heart attack.' He kissed her neck, at the crease of her jaw. 'Besides, at my place I can make you breakfast.'

'You cook?'

'Well, a few things. Huevos rancheros. Bloody Marys . . . '

It wasn't a good idea, she thought. At his place they'd be alone. With no witnesses.

Away from Hacienda Carmen, where people were watching. Or was that a good thing?

If she said no, if she turned him down, then what?

What was safer? She couldn't tell anymore.

'You sure you got the flies out?'

⋆   ⋆   ⋆

Don't think. Just do. Quiet the monkey mind. That was what she needed right now, to shut up the chatter in her head, to just forget about everything. To pretend it was all going to be okay.

'So are you into this?'

'What?'

Even in the dark, she could see the concern in his eyes, the worry — that he wasn't pleasing her, maybe?

'Are you kidding?' she said, trying to keep it light.

They lay side by side on Daniel's big bed, which after the hard pallets of both her hotel rooms felt almost decadent, like being gently held.

'You're kind of tough to read,' he said.

They were touching, her knees brushing his thighs, his hand resting on her hip, their faces inches apart.

You can't panic, she told herself.

She hadn't given him any reason to suspect . . . well, anything.

At least she didn't think she had.

She felt the pulse beat in the back of her throat.

'Look,' she said. 'I'm sorry if I seem . . . I don't know, distant. I'm not always very good at showing how I feel, I guess. But it's great being with you. It's the first time in a long time that I feel like I'm getting out of my own head. And with the stuff that's in my head . . . believe me, it's great not to be there.'

She thought she sounded convincing. She was mostly telling the truth, which helped.

Daniel frowned and then nodded. 'Yeah. I hear you. Sometimes it's good to just get away from yourself.'

He had *that* right, she thought.

She needed to get the focus off herself. Off her drama. He must be sick of it by now. *I'm* sick of it, she thought.

'What about you? I mean . . . are *you* into this?'

Maybe he wasn't anymore, and that would be her out.

Funny. She wasn't sure how she felt about that.

He laughed a little, reached over and touched her cheek. 'Yeah. You're just not catching me at my best. Sorry. I'm kind of an asshole sometimes.'

Weren't you supposed to believe what men said about themselves?

All she knew was that he didn't seem like one now.

'You're not,' she said. 'And you don't need to apologize. I've been so wrapped up in myself, I haven't even asked . . . ' She hesitated. But it was what you'd ask in a normal situation, wasn't it? 'What's going on with you?'

'Just a bunch of shit I never should've gotten involved with,' he said.

They lay there in silence for a moment, and she thought, Do I ask?

His eyes left her face. Looked down. He skimmed his fingertips over her breast. Lightly rubbed her nipple. Her breath caught.

'Let's just forget about all of it right now.' His eyes held hers again. His hand moved along her ribs, lower, to the crease of her thigh, his fingers gently probing inward. 'How's that sound?'

She moved against his hand. 'It sounds good.'

16

Daniel made her breakfast, like he'd promised. Huevos rancheros and Bloody Marys. They sat out on his balcony and ate.

'Really good,' she said, because it was.

When he finished his, he pushed his plate away and leaned back in his chair. Stirred his Bloody Mary with a celery stick.

'So what do you think?'

She was still eating. She put down her fork. 'About what?'

He shrugged. 'Are you going to be sticking around for a while?'

Funny, she thought. Was he really that interested? She wasn't sure. He wasn't smiling the way he usually did. He looked, if anything, thoughtful. Maybe a little sad.

He'd enjoyed himself last night, she was pretty sure. She had, in spite of everything.

She'd managed to forget, for a while.

They were quiet together. Tender, almost. And she'd fallen asleep, which she hadn't really expected to be able to do, and she'd slept well.

She'd woken up to an empty bed, a clatter of pans, and the faint smell of coffee. He'd put a folded robe on the pillow where he'd been, which was a nice gesture, she thought.

Now she stared at the sliver of ocean visible from the balcony.

'I don't know,' she said. 'I do have to get back

at some point. Maybe in a week or so. After that I really don't know.'

'My week's looking kind of crazy,' he said. 'But I hope we can get together again, before you go.'

★ ★ ★

They were refinancing, Tom had told her.

When she thought about it now, that was when she should have demanded an explanation. When she should have stopped trusting him. Even if he hadn't been lying to her, she shouldn't have let it go.

She'd gone online to their bank's bill-pay center to schedule the month's payments, and the mortgage account had vanished. The line where the payee should have been, gone.

'We can get a better rate,' Tom had said. 'The accountant's dealing with the refinancing. He's taken the payments out of the household account, so you don't have to worry about it.'

'And you didn't think we should talk about it first?'

It had really grated on her the last few years, the paternal attitude, that he could just do these things and not even bother to discuss them with her. Of course, it *was* his money, he was the wage earner, but weren't they supposed to be in this together?

'Honey, this kind of thing is my *business*,' he'd said. 'It's what I do. It would be like . . . like me telling you what photos to hang on the wall.'

'But I still ask you,' she'd said. 'I ask you what you think.'

The truth was, she hadn't asked enough.

She'd known that the business hadn't been going well. But he'd told her it was nothing dire, nothing to worry about, just normal ups and downs — a fund that was underperforming. Financing that had fallen through. She could tell that he was more stressed out than usual, working longer hours, keeping a greater distance from her. She'd let him.

That was what bothered her the most now. That she hadn't confronted him. That she'd let him handle things, even when she'd suspected that things weren't right.

Maybe he'd wanted to talk. To confess. If only she'd pushed him a bit, maybe he would have told her. Instead she'd gritted her teeth and nodded. Because she hadn't really wanted to know.

She'd liked the distance between them.

★　★　★

When she got back to Hacienda Carmen in the early afternoon, she changed into her bathing suit and a blouse and sarong and went down to the beach. She had her choice of chairs at the beach club; hardly any were taken.

She got out her iPhone and stared at it a moment before calling Ted Banks.

'Hey, there, Michelle. Nice night?'

It was all she could do not to hurl her phone into the sand. Instead she swallowed hard. Took a deep, calming breath.

'Hi, Ted. Yeah.'

Maybe he didn't know. She was calling him; presumably she had something to report.

Or he had someone watching Hacienda Carmen, who'd reported that she hadn't come home that night.

Either way he could read between the lines.

She didn't know what to say. She kept silent, her chest and throat tight with frustration.

'So are you gonna tell me about it?'

'Look . . . '

The parasail guys finally had a customer. She watched for a moment as the chute advertising a local real estate agent lifted up and soared out over the surf.

'How much longer do you expect me to do this?'

'For now I think we need to play that by ear.'

'Gary . . . ' Her heart was pounding. Deep breath. One more. 'I don't know if I can keep doing this. I . . . it's too hard.'

Gary snickered. 'Awww, don't tell me you're falling for him.'

'Fuck you,' she said before she could stop herself.

'You are, aren't you? Sweetie, I could tell you some things about Danny that would curl your hair.'

'Then tell me,' she snapped. 'Go ahead, tell me! You're always insinuating all this shit — why don't you prove it to me?'

For a moment there was silence.

'Oh, I get it,' Gary said. 'You think you can get

a better deal with him, don't you?'

'What are you talking about?'

'What's he been promising you, Michelle? You think he's gonna give you a cut? Well, let me tell you, you're in for a world of hurt if you believe that.'

Michelle stared at the phone in disbelief.

'I don't know what you're talking about. I don't want a deal, I don't want a cut, I just want to go home.'

'Well then, we both want the same thing,' Gary said. 'So you need to keep your cool and do what I tell you, okay?'

The parasail was landing now. A young guy, bearded and shirtless, laughing as he stumbled onto the beach.

'How long, Gary?' she repeated.

'Not too long. I promise. Just tell me about last night.'

Oh, God, she thought. What was she supposed to tell him? About the sex? About what they'd done? Was that what he wanted to hear?

'Ned came by El Tiburón,' she said. 'He's an American who owns a restaurant.'

'I know who he is.'

'He was looking for Danny. He seemed really anxious about it. Said it was . . . it was time-sensitive.'

'Oh, yeah? So what did Danny say?'

'I . . . ' Michelle squeezed her eyes shut. 'I used the watch. I'll send it to you.'

'I knew you could do it,' Gary said, and the satisfaction in his voice made her cringe. 'Good job, Michelle! Lookin' forward to it.'

A pause. 'Anything else?'

Just a bunch of shit I never should've gotten involved with.

'No,' she said. 'No, nothing else.'

★ ★ ★

Fuck the passport, she thought. I'll just get on a plane, and when I get to L.A., I'll say I lost it. They could lock her up in Immigration, whatever. It didn't matter.

Except . . . didn't she need a passport number to book a flight? Did she know her passport number?

You were supposed to make a copy of your passport when you traveled — how many times had she read that? — but she hadn't done it. Hadn't even thought about it.

Would they even let her on the plane without one?

A bus, then. A bus to Guadalajara, then a bus to Tijuana. Just get to the border.

But Gary knows where I live, she thought. He knows who my family is. He knows my credit cards, my bank accounts . . .

Stop, she told herself. Just stop.

She lay back in the beach chair and closed her eyes.

She could call Daniel. Tell him what was going on. Maybe everything Gary had been telling her about Daniel was bullshit. Lies.

Or maybe it wasn't.

★ ★ ★

Sunday morning she got up and did yoga, but after that she was still restless. The courtyard of Hacienda Carmen felt like a trap, a place contaminated by Gary — he'd chosen it for her, after all.

I'll go have coffee someplace else, she thought. One of those cute breakfast places up on Basilio Badillo, maybe. Buy yesterday's *New York Times* and try to relax.

One of the little markets on Olas Altas carried English-language papers, she recalled. Maybe they even had magazines. *New Yorker*, something like that.

The inside of the store smelled like mildew and heated sunscreen: coconut mixed with chemicals. She perused the rack. Mexican tabloids and papers dominated, but here were the *New York Times* and the *San Francisco Chronicle*.

The Mexican papers printed some really gruesome images, she thought. This one, on the front page, a body scorched and melted by flame in the middle of a burned-out room.

MATARON A NORTEAMERICANO, she read.

Mataron. Did that mean 'killed'?

Her heart started pounding before she could even think why.

There was a hand-lettered sign taped to the rack that said NO READING! in English. She picked up the paper anyway and looked below the fold. '*Incendio*,' she saw. '*Restaurante*.'

And a name. Ned Gardner.

She bought the paper, shoved it in her totebag, and went outside, blinking in the glaring light.

Don't think about it. Not yet. Find someplace to sit down.

She walked blindly down Olas Altas, sweat dripping into her eyes.

Here were some restaurants. Where to sit? Inside, where no one could see her? She thought of fire.

By the window, closer to the exit. Where she could get away.

'Coffee, *por favor*,' she said automatically when the waiter came by. She sat and stared out the window. The newspaper in her bag felt poisonous, something she feared to touch.

Not yet. She'd wait for her coffee.

'¿*Y para comer*? For breakfast?'

'I haven't decided.'

She sipped the bitter coffee and finally pulled out the paper.

Not that she could understand much of what it said, just a few words here and there. But the photo she understood: That charred and melted thing, that was Ned. A man she'd met. She'd talked to him. He'd had to talk to Daniel. And she'd told Gary about it.

She found a twenty-peso note, threw it on the table, and pushed back the chair, acid burning her throat, stumbling a little as she stood.

★ ★ ★

At the Internet café, she searched for the article and found it easily enough, then ran it through Babelfish to see if she could figure out what had happened.

'The official of Firemen information emphasized: in the 2:45 hours, it reported that Ned

Gardner, who was a person of North American, apparently dead by the flame erupted it in a restaurant denominated the Lonely Bull, in the flank of the street Insurgentes in the Emiliano colony Zapata, already by the firemen extinguished . . . '

Okay, Michelle thought. Firemen reported that they'd found him dead at 2:45 A.M. — this morning — in the restaurant. There'd been a fire.

'The agents of the municipal police they went to the place, later the judicial and personal authority arrived from the *Instituto Jalisciense* de *Ciencias* Forenses. It extended that there were no violence tracks and the body did not present/display blows or wounds, but that had a splice of cord or rope in the wrist, reason why thinks that he can be assassinated.'

Cord or rope in the wrist. Tied.

'The authorities expect to the use an accelerator, as liquid lighter or gasoline.'

The online version had additional photos, and they were clearer than the one in the newspaper.

You could still see his sneaker in one shot, a Nike. It hadn't burned all the way. Why was that? she wondered. And bits of fabric from his pants. Were they Dockers?

A giggle rose in her throat. She swallowed it.

You can't lose it now, she told herself. Get a grip.

She forced herself to look at the photo again. The head and torso had burned more than the lower legs.

Now, if this were one of those stupid *CSI*

programs, they'd do some fancy graphics with slow motion and reconstruct the murder, with a few shots of the screaming victim thrown in for shock value, she supposed. She'd always hated those shows.

But she could guess what had happened, from what she could read and what she could see. Tied. An accelerant. Burning from the top down. She could picture it. Bound in a chair maybe. Gas or fluid poured on his head. The match or lighter lit.

She shuddered and closed the browser.

17

Maybe it was just a coincidence. Maybe Ned's death had nothing to do with either Gary or Daniel. What was it that Charlie had said?

He's perpetually in over his head.

She stood outside the Internet café and thought about what she should do.

Maybe nothing. Leave it alone and just try to get through the next few days, until she saw Daniel again.

If she saw Daniel again. They hadn't exactly made plans.

What was she supposed to do? Yoga? Go to the beach? Ignore it all and hope that nothing bad would happen?

I can't keep just letting things happen to me, she thought, I can't. I have to *do* something.

Do what?

Charlie had been friendly. He seemed to know a lot of people here. He knew something about Ned, and about Daniel. Maybe she could talk to him, see what he'd tell her.

Most of the time you run into trouble here, you have to go looking for it.

He's not dangerous, she told herself. He's just a harmless old guy you met at a bar.

An aging drunk with a tactless streak.

★ ★ ★

The only local person whose phone number she had apart from Daniel and Gary was Vicky.

It was nearly 11:00 A.M. on a Sunday, not too early to call, late enough, she hoped, that whatever church service Vicky attended would be over.

Three rings and Vicky picked up.

'Vicky? Hi, it's Michelle. Michelle from Los Angeles. How are you?'

'Oh, fine, just fine.' In fact, Vicky sounded distracted. 'How about yourself?'

'Great, thanks. Listen, I was wondering if you had Charlie's number. Charlie from the board meeting.'

'Well, I think so. Hang on, I'll check.'

Vicky had both Charlie's cell phone and his e-mail address. Michelle jotted them down in the margins of the newspaper she'd bought that morning.

'Did you hear?' Vicky suddenly blurted. 'About Ned? Oh, maybe you didn't know him.'

Of course, this was a small town. No surprise that Vicky had heard.

'The guy that owned the Lonely Bull? I did hear. There was some kind of fire?'

'Oh, Michelle, it's just horrible. They say somebody killed him.'

'It's awful,' Michelle said. 'I mean, I only barely knew him, but what a terrible thing to happen.'

'I don't know what to think.' She could hear Vicky's sigh through the phone. 'I know it sounds crazy for me to be saying this, but that kind of thing just doesn't happen here.'

* * *

Michelle called Charlie around noon. Right about when she figured her call would go to voicemail, he answered the phone.

'It's Michelle. We met at El Tiburón. Danny's friend,' she added.

'Of course, I remember. What can I do for you?'

'Well . . . I'm thinking about moving here, and I have a few questions. I was just wondering . . . if I could talk to you about it.'

Charlie coughed a few times in her ear.

'Sure,' he said. 'I'm not busy. Come on over for the sunset if you'd like. I have a good view.'

She hesitated. He didn't seem dangerous, but how could she be sure? 'I don't want to impose. We could meet someplace for drinks if you'd like. On me.'

'You wouldn't be imposing. I like having people over.'

* * *

Charlie lived north and east of La Zona Romántica and Los Muertos Beach. A Mexican neighborhood, it looked like, without a lot of gringos, the buildings blocks of irregular whitewashed rectangles with tile and tin roofs, trimmed with wrought iron and hand-painted signs. Leafy plants in red ceramic pots dotted the balconies; palm trees and a few ginkgoes and *parotas* thrust up from planters on the

185

sidewalk: places where the earth broke through the thin crust of cement trying to hold it in bondage. The curbs cracked and staggered, wires crisscrossing the street and catching on the window bars, among the bougainvillea.

She'd stopped and bought a fancy bottle of tequila, feeling like she needed to bring something, and anyway, she liked spending Gary's money.

She passed a taco stand that overlapped sidewalk and street, a Formica box with a tin roof ringed by barstools, half occupied. She almost sat down herself, the sizzle of meat fat and onions and chilies reminding her that she'd hardly eaten today.

Maybe I should have brought tacos instead of tequila, she thought.

Here was Charlie's building: a typical concrete block trimmed with rusting iron, perhaps three stories high.

She started climbing up the stairs that ran along the outside. Charlie's apartment was on the top floor. The building looked like a dive — the steep, uneven steps; the smears of green-black mold and trickles of rust; the dismantled gym equipment with dried, cracked vinyl; the abandoned kid's bike, its once-gaudy pinks and purples faded by sun and damp. In the rooms she passed, she could hear televisions, kids playing, someone practicing, of all things, a tuba.

She reached the top of the stairs on the third floor and paused for a moment in front of the metal security screen.

186

Was this really a good idea?

You're here, she told herself. Suck it up.

She knocked on the door.

★ ★ ★

'Well, we will have to open this.' Charlie cradled in both hands the bottle of tequila that Michelle had brought.

'Oh, is it good? I wasn't sure.'

'It is excellent, my dear. Thank you.'

Charlie's place wasn't what she'd expected. The apartment was a series of rooms — two bedrooms, big kitchen, a living room that bordered on a terrace. The walls were carefully painted, washes of color alternating with white — apricot in one bedroom, a red wall in the other — with framed prints hung here and there. The furniture — Michelle supposed you could call it rustic, or 'Mexican country' — was simple, but it worked. There were a couple of bookcases. An old-fashioned stereo with turntable.

'This is lovely,' she said.

'I like to think the best part is outside.' He gestured toward the terrace.

Outside, on the roof of the apartment below, he'd set up a table and chairs, shaded by market umbrellas, a broad bench, almost a daybed, surrounded on three sides by gauze curtains. Plants in tubs lined the perimeter. The view was mostly rooftops, but beyond them was the ocean and, if you turned your head, the mountains.

'I live out here a lot of the time.'

On the table were a platter of quesadillas, a

bowl of guacamole, and small dishes of salsa and spicy peanuts.

They sat down, and he poured out two tequilas into blue-rimmed shot glasses.

'Cheers!'

They both sipped.

'Thanks for seeing me.'

'My dear, anyone who brings tequila of this quality is more than welcome in my house.'

The sun had begun its descent into the bay, staining the surrounding clouds a pale pink that deepened to violet.

Charlie sighed in seeming contentment and stretched his legs out into the spare chair. 'I never get tired of this.'

'Is that what everyone does here? Watch the sunsets?'

'If they have any sense.'

'And if they don't?'

'Party too much, usually. Sleep with people they'd be better off avoiding. Get involved in a whole excess of drama.'

A flush rose on her cheeks. Hadn't she done exactly all that?

Maybe he hadn't been referring to her specifically. It hadn't sounded like a dig or a reprimand. The only thing Charlie knew about her for sure was that she'd been with Daniel.

And he didn't know a fraction of the drama.

At least she didn't think he did.

'What about Ned?'

Charlie sat very still. 'You heard what happened.'

'I did.'

188

'Why do you ask?'

Michelle took a sip of her tequila and thought about what she should say. 'Everybody tells me how safe it is here. But I've had some strange things happen to me. And I don't know . . . '

Who to trust, she almost said, but she stopped herself.

'You told me Ned was always in over his head,' she said. 'And that you had to go looking for trouble here. I just want to know, if I decide to stay . . . what kind of trouble are you talking about?'

'Ah.' He poured himself more tequila. 'Look, you're safer here, probably, than you'd be in Los Angeles. I mean, you've got your theft and your robbery, but most of it's like I said. It's getting involved with the wrong kind of people.'

'Like Danny?'

There. She'd said it.

Charlie drew in another lungful of smoke as the last crescent slice of sun dipped into the bay.

'I hope I didn't give you the wrong impression of him,' he said. 'I don't really know him that well, but he seems like a decent guy.'

Did he mean it? She couldn't tell. He sounded reluctant, as if he were afraid of saying the wrong thing.

Like he didn't want to go looking for trouble.

'I don't know Danny that well either,' she said. 'I like him, and we've been seeing each other, and I'd like to see him more. But . . . what you said . . . I just got the impression . . . It worried me a little.'

Charlie let out a long, smoke-filled sigh.

Sipped his tequila. 'I don't really know his business. He doesn't discuss it much. But the people who hire private jets around here . . . well, not all of them are going to have the most savory connections.'

'You mean they're involved with drugs?'

'Do you have reason to think that?'

'I . . . just . . . ' She wasn't going to tell him about the coke. 'I don't know. I just know it's a real problem here. I mean, isn't it?'

A silence. 'Look, the people Danny works for, I don't really know any of them personally,' he finally said. 'But drug money in this country . . . it's everywhere, and if you have any kind of large business, it's tough to avoid. So maybe they aren't involved directly. But they'll do business with people who are.'

She'd hoped for something else. A defense of Daniel, testimony that he was a good guy, so that she could have some measure of trust in her own perceptions.

Failing that, definitive proof that what Gary said was true.

That was the worst part of this situation in a way, that she didn't think she could accurately read anyone or anything around her.

She used to think she was good at that.

'So what about Ned?' she asked.

'It might have been a robbery.'

'Do you really think it was? That robbers would go to all the trouble to do . . . that?'

'Probably not.' Charlie sighed. 'That restaurant of his never did great business, but somehow he kept it going. A lot of people guessed he was selling drugs on the side. You know, to the gringos who didn't want to deal with the locals. There's all kinds of ways that can go bad.' He paused to refill her tequila. 'But that's just a rumor.'

18

The last year with Tom, she'd promised herself that she was going to make some changes. It wasn't enough, the way she'd been living; she wasn't doing enough, wasn't truly engaged in anything. She'd go back to school, maybe. Get more serious about the photography again. Or go in a completely different direction. Adopt a kid — someone who needed her, whom she could care for. Volunteer to do something, something hard and meaningful. Dig wells in Africa. Build orphanages in Peru. She'd drag Tom into counseling, and if he wouldn't go or it didn't help, maybe she'd leave him. What was even keeping them together anymore?

She was going to make some changes, she really was. As soon as things calmed down a little. When Tom's business had improved.

When she figured out what it was she really wanted to be when she grew up.

Then Tom had died, and the changes weren't choices anymore.

★ ★ ★

'Hey there, Michelle.'

'Hi, Ted.'

'Just wanted to touch base,' he said. 'It's been a couple days since we've talked.'

As usual, he'd called her early in the morning,

six-thirty Vallarta time. He probably did it to keep her off balance, get to her before she'd had a chance to talk to anyone else, when she was still unused to speaking.

'I haven't seen Danny, if that's what you want to know.'

'Well, aren't we cranky this morning?'

'You better fucking believe I'm cranky,' she spit out before she could stop herself. 'Did you hear about Ned? Somebody lit him on *fire*. Like . . . like a fucking birthday candle.'

'Yeah, I heard about it. Listen, we don't know who did it. It might not have anything to do with — '

'Oh, come on, Gary. He talks to Danny. I tell you. And the next day he's dead.'

There was a silence on the other end of the line, then a raspy breath. 'See, this is why we do the things we do, Michelle. I know you've felt . . . well, pretty put out by all this. But this is what's at stake. The people we're up against, this is what they do. You need to understand that.'

Michelle lay on her bed, holding her iPhone at arm's length. 'I do understand,' she finally said. 'But you can't expect me to go up against people who do this kind of thing. I'm not a cop or a spy. I'm just . . . '

A housewife, she almost said. That wasn't really who she was, was it?

'Sure, Michelle. I hear what you're saying. But you're not going to be in any danger as long as you keep doing exactly what I tell you to do. Just give me another week, okay? Can you do that? I promise you, that'll be the end of it. And you'll

193

be compensated for it. Trust me on that.' A snorted laugh. 'Check your accounts in a couple of hours.'

★   ★   ★

After Tom died, she'd figured it out. How he'd used a credit card to put money into the household account. How he'd used another card to pay the first one off. Frantically moved money from one account to the other. Kept up appearances, while the mortgage went into default.

It was, on a much larger scale, what he'd done with his business.

Some of what Tom had told her was true. Financing on a project had fallen through, like he said, and he'd made some bad investments. A hedge fund was involved, the assets of which were 'rehypothecated,' whatever that meant.

He hadn't told her the rest. That he'd counted on the housing market's continuing to rise to make up the difference, and when the bubble had started to deflate, how he'd taken clients' money that was supposed to be reinvested into other real estate and instead used it to pay off clients he already owed.

Her lawyer had tried to explain it to her. How what Tom had done was something between a Ponzi scheme and a shell game. He'd started drawing a diagram, with various investment funds and projects, holding companies, warehouse lenders, brokers, 'holders in due course,' 'asset-backed pass-throughs,' 'tranches.'

'Do you actually understand all this?' she'd finally asked him.

'Are you kidding?' he'd said. 'No one does. Not even the guys who invented this stuff.'

★ ★ ★

The beach was brutally hot. She'd already gone into the water twice to cool off. The second time she stayed in awhile. Bobbed up and down in the surf, thoughts circling in her head like they were caught in some kind of whirlpool.

A week. Would that really be the end of it? How did she know that Gary wouldn't just bury the evidence when he was done with her, like he'd threatened to do?

They find all kinds of things up at that dump!

When she retrieved her bag with her wallet and cell phone from behind the bar, she saw that she'd missed a call.

Unknown caller. A U.S. number, area code 561. No message.

Wrong number?

Her finger hovered over the touchscreen.

She tapped the number.

'Hello?'

A woman's voice. Unfamiliar. American, she thought.

'You called me?'

A throaty giggle. 'I did.'

'Who is this?'

'Emma. We met at María's party.'

'Oh.' Michelle remembered her now, the pretty woman with the forties pinup look.

195

The one whose father Daniel worked for.

'Right,' Michelle said. 'How nice of you to call.'

'Are you busy tonight? I thought we could get together for drinks. And conversation.'

Michelle hesitated.

It was one thing, she thought, to risk going over to Charlie's. Charlie, whom she'd had no real reason to suspect of any involvement in the craziness that had somehow taken over her life.

Emma, however, she'd encountered in the thick of it, at María's party.

'I'm not sure if — '

'Oh, come on,' Emma said. 'Just meet me for a drink. It'll be fun. Besides . . . '

There was a burst of music on the other end of the line, then silence, like someone had turned down a radio.

'I can tell you some things you need to know.'

19

The place Emma wanted to meet was a club north of downtown, past the marine terminal. 'It's new,' she said. 'Close to the Walmart.'

The name was El Pirata, which, if Michelle had to guess, she figured meant 'The Pirate.' She really hoped it wasn't a theme bar.

'This is the place,' the taxi driver said. He hesitated. 'You don't look like the kind of lady who goes there.'

From the street it looked fairly bland: a multistory stucco box with neon trim and an unavoidable Jolly Roger graphic above double doors flanked by bouncers. A few people waited outside, a couple of young women, almost girls, wearing tiny dresses and ridiculous heels, accompanied by young men wearing more gold jewelry than the women, several middle-aged men — Americans or Europeans, she thought — in shorts and polos or Hawaiian shirts. She could already hear the boom of music reverberating through the walls. It was late, midnight — the earliest Emma said she could meet.

Michelle hesitated in the taxi. Do I really want to do this? she thought.

It's a public place, she told herself. It had to be pretty safe. Worth the risk anyway. So far Emma was the only person she'd met who seemed more than willing to speak openly about who and what people really were.

That is, if she was telling the truth.

⋆   ⋆   ⋆

There was a cover charge at the door.

Great, Michelle thought, handing over the two hundred pesos.

Inside, what she noticed was not so much the pirate theme as the stripper pole, and the topless girl gyrating around it.

Just great.

The place was a quarter full at best, dimly lit, with disco lighting on the dance floor where the stripper worked. Michelle scanned the club looking for Emma. Jolly Rogers on the walls, rope rigging, and an exaggerated topless figurehead with huge breasts on a fake ship's prow.

Toward the back, in a high leatherette booth, a woman lifted her arm and waved.

'There you are,' Emma said loudly as Michelle approached. She patted the seat next to her. 'I was afraid you'd wimp out. Isn't this place cute?'

'It's . . . um . . . I haven't been to many clubs like this.'

'I thought about a gay club,' Emma said, 'but my boyfriend doesn't approve. What do you want to drink? We could have champagne. Do you like that?'

'Whatever you're having is fine.'

Emma ordered champagne. Dom, of course. The pirate waitress brought the bottle in an ice bucket.

'Cheers!' Emma said, lifting her flute.

* * *

'So you've known Danny awhile?'

Emma shrugged. 'Oh, like you know the family chauffeur. A couple of years.' She laughed. 'He's sort of in and out.'

Michelle forced a smile and had a sip of her champagne. It was hard enough to talk over the music, nearly impossible when your companion only wanted to drink and chatter and occasionally provoke.

But she had to try. She'd risked coming here to get information; the evening would be a total waste of time if she didn't at least try.

She moved closer to Emma, so that she wouldn't have to shout. 'I like Danny a lot,' she said. 'Even though we got off to a pretty bad start.'

'I heard. Did they ever catch them?'

'Not that I know of.' She shook her head. 'I guess I'm kind of surprised at how much crime there is here. Like with that guy Ned. Did you hear about that?'

Emma gave an odd little lurch. 'You knew Ned?'

'Not really — I mean, I met him a couple of times. But, you know, what happened . . . it's pretty awful.'

'Yeah. Kind of over the top.' Emma looked down at her hands, at her champagne, then back at Michelle. Smiled shakily.

'I'm sorry,' Michelle said. 'I shouldn't have just . . . Were the two of you close?'

'We weren't bosom buddies or anything like that. But I used to go to his restaurant. He did good salads.' She lifted her glass, smile back in

199

place, slightly crooked, just the right degree of irony. 'To Ned's salads.'

Michelle raised her glass and took a sip. 'Danny and I almost went there on Friday,' she said, a lie that could have been true.

Emma sighed a little. 'Ned had such a man crush on Danny. Danny was, like, the guy he wanted to be. The player. Poor Ned. He was never going to be that guy. He shouldn't have tried to hang with Danny.'

'Why do you say that?'

'Look how he ended up.'

Emma stared at her for a moment, eyes wide, lower lip trembling. Then she burst into giggles. 'Oh, my God, if you could see your face!' She reached out and grabbed Michelle's hand. 'I'm kidding!'

'Very funny,' Michelle said. She nearly rose from her seat right then, but she stopped herself. Finish the glass of champagne, she thought. Make one last attempt at getting some information. Then leave.

'What does your father do anyway?' she asked.

'Venture capital. Can we talk about him later?' She sounded almost plaintive. 'I need a few more drinks first.'

A light pulsed inside Emma's little purse — her cellphone.

She retrieved it, stared at the screen. Smiled again. 'It's my boyfriend.'

She slid out the keyboard and started typing. Peered up at Michelle through eyelashes thick with mascara.

'He wants to meet you,' she said.

Michelle nursed her champagne while Emma drank and laughed and pointed out the call girls in the club — 'PV Playmates. They're really expensive. Do you want one?' — wondering when she should make her exit.

The boyfriend hadn't arrived. 'He's working,' Emma explained. Michelle wasn't too sure that she wanted to meet him in any case. Who knew what kind of men Emma liked to play with?

Not worth the risk.

'Look,' she finally said, 'it's really late, and I'm getting tired.'

'But you need to meet Oscar. You'll like him. He knows everything about what goes on here.' She clutched Michelle's arm. She already seemed pretty drunk. 'Come on, you're on vacation! You can sleep in tomorrow. It'll be fun.'

'I'm sure it would be. How about a rain check?'

Emma wasn't going to tell her anything useful. She was just a tease and a drama queen.

What a waste of time, she thought.

Emma's grip tightened. 'No, really. You need to meet my boyfriend. I bet you don't have a clue what you've gotten into.'

'I . . . ' Her mouth had gone dry. 'I don't feel comfortable.'

'You shouldn't,' Emma whispered, and then she snickered.

★ ★ ★

Michelle scanned the street outside the club for a taxi. 'He's on his way,' Emma said, staggering a bit as she followed her out onto the uneven sidewalk. 'Let's go back inside. There's a patio we can go where it's quiet.'

'Emma, it's almost two in the morning. Why don't we do it some other time?'

'Look, I'm sorry. I was just teasing you. There's nothing to be nervous about. And if you're going to keep seeing Danny, you really should talk to Oscar.'

There was a cab coming, and it was empty, but Emma held onto Michelle's arm and a couple of college students stumbling out of the club flagged it down first.

'Just wait,' Emma said. 'He's on his way.'

Enough, Michelle thought. 'Emma, I don't have time for this. Danny works for your father — if there's something I need to know about him, why can't you just tell me?'

'Because I don't want to,' Emma said sharply. 'And Oscar wants to meet you.' She leaned toward Michelle, then put her hands on either side of her face, like someone taking in a sculpture.

'Unless this whole thing of yours, this innocent-lady-from-L.A. thing, is just an act and you already know. Is that it? Are you playing all of us?' She smiled. 'That would be funny.'

Michelle swallowed hard. 'I'm not,' she said, trying to keep her voice steady. 'My husband died. I used to work in a photo gallery. I came here on vacation, and I met Danny. That's all.'

Emma studied her face a moment longer.

'Okay,' she said brightly. 'Then let's go back inside and have a drink. Little Ms. Michelle from Los Angeles.'

★ ★ ★

She followed Emma back inside the club, first stopping at the bar so Emma could buy shots of tequila, then past the dance floor where another stripper hung upside down from the pole, wrapping her legs around it and doing a sort of handstand, her big breasts flopping down toward her collarbones. Behind the dance floor was a corridor lit with black lights, a Plexiglas door at the end. 'This way,' Emma said loudly over the music. 'There's a patio — it's nice.' She pushed the door open. Michelle trailed behind her.

It was much quieter outside, the music turned down low, so that what Michelle mostly heard was the ringing in her ears.

Emma led her through the patio, which was larger than it seemed at first glance, winding back between two buildings into a narrow passage and then into a larger alcove. Hardly anyone was out here, probably because it was much cooler inside the air-conditioned club.

There, in the back, behind a fountain, was a statue dressed in bone-white cloth robes trimmed in lace like a bridal gown: a life-size statue of a skeleton. In one outstretched hand, she — it? — held a globe, in the other a scythe. Different-colored candles ringed the statue's base.

'Santa Muerte,' Emma said, making a curtsy

in the direction of the statue. 'The patron saint of prisoners and criminals.'

'Is this from the Day of the Dead?' Michelle asked.

'No. The Church calls it a cult. But it's more than that.'

Emma leaned over, passing her fingers through the candles' flames, the way Michelle and Maggie used to do when they were kids, taking such delight that the fire didn't burn them.

'The colors she wears and the candles you light depend on what you want. Bone is for peace and harmony. Gold to achieve wealth and power. Red brings love and passion. Green for justice, yellow for healing, from disease or addiction.'

She grinned. 'Guess which color candle Danny lights?'

'I don't know,' Michelle said. 'Why don't you tell me?'

Emma giggled. 'Wait, I forgot one.' She put her shot glass down on the brick that ringed the statue, pulled her blouse off her shoulder, and half turned.

On her shoulder and back was a tattoo, a background of red and purple roses. Against it was a skeleton holding a globe and a scythe, robed in lace-trimmed black, the outlines still red, as if it had been recently inked.

'Black is for protection against bad magic and evil spirits,' Emma said. 'And to bring harm to your enemies.'

She tugged her blouse back up over her

shoulder, stumbling a little. 'Why don't we sit down?' Michelle suggested.

'Okay.'

They sat. Emma rested her chin on her hands. For a moment she looked older than Michelle had thought she was. Maybe it was just a trick of the light.

'Emma?'

A man approached their table. Youngish. In his mid- or late twenties, Michelle thought.

'Oh, it's Oscar!' Emma said, lifting her head, smiling broadly. 'Oscar, *mi novio*.' She let her head fall back against the chair, tilting up her face to receive his light kiss on her lips.

'This is your friend?' he asked. He had a soft voice, soft brown eyes. He was clean-shaven and wore a short-sleeved shirt with a button-down collar, open at the neck. Good-looking in a pleasant sort of way.

He didn't look dangerous. He looked like a businessman, or an accountant.

That didn't mean anything, Michelle knew.

'Michelle,' Emma said with a giggle. 'This is Michelle.'

'*Mucho gusto*,' Oscar said.

What was she supposed to say?

'It's very nice to meet you.'

He pulled up a chair and sat down. 'I am sorry I've come so late,' he said. 'I can see you both are tired.'

'I'm not tired,' Emma said, stretching out her hand, stroking his thigh.

'Oh, I know you, sweetheart,' he said with a small smile. 'Here, we can all have one drink before I take you home.'

The bartender came out with a tray of shotglasses — tequila, accompanied by orange-red sangritas.

'*Salud*,' Oscar said, lifting his glass.

Michelle tasted the tequila. This was much better quality than what she'd had before, and the sangrita, a blend of fruit juices and chili, was perfect to cleanse the palate between sips.

'Delicious,' she said. 'Thank you.'

'This is your first time in Vallarta?' Oscar asked.

'Yes.'

'Are you enjoying yourself?'

'Very much.'

Emma laughed. 'Liar.' She picked up her shot glass and drank half of the tequila down.

Oscar acted as though he hadn't heard her. 'This place, do you like it?' He meant the club.

'Oh, well, it's . . . a change of pace for me.'

Oscar smiled a little. 'I don't like it very much myself. It's loud. And tasteless. But useful, as an investment.'

'Do you own it?' Michelle asked.

'I work for an ownership group. We recently have bought it.'

'Are you from Vallarta?' she asked.

'No. From out of town.' He gestured toward the skeletal statue dressed in a bride's gown. 'Like her. She is still new to Vallarta. Not as popular here as Jesús Malverde. Have you heard of him?'

Michelle shook her head.

'An outlaw who was hanged a hundred years

ago. The patron saint of border crossers.'

'And smugglers,' Emma mumbled, resting her head on his shoulder. Now she looked impossibly young.

'Emma does not understand as much as she thinks,' Oscar whispered, still smiling. 'About Santa Muerte. She came from the barrios. She is the saint of the poor. And the desperate. The hopeless. When you are always so close to death, you should befriend her.' He raised his shot glass. 'Maybe you will see more of her here soon.'

⋆   ⋆   ⋆

'Baby, I'll stay awake.'

'No, Emma, I know you. You can ride in the back and sleep.' Oscar guided her into the third row of the black Suburban, which he'd parked a block away from the bar, half up on the sidewalk. 'Michelle can sit in front and keep me company.'

Michelle didn't want to ride in front. She didn't want to ride in the Suburban at all. Black? Tinted windows?

He hadn't asked her anything. Had told her nothing. Why had he wanted to meet her?

'Thanks, but I think I'll just catch a taxi,' she said.

Oscar laughed. The street they stood on was empty. Quiet, except for the vague echo of music from the bar.

'You won't find a taxi now,' he said.

'I'll find one,' she said. 'I really don't want to take you out of your way.'

'I think you should come with us,' he said. 'Vallarta, it's not so safe this time of night.'

He pointed down the end of the block. 'You see those guys?' he asked, his voice hushed.

She looked to where he pointed. A couple of young men, wearing oversized T-shirts and surf trunks, laughing and drinking from paper bags, had just stumbled around the corner.

'They see an American lady like you, maybe they will try to rob you. Because they don't have money, and they think you do.'

He gave her arm a little squeeze. 'Can I show you something?'

She nodded mutely.

He reached down, hitched up his pants leg. There was a holster strapped just above his ankle. A black gun.

'I think you should let me take you home.'

*   *   *

They drove south — or at least she hoped they did. It felt to her like they were going in the right direction, and finally she glimpsed the ocean over her right shoulder.

We're going the right way, she thought. We're going the right way. The gun, it's for protection. He's going to take me home.

They drove through city streets, but this time of night there were few cars; between that and the sealed Suburban it was eerily quiet, like being inside a space capsule.

'When Emma told me about you, I knew I wanted to meet you,' Oscar said.

'I'm just a tourist from Los Angeles. I'm really not that interesting.'

'She knows what interests me.' He glanced briefly over his shoulder at Emma, who lay curled on her side in the back-seat, asleep. 'She is very intelligent. It is too bad, about her weaknesses.'

Get me home, Michelle thought. Just get me home. Or to Hacienda Carmen. Close enough. 'She doesn't really know me. We only met once before tonight.'

'She told me about your friends.'

Michelle thought she recognized the road they were on now, one of the main north-south-running streets that crossed over the river. She couldn't remember what it was called. Something having to do with a revolution, probably.

'I don't have many friends here,' she said. 'I'm new. The friends I've made, I don't know them very well.'

Almost home, she thought. She'd lie on the hard bed, and it would feel like salvation.

Oscar chuckled. 'When I was young, I prayed to Santa Muerte all the time. My family was poor. I think probably you don't know what being poor this way is like.'

'Probably not.'

'You think all the time about wanting things. Simple things. Food. Shoes. A bed. I could only dream about a car like this. In another world they drove them. I could see this world sometimes, passing me on the streets. So close.'

'You're doing well now.'

'Yes.' He nodded. 'Maybe Santa Muerte heard me.'

'Or you're talented and capable.'

He grinned. He had a gold tooth, just next to his canine. 'And lucky.'

He turned the steering wheel left. Away from the ocean, toward the mountains.

'This isn't the way to my hotel,' she said. Her mouth had gone dry. She swallowed, the sides of her throat sticking together.

'I know. I just want to show you something. Something interesting.'

It must have shown on her face, the fear. Oscar smiled. 'Don't worry. You will be home soon.'

They drove on a narrow road along the river, a rippling shadow that she could now and then glimpse through Oscar's window, through gaps in the drooping trees.

'Across the river, that place is called Gringo Gulch,' Oscar said. 'Very rich people live there. I will have a house there, someday soon.'

'Please,' she said, 'could you just take me to my hotel?'

He shook his head. 'In a few minutes. I promise. Don't worry.' He tilted his head toward the backseat. 'You are a friend of Emma's. You're safe with me.'

She could hear Emma moan and sigh from the backseat, then settle into sleep again.

They drove a while longer.

'Here we are,' Oscar said.

They had reached a rise that Michelle thought might be the first undulations of the mountains that cordoned off Puerto Vallarta from the interior. Nestled here were a series of buildings under construction, gray slabs of concrete studded with rebar that thrust out of half-built walls like bamboo shoots. They looked to be five or six stories high.

Oscar drove along the chain-link fence that that ran from the first building to the second, and then he parked the car, leaving the engine idling, the headlights on, pointing toward the blank gray wall of the next building.

'Get out,' he said, 'so you can have a better look.'

I don't want to get out, she thought.

Or maybe she wanted to get out and run, run fast and far away.

'It will only take a minute,' Oscar said. 'Don't worry.' He opened his door and hopped out.

Michelle stared at the keys in the ignition. Could I do it? she thought. Scramble across the bank of cupholders and storage compartments and into the driver's seat? Put the car in reverse and pull out of here?

By the time she'd thought it, Oscar had reached the passenger door. He opened it. Extended his hand toward Michelle.

'Let me help you.'

Behind her, Emma giggled, then smacked her lips a few times, her sigh catching on a snore.

It's a game, Michelle thought, it's one of Emma's games. Nothing bad will happen.

She took Oscar's hand, her own hand trembling, and climbed out.

Their footsteps crunched on gravel, the car's

headlights throwing their shadows ahead of them.

Along the wall were heaps — bundles of clothing.

'Go on,' he said.

She took a stumbling step forward, then another, and she knew that he was going to kill her, no matter what he said, and she didn't even know why.

'Don't worry,' he said again from behind her.

It wasn't clothing; she knew it wasn't, but it was easier to pretend that it was, just for another moment or two. Like when she was driving and would see a dead animal on the road and she'd tell herself, it's not that, it's a plastic sack, it's someone's lost sweatshirt. And sometimes it was, and she'd feel a flood of cool relief, that she wasn't going to see some poor mangled cat or dog with its guts spilled out on the asphalt.

The bundles were bodies, propped against the concrete wall, and she knew that they were; she could already smell the spoiled-meat smell of them; if she drew closer, she'd see the maggots, like on the pig's head, except she couldn't see their heads. They didn't have them anymore.

Just ragged necks, like the stems of hacked-off flowers.

She could see the blood on their shirts, almost black in the beams of the headlamps, their legs kicked out in front of them.

The third body was different. Burned to the point where the charred flesh barely covered the bones. It looked like a prop. Like a horror-movie skeleton. The flesh had been seared away, down to the skull, to a few leathered scraps of skin.

Draped on the skull was a white headdress and veil, like a bride's.

Behind her, Oscar asked, 'Do you want to go home now, Michelle?'

Her stomach twisted and roiled. Don't get sick, she told herself. Pretend you have your camera and you're looking through the lens. It's just an image. It's not real.

She nodded.

★ ★ ★

He didn't say anything. He helped her into the front seat of the Suburban. Emma was still sprawled out in the backseat, snoring softly.

He isn't going to kill me, she told herself. He isn't. He would have done it there if he were going to. He wanted to show me those . . . those things.

Why?

He drove her back to Hacienda Carmen, not saying a word. Neither did she.

When they reached the gates, he said, 'I like that you pay attention and that you don't talk too much.'

Her hand clutched the door latch. Oscar reached across and pressed the button to release her seatbelt.

'Tell your friends,' he said. 'Tell them that I've come to town.' He smiled. 'Tell them that you met me.'

20

She made it to the bathroom in her room at Hacienda Carmen before she threw up. She crouched over the toilet seat, puking up the red snapper she'd had for dinner and the champagne and tequila she'd drunk with Emma until bile burned her throat, and when she was finally done, she lay on the bathroom floor curled on her side, shivering, the glazed tiles cool against her cheek.

Eventually she sat up, then stood, grasping the edge of the sink for support.

She rinsed out her mouth with water from the sink, wet down a washcloth with cold water and washed her face, cleaned up the splatters of vomit on the toilet seat and the floor where she'd missed the bowl. Brushed her teeth.

Then she changed out of her clothes, tossing them on the bathroom floor. Stood there naked for a moment, still shivering in the damp heat.

What clothes to put on?

What should she do now?

Four in the morning, she told herself, it's four in the morning.

She put on an oversized T-shirt and went and sat on the edge of her bed.

He hadn't killed her. He wanted her to see . . . he wanted her to tell . . .

To tell someone.

Tell your friends.

She wanted to cry, but she was too empty for that. Too exhausted. Instead she stood and got a bottle of water out of her refrigerator, took a few sips of it, then sank back onto the bed.

Daniel. It had to be Daniel. Who of her 'friends' here did Emma even know about, except for him?

You can't be sure, she told herself. You don't know what's going on behind the curtain.

But all this had started with Daniel, hadn't it? Emma had seen the two of them together. It was the simplest explanation. The simplest explanation was usually true. What was that called again? Someone's razor, something like that.

It couldn't be Gary. Emma couldn't know about Gary. Could she?

Whoever Gary worked for, she knew that he wasn't her friend.

She rested her forehead in her palms for a moment.

Were there buses running this time of night? Buses to anywhere that wasn't here?

You have to call him, she thought. That wasn't a request from Oscar. It was a command. If she didn't . . .

She got her iPhone out of the little black purse she'd carried with her tonight. Tapped on her contacts and dragged her finger to Daniel.

'*Howdy*,' his voice said. 'Leave a message.'

Fuck.

Well, what did she expect? It was four in the morning.

'It's Michelle,' she said. 'Sorry to call so late. But some things have happened . . . '

Don't lose it, she told herself. You can't.

'Some things have happened. And I have to talk to you. It's . . . '

What was she supposed to say?

'Please call me. It's really important.'

She lay there on the bed staring at the iPhone, at all her apps, at the lie of connection, its blank promises.

Finally she got up and took one of Tom's Ambiens and a couple of Advils. Drank the rest of her bottle of water. Stretched out on the bed staring at the fan on the ceiling, at its slowly rotating blades.

★　★　★

The phone. She lunged for it. 'Hello?'

'Hey.'

'Danny?'

'Yeah.'

Eight A.M. She'd dozed a little. She was wide awake now, her heart thudding hard.

'I . . . ' How could she even begin to explain? 'Are you in town?'

'No.' He sounded a little irritated. 'What's up?'

'Something happened last night . . . with Emma . . . '

'Emma?' Right away his tone changed. To a sort of wary concern. 'Is she . . . is she okay or . . . ?'

'Yeah. I think so. But . . . look, I need to see you. I can't . . . It's too hard to explain on the phone.'

And what if someone were listening?

She could hear his harsh sigh on the other end. 'I've got a lot going on. But I can meet you tomorrow morning. Is that going to work?'

It would have to.

★ ★ ★

Maybe it was time to go to the consulate. She tried to imagine it, what she would say to them, how they would react.

They'll think I'm crazy, she decided. Or guilty of something. But as long as they'd help her . . .

Would they?

Oh, I wouldn't do that, Michelle. I really wouldn't.

She showered, dressed, and went downstairs for coffee.

Two men waited at the reception counter. At first she didn't realize they were waiting for her; the older of the two leaned against the counter chatting up Paloma, the woman with the rose tattoo who worked the front desk. The other hung back, sipping a cup of coffee, smiling and then laughing at something one of them had said.

Michelle approached the counter, where the coffee pot sat surrounded by an assortment of mismatched cups.

The younger of the two men straightened up. 'Ms. Mason?'

She recognized him then — the policeman who'd come to her hotel the night of the assault, the one who'd spoken better English. As before, he wore a white polo shirt and khakis; his badge hung around his neck on a lanyard.

'Inspector Morales with the judicial police.'

Her heart started to pound, so hard that for a moment she felt dizzy, cold sweat prickling on her back.

Did they know? That she'd been there, that she'd seen . . .

They couldn't, she told herself. Calm down.

Unless someone told them.

'I remember you,' she said. 'You came to the hotel.'

He smiled, showing even, white teeth. 'Right.' He gestured at his companion. 'This is Inspector Dos Santos. Can we speak to you for a few minutes?'

'Of course,' Michelle said.

He gestured toward an empty table behind the fountain, by the wrought-iron fence. Michelle nodded and started to follow him, then stopped. 'I'd better have a cup of coffee,' she said, smiling at him.

'Sure,' he said, lifting his mug, and he and Dos Santos went to sit down at the table.

She watched his retreating back. She could see the edge of a tattoo where his neck met his shoulder. A spiderweb, it looked like.

She filled her mug, her hands shaking, topped the coffee off with milk, thinking. What could she say? What would they think?

Never offer information. She remembered reading that somewhere, that you should never give the police information if they suspected you of something, not without a lawyer. You could get yourself into a lot of trouble that way.

But this was Mexico. She wasn't innocent until proven guilty. It was the other way around.

A spiderweb. Was that a gang tattoo?

Don't say anything unless you have to, she told herself. Find out what they want first.

She followed the two men over to the table. The yellow dog that hung out in the courtyard trotted over and flopped beneath its shade.

'Is this about what happened at the hotel?' she asked.

Morales shook his head. 'No. Unfortunately, we haven't caught those guys. They probably left town, to be honest.'

'Oh. Then why . . . ?'

'Ned Gardner.'

'Ned?'

For a moment she felt absurdly relieved. She'd only seen Ned's body in photographs. She hadn't been there. They couldn't possibly think she'd had anything to do with what happened to him.

'The American who ran the restaurant. You knew him?'

'I'd met him.' She took a moment to sip her coffee, to think about what she should say. 'I heard about what happened. It's really awful.'

'Yeah. So we want to be very thorough in our investigation. And we understand you talked to him the night he died. At El Tiburón. Is that correct?'

'I talked to him for a couple of minutes.'

'Can you tell us about your conversation?'

'Well, there wasn't all that much to it.'

219

Dos Santos leaned back in his chair, smiling, saying nothing. Maybe he didn't speak much English.

She thought about what she should say, if she should mention Ned's 'business' with Daniel, then realized she didn't have much choice.

Charlie had heard the whole thing.

'He was trying to drum up business for his restaurant,' Michelle said. 'You know, offering two-for-one specials, that kind of thing. I got the impression the place wasn't doing that well.'

'Was there anything else?'

'He was mostly talking to my friend, to Danny.'

'Oh,' Morales said. 'The man from the hotel. Okay.'

The way he said it, so carefully neutral — he found that interesting.

Or he knew something already.

'What about?'

'Trying to get some advice, I think.' She gave a little shrug. 'I wasn't really paying that much attention.'

'Do you know where I can reach him?'

'I think he's out of town.'

'A phone number?'

She hesitated. 'Sure.'

Daniel wasn't going to like that. But lying didn't seem like an option.

Underneath the table the yellow dog's tail beat against the ground, in slow steady time.

She gave Morales the phone number. He made a note in a little pad, the first note he'd taken.

Were they recording the conversation? she wondered.

'I didn't think you would still be in Vallarta,' he said. 'I guess I thought you were only here for a week or so. On vacation.'

'Well, that was my original plan.' She shrugged. 'I like it here.'

'In spite of your troubles.'

'Yes. In spite of my troubles. But I'm probably going home next week.'

'I see.' He reached into his pants pocket and extracted a small plastic card case. 'If you think of anything else, you can reach me at these numbers. And I still have yours.'

'Thanks,' she said, taking his card. Dos Santos stood as well, still smiling, still saying nothing.

'Did you spend time in the States?' she said. Because it suddenly occurred to her, what was familiar about Morales. It was his accent, the way he carried himself.

'Yeah, I did. In L.A., in Van Nuys.' He grinned. 'You know Van Nuys?'

'Of course. I live in L.A.'

'No kidding! Yeah, I was there from when I was a little kid till I was in high school. You can still tell, huh?'

She nodded. 'You sound American.'

He shrugged. 'I used to think I was.'

* * *

By late afternoon it had made the online papers.

¡MASACRE EN VALLARTA! the headline said in huge type. *'Calcinaron a una persona y*

221

decapitaron a dos más,' read the subhead halfway down, just above the photos.

There were the bodies, posed against the concrete wall, the two headless and bloody, the third burned clear to the bone.

★ ★ ★

'Beltrán Leyva. It's got to be.'

'Maybe it's Sinaloa, Chapo's boys setting an example.'

'Dumped at the Aguilars' building? No fucking way. That's a message to Sinaloa — *and* to this town.'

Michelle clutched her Perrier, drank, and nodded. Like she had a clue what they were talking about.

She'd gone to El Tiburón early in the evening, before sunset. It wasn't Friday, but she'd hoped there would be people here she knew, engaging in the town sport of gossip.

She hadn't been disappointed. Charlie sat at a table by the railing overlooking the sand. With him was the Asian-American man she'd seen here the first time she'd come, who'd gone on about how crime was bad for business. Broad-faced, red-cheeked, and sweating, he tilted back in his chair and drained his beer, rested his hands on his thick thighs. 'Fucking craptastic,' he said.

His name was Nate — 'Except around here they call me 'El Chino.' Nice, huh?' — and he was a structural engineer and contractor. 'The Aguilars hired me to fix their sinkhole of a condo

222

project,' he told Michelle. 'First they tried building on unstable ground. Then they didn't grease the right palms when the new mayor came in. Now they've got fucking *narcos* doing some voodoo Santería shit and dumping bodies on the property.'

'Santa Muerte,' Michelle said.

'Huh?'

'That's what it looked like. The skull. Santa Muerte. The patron saint of the poor. And criminals.'

'Whatever. All I know is the job's a crime scene now, on top of everything else.'

'Santa Muerte's always been more of a Gulf cartel icon than a Sinaloa one,' Charlie said thoughtfully. 'But supposedly Sinaloa and Gulf are allied these days. I'm not sure what to make of this.'

Oscar had said he was from out of town. Like Santa Muerte. Did that mean he was from Gulf?

'Maybe I'm wrong,' Michelle mumbled.

'Just tell me it's not the fucking Zetas,' Nate said, pushing his lank hair out of his face. 'Because that would just be the shit icing on my crap cupcake.'

★ ★ ★

'Are you all right?'

'What?'

Charlie was looking at her, his blue eyes bright even after all the beers and tequila.

'You seem kind of shook up.'

She'd been tearing off strips of napkin and

twisting them into tight little spirals. Maybe that's how he could tell she was upset.

'Nothing . . . just . . . I went out with this woman named Emma last night. Do you know her?'

'Emma? Emma Dellinger?' Charlie leaned back in his chair and snorted. 'Yeah, I've met her.'

'Do you know anything about her father?'

'Not really. Just that he's loaded and she's daddy's little girl. I hear the family compound up in San Pancho is something to see. Why do you ask?'

Michelle forced a smile. 'It was just a strange evening.'

'I can imagine. She's not the most stable. Unlike me.' He grinned and lifted his hand to call the waiter. 'Join me in a Cazadores?'

★　★　★

They sat and sipped their drinks and watched the inevitable sunset. Michelle had a Bohemia. Cazadores was a tequila, and the thought of drinking tequila made her feel sick.

'This thing everybody's talking about,' she finally said. 'The bodies, the ones they found last night . . . I thought you said . . . that it was safe here.'

'Well, if you're not involved in the drug trade, I stand by what I said.' He sounded annoyed. 'I swear, from some of the shit you read, you'd think there were corpses on every street corner in Mexico.'

224

She thought about Gary's claim, that they'd found bodies at the dump, which Vicky had known nothing about.

'But they found bodies here,' she said. 'At that condo complex. What did Nate mean when he said it was a message?'

Charlie took a long moment, seeming to consider.

'Traditionally this has been Sinaloa territory. The cartel. You've heard of it?'

She nodded.

'The most influential cartel in Mexico these days. People like the Aguilars, the local power brokers, many of them have business tied up with Sinaloa. It's like that in a lot of Mexico. The cartels have to put all that drug money someplace. Around here they invest in real estate, hotels and condos. Clubs. Helps them do their money laundering. That's how it's been for years. Overall, pretty quiet and stable. A vacation town. This isn't where they do their real business.'

He lit a cigarette. The first since she'd arrived. 'I'm cutting back, I swear,' he said, taking a long drag. 'Anyway, things are changing. For one, the drug market in Vallarta is lucrative enough that it's worth fighting for, what with all the gringos in town. So there've been some incidents. But nothing like what you get up along the border. They're playing for the big money up there — for the *plazas*, the smuggling routes into the States.'

'Serapes?' A stocky vendor approached them, arms draped with blankets woven in bands of bright colors.

'No, *gracias*,' Michelle told him. 'So what's changed?' she asked Charlie.

'Calderón — he's the current president — he's gone to war against the cartels. Or so he says. Using Mexican military units to do the fighting, because the local and state cops are too corrupt. The last few years they've mostly gone after Gulf — Sinaloa's main rival. To hear some tell it, the government's been playing favorites, with the military taking out Sinaloa's enemies for them.'

'Do you think that's true?'

Charlie laughed. '*Forbes* magazine has the head of the Sinaloa cartel as one of the richest men in the world. Do you think that happens without friends in very high places? I don't.'

He stubbed out his cigarette before it was half smoked. 'It's the butt end that kills you,' he said. 'Or so I've heard.'

'I think it just kills you faster.'

'Well, in that case . . . ' He lit a fresh cigarette. Coughed a bit. 'Every time somebody high up in one of the cartels gets taken out, it puts things in a state of flux,' he said. 'Chaos, even. Alliances keep shifting. The last year or so, Sinaloa's been knocking heads with their old allies Beltrán Leyva. And you ever heard of the Zetas?'

She tried to remember from her reading at the Internet café. There were so many names that she hadn't come close to understanding who was who, whose side they were on. The Zetas . . . it was something about an army.

'They're an armed paramilitary, started out as the Gulf cartel's enforcers,' Charlie said. 'Became the tail that wagged the dog and turned

226

on their former masters. They're mercenaries —
they'll fight Sinaloa, Gulf, the police, anybody.
And they think like a military unit. Complete
with military-grade weapons, which, by the way,
they get smuggled in from the U.S. They're so
well organized that the big cartels — Sinaloa,
Gulf and La Familia — have formed an alliance
to wipe them out. Now, supposedly the Zetas are
working for Beltrán Leyva, and that's what's
getting everyone around here so stirred up.'

'Because . . . they're coming here? To fight for
the drug trade?'

Charlie nodded. 'Rumor has it.'

He leaned back in his chair, seeming to watch
the sunset. 'That's one story. I got another one
for you, if you're up for it.'

She wasn't sure that she was. 'Why not?' she
said anyway.

'The Zetas' founders were Mexican military
officers trained at the School of the Americas,
did you know that? Them and half the dictators
and torturers in South America over the last
couple of decades.' He sipped his tequila. 'You
can look it up.'

'School of the Americas?'

'The army school at Fort Benning. Which is a
CIA front, of course.'

'Of course.'

Calm down, she told herself. This is Charlie
talking over tequila. Next thing you know, he'll
be telling me that 9/11 was an inside job.

'So what exactly are you saying?' she asked.
'The CIA hired the Zetas to . . . to take out
Sinaloa?'

227

She knew that she'd sounded sarcastic. Disbelieving.

The last thing she wanted was for all this to be true.

'Not necessarily,' Charlie said, waving his arm, cigarette making an orange trail in the dark. 'Sometimes you create something that you can't control. Blowback. Like Osama. The mujahideen. Religious fanatics that the U.S. government armed to fight the Soviets in Afghanistan.' He snorted. '*That* worked out well.'

He finished off his shot, then raised his hand to call the waiter for another. 'But who knows? Look at it this way. A war breaks out between two cartel factions. People get slaughtered. It's out of control. And who do you think comes in next, to restore the peace?'

'The Mexican military?' she guessed.

'Got it in one. And then ask yourself, who ends up in charge?'

She tried to think it through, but she couldn't. She hadn't slept. Her head hurt. She closed her eyes and saw Oscar lifting his shot of tequila, saw the statue of Santa Muerte lit by flickering candles.

'I don't know, Charlie. I'm pretty confused.'

'If you're an optimist, the president.'

The president who'd had officials corrupted by Sinaloa. Who'd been accused of favoring them. 'And if I'm not?'

'The military itself. Which has been infiltrated by the cartels, too.' Charlie shrugged. 'Everything has.'

★ ★ ★

She walked back toward Hacienda Carmen along the packed sand by the water's edge. The ocean scent, the kelp and the brine, soothed her a little, though not nearly enough. Nothing really could.

She stepped off the sand onto the cobblestones and headed up the hill to Hacienda Carmen.

A block up from the wrought-iron gate was a late-model white SUV; she could see it glowing under the street lamp.

She froze in place, heart thudding. *Stupid*, she thought. Many people drove SUVs. Not all of them were interested in her.

She thought some more, about articles she'd read. About people getting kidnapped in Mexico in broad daylight. And it wasn't even daylight now.

Walk slowly, she told herself, Watch closely. If anything looks off, run like hell.

The SUV was a new Navigator with gold trim, its engine idling, white exhaust wafting from the tailpipe.

She walked up to the gate of Hacienda Carmen, opened it, and went inside.

★　★　★

Just after 9:00 P.M. She'd gone beyond exhaustion to that point where she knew she wouldn't be able to fall asleep; she was too wired. Now and again her mind would make pictures, like snapshots, of what she'd seen the night before. She tried to push them away, but it didn't work.

As she went into the bathroom to brush her teeth, she heard three short knocks on the door.

Don't answer it. Just don't. Hide in the bathroom. Lock the door.

Okay, she told herself. That's not a rational response. Probably.

It was probably just Paloma, from the front desk.

She went to the door and opened it as far as the door guard would allow. A woman stood there, middle-aged, dark hair and dark eyes.

'Michelle,' the woman said. 'Is this Michelle? Danny's friend?'

'Who is this?'

'María. María Aguilar.' A pause. 'You were a guest at my party.'

She'd come alone, as far as Michelle could see; there was no one on the little balcony or on the stairs behind her.

'May I come in? I won't take up too much of your time.'

Michelle hesitated.

'It's important,' she said. 'And I would be very grateful.'

★   ★   ★

'I'm sorry to disturb you.' María sat in one of the room's two chairs, twisting around the chunky ring that she wore on her left hand. Her eyes were red, the lids puffy.

Michelle had met María for all of five minutes. Maybe ten. And now the woman was sitting in her hotel room.

Given the last couple of days, this could not be good.

'Would you like a glass of wine?' Michelle asked. She still had the bottle of white in the mini-fridge.

María nodded, twisting the ring on her finger. She wore a black lace shawl over a gray silk blouse this evening, a small gold cross hung on a gold chain around her neck.

'Sorry, I don't have proper glasses,' Michelle said, handing her a tumbler. She poured her own into a coffee cup and sat down in the other chair.

'Do you know how to reach Danny?' María asked.

'I . . . ' She wasn't sure how to answer. Should she offer Daniel's cell number? Wouldn't María have that already?

'I have his number, of course,' María said with a wave of her hand, as if she'd anticipated the question. 'But he does not pick up. And it's important that I speak to him.'

'Well, if you can't get a hold of him, I don't know that I'll be able to,' Michelle said. 'He speaks highly of you. I think he's just very busy.'

Now María gave her a look, a half-raised eyebrow, head tilted back, the way she'd looked her over at the party. 'Really? I had the impression that the two of you are close. That you are . . . important to him.'

'I'm not sure why you think that.' Which was the truth.

'He brought you to my party,' María said simply. 'He introduced you to everyone. He

231

wanted us to know about you. And you are still here, in Vallarta.'

She'd wondered why Daniel had brought her to that party. Now she thought she knew.

She'd been chum, tossed out to attract the sharks.

She felt a surge of rage. She took a sip of wine and swallowed it.

'I should be seeing him soon. I could give him a message for you. If you can't reach him before then.'

María closed her eyes and rocked back and forth in the chair.

'Yes,' she said, suddenly still. 'Yes. Tell him we are loyal. No matter what has been said. Tell him that. Whoever is responsible, we deserve protection.'

She shook her head and gulped some wine. 'What's important is stability. Chaos will only benefit the most wicked.'

'Right,' Michelle said. 'I'll tell him.'

María stood up slowly, her hands shaking. She put the tumbler down on the credenza by the door.

'My husband did not deserve this,' she said. 'Tell him that.'

21

'Morning, Michelle.'

'Hi, Ted.'

He'd let her sleep in till seven this time, and she had managed to sleep, a little, thanks to Tom's Ambien.

'It's been a couple days since we've talked. What's going on?'

'I . . . I haven't seen Danny.'

'So you been keeping busy?' A pause. She could imagine him smiling on the other end of the line. 'You take any good photos?'

'No, I . . . '

How much should she tell him about the last two days?

'I had something strange happen last night,' she finally said. 'María — María Aguilar, the woman who had the party I went to. She came here wanting to get in touch with Danny.'

'Oh, yeah?' Gary sounded suddenly alert.

'She said something about her husband. That he didn't deserve what happened to him. Do you know anything about that?'

A pause. 'Well, it's a sad thing. He got killed the other night. Him and a couple other guys who I guess were *narcos*. It took a little longer to ID him because they burned his body.'

For a moment she couldn't speak, only nod, even though he couldn't see her. 'Do they know who did it?' she asked. 'Or why?'

233

Maybe Gary could at least tell her who Oscar was. Who he worked for.

'Couple of possibilities. He got caught out in the middle of something either way.'

'Is it . . . is it the Gulf cartel? Or the Zetas? Or . . . ?'

Gary chuckled. 'My, my. Sounds like you've been doing a little research. That's great, Michelle. I like to see someone who has a genuine interest in the job. I can tell, you've got a real future in this line of work.'

'You didn't answer my question.'

'Well, it's too soon to say. These guys, they're always fighting about something. It could be an internal dispute, for all we know.'

She swallowed her frustration. It was as much of an admission as he'd ever make, and it told her nothing.

'Anything else going on I should know about?' he asked.

Through the open window behind her bed, she could hear the donkeys braying on the hillside.

'Look, I'm going to have to call you back,' she said. 'I'm meeting Danny for coffee, and I'm running late.'

'So early?' She could picture his smile. 'He must really like you.'

'He's busy,' she said. 'I'll call you after.'

'All right, Michelle. Just make sure you do that.'

* * *

She'd lied. Not a big lie, just a small one. She wasn't meeting Daniel for a couple of hours. But she'd needed a little time. Time to decide what to tell Gary. She wasn't sure if he needed to know what had happened that night with Emma and Oscar. Or if it would be dangerous for her to tell him.

'I don't have a lot of time, but I can meet you at your place around nine,' Daniel had said.

'No, let's . . . let's meet somewhere else. Like, on the beach, maybe.'

'Okay. Your old hotel, how about that? It's a big place, we can probably grab a coffee somewhere quiet.'

★ ★ ★

It felt strange, walking into her old hotel. Like walking into another life. It felt so long ago. But it had been, what? Two weeks? Less than that. A week and a half.

'Señora Mason,' the woman behind the front desk said. 'How nice to see you! But I thought that you'd left Vallarta.'

Michelle managed a smile. 'So did I.'

'Have you come back to spend some time with us?'

'Well, no, just . . . I wanted a place to meet my friend, for breakfast. And I thought this would be a nice place. Is it okay, if I'm not a guest?'

'Oh, of course. Where would you like to sit?'

★ ★ ★

She chose a table in the corner of the terrace below the swimming pool that overlooked the beach. Far enough away from the few guests who swam morning laps and drank coffees in the shade of the rear patio. Eighties rock played from the terrace bar, in spite of the early hour and the lack of customers.

She'd gotten there a few minutes early, so she could have a chance to catch her breath, decide what she wanted to say and how she was going to say it. But she couldn't think of any words, not any good ones, nothing clever or strategic.

She was waiting for a man she couldn't trust, to give him a message from a killer. She didn't know where she'd be left after she delivered it.

Her heart skipped as Daniel appeared at the edge of the terrace.

He wasn't going to solve her problems. He'd caused them.

'Hey.'

She rose to greet him. He wore wrinkled khaki cargo shorts and a light madras shirt, and he carried a small canvas duffel bag over one shoulder.

They hugged, and she felt awkward, rigid. He could tell. He took a step back and studied her face.

He looked tired, she noticed. Red-eyed and stubbled.

'What's up?' he asked.

'I don't really know where to start.'

'How about with breakfast? I'm hungry.' He grinned, but there was nothing light about it.

He ordered chilaquiles. Michelle got a fruit plate.

'So?' he said after the waiter had brought their coffees.

You have to tell him, she thought.

'I went out with Emma the other night.'

He put his hand to his forehead and winced. 'Jesus. Emma? Why?'

'Because she asked me. Because I thought . . . She said she was a friend of yours.'

She didn't want to lie, she was sick of lying, but it was close to the truth, at least.

'Emma is fucking crazy.'

'Yeah, well, I get that now.' Stay calm, she told herself. Keep your voice low. If anyone was watching, they were just having a conversation.

'I met her boyfriend, a guy named Oscar. He was supposed to take me home. He took me to . . . up to the condos. Where the bodies were. Did you hear about that?'

He nodded. He'd gone pale beneath the tan.

'He told me to tell my friends. He meant you. Didn't he?'

The waiter approached with Michelle's fruit plate.

'Hell of a place to have this conversation,' Daniel said, his voice rough. 'Let's go somewhere more private.'

'No.'

'Your breakfast will be out in just a minute, señor,' the waiter said, depositing Michelle's plate.

As the waiter retreated to the kitchen, she took

in a deep breath. 'I'd rather talk here. In a public place. I'm just . . . I don't really know you. And ever since I met you, all kinds of shit keeps happening.'

'I told you to stay away from Emma,' he said. He sounded pissed.

'You took me to María's party! That's the only reason Emma even knew who I was.'

She was so angry that it was easy to forget the lie she told every moment she was with him.

'Is that why you brought me along, Danny? To see what I stirred up?'

'No, I just . . . I just wanted a date. I told you, I hate those parties.' He tried the half-smile again. She wasn't buying it.

'You want to hear the rest?' she asked.

'Guess I'd better.'

'María came to see me. She was looking for you. One of those bodies was her husband.'

Daniel stared at the table. 'I heard. He didn't deserve that.'

'That's what she said to me. She wanted me to tell you that. And that they were loyal and deserved protection.'

'It's a fucked-up situation,' he muttered.

'You think?'

'Look, you don't have to worry about it. None of this is your problem.'

'Seriously, Danny? *Seriously*? I was at a crime scene! With dead people! I've got the police coming around asking me questions. And it's not my problem?'

'I didn't think you were going to get dragged into this.'

238

'What *did* you think, then?'

'That we were having a good time together. That I could . . . forget about this shit for a few days. I like being with you, that's all.'

She wished she could believe him.

The waiter arrived with Daniel's chilaquiles. 'Anything else? Maybe something to drink? A mimosa?'

'No, thanks,' Daniel said. 'The police?' he asked after the waiter had left.

'Yesterday morning. Asking about Ned and that night at El Tiburón. I'm guessing you heard about Ned, too.'

'Yeah. Some detective called yesterday. I haven't returned it yet.' He stared at her. 'You give them my number?'

She repressed a shiver. 'I had to, Danny. They were going to get it from someone, and I didn't want to lie.'

He sighed. 'Okay. I get it.'

He pushed his eggs and tortillas around the plate, took a couple desultory bites.

'Look,' he said, putting down his fork. 'I'm heading out of town in about an hour. Just down the coast, to this little village I like. I'm meeting a buddy of mine. For fishing. I think you should come with me.'

'Why?'

'Just . . . There's a lot of shit going on right now. It might be better if you get out of town for a few days.'

'Then why don't I just get on a plane and go home to L.A.?'

He shrugged. 'Might not be a bad idea. If you

239

think you can get on a plane today. Otherwise . . . you don't want these people looking for me and coming to you.'

She tried not to let any of it show. That she couldn't get on a plane today. That she didn't know if going with him was any safer than staying here.

'Fishing?' she asked. 'A lot of shit going on, and you go fishing?'

'It's complicated,' he mumbled.

'I guess.'

'I know what you're probably thinking.'

'I'm pretty sure you don't.'

He checked his watch. 'If you're going to come with me, you have to decide fast. Water taxi leaves at eleven.'

'Why is everyone looking for you, Danny?'

He sighed. 'They want me to take sides,' he said.

⋆　⋆　⋆

He walked with her to Hacienda Carmen. 'Think about it while we walk,' he said. 'If you want to go, you have time to pack a few things.'

They climbed up the stairs to her room, Paloma at the front desk greeting her with a slight smile and a nod. Went inside.

They stood there by the bed, facing each other.

'Danny,' she finally said, 'I don't know if I can trust you.'

'I guess I haven't given you much reason to.' He looked at her, his expression steady, and if

240

she hadn't known anything about him, she would have thought he was utterly sincere. 'All I can do is promise you that I'll do my best to keep you safe.'

Funny. What had Oscar said?

You're safe with me.

She thought about it. There were no good choices here, but that had been the situation ever since she'd met him.

'I guess I'll go with you,' she said.

★ ★ ★

'It's a casual place,' he said. 'You don't need anything fancy. Definitely bring your bathing suit.' He grinned as he said that, a mock leer, and for a moment it felt like they were going off on a romantic getaway somewhere. But the look on his face as he watched her gather up her suit, sarong, a pair of shorts, a few blouses and stuff them in her tote, there was nothing romantic about that.

She went into the bathroom to retrieve her small toiletry kit, then thought maybe she should bring her good camera, just because she didn't want to leave it behind.

And remembered: the watch. Sitting in the bottom of her hobo, where she'd put it the night she'd gone over to Daniel's.

She felt a wash of cold sweat. She'd left the purse on her bed. Could she get it out without his noticing, leave it here? Was that even smart?

If Gary found the watch here and her gone, what would he do?

She stood in the bathroom and thought, This is a mistake.

She'd told herself that going with Daniel was safer than staying behind, that Oscar was a killer and asking Gary for protection was absurd — he didn't give a shit about her, and she knew that. But she didn't know who Daniel was.

He was attractive, and he seemed kind at times, and he knew how to make her come. None of that meant she was safer with him.

'We should get going,' Daniel said from the other room.

For a moment she stayed where she was, thinking, there must be a way out of this. There must be something I can do.

But there was nothing else to do except to face him.

He sat on the chair next to the bed, legs stretched out, arms crossed over his lean belly, expression tense and watchful.

Tell him you changed your mind, she thought. That you decided to try to get a flight home. Just lie and figure out something later.

'You ready?' he asked.

She dropped the toiletry bag into her tote, grabbed the purse from the bed and slung it over her shoulder.

'Yeah,' she said.

22

They picked up the water taxi on the cement pier at Los Muertos Beach — a flat, fiberglass boat with benches and a canvas canopy to shield the passengers from the sun. The wide, square bow was piled high with boxes and bags: cases of beer, suitcases, crates of fruit, a packaged television.

'It's the easiest way to get stuff down there,' Daniel said. 'They ship a lot of the garbage back this way, too. The stuff that doesn't get burned or dumped.'

'They can't use trucks?'

'No real roads in town. No cars. There's a road through the mountains that gets you close, but it takes hours. Water taxi's the quickest way.'

They sat near the stern. Michelle could smell the gas fumes from the outboard engines. As the *panga* pulled out from the pier and picked up speed, the wind blew the fumes away. Then she caught the salt tang of the ocean, mixed with an occasional waft of rotting kelp.

The passengers were a mix of tourists, other foreigners Michelle guessed were long-term residents, just from the depth of their tans and the wear of their clothing, and locals, mostly workers at the beach resorts.

They passed several resorts along the way, a couple that looked like actual villages, another that seemed to be nothing but the resort:

wooden docks with Jet Skis, thatched huts, and open-air bars, tourists swimming in a protected inlet.

The wind off the ocean made it cooler here than on the shore, the salt spray hitting her face, refreshing, the thump of waves against the boat's hull almost hypnotic.

'Pretty great, huh?' Daniel said, raising his voice over the noise of the engines.

Like they were on vacation.

She felt the pressure of his thigh against hers.

'Beautiful,' she said.

* * *

About forty minutes after they'd left the Los Muertos dock, the jagged coast opened up into a wide, deep bay surrounded by mountains, with a beach on the left and what looked like a little town on the right that staggered up into the hills.

'Used to be if you were going to the hotel, they'd get as close as they could and you'd have to wade through the surf up onto the beach,' Daniel said. 'Or get off at the dock in town and wade across the river. Some times of year, that's pretty tough.'

Now there was a new dock on the left side of the horseshoe-shaped bay, flanked by a few cement-walled, thatched roofed cottages and a flagstone path that led past them to the beach. 'That's our hotel,' Daniel said.

The boat went to the dock in town first.

'Hey!' Daniel shouted. 'Hey, Rick!'

The man on the dock was older, maybe in his

late sixties, but wiry trim, holding a fishing rod that he'd just cast sideways into the water. He wore cargo shorts, a vest with many pockets, and a floppy khaki hat.

Daniel's fishing buddy, Michelle presumed. American, she guessed.

'Rick!' Daniel shouted again. And then, 'Punch!'

That got his attention. Rick lifted his hand and grinned as the water taxi reached the pier and the crewman on the bow jumped onto the dock and looped a rope around a pitted iron cleat.

'You dog, what do you think you're gonna catch here?' Daniel said.

'Saw a whale yesterday. Breached right out there.' Rick waved vaguely at the bay.

'You had lunch?'

'Don't think so.'

'Let's get off here,' Daniel said to Michelle. 'We can hire somebody to sail us across if you don't feel like walking with your stuff.'

They climbed onto the dock, the crewman giving Michelle a hand up. Rick, meanwhile, rested his fishing pole on his shoulder as if it were a rifle and ambled over. Slapped Daniel on the shoulder.

'You look good, Jink,' he said. 'Life treating you okay?'

Yeah,' Daniel said with a neutral grin. 'Rick, this is Michelle.'

'A pleasure.' Rick bowed a little and brushed his lips against the back of her hand.

'Likewise.'

He had hooks and fishing flies stuck in his

floppy hat, a pleasant, unfocused expression, like he might be farsighted. She could feel some of the tension she'd been carrying drain away — the hard edge of fear at least.

You can't relax, she told herself, just because he looks like a cartoon fisherman.

'You ready for some lunch?' Daniel asked.

Rick nodded. 'This place here is pretty good.' He gestured at a patio to the right of the dock with canvas umbrellas emblazoned with the logo for Pacífico beer. 'I think Marissa might be there already.'

As they approached the restaurant, a woman sitting at one of the tables rose.

'Hey, Marissa!'

She and Daniel hugged. She was younger than Rick by twenty years, Michelle figured, a tall blonde with a tanned, lined face, impressively muscled arms, and tight beach braids.

So someone actually does get braids, Michelle thought.

'This is Danny's friend,' Rick said. 'I'm sorry, I didn't catch your name. It takes me a few times.'

★   ★   ★

The restaurant was run by a couple of Australians and featured mostly sandwiches and pastas. 'And the margaritas here are really good,' Marissa said.

Daniel lifted his hand to call the waiter. 'Round's on me.' He turned to Rick. 'So how's the fishing been?'

246

'Haven't done too much yet. Waiting for you. And Bagger said he might be coming. Right, Marissa?'

'Right. On the late boat.' She smiled at him. 'In a few hours.'

'Bagger? Oh. Wasn't expecting him.'

Michelle knew Daniel well enough by now to read between the lines. The friendly tone, the smile — they didn't mean he was happy to hear this.

'Bagger?' she asked.

'Nicknames,' Marissa said. She gave Rick a hug. 'He's 'Punch' because he had to eject once.'

Rick stretched out his left arm. A thick white scar ran down it, from wrist to elbow. 'Bolts didn't fire right. Blasted clear through the edge of the canopy.'

'You were a pilot?' Michelle asked.

'Back when dinosaurs walked the earth,' Daniel intoned, like the narrator of a nature documentary.

'I still taught you a few things, though,' Rick said.

'That you did.'

'So have you known Danny long?' Marissa asked Michelle.

Obviously not, Michelle thought, and obviously Marissa knew that.

'Just a few weeks.'

'Wow.' Marissa leaned back in her chair, studying her, her smile pasted on. 'It's not like Danny, bringing someone new to meet Rick. You two must have something pretty special.'

'Well, it's been a pretty exciting couple of

247

weeks,' Michelle said.

Daniel draped his arm around her shoulders and gave her a little hug. 'Yeah. Michelle's a trouper.'

'You're going to have to tell me more about that, Danny,' Rick said, and suddenly there was nothing vague about him.

Daniel nodded. 'There's a few things we need to talk about.'

'Okay,' Rick said. 'Tonight.' He smiled and sipped his margarita, adjusted his fishing hat, and turned his gaze back out over the bay.

Looking for whales, maybe.

'How long are you staying?' Daniel asked.

'A week. We're comfortable here.' Marissa gave Rick's arm a squeeze. 'Right, sweetie?'

'Yep. I know where the ocean is. Big target.' Rick grinned, and for a moment he reminded Michelle of Daniel.

* * *

'You and Rick, you worked together?'

'Air force. My IP, my instructor. He trained me.'

She and Daniel walked through town, what there was of it, on their way to the path that led down to the town's tiny beach so they could cross the river to their hotel. The air felt thick, an almost physical barrier. The town was quiet, save for the buzzing of flies and an occasional hammering up the hillside. No cars. It took her a while to absorb the quiet, to realize what was missing here.

248

They passed a few businesses along the road: a little market, a coffee shop and Internet bar. Signs tacked to trees and posts advertised a woman who would do your laundry, apartments to rent, restaurants farther up the path, by the waterfall, near the bridge. The few people she saw moved slowly as well. The burro tied up at a telephone pole barely flicked its tail at the flies.

'You were in the air force,' she said. Hoping that would prompt him to say more.

He nodded, mouth tight.

They passed a giant black barrel up on stilts — a water barrel? Michelle wondered. An arrow-shaped sign on one of its legs said, TO THE BEACH — A LA PLAYA.

'Here we go,' Daniel said. The narrow path plunged and wound around a cement-covered bank and a skinny concrete house topped by palm fronds, the steps cracked and slick with mold. Dark, like some Disneyland ride.

'Operation Noble Anvil,' he said suddenly, pronouncing the words like a punchline to some joke. 'You heard of it?'

'I don't think so.'

They emerged into the light, into the open patio of a crumbling restaurant, abandoned by the look of it.

'Kosovo,' Daniel said, taking her arm. 'Watch your step.'

The concrete deck had rotted in places, exposing twisted, rusting iron rebar, the sand and kelp and water beneath.

'I think it's shallow enough for us to cross,' he said. Michelle looked to the right. There was the river that bisected the town and fed into the bay, a narrow channel that spread on the exposed sand of the low tide. Farther up, the river was broad and shallow; she could see riders on horseback crossing it, the water not reaching the horses' knees. Beyond that the river narrowed again, disappearing into the mountains and the browning jungle that waited for the summer rains.

She wanted him to talk, to say something that might explain who he really was, but he didn't. They climbed off the deck and onto the sand.

'When did you leave the air force?' she finally asked.

'In 2000.' He shrugged. 'Private-sector opportunity came up. I took it. Figured I'd get more flying time that way.' Now he snorted. 'Sometimes I'm kind of a dumbfuck. Who knew there'd be all these wars?'

Michelle wasn't sure what to say to that.

Sandals in one hand, bag slung over her shoulder, she followed him through the river water and onto the sands of the big beach on the other side.

'And you're Jink?' she asked.

He laughed. 'Yeah.'

'What's that mean?'

'Maybe I'll tell you later,' he said.

★　★　★

The hotel was a series of cabanas, with thatched-palm roofs like the *palapas* back on the beach in Vallarta, its reception counter in an

250

open bungalow that looked like one of the guest rooms.

'Make sure you put on shoes if you get up in the middle of the night,' the woman at the counter told them. 'And check inside your shoes for scorpions before you put them on.'

They went to their cabin, past the saltwater pool, by the stone walkway above the sea, just below the pier.

'It's a little rustic,' Daniel said.

There was a gap between the palm fronds of the roof and the walls, mosquito netting surrounding the beds like a loose cocoon. The floors were cracked cement, patched and painted a reddish brown. There was no air conditioner, only a floor fan and shuttered windows across the front of the bungalow that could be opened up to let in whatever breeze there might be.

'So,' Daniel said. 'You wanna unpack, maybe hit the beach for a while before dinner?'

'I don't really have much to unpack.'

'Change into your bathing suit, then? It's too hot to stay in here.'

He laid his duffel bag on the luggage cart, unzipped it, and started taking out his things. Swim trunks. Shaving kit. T-shirts.

'I . . . ' She sat down on the edge of the bed. 'Are we going to talk about any of this?'

He put his T-shirts and extra shorts in the dresser drawer, carried his shaving kit into the bathroom.

'There's nothing much I can tell you,' he said when he returned.

'Why are we here? Can you tell me that?'

'I already did. It's not a good time for either of us to be in PV.'

'Because of . . . because of what's going on with Oscar, and . . . ?

'Yeah,' he said shortly. 'The best thing we can do is stay out of it. Let them fight it out till it's settled.'

'And . . . then what?'

He shrugged. 'I still have a job to do.'

'Are you going to tell me what that is?'

He shook his head.

'Danny, I don't even care anymore. If you're . . . if you're some kind of smuggler or whatever, I don't care. Just tell me, so I know.'

He sat down on the bed next to her. 'I'm not a bad guy,' he said. He rested his arm on her shoulder. Cupped her neck. 'Sometimes I've done stuff I haven't liked doing.'

She felt his hand on her neck, his fingers outlining her jaw, and it felt good. But you can't trust that, she told herself. The hand could tighten, and he was stronger than she was.

'You have to tell me *something*,' she said.

The fingers on her neck gripped for a moment, then moved down, massaging the tense muscles of her shoulder.

'Okay. 'Jink' means a quick turn. An evasive maneuver.'

'Seriously?'

'Yeah,' he whispered, his warm breath tickling her ear.

She laughed. 'Great,' she said.

He eased her down to the bed. 'I'll show you a few.'

When he went into the bathroom, she got out her iPhone. She didn't want to, but she should at least text Gary, let him know that she hadn't tried to run, that she was 'keeping an eye on Danny,' like he wanted her to do. Even though she wasn't sure if that was true.

She didn't know what she was doing anymore.

No signal.

He came out, wearing his swim trunks. 'You ready for the beach?'

'Sure.' She held up her phone. 'Is it just me? I'm not getting any reception.'

'Nope. No cell service here.' He grinned. 'One of the reasons I like this town. Why? Somebody you need to call?'

'Not really,' she said, putting the phone back into her tote.

23

It was still light when they crossed the river, but the tide had risen, the water nearly up to their knees.

'Are we going to have trouble on the way back?' Michelle asked.

'Maybe. But we can always hire a boat to take us across.'

They started to climb the stairs that led from the beach to the road into town. The remnants of the day's light barely penetrated here, and the steps were slick with moss.

Her foot slipped, and she rested her hand on the pitted concrete wall.

Behind her, Daniel put a steadying hand on her waist.

'Watch it,' he said.

'Why do you need to talk to Rick?' she asked.

'He's an old friend.'

'What do you have to talk to him about?'

He was silent. They stood there, in the near twilight, his hand on her waist. She heard birds and cicadas and the lap of waves from the bay.

'Getting out,' he finally said.

★ ★ ★

They were meeting Rick and Marissa at a restaurant in the pueblo. The place was an open patio that jutted out over the bay, supported by stilts, roofed by tin.

By the time they got to the restaurant, Rick and Marissa already sat at a table pushed up against the wooden railing that circled the seating area, along with another man, a stranger. Younger than Daniel. Buzzed hair, cut build.

'Hey, Jink!' he shouted out as they approached.

Daniel raised his hand.

'Hey, Bagger. This is my friend Michelle.'

Bagger rose. 'Pleasure,' he said. Then belched and sat. A beer and an empty shotglass in front of him. 'What are you drinking?' he asked.

Daniel shrugged. 'What you're having.'

Marissa patted the seat next to her. 'Sit next to me,' she said to Michelle. 'Otherwise, believe me, all you're gonna hear about is flying and titty jokes.'

'Sure,' Michelle said. 'Thanks.' She sat.

They ordered drinks and quesadillas, platters of chicken and fish, beans, rice, and guacamole. Towering clouds had begun to stack up over the water, illuminated by the last rays of the falling sun.

'It's going to rain soon,' Rick said.

'So,' Marissa said, 'tell me about your life in Los Angeles.'

Michelle smiled and thought about what version of the truth she'd tell this time.

The standard version, she decided. That her husband had died. How she was between things. Trying to figure out her next move.

How great Danny had been.

'He's a special guy,' Marissa said with a narrow-eyed smile.

255

The music got louder as the sun went down, eighties hits, mostly, competing with low rumbles of thunder echoing from the mountains up the river. More drinks came.

'So what got you off your ass to come down here?' Daniel said to Bagger.

Bagger grinned. 'A chance to hang with my old bubbas.'

'You on leave?'

'Kind of. Changed my line of work. Thought I'd come play in your sandbox.'

Daniel was good at covering, she'd learned, but she still caught the ripple of dismay, maybe of anger, before his expression settled into its familiar grin.

'Dude, why'd you go in that direction?'

Bagger shrugged. 'Jocks like me, we're fucking dinosaurs. In a couple of years, we'll all be sitting in front of a computer in Nevada, joysticking drones. Kiss the wife in the morning, drive to your cubicle, deliver a few smart bombs to hajji wedding parties, and you're home for dinner.'

Lovely, Michelle thought.

Daniel lifted his hands. 'Hey, there's worse ways to make a living. Right, Punch?'

'Yeah,' Rick said, gazing out over the water. 'Yeah, there are.'

The waitress brought another round of beers and shots.

'You had the right idea, Jink. Getting out,' Bagger said, lifting his shot. 'I'm just following in your footsteps.'

'Oh, yeah? That why you came down here? So you could catch up?' Daniel still smiled, but now he wasn't trying to hide the anger. 'Maybe work my hop?'

'Hey.' Bagger had tensed up in his chair. Like he was expecting a fight. 'Look, man. I'm just here to back you up. Sounds like you got a little bit of the leans.'

The leans?

'You tell him that, Punch?' Daniel asked. 'You tell him I need backup?'

Rick frowned, as if he were trying to remember. 'I don't know. I might have.'

Marissa put her hand on Michelle's arm. 'They talk like this all the time once they start drinking,' she said, like she was sharing a secret. 'It doesn't really mean much.'

''Scuse me,' Rick said, pushing his chair back. He stood up, swaying slightly. 'I gotta find the head.'

Thunder cracked like an explosion, and a bolt of lightning shot across the bay.

Bagger flinched, then lifted his shot glass and pounded the tequila. 'Check out the light show,' he said.

Spiderwebs of lightning lit up the sky above the water, turning the clouds white and then purple and indigo as they faded. A few fat drops of rain spattered on the rail, blown by a cooling breeze. The lightning was so spectacular that Michelle thought it seemed almost unreal, like some kind of special effect in a movie.

Then there was a series of loud pops, and the lights went out and the music stopped.

'Must've hit a transformer.'

Several wobbly flashlight beams crisscrossed

the restaurant — from a waitress and Daniel and another customer over by the bar. Bagger stood and looked around. 'Shit, it's the whole town.'

'The grid here's so shaky it doesn't take much to bring it down,' Daniel said.

'The hotel's got power,' Bagger said, peering across the bay.

'Backup generator.'

'So let's go over there,' he said. 'They got a bar, right?'

'Shit,' Marissa said in a low voice. 'Rick isn't back.'

'He said he was going to the restroom,' Michelle said.

'That was at least ten minutes ago.' Marissa stood, the tendons in her sculpted arms standing out like wires. She looked like she was about to cry.

Daniel frowned. 'What's up with Rick?'

'Nothing,' Marissa said quickly. 'With the power off . . . he just . . . he gets confused sometimes.'

'I'll come with you,' Michelle said. 'I need to use the restroom anyway.' She turned to Daniel. 'Can I borrow your flashlight?'

'Sure.' He handed it to her — a little metal flashlight with a bright halogen beam. He looked uncertain. Unmoored.

★ ★ ★

The bathroom was around the back of the kitchen, down an uneven path with tipped cement slabs for pavers.

258

'Thanks,' Marissa said. 'Thanks for . . . He doesn't want the guys to know he's having problems.'

'What kind of problems?'

'Oh, just . . . Really, he's fine most of the time. Especially someplace like this, that's familiar. You know, comfortable. But if things are confusing, or if he drinks . . . '

Marissa knocked on the wobbly door of the men's room. 'Rick? You in there, hon?'

No answer.

Marissa opened the door, and Michelle aimed her flashlight inside. A urinal, a tiny sink, a screened widow up high on the wall. Empty.

'Could he have gone back to where you're staying?'

'Maybe . . . maybe he just got tired.' Marissa wiped tears from her eyes. 'You know, a lot of the time he's fine. They're not even sure what's wrong. TIAs, mini-strokes, maybe. He's in and out.'

Marissa rummaged around in her purse. 'I have a flashlight,' she said. 'Maybe I should go to our place. I'll let you know if he's there.' She smiled shakily. 'No cellphones, so I'll have to come back.'

She started up a steep path behind the restaurant. 'I'll be back in about fifteen minutes,' she said.

Michelle nodded and watched her go.

If Rick was confused, where might he go? she wondered. The path to the left, up the hill, where Marissa had gone? Or to the right, a gentle incline that curved down toward the water?

She followed the path to the right, between the restaurant and several tall houses that looked as though they hadn't been built to any plan, just added onto when the owners had the time, money, and inspiration. Cicadas and grasshoppers chirped and buzzed beneath the cracks of thunder; it was utterly dark between flashes of lighting, and the only human noises were occasional snatches of conversation and laughter.

Ahead of her was the pier.

She could see the dark shapes of two men sitting on a bench at the pier's foot, one smoking a cigar, the other drinking from a bottle of beer. Not Rick. On the pier itself were another man and a woman, sitting close to each other, holding hands, watching the storm. And at the very end of the pier, a lone man standing at the edge.

'Rick?'

He turned as she approached, blinking in the flashlight's bluish beam. 'Who is it?'

'It's Michelle. Danny's friend.'

'Oh,' he said.

She was next to him now. Dark as it was, she didn't want to aim the light at his face, so she held it up like a candle.

'Are you okay?' she asked.

Tears ran down his cheeks, but his expression was strangely calm. As if the tears were just water, something external.

'Oh, I'm fine,' he said. 'Just wanted to . . . ' He frowned and gestured vaguely at the bay. 'Get some air.'

'We were wondering where you went. Maybe we should go back.'

He nodded. 'Yeah. Probably should.'

They started walking up the pier.

'Can I ask you something?'

'Sure,' Rick said.

'What are the leans?'

He chuckled. 'Happens when you're flying sometimes. When you can't see the horizon. You don't know you're in a turn, you're in it for a while, and then, when you're flying straight, you think you're banking the other way. It's, uh . . . what do you call it? Not a mirage.' Suddenly he smiled and closed his fist, as if he'd caught the word he wanted. 'It's an illusion.'

'So why did Bagger say that Danny . . . that he had the leans?'

'Danny's trying to change direction. It's tough to do when you've been going the same way a long time.'

'And . . . he came to you, right? To help him.'

Rick nodded.

'Are you going to?'

'I don't know if I can. I don't have the juice I used to.'

'Rick, I'd like to help Danny. Tell me what to do. How to help him.'

Rick shook his head. 'You can't. Unless there's something about you I don't know.'

There it was again, awareness cutting through the fog, and she realized she might have assumed too much, that Rick wasn't as far gone as he'd seemed.

'No,' she said. 'But he told me he wants out.'

'Yeah. And I guess I owe him.'

She had to risk it. If he was already suspicious

of her, then asking more questions couldn't make it that much worse.

'Why, Rick? Do you want to talk about it?'

'I hooked him up.'

They'd reached the path that led back to the restaurant. Rick paused there, head swiveling, like he was trying to get oriented.

'I worked with the boys, in Vietnam,' he said. 'In Laos. Did mission support.'

'The boys?'

He grinned. '*You* know.'

'No. I don't.'

'Sure you do. The cowboys. Spook stuff. Black ops.' He patted her on the back. Started walking again. She caught up.

'Anyway, we stayed connected, after. They came looking for recruits, and I recommended Danny.'

She couldn't tell whether it was a chuckle or a sob, the sound he made in his throat. 'I thought I was doing him a favor. I know Danny. He wasn't gonna be happy being an IP or a bus driver.'

'A bus driver?'

'Yeah. He'd hate it. He'd get so bored. He needs to be out booming. Doing something fun.'

Suddenly he stopped and took Michelle's hand. He stared at her, though she could barely see his face in the dark.

'I should've been a better teacher. I should've told him not to.'

★ ★ ★

She guided Rick back to the restaurant, steadying him when he stumbled on the uneven slabs. Once they got there, she could make out Daniel and Bagger sitting at the table, illuminated by a Coleman lantern, Bagger hunched over the table, Daniel leaning back in his chair in a pose that seemed like a parody of relaxation.

'Hey,' Daniel said, rising. 'Shit, Punch, you trying to get out of buying the next round?'

'No, no. Just stretching my legs.' He looked around. 'Where's Marissa?'

'Here I am, sweetie.' Marissa crossed to the table and gathered Rick up in her muscled arms. Even in this dim light, Michelle could see the puffiness of her eyelids, her reddened nose. 'Thanks,' she mouthed to Michelle.

'Did you want to talk about something, Danny?' Rick asked.

'Why don't we call it a night? I'm kinda tired.' He slapped Rick on the shoulder. 'We can talk in the morning. Over some fish.'

* * *

They hired a *panga* to take them across the bay to their hotel: Daniel, Michelle, and Bagger, who'd gotten a cabin there.

'You wanna get another round?' Bagger said after they'd clambered up onto the beach, wading through knee-high surf.

'No, buddy. I'm done for the night.'

'Look,' Bagger said, 'don't take me coming in the wrong way. All I'm trying to do is keep you

263

out of the graveyard.'

Daniel stopped. Turned to him. Gave him a dead-eyed look. 'Right. Appreciate that.'

Bagger raised his hand in a mock salute and shuffled up the beach toward the bar.

'Jesus, Danny. The graveyard?' Michelle said.

'It's a flying term. Don't worry about it.' He turned and headed for the stone path that led to their cabin. Michelle followed.

'So what's a bus driver?' she asked him.

'Depends. Airbus pilot, usually. Why?'

'Something Rick said.'

Daniel stopped. 'You talked to Rick?'

'Well, yes. What do you expect? You won't tell me what's going on. I was hoping *he* could.' She was getting angry again, raising her voice. She tried to calm herself. 'He talked about 'the boys.' Some people who recruited you to do . . . whatever it is you do.'

'He was drunk,' Daniel said as they passed the saltwater pool. 'You can't take anything he said too seriously.'

'He wasn't just drunk. There's something wrong with him, I don't know what. Dementia or Alzheimer's or — '

'You don't know that.'

'Marissa told me there's a problem. He didn't want you to know.'

He didn't say anything. He flinched and kept walking.

They'd reached their cabana.

'What if he can't help you, Danny?'

His shoulders slumped. 'I don't know. Figure something out, I guess.'

He looked so lost suddenly, and she thought of that first night in the hotel, when she'd wanted to reach out to him and hadn't.

He fumbled around in a pocket of his cargo shorts for the key. She watched as he unlocked the door. Opened it for her. She stepped inside.

There was a man sitting on the bed. Another one standing against the wall. She could just make out their shapes in the dark.

'Don't scream,' the man on the bed said. 'Okay?'

24

'This isn't the way I wanted us to meet.' Oscar rose from the bed. 'But, Danny, we give you hints, and you don't appreciate them.'

The man standing against the wall had switched on the light. Daniel and Michelle stood inside the cabana now, with the door closed behind them and a third man whom they hadn't noticed waiting outside, standing in front of it.

'I don't know you,' Daniel said, his voice hoarse.

'Oh. But you know *about* me,' Oscar said. 'Your friend Michelle has met me before.'

'It's . . . he's the man I met with Emma.'

Headless bodies. Burned bodies. She could see the nose of his pistol nudging out from beneath his hitched-up trouser leg.

'There's no need for us to talk this way,' Oscar said. He waved a hand at the man standing by the door. 'We can sit if you'd like.'

Daniel hesitated, then nodded.

The man by the door opened it and stepped outside.

'What about him?' Daniel said, tilting his head in the direction of the man who stood by the wall. He looked so ordinary, Michelle thought. Short, wiry, and dark, wearing a blue-gray short-sleeved shirt, like one of the Mexicans she'd see around L.A. every day and not even think about. A gardener. A busboy.

Oscar shrugged. 'I don't need him here.'

He rattled off something in rapid Spanish, and the man nodded and moved past them and out the door. Daniel cocked his ear, as though he understood.

'I sent him to get us something to drink,' Oscar said, smiling at Michelle.

'She doesn't need to be here either,' Daniel said.

'Oh, I think maybe right now it's better if she stays. Except, Michelle, you will have to sit on the floor. Because there is only one chair, and Danny and I, we need to talk about our business.'

She sat down on the floor by the door. In case she had a chance to slip away.

Oscar nodded at Daniel and indicated the room's lone chair. Daniel pulled it out from under the desk, his eyes fixed on Oscar, the legs scraping on the bare concrete, and sat.

'What do you want to talk about?' he asked.

'I think you should know.'

'I don't. Look, I think you might have the wrong idea about me. About what I do.'

Oscar snorted. 'Please don't insult my intelligence. I know what you do.'

Daniel crossed his arms over his chest. 'Okay. Let's say you have an idea. What is it you want from me?'

'You have the route. You have the connections. On the demand side. We have the product.' Oscar shrugged again. 'It is obvious what we want.'

'And what are you offering?'

267

'A better price. More . . . efficiency.'

'What about export clearances?' Daniel stretched out his legs. 'I don't know what you were thinking, taking Carlos Aguilar out of the picture. He had that piece wired.'

'He didn't wish to deal with us. He had his loyalties.' Oscar shook his head. 'It's regretful. But, you know, some people, they don't like change. They think, because they had the business for a long time, they should always have it. They don't understand that you must always compete.'

'You haven't answered my question,' Daniel said.

'We can manage this if you give us a little time. We have more and more influence here, every day.' Oscar smiled. 'Soon you won't be able to do business here without us.'

Michelle stayed where she was, sitting on the floor by the door, thinking that no one was paying any attention to her right now and that this was a good thing. And the way they were talking, it didn't sound like Oscar planned on killing Daniel. But that didn't mean she had any value to either of them.

'Look,' Daniel said, 'I'm just a driver. This kind of decision, it's above my pay grade.'

'But your word has some weight, I think.'

'Maybe.' Daniel gave him that little half smile, the one that Michelle now knew meant absolutely nothing. 'I guess I'm kind of surprised that you'd go to so much trouble just to talk to me. It's not like I'm doing that much volume. There's way bigger accounts out there.'

At that, Oscar became very still, and suddenly Michelle wondered if she'd read the situation wrong. Maybe Daniel wasn't safe at all. And if *he* wasn't . . .

Oscar could draw his pistol and shoot them both, and there wasn't anything either of them could do about it.

She felt a moan rise in her throat. She stifled it.

Then Oscar relaxed, the stillness giving way to amusement.

'It's what your account represents,' he said. 'Securing your business would help our position. And we would reward you for it.'

From outside she could hear jogging footsteps, and for a moment she thought that maybe it was the police. Or Bagger, come to save the day.

But no. There was a brief knock on the door. A burst of muttered Spanish.

'Our drinks,' Oscar said.

* * *

They had a round of tequila, at Oscar's insistence.

'To a new partnership, I hope,' he said, lifting his shotglass.

Daniel held his glass level. 'We still have a lot to work out,' he said.

'I know. But consider our bid on its merits.'

'Okay,' Daniel said. 'We'll do that.'

'And consider that the terms you get now are maybe better than what we offer in the future.'

'I see.'

269

Oscar nodded, and then he drank. After a moment Daniel did, too.

★ ★ ★

'I'm sorry,' he said. 'I'm really sorry.'

Oscar and his men had left. Michelle sat on the edge of the bed, shaking.

'You're a good guy, Danny?' she managed. 'Really?'

Daniel's back was to her. He stood by the dresser, where Oscar had left the tequila. He poured himself another shot.

'You tell him we were coming here?' he asked.

'Are you kidding? How the *fuck* can you even think . . . ?'

'Okay,' he said. 'Okay. Sorry.' He held out the tequila bottle. 'You want any?'

She hardly knew how to react. She just kept her glass steady when he poured more tequila into it.

'He probably had someone watching you,' Daniel said, sitting down next to her. 'Once we got on the boat, it was easy to figure out where we were going.'

'I guess.'

'I didn't think he'd be that aggressive. Pretty fucking stupid of me.'

'You didn't? Why not? He *kills* people!'

'I'm sorry,' he said again.

'What's so special about your . . . your account?'

He shook his head, mutely, and drained his tequila.

She finally drank. He wouldn't answer; she knew that.

'What do we do now?' she asked.

'Sleep.'

'Sleep?'

'Yeah. It's done for the night. He got his meeting. That's what he wanted.'

'What are you going to do?'

'That's nothing you need to worry about.'

She took the shot glass and hurled it against the wall. 'I'm so sick of people telling me that!'

Daniel stared at the streak the tequila made on the wall and said, 'In the morning I'm going to do some fishing. After that . . . ' He shrugged. 'We'll see.'

25

She didn't sleep. Daniel did, his breaths slow and even, with an occasional quiet snore.

Things fluttered and scrapped in the palm fronds above her head, small bits of leaf and fiber falling on the gauzy web of mosquito net that surrounded them.

How much more fucked up could this get? Then she told herself not to ask. It could always get worse.

There'd been some room for doubt about Daniel before. There was none now. Everything was out in the open.

Except that it wasn't.

Cowboys. Spook stuff. Black ops.

Back in the world of Gary. The world Gary *claimed* to be in anyway.

But if that were true, if Daniel worked for some kind of government agency, why would Gary want her to spy on him?

Maybe Daniel had done something he wasn't supposed to do.

Or Gary wasn't working for the government at all.

He could be a rival drug runner, for all she knew.

Fucking Gary, she thought. She'd told him she was going to meet Daniel, and then she'd dropped off his radar. If he'd tried to call her, what would he be thinking? That she'd screwed him over? That she was dead?

Or maybe he knew exactly where she was.

Maybe he was the one who'd had her followed here. Hadn't he been keeping track of her movements all along?

Her gut hollowed out, like something pulled it from beneath.

Maybe he and Oscar were working together.

'Oh, Jesus,' she whispered.

If there were taxis, if there were a boat, she'd leave right now. But there weren't. There were no good ways out of here until the morning.

Maybe in the morning, she thought. Maybe in the morning I'll leave.

And then what?

$\star$ $\star$ $\star$

Just after dawn an alarm beeped softly — Daniel's watch, maybe. He rose, went into the bathroom. She pretended to sleep.

He came out wearing swimtrunks and a batik shirt, found his sunglasses on the dresser, put a tube of sunscreen into a worn canvas bag.

'You awake?' he asked. He knew that she was.

'Yeah.'

'I'll be back in time for lunch.' He grinned. 'Maybe with some fresh ceviche.'

'Okay.'

He hesitated by the side of the bed, the smile no longer in place. 'Look, just hang tight. Can you do that? There's nothing to worry about, and you're not going to have any problems. Just stay here and try to relax.'

She almost laughed. 'Right.'

'Go to the beach. Read a book. Have a margarita.' He smiled again. 'It's going to be fine.'

★ ★ ★

She lay there a while after he left, but of course she wasn't going to sleep, not here, with no air-conditioning, not after last night. She got up, put on shorts and a gauze top, went out to the little coffee stand by the bar, and ordered a double cappuccino. Stood there in the coarse sand, drank it, and ordered another. The sun had just begun to rise above the eastern mountains, bringing with it bird sounds and fresh heat.

She wasn't going to get on the water taxi back to Vallarta. She knew that already. All that would do was piss off Daniel *and* Gary. Gary wanted her here, 'keeping an eye' on Daniel.

But she had to get in touch with Gary somehow. Just to cover her ass, whether he knew where she was or not.

E-mail, she thought.

'Sorry,' the woman at the reception counter said. 'We don't have it.'

Michelle stood there in disbelief. 'No e-mail. Really?' She could see the graying computer sitting on the counter there; they had to have e-mail.

'We can in an emergency,' the woman told her. 'But no, no Internet for guests.' She smiled. 'Our guests mostly like that. Being out of touch.'

Was this an emergency?

'There's an Internet bar in the pueblo. It's still open in the summer, I think.'

'Okay,' Michelle said. 'I'll try that.'

★　★　★

She walked across the packed wet sand, along the beach toward the river. The bars were empty at this time of day, not surprisingly. One couple dozed in loungers. A few workers piled empty blue tanks of some sort onto the beach, waiting, Michelle supposed, for a boat to haul them back to Vallarta.

It was so quiet here after Vallarta, where the bars and hotels played music directed at the beach, where there was the constant noise of cars and horns. No music playing here, no cars. Just the birds and the waves. Riders on horses splashed across the shallows of the river. Farther upstream, women beat clothing on rocks and a group of schoolkids in blue-and-white uniforms headed east, up the river and into the hills. There must be a school up there, Michelle thought. She wondered how far they had to go.

By the time she reached the pueblo, sweat had soaked her blouse, her hair, the brim of her raffia hat. She found iced tea and a muffin at a tiny café that claimed to be an Internet bar — three aged computers on dial-up, two of which worked. The café was a U-shaped cinder-block building with a tin roof, and even with the front open to the air it was stifling hot inside.

She logged on to her e-mail account. Several from Maggie, asking how she was, when she was coming home, if she needed a ride from the airport. '*I'm fine,*' she replied. '*I'll be home soon.*'

She hesitated, wondering if she should say anything else.

No. It might not be safe.

She got out her phone and looked up the contact information for 'Ted Banks.'

'*Hi, Ted,*' she typed. '*Sorry to be out of touch. Am with a friend, a last-minute getaway. No cell reception. Will contact you as soon as I'm back in PV in a day or two. Lots to discuss.*'

Reading it over, she felt a sudden fresh wave of heat and sweat. She'd told him something without telling him everything. Splitting the difference, as usual.

She hoped it would be enough.

She hit SEND, then cleared her browsing history and closed the browser.

★   ★   ★

After that she didn't know what to do.

Go to the beach. Read a book. Have a margarita.

Might as well.

She went back to the hotel, changed into her bathing suit, put a few things in her totebag. She didn't need her wallet — she could charge anything she wanted to the room — but was it safe to leave it behind? The cabanas didn't seem very secure.

She carried her purse to the reception desk. 'Do you have someplace I can check this?'

'Sure, I can take it for you,' the woman at the reception counter said.

'Thanks.'

Michelle grabbed a blue beach towel and chose a chair under a *palapa* at the crest of the rise of sand, so she could look down at the bay.

'Pie? Pie?'

A stout, middle-aged woman wearing a white peasant dress and a straw hat approached her. On her head she balanced a covered platter, big enough to shade her from the sun. 'Pie, miss?' she asked. 'Best in town.'

'Maybe later, thank you.'

Pie. It's not just for breakfast anymore.

She tried to read her British mystery. Her eyes were sore, like they'd been rubbed with sandpaper.

She closed them. Just for a minute.

It was so quiet here. She listened to the waves. I'm tired, she thought.

★ ★ ★

'Hey.'

Michelle opened her eyes. Daniel stood there, a shadow backlit by the sun. 'Hi,' she said slowly.

What time was it?

'How was the fishing?' she asked.

'Kind of sucked. Nothing out there, and then Rick wasn't doing too good, so we figured we might as well call it.'

'Sorry.'

He shrugged. 'It was okay. But no ceviche for lunch, I guess.'

'Well, there's plenty of ceviche around,' she said. 'They've got a great one here, everybody says.'

'There's a place up the river I thought we could try. I've heard good things about it.'

She thought, First he goes fishing, now he wants to try restaurants? 'Do you think that's a good idea?'

'Like I told you. There's nothing to worry about. And it's not far.'

She hesitated. What were the odds that he'd answer her if she asked?

Not good.

'So Rick couldn't . . . He didn't have any advice for you?' she asked anyway.

He seemed to tense, like the outline of a shadow sharpening. Then relaxed. 'Actually, he had a couple good things to say. I'll tell you about it over lunch.'

★   ★   ★

She took a few minutes to change. Put on shorts and a T-shirt and her Mephisto sandals.

'You have any aloe?' he asked. 'I got a little burned out there.'

'Sure,' she said, handing him the tube from her toiletry kit. 'Look, why don't we just have lunch here?'

She didn't like the idea of going up the river someplace, no matter how safe he claimed it was. She still didn't know how safe she was with him.

He screwed the top on the aloe and handed the tube back to her. He wasn't smiling. In a way that comforted her. She'd learned not to trust the smile.

'It's a better place for us to talk. That's what you've been wanting, right? And I figure I owe you.'

* * *

'I should get my purse,' she said as they passed the office.

'Seems like a pain to carry. Anything you need in it?'

'Well, my wallet.'

'Come on, you don't need that,' he said, rubbing her shoulder. 'You can treat me next time.'

* * *

They walked up the trail on the north side of the river, winding past shacks and makeshift corrals where horses grazed and stamped at flies. Cicadas rasped, so loudly that they took on the quality of machinery. The heat in the late afternoon was as oppressive as ever, and with the dirt from the trail powdering her feet and calves she longed for an ocean wave to wash her clean.

'How long do you want to stay here?' she asked.

'Maybe another day.'

'Do you think . . . Is it safe back in Vallarta?'

'Yeah. I mean, look . . . Whatever's going on up there, with . . . with the guys competing, it doesn't have anything to do with us.'

That stopped her in her tracks.

'How can you say that? After last night — '

'He wanted to get my attention,' he said quietly. 'Well, he's got it. But it's their fight. Let them have it.'

'And you don't care who wins?'

'Can't afford to.'

Chaos will only benefit the most wicked.

Up ahead was a skinny trail that curled into a thicket of banana trees and out of sight. A hand-painted sign for 'Casita Alma' hung crookedly on a fence pole, strung up with wire.

'Here,' he said.

The path led to a clearing by the river: a cracked cement patio and two tiny buildings made of wood and tin. No one was there. Padlocked wooden shutters covered the windows. Daniel stood behind her, at the entrance to the path.

'Looks closed,' she said, turning to him.

Daniel nodded.

He'd known that all along, she realized.

He reached into his pocket. 'What are you doing with this?'

She saw what he held in his hand.

Gary's watch.

26

She thought about running. Or nearly bolted before she thought again. Where could she run? Daniel blocked the path. Trees and banana plants surrounded the little clearing. The river? Maybe. Over the rail, into the shallows . . .

But if she tried it and he caught her, then what?

'It's not — '

'Don't fucking tell me what it's not.' He gripped the watch like he'd crush it if he could. 'Tell me what it is. Why do you have this?'

It was a gift. From my nephew. So I can take pictures without people seeing me. I promised him I'd . . .

She thought all that. Maybe she could sell it. Maybe he'd buy the lie. Maybe he wouldn't.

'Gary,' she said.

He didn't say anything right away. She couldn't read his expression clearly, behind the sunglasses. She had the impression that he was looking at her but not seeing her. That he was thinking it through.

'Fucking Gary,' he finally said.

He stood there, staring at the watch. 'You really had me going, you know? You're a real fucking pro.'

'I'm not,' she said. 'That's not it at all. I didn't want to — '

'But the way you kept turning up, I had to be

281

sure.' He tossed the watch around in his hand. 'How much did he pay you? Or are you a regular?'

'There's hardly anything on it. If you looked, you saw — '

'How long have you been working for him?'

'I — '

His fists clenched, and he took a step toward her, and then he threw the watch to the ground.

'If that asshole thinks a dick move like this is what's gonna keep me in line, he just fucking screwed the pooch, because I am *done* with this bullshit job.'

'Please,' she said. 'Please let me explain. I didn't want to do this.'

'You know, I should fucking kill you.'

She stared at him.

If he takes another step, a single step, run.

'Can we talk?'

He stared back, light reflecting off his sunglasses, making them a mask.

'Please,' she said. 'After everything we . . . You said we'd talk. That's all I'm asking. Just . . . Don't you want to know?'

He swallowed. She could see the bulge of his throat move, and then he gestured at one of the tables. 'Okay. Let's talk.'

★ ★ ★

She told him everything, all of it. She'd heard about people confessing things, to police or interrogators, and she got it now, how releasing the tension of keeping the guilty secret felt something like joy, regardless of the consequences.

When she finished, he sat there, the muscles in his jaw working.

'I'm sorry,' Michelle said.

Something seemed to break in him. His expression cracked. He looked away.

'Yeah, aren't we all?'

He reached down, scooped up the watch and put it back in his pocket. Stood. 'Come on.'

'Where — ' Her voice caught. 'What are you going to do?'

'I'm not going to hurt you. Jesus. I'm not . . . ' He ground the heel of his hand into his forehead. 'Just forget it.'

He turned and headed to the path that led out of the clearing. She got up and followed him.

They walked back to the hotel in silence. Questions pinballed in her mind, but she wasn't about to ask them.

'Pack your stuff,' he said when they reached the cabana. He pulled the door open, hard enough that it banged into the wall, and went inside.

The room smelled like heated dust.

'Where are we going?'

'You're getting on the next water taxi out of here. It's none of your fucking business where *I'm* going.'

For a moment she was speechless with rage. *This isn't my fault!* she wanted to scream. *I'm not the criminal here* — you *are!*

And then she thought, What's wrong with you? He's letting you go. Just get out.

She nodded and went into the bathroom and packed up her toiletry kit. Grabbed her bathing suit and sarong.

When she came out, he was sitting on the bed, shoulders slumped, hands resting slack on his lap. He didn't look up.

'I'll talk to Gary,' he said. 'I'll tell him to lay off you.'

She almost laughed. 'You think he'll listen?'

'He should. This is between him and me anyway. He didn't have any business bringing you into it.'

'So who is he, Danny? Is he your boss? Who does he work for?'

'I can't talk about that.'

'Give me a break.'

She gathered up the rest of her clothes and stuffed them into her totebag. Daniel still sat on the bed, staring at his hands. 'Look,' he finally said. 'You don't have to go.'

'You know what? Fuck you.'

Just say something, she thought as she walked toward the door. Say one thing, to stop me.

He didn't.

She walked outside. Clouds had started to pile up over the bay.

It looked to be another beautiful fucking sunset.

27

Michelle sat in the water taxi, toward the back, against the side of the boat. Felt the ocean spray hit her face, the hull of the *panga* lap against the waves, a rhythmic series of thumps. And wondered what the fuck she was going to do now.

It was stupid to have hoped that Daniel would be her way out of this; she'd known that all along, but a part of her had still hoped it. Because he'd been nice. Because she'd liked sleeping with him.

Because in spite of everything that had happened, she'd still wanted some guy to rescue her.

Stupid, she told herself, you really are stupid.

By the time she stepped onto the cement pier at Los Muertos, she realized that her options had narrowed down to one.

Get out of town. Just get on the next bus, going anywhere. To Guadalajara or Mexico City. To someplace far away from here. As far from Gary as she could get.

She couldn't trust that Daniel would intercede with him on her behalf. Didn't know that it would do any good if he did. Whatever this thing between Gary and Daniel was about, people were getting killed over it, and she was pretty sure that Gary didn't care if she lived or died.

Maybe Daniel cared, a little, but not enough

to do anything about it.

She walked up to the street that ended at the pier and ran up to Olas Altas, paused for a moment by the shop that sold the Frida and Che totebags and cheap inflatable water toys that smelled of sticky plastic, scanning the street for a cab.

Then she remembered the money.

Gary's money.

She had about seven hundred dollars with her. The rest of it, more than three thousand dollars, sat in the safe of her room at Hacienda Carmen.

'Shit,' she muttered. Sure, she had her credit cards, some of which were paid off now, thanks to Gary. But if he could pay them off that easily, couldn't he just max them out again? Even put out a fraud alert or something.

She didn't want to go back there. Didn't want to risk it. But the money. She needed the money if she was going to run.

You couldn't get very far without money.

★   ★   ★

Just go inside, grab the money, and get out, she told herself, as she unlatched the heavy wrought-iron gate that barred Hacienda Carmen's driveway.

'Hello, Senora Mason!' Paloma called out from her station at the front desk. 'Did you have a nice time?'

'It was great,' she said, mustering a smile. 'Really nice, thanks.'

Walk upstairs, she told herself. Just walk

286

upstairs and get the money. Even if Paloma was Gary's spy, she wasn't doing anything suspicious. She wasn't going to look like she was running. She was going to get the money and walk out with her totebag and her hobo, and that was all.

She was going out for a coffee. Or to drop off some laundry. That made sense, didn't it?

Her room was closed up and stifling hot, but she wasn't going to take the time to do anything about that. She grabbed the money from the safe, stuffed half in her wallet. The rest . . . she thought about it. In the small toiletries kit she'd taken with her to the village. That would be good.

As long as she was here, what else? A couple pairs of clean underwear and a fresh bra. The light sweater she'd worn on the plane. A blouse she particularly liked.

She hesitated, then told herself, Don't get caught up in this. Leave the rest behind, so it won't look like you're running. You can buy what you need on the road. Get out, and get out now.

She'd been there five minutes at most.

She closed and locked the door and walked through the courtyard, tote bag on one shoulder, hobo on the other, nodded at a couple having drinks by the fountain, and waved to Paloma at the front desk as she opened the wrought-iron gate.

She stepped out onto the uneven sidewalk. Looked down the street for a cab.

'Hey, Michelle. You have a nice vacation?'

★　★　★

287

He'd waited for her by the gate, and now Gary stood close to her, too close, resting a hand on her upper arm, foot practically touching hers.

'It was interesting,' she said.

How could he know? Even if her room was bugged or Paloma was a spy for him, how could he have gotten here so quickly?

'Why didn't you call me?'

Maybe there was someone else, someone following her. One of Oscar's men. Someone on the boat.

'I just got back.'

'Oh?' His hand gripped her arm now, hard enough to bruise. His other hand reached into her tote bag, pulled it open. 'Where are you going with all this?'

'To the laundry. Let go of me.'

His grip tightened. 'You weren't thinking about running, were you, Michelle? I'd hate to think you'd try something stupid like that.'

Maybe Daniel had called him.

'Let go of me, Gary.'

He held on a moment longer, then released her.

'Why don't we go sit down and have a drink?' he said. 'You can tell me all about your trip.'

⋆　⋆　⋆

Olas Altas was eerily quiet. A few customers sat outside at the tables that lined the edge of the sidewalk, drinking beers and margaritas, but the music from the bars was muted. Signs on some restaurants announced that they were closed

288

until the fall, until after the summer rains, when the tourists would return.

'Kind of nice this time of year, isn't it?' Gary said. 'If you can take the heat and the rain.'

Michelle nodded and sipped her Perrier and thought about what she should say. What was safe to tell him.

'You never told me that Danny was in the air force,' she said.

Gary gave a little half shrug, like this was nothing very important. 'Yeah, he was. He tell you about that?'

'So he just went from the air force to being, to being some kind of criminal?'

Now Gary eyed her with more than usual attention. 'Just what are you getting at, Michelle?'

'I don't know, Gary. Why don't you tell me? Who does Danny really work for? And you?'

Gary took a moment to swirl the ice around in his tumbler. 'Well now, it's complicated. But I can tell you this much, okay? Danny's gone off the reservation. That's what's motivated a lot of this. That's why it's so important for us to know what he's up to.'

Of course he wasn't going to tell her. Why had she even bothered to ask?

Just to let him know that she wasn't stupid enough to believe all his lies.

'You're going to have to find someone else to do it,' she said. 'I'm done.'

'Now, we've been over this before, Michelle. You're done when I say you're done.' He smiled, the smile that pushed up his cheeks but didn't reach his eyes. 'And haven't I been making it worth your time?'

She might as well tell him the truth. A lie wasn't going to help.

'You don't understand. He found the watch, Gary.'

For a long moment, Gary sat there staring, a puffy-eyed predator making his evaluation of her from across the bar table.

'Well, shoot,' he said. He took a long sip of his whiskey. 'So how'd he react?'

'How do you *think* he reacted? He was furious! I thought he was going to kill me. Jesus.'

'Now, now.' He reached across the table and patted her hand. 'I don't blame you for being upset. I warned you, Danny's a dangerous guy. Just tell me what happened.'

She jerked her hand away. 'Why don't you ask him yourself?'

'Because I'm asking you.'

He didn't have to say anything else. She knew that it was a threat.

You have to calm down, she told herself. You have to play this right.

'Start from the beginning,' he said. 'Where you went, who you saw, and what you did.'

She told him. How Danny wanted to meet a friend of his for fishing and for advice. How he'd invited her to go along. She didn't mention Oscar. It was too late for that, she thought. Too hard to explain without admitting that she'd kept it from him before.

Then the watch.

'I don't know what set him off,' she said. 'Just

that I kept turning up everywhere, that's all he said. I don't know, maybe that's why he wanted to go out with me in the first place. So he'd have a better chance to check me out.'

'You tell him about me?'

'I had to, Gary. I had to tell him something. What else was I supposed to do?'

He let out a huge sigh. 'Fair enough, I guess. What'd he say when you told him?'

'That it was a dick move. That he'd had it with you and your bullshit and the job. That you never should have involved me in the first place.'

Daniel's words, but they could have been her own.

Fucking Gary.

'He said all that, did he?'

Gary leaned back in his chair and appeared to consider.

'Well, I guess that's that,' he said. 'Give me a couple of days to sort things out, get you your passport. In the meantime you just hang tight, okay? Don't go running off anywhere. You're safer if you just stay put.'

He clinked the ice against the side of the tumbler and chuckled. 'Guess you were right about that watch. Not such a good idea.'

★ ★ ★

She couldn't believe that he would just let her go. It couldn't be so easy. Could it?

What to do now?

Maybe exactly what she'd planned to do. Okay, she could believe that Gary had people spying on her, who'd maybe even followed her down the coast. Paid some local kid who needed the money to keep an eye on her. Easy enough to do.

But there was simply no way Gary could find her wherever she went. Was there? If she just started walking north along the Malecón, caught a taxi somewhere on the way, and went to the bus station, how could Gary possibly find out?

Unless he'd put something — one of his stupid spy toys, some kind of bug or tracker — in her things. Maybe she hadn't looked carefully enough.

She stood there on the corner of Olas Altas and Basilio Badillo, sweat running down her forehead, dripping down her back. The sun was setting, but it wasn't taking the heat with it.

I won't try to run again, not tonight, she thought. Gary was already on the alert. She'd have to wait awhile, a day at least, pretend she was going along with him.

In the meantime was there anyone here she could talk to? Anyone who could help? Who knew who the players were, who could at least give her some advice?

Anyone at all?

28

'Just in time for the sunset,' Charlie said. 'And look, I still have most of the tequila.'

She'd stopped at the taquería and loaded up on carne asada and guacamole, which Charlie arranged on a platter and now carried out to his terrace.

'Sit,' he said.

She did, and he poured two shots and sat down in the other chair.

She'd gone back to Hacienda Carmen and dropped off most of her stuff. Split up Gary's money, putting half back in the safe and carrying the rest, just in case. Had with her only the small purse she'd bought on Basilio Badillo, her wallet, and her phone. If Gary'd put a bug in her Marc Jacobs, she hadn't been able to find it, but no sense taking chances.

They sat in silence for a while, sipping tequila as the sun stained the surrounding clouds a pale pink that deepened to violet.

'What is it you wanted to talk to me about?' he finally asked.

She didn't answer right away.

What did she know about Charlie, really? How could she be sure that she could trust him?

You can't, she thought. You can't be sure.

All she had were her instincts, and so far her instincts hadn't exactly been reliable.

But trying to deal with this alone, she just

couldn't do it anymore.

It was resignation more than anything else that she felt when she said, 'I don't know how to talk about this. I've had some things happen to me here, and I don't know what to do.'

'Why me? I mean, I'm flattered, but . . . ' He laughed, coughing a little at the end of it. 'I'm not exactly a model of wisdom and sobriety.'

'Just some things you said the last time we talked. I thought maybe you might . . . understand this better than I do.'

'Don't tell me you've hooked up with a rent boy.'

'I wish.' She hesitated. 'What do you know about Gary?'

'Not much. He's more a friend of Vicky's. Someone she knows anyway.'

'If I told you some things about him — about him and Danny . . . '

'You can tell me.' He grinned. 'What's it gonna hurt?'

★ ★ ★

She told him. When she finished, Charlie leaned back in his lounge chair and shook his head. 'I have to say, that's not what I was expecting.'

'What *were* you expecting?'

'Oh, just about anything but that.'

'I know it sounds ridiculous.'

'I was thinking more along the lines of absurd.'

'There's a difference?'

'Absurd implies a certain existential irony.'

294

'Great.'

'I'm not saying I don't believe you.'

Charlie fiddled with a cigarette, lit it, sucked down a deep draw of tobacco, cheeks concave with the effort. Coughed twice.

'Jesus. You know, I've been reading about this kind of thing for years. And I do believe it's the way the world works. I just never happened to encounter it in person.'

Out in the bay, the pirate ship boomed its cannon.

'What do you think I should do?' Michelle asked.

'I have no idea.'

★ ★ ★

They sat and drank a while longer. The drinking didn't make her feel any better, but being in the company of someone else, someone who believed her, helped a little.

'So if this is about drugs, what does that make Danny?' she asked.

'Any number of things.' Charlie steepled his fingers. Like it was some kind of puzzle to figure out. A game. Not something real that had left burned and beheaded bodies only a few miles away.

He lives here, but it hasn't really touched him, she thought.

'Maybe just a smuggler,' Charlie said. 'But with all this other shit floating around . . . More likely he's a spook. You know, the CIA's been running drugs for years.'

She must have looked skeptical. Hell, she *was* skeptical.

Charlie grinned. 'Really. There's plenty of documentation. Heroin from Laos during Vietnam in the Air America days. Cocaine from South America. That's how Ollie North financed the Contras. Traded guns for coke. You didn't know that?'

'I guess I missed it,' she said. She felt angry and tired and hollow.

'There's a reason they call it 'the Company.'' He tapped a cigarette out of its pack, fumbled around for his lighter. 'They sell the drugs in the U.S. Use the money to fund black ops. Like the Contras. Or buying elections, overseas, in the States.' He paused to light the cigarette. Took one deep inhale, coughed, and stubbed it out. 'No record. No congressional testimony. They do what they want. It has a kind of elegance, you have to admit.'

'No I don't. I don't . . . I don't have to admit any of this.' She reached over and poured herself more tequila. She was getting pretty drunk. She knew that wasn't a good idea, but she drank more anyway.

'Think about it. You've heard the names of the drug lords in Mexico. Chapo Guzmán. Beltrán Leyva. Before that, in Colombia, Pablo Escobar. Nobody knows the names of those kinds of men in the United States. When have you ever heard them?'

'Maybe there aren't any,' she said sullenly.

'Of course there are. How do the drugs get distributed? Who controls the pipelines? How do they end up on the street?'

'I thought it was the Mexicans.'

That sounded dreadful, she realized. Next she'd be saying, 'the blacks.'

'Sure, up to a point. The cartels have amazing distribution networks, and they're expanding all the time. Growing pot in American national forests. Laundering money and kidnapping for ransom in San Diego and Phoenix. But all the corruption that lets them do all that here, in Mexico — you think there isn't any on the other side of the border? That everyone's hands are clean?' He sipped his tequila. 'Occam's razor, my dear. The simplest explanation.'

So that's what it was called.

'What about Gary?'

'Who knows? DEA? ICE? Probably another spook. If Danny's an asset, people like that get burned all the time. Look at Manuel Noriega.'

'Noriega?'

'CIA asset. Even says so in the papers. And all of a sudden, we're invading Panama and prosecuting him for drug trafficking. Like no one knew he was dirty before?'

Manuel Noriega. Ollie North. The CIA. Great, she thought.

'I don't know,' she said. 'I mean . . . there aren't any Contras anymore, right? The Cold War's over. So what's the excuse? What's it all for?'

'Well, you've still got your leftist movements. Guys like Hugo Chávez in Venezuela. Or terrorists. You can always blame terrorists.' Charlie shrugged and topped off their tequilas.

297

'Maybe they just like making money.'

They sipped their drinks and watched the fireworks from the pirate ship.

'I should go,' she said eventually.

'Why don't you stay here tonight? My couch is very comfortable. I've passed out many a night on it myself.'

'I appreciate that, but . . . '

'At least have some coffee.'

She thought about it. Probably a good idea. 'Thanks.'

They went inside, and she sat for a while on the couch while Charlie went into the kitchen. When he returned, bearing a tray with coffee, cream, and sugar, he sat down across from her.

'Look,' he said, pouring a shot of tequila into his cup, 'I know a fellow at the consulate in Guadalajara. Why don't you and I just go up there, talk to him? He's a decent guy.'

'I don't know . . . I mean, I'm sure he is, but . . . ' She nearly laughed. 'Gary's already had me arrested for drugs. At least I think it was Gary. Why would your friend believe anything I have to say?'

'Well, I don't know that we need to tell him all of it. You've got a guy who's threatening you, and you need your passport so you can get home. That's the main thing.'

'You think it'll end when I get home? You think it'll be over?' She'd meant it as sarcasm, but she could hear the pleading in her voice, the need for reassurance, like a little girl wanting to know that someone could make it all okay again.

'I don't know. The rest of this . . . I don't know

what you can do about it. But let's get you home first thing. Away from Gary, whoever he is.'

She thought about what Charlie said. It made as much sense as anything. But if Gary really was watching her, was spying on her, what would he think if she went off someplace with Charlie?

'Okay. But maybe you should just call him, and I'll go on my own.'

'I don't mind going with you. There's some shopping I could do in Guadalajara.'

It was tempting to agree, to have somebody with her, someone on her side. Assuming that Charlie really *was* on her side.

Don't go down that rabbit hole, she told herself. He's a nice old guy who drinks too much and studies conspiracy theories for fun. And he believes you.

What would Gary do if he saw her with Charlie?

'I don't think it's a good idea,' she said.

'Why, because of Gary?' Now Charlie laughed. 'Darling . . . I do believe you, don't get me wrong. But I'm too old and too tired to let that dickhead dictate my behavior.' He poured another slug of tequila into his cup. 'Gary can kiss my wrinkled ass.'

'I think I should go by myself,' she said. 'That way maybe it'll look like . . . like I just came over for drinks. Like you're not involved. And I don't think you want to be.'

After that she finished her coffee while Charlie retrieved his friend's number, writing it down on the back of an envelope. 'I'll call him tomorrow,' he said. 'That's a promise. And I'll let you know what he said. But you take this so you have it, too.'

She nodded, folded the envelope in half, and put it in the pocket of her shorts. Then she rose to leave.

He stood as well. 'Now, you call me when you get there,' he said. 'There's ETN buses going to Guadalajara from the main bus station all day — last one's not till after midnight. Just go and get on one.'

'That's what I tried to do when I got off the boat today. It didn't quite work out.'

'It'll work out this time.' He gave her a quick hug. 'Try ditching him in the Costco.'

Now she did laugh. 'Like, hide behind the paper towels?'

'I'd go for the condiments aisle.'

She slung her purse on her shoulder. 'Thanks, Charlie. Thanks for listening.'

'Take care of yourself,' he said.

'You, too.' She hesitated. 'And . . . just take care.'

★ ★ ★

Maybe I shouldn't have come here, Michelle thought, picking her way down the darkened stairs. If Gary found out she'd been talking to Charlie . . .

Well, so what? she told herself. She was supposed to be 'hanging tight,' wasn't she? Acting normal. Normal people went and visited friends, didn't they?

And she'd needed some help. Needed to talk

to someone. Charlie wasn't going to have any problems just because she'd talked to him. Was he?

'Jesus.'

She'd banged her shin on something — the old weight bench. She remembered it now from her first visit. It hadn't moved. Why would anyone leave a thing like that out on a landing, where it just sat and rotted and rusted? She'd hit her shin hard — *that* was going to leave a nice bruise.

A burst of laughter and a flicker of color from a television set in the next apartment. She flinched and kept walking. She should have thought more about it, at least, what the consequences of her unburdening herself might be, for Charlie.

When did I get to be so selfish? she wondered. Or maybe 'selfish' wasn't the right word. So self-centered.

So oblivious.

She'd reached the street. It was close to 11:00 P.M., and the night was quiet, the air sullen with clouds.

It was about a twenty-five-minute walk to Hacienda Carmen. She supposed she had to go back there. Anything else would look suspicious. I'll get an early start in the morning, she thought. Head north. Take just my hobo, the camera, and the money, leave everything else. Maybe even go to Costco first. Who knows, it could work.

She should find a cab. The walk would have been nice, a way to clear her head, but how many people had told her that it wasn't always safe here at night?

Charlie's building was on a hill, exiting onto a narrow lane that wound down to a broader avenue, where the taquería and other businesses were. She could probably find a cab down there. Here there was nothing but a few skinny buildings and a cement retaining wall pressed against a cut in the hill, crumbling from an onslaught of knobby roots that seemed to grip it like arthritic fingers.

She'd nearly reached the bottom of the block when something, a darker shape in the dark of a doorway, moved in a blur that caught the corner of her eye. She half turned, and something whirred and slammed into her head, and everything exploded into red and white sparks, and she knew she was falling. Her hip, her shoulder, struck concrete, and she lay there for a moment on her back. She saw darkness above her, darkness that moved, a man crouching over her; she tried to hold the picture together, but it dissolved into sand, into nothing.

29

Bumpity-bumpity-bump.

There goes the train, over the hill.

Bumpity-bumpity-bump.

Here comes the car, out of the drive.

Sleeping in cars, that was the best. When she was little, dozing in the backseat at night, wrapped in her blanket, Maggie next to her, the wheels on the road, the hum and rumble of the engine. Sometimes she wanted to stay there forever, in the dark, always moving. She wished they'd never get home.

The blanket. She'd gotten tangled up in it somehow; it was in her mouth; she couldn't move. I have to move, I have to get up, she thought. We're almost there.

Bumpity-bumpity-bump.

Smell of raw gas. Of exhaust. Warm metal. Pressed into her cheek. Dark, all dark. A bump, a jolt. Her skull slammed against the metal. Pain echoed through her head like a struck drum, and there was something in her mouth — a washcloth, maybe. She couldn't spit it out, and for a moment she couldn't breathe. She tried to move, to sit up, to do something. Her hands — her hands were behind her back, tied there, she could feel the rough twine rubbing her wrists raw, and she thrashed around, struggling to draw in a breath, her chest aching from the strain, until finally she lay still.

Breathe. Breathe. Breathe.

A car trunk. She was in a car trunk.

What had happened?

She'd come out of Charlie's place, and something . . . someone . . . Her head hurt. Someone had hit her.

Hit her and tied her up and locked her in the trunk of a car.

She screamed, once, twice, but with the cloth in her mouth it hardly made a sound. She kicked out with her feet, striking metal with her bare toes, and the pain from that was enough to make her stop. Think.

Did she want whoever was driving to hear her?

He was going to kill her.

She was sobbing now, and she told herself, I have to stop. I won't be able to breathe.

But he was going to kill her. How could there be any doubt? The way he'd hit her . . . He'd hit her *with* something. A blow like that, that could have killed her, and he didn't care.

Where was he taking her?

The car bounced and swerved, moving slowly. There was something else: a smell. What was it? She'd smelled it before.

Think. Think.

Her wrists were tied, but her feet weren't. She could run if she got the chance.

The car stopped. She lay there in the trunk, waiting. Lie still, she told herself. Don't move.

Spoiled babyfood. That was what it smelled like.

He was opening the trunk — she knew that from the click and creak of metal — and a little light came on inside the trunk. Don't look, she told herself. The man leaned in and scooped her up, grunting, like he was lifting a heavy sack of flour. She let herself go limp in his arms. Corpse Pose. Don't resist the pull of the earth.

He walked a few paces. Who was he? The policeman? Dark as it was, with her head purposefully lolling, eyes half-closed, she couldn't really tell.

Abruptly, he released her, letting her roll off his arms. She cried out a little; she couldn't help it, the cry muffled by the cloth in her mouth. But the landing wasn't what she expected: The ground yielded.

Plastic bags. She'd landed on plastic bags. Fast-food wrappers and Styrofoam. Soiled napkins, plastic forks. Banana peels and melon rinds. Animal parts: A flapping of birds.

The dump. They were at the dump.

She lay there and didn't move.

The man walked away. She heard his footsteps, making soft hissing noises from the exhalation of air trapped in layer upon layer of plastic bags.

Was he leaving? Maybe he thought she was already dead, or dying.

She lifted up her head. She could see him lean over the open trunk of the car, pull something out, and in the light from the trunk she could see what it was. A baseball bat.

Now — move *now*. She rolled up to a sitting position, got to her knees, managed to stand, took a few staggering steps. He caught up to her easily. Her arm took the first blow, right above the elbow. She stayed on her feet, stumbled forward, and he swung again, and this time the bat smashed against her hip. She fell, landing on her side, but her legs kept moving, scrabbling through the plastic bags and garbage, her chin scraping on a dented can, and the bat struck again, hitting her shoulder, and she rolled onto her back, and she could see him standing over her, resting the bat on his shoulder.

She rolled over again, onto her side, then onto her stomach, too slowly, and the bat slammed against her ribs, and she rolled once more, and suddenly she was falling, falling into space, into nothing again.

There was a rush of birds crying out, beating their wings, feathers and claws brushing against her as she landed. She lay there, stunned. Took in what she lay on: stuffed garbage bags and cracked tires. From above she heard a bird scream, the man give a surprised shout, and then a chorus of barking dogs. She struggled to sit up, crawled on her knees, then half fell off the pile she'd landed on and crawled behind it. Crouched down. Could he see her? The dogs kept barking. A couple men, shouting at them. Then, finally, a car engine starting and the car driving away.

She stayed where she was. She thought she might pass out. It was so hard to breathe, and everything . . . everything hurt. Her head . . .

Just lie down. Just for a few minutes.

Then she heard the car engine and saw the headlights coming around the hill.

She burrowed into the garbage, curled herself

306

into a ball. The car moved slowly down the road. She couldn't see it, couldn't see anything except the black garbage bags around her, but she could hear its low idle, the crunch of tires on dirt and gravel.

Had it stopped?

No. The car kept moving, slowly, until finally she couldn't hear it anymore.

She stood up, dizzy and shaking.

There was some light here, from a few utility lamps strung here and there on skinny poles, and ambient light from town, too. Not enough to see much about where she was, but enough to look up and have some idea how far she'd fallen. A story's worth, at least. Maybe two. The way she'd landed, on decades of garbage bags and tires, it was like one of those stuntpeople falling into an air mattress. If she hadn't been at a dump, she really would have been hurt.

That thought made her laugh.

Don't laugh, she told herself. You'll choke.

She had to get rid of the gag somehow.

She tried lying down again, thinking maybe she could bring her arms from behind her back under her legs, get them in front of her. She'd seen that done on TV, hadn't she?

The pain in her arm and shoulder sent a wave of white across her eyes, and for a moment she didn't know where she was. No use. The way her hands were tied, rope looped multiple times around her wrists and forearms, she couldn't do it.

She stood up again. It was harder this time.

In the dim, gray light, she made out a

rectangular shape, large, tilted at an angle, about her height, just a few yards away. What was it?

A refrigerator. She moved toward it.

The doors had been removed. Where the bottom of the freezer door would have been attached, there was still a metal hinge, a blunted projection with a ragged hole where the bolt had once been.

Could that work?

She knelt down so the hinge was roughly even with her mouth. Came at it from the side, opened her mouth as wide as she could, pushed against the hinge, trying to catch it in the folds of the cloth, but it slid off. She tried again. Same result. And again.

She cried out in frustration but could barely make a sound. I just want to sleep, she thought. Curl up right here.

No, she told herself. No. You could die if you do that. Suffocate. Try again. One more time. Just try.

The hole in the hinge, she thought. It had sharp edges on it from where they'd pried out the bolt.

She tried to slide the hinge underneath the cloth. On the first attempt, she shoved the cloth in even further. Gagged on it. Tried again. It moved but caught on her teeth. Again. This time she could feel the cloth catch, just a little. She opened her mouth so wide that her jaw hurt. A little more. Just a little more. The cloth moved, inch by inch.

And then it was out.

She fell back, gasping. The air was so sweet.

Even the dump smells were beautiful.

She let herself lie there for a minute. Just to rest.

But I can't stay here, she thought vaguely. The man had left, but would he come back? Could he be looking for her now? Driving on the road that circled the dump? She hadn't thought of that.

A fresh rush of adrenaline got her to her feet.

Her feet. She'd lost her flip-flops at some point. It wasn't too bad at first — no cans or glass, that stuff had already been sorted and gleaned. But still she stepped on things, things that hurt, and she couldn't stop to look and see what they were. Animal bones, maybe. Shards of hard plastic.

She picked her way through the bags and tires, trying to find some kind of path. Her hip was stiffening up; every step on that side sent bolts of pain shooting down her leg, and she hadn't gone very far before she lost her balance and fell. She didn't know if she could stand up again, with her hip like that, without her arms to aid her, with no firm surface.

Use your core! Use your core! She'd had a trainer once who said that nearly every set, regardless of the exercise, and Michelle heard her voice now.

She'd never liked that trainer.

Somehow she stood.

The third time she fell, she thought, That's it. I can't do it. Maybe she could lie there for a while. Maybe in the morning someone would find her. Someone who could help.

She thought about that some more. Remembered the first time she'd come here, the buzzard sitting on the cow head, picking at the hide and the scraps of flesh the butchers had left. That's what the man had wanted for her. He'd wanted to beat her to death and throw her body over the side, into the garbage, for the birds to eat.

Well, fuck that.

Use your core!

She stood.

She just had to get to the road. It wasn't too far. She risked running into the man in the car, she knew that, but it had been a while now, and he hadn't come back, and she knew she could not continue much longer through this landscape of garbage bags and abandoned couches.

She could see the road, just over a ridge of trash.

Only a few more steps. Past the crumpled baby carriage. Around the torn mattress, bleeding springs and stuffing.

Here was the road. She stepped onto it, feeling like she was climbing off a rocking boat onto solid land. Beautiful road, she thought.

She hesitated for a moment, swaying. Up or down?

How had the man gotten into the dump? It couldn't be open now, could it? Were there gates at the bottom? She couldn't remember. There was a guard shack, she remembered that. What had he done, bribed the guards?

The man had gone down, hadn't he? Could he be waiting for her there?

She wasn't sure she could even make it that far.

Up. What choice did she have?

Was there anyone up on top who could help her? Anyone at all?

I'll get to lie down, she told herself. There were shacks up there, she remembered those. A table, with umbrellas. Maybe someone had some water. People lived up there, didn't they?

Up and up and up.

Her feet hurt. She'd cut them, she thought, but she wasn't sure. Stepping wrong, the pain in her hip made her cry out. A lot of things hurt, actually. It hurt when she breathed. Her arm, too, every time it moved. Her head.

Count to ten, she told herself. Take ten steps. One step at a time. Okay. Now ten more.

Ten more steps. She could do that.

She could see the top of the dump now, stretching out ahead of her, a vast plateau ringed and dotted by mounds of garbage that in the near dark took on the contours of hills and shrubbery, the resting birds moving now and again like ripples on a wave.

Over there were some shacks, she thought — rectangular, hard angles against all the softer curves. There were little lights on in some of them, and she thought she even heard music.

She stumbled toward the lights.

'Hello?' she called out. Tried to anyway. Her voice cracked and broke. 'Hello,' she said again. It came out a whisper.

She kept walking. Were there people there, sitting at a table? Drinking beers, playing cards?

Waiting for sleep, and then for the next day to begin? There would be work for them in the morning, wouldn't there? Garbage to sort. Cans and plastic bottles. Copper wire from junked appliances. Maybe a T-shirt to wear.

She thought she saw someone at a table stand up, someone else pull him down. Were they ignoring her? How could that be? She had her hands tied behind her back, for fuck's sake.

They probably hadn't seen what the man had done to her. Or maybe they'd seen it and were afraid. Well, no one wants trouble, right? She could understand that.

'Can someone help me anyway?' she whispered. Or thought.

When she fell this time, she didn't get up again. That's okay, she told herself. It's warm enough out here. I can just rest awhile.

30

Look at the pretty lights.

Michelle opened her eyes and saw diamonds reflecting gold. She closed her eyes again. That couldn't be real.

When she opened her eyes once more, she saw an old woman crouching at her side, dabbing at her face with a wet cloth. The old woman wore a lace-embroidered dress and long white gloves. It was dark, except for the warm yellow light that bounced off crystal twinkling behind her.

The old woman smiled at Michelle and said something. '*Tranquila*,' it sounded like.

'Okay,' Michelle said. She lifted her hand. I can lift it, she thought. The rope marks around her wrists were livid, even in the dim light. 'Water . . . Do you have . . . ?' She tried to think. '*Agua.*'

'Cola,' the old woman replied. She held up a half-full plastic bottle of Coke in her gloved hand.

Michelle tried to sit up. The pain in her head and ribs made her fall back on the . . . What was she lying on?

A mattress. An old mattress, covered with a tattered blanket.

Where was she?

'*Le ayudo*,' the old woman said. She cradled one arm around Michelle's head, lifted it up, tilted the Coke bottle to Michelle's lips.

313

Michelle drank. Sweet, warm, and sticky. Nectar.

It was a shack, constructed of crates and cardboard and scraps of canvas. The light, two lanterns, like Coleman lanterns, one sitting on a tilted card table covered with . . .

Little bottles. Little bottles everywhere, reflecting the light. What were they? Perfume bottles?

'*Descanse*,' the old woman said.

Rest.

Michelle laid her head back down on the mattress and closed her eyes.

★ ★ ★

When she opened them again, it was day. She knew that from the light leaking in through the cracks in the makeshift walls, the scented heat rising up from the tainted ground.

The old woman . . . Michelle hadn't dreamed that, had she? The rest of it seemed to be true. The shack. The tiny bottles everywhere. Next to the mattress was an upended crate, a sort of nightstand. There were bottles there, perfume bottles, just like she'd thought last night.

And a half-full bottle of Coke.

Definitely half full. She was alive. The man hadn't killed her. He'd tried, but she'd survived.

Michelle reached out for the Coke bottle. Gasped. Her arm . . . He'd hit that arm, her left, with the bat. Maybe it was broken.

Sit up, she told herself. Just sit up.

Christ, she hurt. She couldn't even separate out the pain right now.

But the Coke, the Coke still tasted good.

Leaning against the wall between the mattress and the crate was an umbrella, an old-fashioned black one with a wooden handle. Michelle used her good arm to prop up her injured one, grasped the umbrella, and dropped it onto the mattress. She gripped the umbrella in her good hand, leaned on it as much as she thought it would bear, and pushed herself up.

Outside, the heat felt like a living, malign thing that had swallowed the world and her with it. Bulldozers pushed garbage from one spot to another, making the mountain shudder, the noise reverberating, confined by the heat. The gleaners, too, were moving, ripping open bags, sorting through the contents. Heat rose off the plastic in waves.

No one paid much attention to her. They had other things to think about, Michelle supposed. Getting through the day, for one.

What time was it anyway?

She'd assumed it was morning — she'd just woken up, after all — but looking at the sky, the sun hanging over the sea, she thought, it couldn't be morning, could it?

Too bad she wasn't wearing Gary's watch.

Her phone, she didn't have that. Her purse . . . Who knew what the man had done with her things? She wouldn't get them back, she was sure of that.

No passport. No driver's license. No credit cards.

It doesn't matter, she told herself. She'd figure something out.

She wasn't sure where she was, other than at the top of the dump. I'd better find the road down, she thought. Find a phone. Get some help. Maybe call Charlie's friend. At this point why *not* call him? As if she needed any more proof that she was in trouble, that this wasn't some crazy paranoid story she'd made up. Wasn't this enough?

Just get me home, she thought. All I want to do is go home.

She limped toward the roar of machinery, where the bulldozers were.

Here was a donkey, attached to a wooden cart heaped with flattened cardboard boxes. The donkey just stood there. A dog slept underneath the marginal shade of the cart. They looked familiar. She'd seen them before, she thought.

'Hello,' she said. To the dog, maybe. She wasn't sure.

'Michelle?'

The voice was incredulous. Michelle turned.

There was Vicky, wearing yet another Hawaiian shirt, this one featuring a pattern of pink flamingos.

'Hi, Vicky,' she said.

It made sense for Vicky to be here, didn't it? She'd seen Vicky up here before. Vicky came up here nearly every day or something. Michelle couldn't remember for sure.

'Oh, my God, what's happened to you?'

Vicky clasped Michelle around her shoulder. Michelle cried out. She couldn't help it.

'Sorry,' she said. 'It's just that . . . ' She started to cry. 'Sorry. That really hurts.'

'Oh, honey, I'm so sorry. Let me . . . ' For a moment Vicky stood there with a helpless expression. Then she seemed to shake herself. 'Okay,' she said. 'We're going to get you some help, okay? My car's not too far. Can you walk?'

'I can walk,' Michelle assured her. She laughed. 'I can walk. You wouldn't believe how far I walked.'

'Okay, honey. Now, let me help you, okay? Here's my arm. Is that okay?'

'It's fine.'

They started walking together, away from the donkey, Vicky's arm circling Michelle's waist, which hurt a lot because the man had hit her ribs with his bat, but Vicky was being so nice, and Michelle didn't want to hurt her feelings.

'Oh,' Michelle said. 'I have the old woman's umbrella. I don't want to take it away. Can we give it back to her?'

'The old woman?'

'She wore gloves and lace. And her shack is full of little bottles. Like, perfume bottles. I'm not making that up. I really saw it.' It felt important to say that to Vicky, that what she saw was real.

'Oh, I know who you mean. That's Ascención. Don't worry. I'll make sure she gets her umbrella.'

They came to Vicky's 4Runner, and Vicky opened the passenger door and pushed the seat back as far as it would go to make it easier for Michelle to climb inside.

After the heat of the day, the air-conditioning in the truck was almost too cold, raising

317

goosebumps on her bare arms and legs. Sitting there as Vicky steered the truck along the road that led to the exit of the dump, Michelle stared down at her hands resting in her lap, at the rope burns on her wrists.

'Can you tell me what happened to you, honey?' Vicky asked.

Michelle thought about it, about what she wanted to say. 'Someone robbed me.'

'You were up here and someone robbed you?'

'No. No, he brought me here, after. I don't know why.'

'It doesn't make much sense,' Vicky said, frowning. 'You can't just come here without permission.'

'Maybe he works here,' Michelle whispered. She closed her eyes and leaned back in the seat.

They drove for a while, over rutted roads and then onto smoother avenues.

'Where are we going?' Michelle finally asked.

'To a hospital, sweetie.'

'No. I need to . . . I want to . . . I have to make a phone call.'

'You can do that at the hospital. Trust me, if you could see yourself . . . We're going to a hospital.'

Michelle supposed that was a good idea. 'My head really hurts,' she said.

'I'm sure it does. Don't worry, we'll be there pretty soon.'

They drove awhile in silence. Funny, Michelle thought, how Vicky always seemed to just turn up. Like that first time at El Tiburón. Then later, on the street.

Vicky had permission to enter the dump. Vicky and her group.

Michelle shuddered. Her hand clutched at the armrest, feeling for the door latch.

'What's wrong, Michelle?'

'Nothing. Nothing.'

Vicky stared at her, her round, pleasant face set in an expression of concern. Of caring. The appearance of it anyway. 'We're almost there, I promise.'

Michelle swung her head around to look out the window, trying to ignore the stabbing pains behind her eye, down her neck. She didn't know where they were; they could be anywhere. Bland stucco buildings. Hotels. Chain stores. A Starbucks. The north end of town, the Hotel Zone maybe. Where she'd met Gary.

'Can we stop for a minute? I have to . . . I think I might . . . '

'Are you feeling sick? Do you need a bag?'

'I just need to stop.'

Vicky pulled over to the curb. They were in front of a Chili's. Michelle reached out blindly for the door handle, found it, opened the door. Tried to stand. Grabbed the umbrella to steady herself.

'Michelle, what are you *doing?*'

'I'm going. I'm just . . . I don't need your help.'

There, she'd stood. She took a few steps. One foot in front of the other, right? She'd done it before.

Behind her she heard the car door slam. Just keep walking, she told herself. Vicky couldn't kidnap her in broad daylight.

'Honey, come back to the car. You're not thinking clearly. You really need to see a doctor.'

It's so fucking hot out, Michelle thought. It was just too much. A great wave of dizziness washed over her. Maybe she should've had more of that Coke.

There was a lamppost just ahead. She reached out, wrapping her hands around the hot metal, rested her head against it, the heat seeming to pulse with the beating of her heart.

Then a gentle hand on her back. 'Let me help you,' Vicky said.

'Okay,' Michelle whispered.

31

The hospital looked clean, modern. 'One of the best in Vallarta,' Vicky had assured her. 'Just as good as — or better than — what you'd get at home.'

It was a hospital; that was all Michelle cared about.

'Anyone I can call for you, honey?' Vicky had asked.

Michelle had thought about it. 'Charlie,' she'd said. She didn't know his number, and her phone was gone. She could call Maggie herself; that number she knew by heart.

Okay, so maybe Vicky wasn't in league with Gary. Or whoever it was who'd tried to kill her. Michelle was feeling pretty stupid about her panic attack in Vicky's car, now that she could think a little more clearly. The IV fluids and the pain meds helped.

'You have a concussion,' the doctor told her. 'Luckily, no skull fracture. Two broken ribs. A hairline fracture here' — he pointed to his upper arm, near the shoulder — 'and a probable shoulder sprain. We don't see any fracture in your hip, but those are hard to find sometimes. A deep bone bruise at least. Altogether you are a lucky woman.'

'I am.' Michelle laughed. 'Right.'

'We want to keep you for a day, minimum, because of the head injury. The other injuries we

321

immobilize as best we can, and then you just must rest.'

'Okay,' she said.

They moved her into a private room after the ER and all the X-rays and even an MRI for her hip. She supposed the privacy would help her rest, and truthfully, she craved isolation now, wanting nothing more than a hole to crawl inside while she licked her wounds.

But how was she going to pay for all this?

The money, Gary's money — some of it was in the hotel safe. The remainder was gone, along with her wallet, her phone, her credit cards.

I'll call Charlie's friend, she thought. If rest was what she needed, she could rest at home. Funny to be thinking of Los Angeles that way, but right now even the spare bedroom in Maggie's Torrance condo sounded better than good.

She dozed awhile, vaguely aware of nurses coming in and out a couple of times. The third time she smelled food.

'Some dinner,' the nurse said, smiling.

Chicken, mashed potatoes, limp green beans. Just like home.

'Can I use that to make a long distance call?' Michelle asked, pointing at the phone on the nightstand by her bed.

'Of course. You can call in Mexico, and also international.'

'Thank you.' Michelle looked around the little room. Across from the bed was a floor-to-ceiling cupboard. Maybe her clothes were in there, her shorts, with the piece of paper from Charlie in the pocket.

'Is that where my clothes are?' she asked the nurse.

The nurse frowned. 'I don't think so. Didn't they . . . ?' She mimed a cutting gesture. 'And the clothes, they were very dirty, too, I think.'

Michelle tried to remember what they'd done when they brought her in. Jesus. Right. They'd cut the clothes off when she couldn't lift her arm and they thought her hip might be broken.

'There was something . . . A piece of paper . . . Something I need,' she said.

The nurse smiled at her. 'Don't worry. I can go ask about it.'

After the nurse left, Michelle lay back on her pillow and closed her eyes. I should eat some of this, she thought, some of the chicken at least, but it seemed like too great an effort. I will in a minute, she told herself. Just being able to lie there, on clean sheets, felt like the most wonderful thing in the world.

'Ms. Mason?'

There was only one person in Vallarta who called her that.

'Detective,' she said. She couldn't remember his name, but she recognized him: the youthful appearance, the khakis, the glimpse of a spiderweb tattoo.

'Morales,' he supplied. 'I'm sorry to have to bother you now, but we need to talk.'

'Right.' She tried to sit up, gasped at the pain that caused.

'Here.' Morales came to her bedside, dug

around for a control pad attached to the bed by a thick cable. 'You can push this one for the bed.'

She took the controller with her good hand and pressed the button he'd indicated, till the top half of the bed lifted enough to prop her up to a sitting position.

Morales pulled the room's heavy, vinyl-upholstered chair over to the bed and sat.

'Who did this to you?' he asked.

'I don't know.'

'Any ideas?'

She didn't say anything.

'Okay,' he said. 'Can you just tell me what happened?'

She told him. It sounded dry and impersonal to her ears, like she was reciting a story that had happened to someone else, someone she didn't know very well.

'What did he look like? Can you describe him at all?'

She gave a one-shouldered shrug. 'Just . . . big. Maybe a mustache. It was dark, and I was too busy — '

Suddenly she couldn't continue. She saw the bat coming down. The bags of garbage. The birds waiting.

He gave her a moment to calm herself, or maybe he was just watching her, trying to see what she might be hiding. 'I'm sorry,' he said. 'What happened to you is terrible.'

'I was lucky.'

Morales cocked his head back, his expression some combination of puzzled and amused. 'It's interesting you say that. You know, the first time

I met you, that night at the hotel, I thought, here's this nice lady who's had some bad luck. Second time we were just talking to anybody who'd seen Mr. Gardner close to when he died. But this time . . . ' He shook his head. 'This time, Ms. Mason, I really have to wonder if there's something you're not telling me.'

'I'm not feeling well,' she said.

'I understand that. But if someone is targeting you, why do you think it stops here?'

He sounded so concerned. Like he actually cared.

'It was a robbery,' she whispered. 'Look, my head hurts. I can't talk any more right now.'

'Sure, okay.' He reached into his pocket. 'I'm going to give you my card again. For when you're feeling better.'

He put the card on the nightstand. 'Oh, the lady who brought you here? Vicky? How do I get a hold of her?'

'I don't know.' Michelle squeezed her eyes shut. 'My phone's gone. I don't know her number. But she's easy to find. You don't need me. You can figure it out, right?'

You're a detective, she almost said.

'Okay, Ms. Mason.'

When he got to the doorway of her room, he paused. 'We'll talk more soon,' he said.

After he left, she closed her eyes again, leaning against the hard mattress of her hospital bed. He'd be back. He'd said as much. What should she tell him? The truth? She didn't even know what the truth was.

Besides, the police, a lot of them were corrupt

here, weren't they? Starting with the one who'd pulled her over and hauled her off to jail. Who'd spied on her.

Who'd maybe tried to kill her.

Now she tried to remember instead of pushing the images out of her head, tried to summon up his face, the man who'd attacked her. Was it the same man, the policeman?

She honestly couldn't be sure.

Morales seemed like an honest man. That's what her instincts told her, if she could only trust them.

But the things she'd read, the things Charlie had told her, about the drug wars, the corruption — *presidents* were involved in that here. Attorney generals. Judges. Army officers. How could she trust a local detective with a spiderweb tattoo?

Her dinner had gotten cold. I should eat some of it anyway, she thought. When was the last time she'd eaten? She'd had some tacos at Charlie's the night before. And a few swallows of Coke since then.

The chicken wasn't too bad, and at least it was lean protein. She ate most of it. Tried a few green beans. A bite of the congealed potatoes.

After that there was nothing to do but wait. Wait for the nurse to return with the scrap of paper she needed. Or for Vicky to come back. Or for Charlie to call.

For someone, anyone, who cared about her.

★　★　★

'I'm sorry,' the nurse said. 'But the police came and took the clothes. Maybe you can ask them for the paper?'

'Great,' Michelle muttered. 'He was just here.' Assuming that Morales was the policeman in question. 'Okay. Thanks.'

I should call Maggie, she thought, but she didn't want to. What could she say? *Hello, I'm in the hospital, and I'm in more trouble than I was the last time we talked. And oh, I lost my driver's license, my credit cards, and most of my money. That is, the money that doesn't really belong to me. So can you help me out?*

Like Maggie had money to spare. She was barely making it as it was, and she had a kid to worry about.

Shit, the credit cards. How could she even report them stolen from here? Who could she call? What cards were they anyway? She tried to remember. A Working Assets Visa. An auto teller card. Did she still have the AmEx?

She was crying now. 'Fuck this,' she whispered.

What a stupid thing to cry about. Fucking credit cards. Plastic. Who cares?

I'm alive, she told herself. Focus on that. Worry about the rest of it tomorrow.

*   *   *

'You're doing really well, Ms. Mason,' the doctor told her the next morning. 'I think we can release you today, but I would feel better about that if you have someone to watch you,

327

just because of the concussion.'

'Oh, I do,' Michelle lied. 'And I'm really feeling pretty good.'

Which was another lie. She felt like shit.

The narcotics had made her drowsy, but she hadn't slept well. She hadn't felt safe. Her room was unlocked, unguarded — anyone could come in. Nurses had, every hour or so, to check on her.

'The humerus fracture we immobilize with a sling and swathe, probably for about six weeks. It's difficult with ribs, because we don't want to compromise breathing, so you will just have to take it easy for a while, until you heal. It is important to breathe deeply and therefore to manage the pain. I don't think you can use crutches now, for the hip, but we will fit you for a cane. Ice, anti-inflammatories, and rest are the best treatment for that.' The doctor smiled. 'Luckily, Vallarta is a good place to rest.'

Michelle nodded.

'For the shoulder injury, you will want to look into physical therapy. You can probably treat it that way. Otherwise there are some very effective surgeries now that aren't too invasive.'

'I'll look into that,' she said.

Like I can afford it, she thought.

Funny, so far no one had said anything about her bill. Maybe they were waiting to hit her with it when she checked out. But you'd think they would at least have asked her about insurance. Or a deposit.

Maybe they were just kinder about things like that here.

'I will check back with you after lunch,' the doctor said. 'And we can make a decision then.'

After that she lay in bed. Try to rest, she told herself, as impossible as that seems.

Exhaustion, injury, and drugs pulled her down like leaded weights into dark water. She dozed, the air conditioner making a sound of gentle waves.

She was aware of someone sitting by the bed almost before she opened her eyes.

'Hey, Michelle. Hope I didn't wake you.'

A part of her wasn't afraid of him even now. She'd never been able to take Gary completely seriously.

Except she was pretty sure he'd tried to kill her.

'What are you doing here?' she said, heart pounding.

'Vicky sent me.' He scraped the heavy chair closer to the bed.

'Vicky?' All those thoughts she'd had, the things she'd told herself were crazy and paranoid, all this time, Vicky, with her fanny pack and her Hawaiian shirts and her charity — *Vicky* was a part of this?

'Yeah.' Gary shook his head. 'You know, she's pretty shook up, and somehow she knew that I'd helped you out before, so she just figured she'd ask me to give you a hand.' Now he smiled at her. 'How'd she know that, Michelle? Did you tell Vicky about our little arrangement?'

'Christ, no, I . . . Just that you'd given me some legal advice. She wanted to know about the

329

two of us after that day at the dump. I had to say something.'

'Ah.' He nodded. 'Good thinking. You really do think on your feet, you know that?' He lifted up a plastic tote bag, the Frida one they sold by the beach. 'Anyway, I brought you some clothes. From what Vicky told me, I guess you need them.'

'What did Vicky tell you?'

'That she found you on top of the dump, that you were pretty messed up.' Gary looked her up and down, a smile lurking at the corners of his cherub mouth. 'Somebody really did a number on you, didn't they?'

She wanted to kill him.

'Yeah, Gary. *Somebody* did. You fucking son of a bitch. Like you didn't know? And you just sit there like, like . . . '

It wasn't fair. She wanted to take something, anything, hit him with it, pound him to a pulp, but she couldn't. She couldn't even lift her fucking arm above her head.

Gary half rose and grimaced — from the pain in his back, probably. 'Well, that's nice, Michelle. *I'm* the one who shows up to help you. What makes you think I had anything to do with it?'

'Don't try to bullshit me,' she said furiously. 'It was that policeman, wasn't it? The one who arrested me, who planted drugs on me — '

'And you think I'm behind that?' He settled back down in the chair. 'Okay, I get it. I know how women like you are. Some guy gives you a good fuck, and all of a sudden you'll do anything for him. 'Oh, he wouldn't hurt me. He *loves* me.' Jesus. I thought you had a little more sense.'

'Fuck *you*, Gary,' Michelle said. She had the controller in her hand, the one that worked the bed and the TV and called the nurse. Her finger brushed against the call button. 'You think I care about Danny? Well, I don't. But he didn't steal my passport. And he didn't blackmail me into some bullshit spy scheme with a fucking James Bond watch.'

'But he did try to kill you,' Gary said. Then he shrugged. 'Fine if you don't believe me.' He stood up, reached into his pocket, pulled out something flat and dark blue. 'Here's your passport.' He tossed it at her. It landed on her lap. 'My advice is, soon as you get out of this hospital, get yourself on a plane to the U.S. Forget about all this. And keep your mouth shut.'

He picked up the Frida tote bag and dropped it in the chair. 'Though you might want to check in with Vicky first. She's pretty upset, and I know the two of you are tight.'

Michelle knew she'd been out of it yesterday, but if anything, Vicky had seemed calm. Concerned yes, but certainly not hysterical.

'About what happened to me?'

'Oh. Right. There's no way you would have heard.'

Gary stood behind the chair. Rested his hands on the back.

'You know Charlie Sloane? Older guy, kind of a drunk? Well, I don't know the whole story, but

331

Vicky went over to his place for some reason, and she found him there, dead. I guess he slipped and fell in the tub. Crazy, huh? But you drink the way he did, something like that's bound to happen.'

32

'Here are your prescriptions,' the nurse said. 'You can fill them at any pharmacy. Here are your instructions for managing the . . . the healing. Remember, for the ribs you must breathe deeply and cough every hour. You do not want to get pneumonia. Try to lie on the side of the injury when you rest. It will actually feel better.'

'Thank you,' Michelle said. 'I will.'

She'd put all the pills and the papers in her Frida tote bag. She didn't have anything else to put them in. The clothes Gary had brought fit her at least, the shorts a little on the baggy side, the T-shirt a turquoise color she'd never wear, with cap sleeves, a scooped neck, and an embossed dolphin above one breast, with a Puerto Vallarta logo. He'd brought flip-flops for shoes. With her feet bandaged up, they barely fit, but they would do for now.

'What about the bill?' she finally asked.

'Oh, I think it's taken care of. But we can check at the front desk.'

An orderly wheeled her to the lobby in a wheelchair. That was something she'd never understood: why they thought you were well enough to leave a hospital but not strong enough to walk on your own.

'The bill is all settled, Señora Mason,' the clerk at the front desk confirmed. 'Please take care of yourself and feel better.'

Fucking Gary, she thought.

They'd called a taxi for her. It waited at the curb, in the full glare of the afternoon tropic light.

The orderly helped her into the backseat of the cab, handed her the specially fitted aluminum cane. 'Take care, Señora Mason,' he said.

'Thank you.'

The cabdriver craned his head toward her. '¿Adónde vamos?'

Where to?

'Hacienda Carmen.' That was where her stuff was, what was left of it. And the money she had, so she could pay the driver.

Charlie was dead. He was dead.

'Oh, fuck,' she whispered. She wanted to cry. Don't do it now, she told herself. Wait. Just wait.

He was dead. He'd tried to help her, and they'd killed him.

It's my fault, she thought. If I hadn't . . . if I'd stayed away . . .

They drove south along the Malecón. The sun glared off the ocean like spotlights on broken glass.

He'd just wanted to enjoy the rest of his life. Drink tequila. Watch the sunset.

No one had the right to take that time from him. No one.

★ ★ ★

'Oh, Señora Mason, what's happened to you?' Paloma came out from behind the counter, putting a tentative hand on Michelle's uninjured shoulder.

The taxi driver, who had opened the gate for her and helped her through the courtyard, leaned the Frida totebag against the counter.

'Can you pay him?' Michelle asked. 'I have the money. I can . . . I can give it to you . . . '

'Of course, of course. Please don't worry.'

'Thanks.'

★   ★   ★

'This is terrible,' Paloma said, as she helped Michelle up the short flight of stairs to her room. 'The crime here these days — I have another friend, and she has been robbed in her apartment three times! The thieves, they break in and they steal everything. Her iPod. Her laptop.'

'Sorry.'

'I tell her it's the part of town she lives in. It's better here, where we are.'

Paloma unlocked the door. 'Can I bring you anything?' she asked. 'Maybe some dinner, later?'

'Thank you,' Michelle whispered. 'Some ice would be great, if you have it.'

Her little suite was closed, dark, and hot — hot like an oven. Michelle stood there in the sitting room while Paloma opened all the windows, turned on the fans, the air conditioner that barely worked.

'Okay. I'll bring you some dinner later. The ice, I can bring you that now.'

Michelle nodded. She limped over to her bed,

leaned the cane against the nightstand. Lay down on the bed, on her left side, where the broken ribs were.

It didn't actually feel good at all.

Breathe deeply, she reminded herself. Cough. Wouldn't want to get pneumonia.

'Do you have an Internet connection I could use?' she asked Paloma when the woman returned with several small bags of ice. 'Just to write one e-mail to my sister. To let her know what happened.'

'Oh, of course. You can use my computer at the desk.'

She lay there for a while with the bags on her hip and her ribs, until water from the melting ice started to soak her clothes. Then she limped downstairs. By now some of the residents had gathered in the patio for their evening cocktails.

'What happened to you, dear?' one of the elderly women asked. 'Did you have an accident?'

Michelle forced a smile and nodded. 'Yes. Doing better now, thanks.'

She made her way to the front desk. Paloma guided her over to the round table where the grimy computer sat. 'Take as much time as you need,' she said.

Six o'clock here. Four o'clock in Los Angeles. Maggie would still be at work. Wouldn't she?

'What day is it today?'

'Saturday, Señora Mason.'

'Oh.'

Michelle typed Maggie's home e-mail in the address line, and CC'ed her work account, just in case she was pulling overtime. Maggie had gotten cautious about personal e-mails in the office in the last couple of years, with all the surveillance that went on by management, but this qualified as an emergency, didn't it?

'*I have a problem,*' Michelle typed. '*I was robbed and just got out of the hospital. I'm okay, but I need you to cancel my credit cards and report my phone stolen. Can you do that? There's a folder in the bedroom in the green file box with all my personal accounts in it. That should have all the credit cards. The phone I think you can do just calling AT&T and giving them my number. Would you mind?*'

Her head throbbed. '*I am going to get a flight home ASAP. I'll let you know as soon as I book it.*'

How to get home?

She'd never actually bought a plane ticket with cash, and cash was all she had. How did one even do that? Go directly to the airport? Buy a ticket at the airline counter?

Maybe a travel agent, she thought; they had them here, didn't they? All those people who stood on street corners, in shops, asking you if you wanted to take a boat ride, a jungle-canopy tour, maybe they could book plane tickets, too.

She could ask Vicky. Vicky would know how.

Then she thought about what she'd already asked Vicky. Vicky had helped her, and she'd sent her to find Charlie. Vicky could have walked in on whoever had killed him.

People who helped her died.

I'll figure it out myself, she thought.

337

Besides, she didn't have Vicky's number anymore.

Was there any point in trying to warn Maggie about what had happened? Would it do any good? Could she tell her to take Ben and get out of town?

'With what vacation?' Maggie would snort.

Besides, if anyone else read this e-mail . . .

There was something more she wanted to say, but she wasn't sure what it was; she couldn't come up with the words.

'Hope everything is okay there. Will see you and Ben soon. Take care.'

Forget all this. Keep your mouth shut.

⋆   ⋆   ⋆

Back in the courtyard, the older woman who'd greeted her listened to her companion telling some kind of story, the other woman gesturing animatedly, leaning over and whispering.

When they saw Michelle, they stared for a moment and quickly looked away.

⋆   ⋆   ⋆

She turned down Paloma's offer of dinner. 'I think I'll just go across the street,' she said. She didn't want to be in her closed little room, trying to eat at the desk or on her bed, listening to the noise from the bar up the block. I can walk across the street, she told herself. It was probably good for her to try to walk. Of course, the doctor had told her that rest was what she needed, but

338

maybe walking would ease the horrible stiffness in her leg and her back, the pain across her shoulders.

Failing that, there were always the pain meds, which she thought might be Vicodin.

The restaurant, with its gaily painted murals of skulls and skeletons and musical instruments, was practically deserted.

'Something to drink?' the waiter asked her.

'Just water, please.' A margarita was probably out of the question.

She thought about drinking tequila with Charlie, up on his balcony.

Don't cry, she told herself again. You can't cry here.

She ordered chicken enchiladas, beans and rice.

It was hard to eat. Maybe the meds were affecting her appetite. She picked at the food, had a few bites of rice, of chicken.

'Ms. Mason?'

'Can't you just leave me alone?'

She'd nearly shouted. Morales shook his head, pulled out the chair across from her, and sat.

'I'm sorry about your friend,' he said.

'So am I.'

Do not cry. Don't.

'I talked to Vicky. Vicky Fallows. She told me a story that was pretty interesting. Something you'd told her, about how you went to jail. Something about a car accident.'

Oh, Christ. What had she told Vicky? She could hardly remember it now.

'But that wasn't the truth, was it? There were some drug charges, right?'

She closed her eyes. 'I didn't have drugs,' she said. 'It was some kind of a setup. Extortion. I don't know, whatever you want to call it.'

'Well, the charges weren't ever filed, which is good for you. But I still have to wonder. Charlie Sloane, right now they say that was an accident. Maybe it was. But now we've had two Americans die in Vallarta, in just a week. One was your friend. And you, almost killed.'

'So it's my fault?' Her voice shook. 'My fault someone beat me half to death with a baseball bat? Is that what you're saying?'

'No. What I'm saying is I don't want to arrest you.' His voice was gentle. 'I don't think you killed anyone. And jail wouldn't be good for you. You get arrested here, you can sit in prison for a long time before you even have a trial. And the trial . . . ' He shook his head. 'Things are different here.'

'So what do you want? What do you want from me?'

He sighed. 'You know about the economy in Mexico, don't you? How bad things are? A place like Vallarta, we depend on tourists and foreigners who live here. And they come because it's safe. If it's not safe, if nobody comes . . . ' He lifted his hands, a gesture of surrender. 'Then what happens?'

'I'm sorry,' she said. 'But I don't see what this has to do with me.'

'I need to know why these men died and why you were attacked. Maybe I can't fix the problem, but I need to know what it is. If it's *narcos*, okay. We tell people, they know if they don't get involved, it's safe here for them. But if it's something else . . . '

There was a passion, a sincerity to his voice, and she wondered if it was real, if an underpaid Mexican detective in a seaside resort town might actually care.

'Just tell me the truth, Ms. Mason. Tell me what's going on, before this gets any more out of hand. We can get you some protection — '

'Really? When your cops plant drugs on me? When they . . . ?'

She couldn't finish.

'I'll see to it myself,' he said, but she could see the doubt in his face.

'And I'm supposed to believe you're one of the good guys? Why should I?'

'Maybe because you don't have a choice.'

'So that's a threat?'

A frown furrowed his brow, and he appeared to consider. 'I don't like making threats.'

He leaned back in his chair, cocked his head like he was stretching out his neck, and sighed.

'You know why I left the States? I got deported when I was eighteen. All the time till I was sixteen, I thought I was a citizen, but I wasn't. Then I wanted to get a driver's license, and my parents told me the truth.'

He smiled at her. 'I was so dumb. I got caught with a bunch of weed. No jail time, but they checked my status, and that was that.' A shrug. 'So here I am. At first I was pretty pissed off, but then I decided I could have a good life in Vallarta. And I do. That's the most anyone can ask for, right?'

341

She wondered if it was really that simple. Was that the best you could hope for?

A good life. What did that even mean?

Then he shrugged again. 'Okay, I'm not a hero. There aren't too many heroes in my position, you know? But I want Vallarta to be a good place to live. And I'll do my best to help you. I promise you that.'

She nodded. She didn't trust herself to speak. Except he sat there, waiting for her to say something.

'Thank you,' she managed at last. 'But I don't know what's going on. I really don't.'

'Okay.' He suppressed another sigh. 'You'll need to stay in town until this is settled. Call me if you want to talk.' He stood up. 'It's better if you don't wait too long. I don't want to take your passport.'

Her passport.

She stared at him for a moment, and then she started laughing.

* * *

Lying in the dark of her room, she wondered what Morales would be willing do to keep her here. Could he have her arrested? On what charges? Or maybe he didn't need any. Maybe being a witness, a material witness, or whatever you called it, maybe that was enough.

Or he could just phony up some more drug charges. Or file the ones that were already there . . .

Would he try again? The man who'd hurt her?

Morales must be counting on that, she thought, that she'd feel threatened, would want to turn to him for protection.

It was tempting. Maybe she was being stupid, naïve, but she thought that he meant what he said. That he actually wanted to help her.

But what could she really tell him? About Gary? About Daniel?

If he really is honest, he's better off not knowing, she thought.

By now it was about 10:00 P.M. Early for Vallarta. Late for her. She felt doped up, drowsy, but everything still hurt. Maybe a book, she thought. Maybe she could read, if the pain in her head would let her.

There was a knock at the door.

She felt her heart jump into her throat. Stupid, she told herself. It's probably Paloma. Probably.

As long as it wasn't fucking Gary.

'Just a minute.'

She hobbled to the door.

It was Daniel.

33

'What happened to you?'

'You don't know?'

'I . . . ' He looked past her, into the room. 'Can I come in?'

She hesitated. All her trouble had started when she'd let Daniel into her room the first time. And she still didn't know how dangerous he really was.

Maybe I'm being stupid, she thought. Maybe Gary was right.

She stepped aside and let him pass.

He had his small canvas bag slung over one shoulder, and as soon as he shut the door, he reached into it and pulled out what looked like a walkie-talkie, like the kind her friends in TV production used.

'What — '

He shook his head a little, touched a finger to his lips. 'Got anything to drink?'

'I think there's beer in the fridge,' she said.

She lowered herself, with difficulty, onto the bed, watched him as he pushed a button on the device, stared at it, and opened the refrigerator door.

'There's a few. You want one?'

'Sure.' Might as well.

Daniel pushed another button on the device. It started playing a sound, something between running water and one of those rain sticks that the pseudo-hippies at Venice Beach liked to shake. He put it on the nightstand.

'It's white noise,' he said quietly. 'Just in case anyone's listening that this didn't pick up. Where's your cellphone?'

'I don't know. Not here. Gone.'

'Good.'

'Good?'

'I know Gary. A cellphone's the easiest thing in the world to use. He could hack the GPS, and there's spyware you can put on it that turns it on, makes it act like a microphone. So he'd have some idea when you were coming and going, where you were. And he could hear some of what you said if the phone was close by.'

'Oh, God.' She thought about it. Her stomach twisted. 'Charlie. And you and me. That's how . . . '

'Yeah.' He pulled the desk chair up next to the bed and opened the beers with a pocketknife, handed her one. 'Okay,' he said. 'What happened?'

'Someone hit me on the head, threw me in a car trunk, took me up to the dump, and tried to kill me. Then they killed Charlie. And where the fuck were you?'

'I . . . ' He stared at her. He'd gone pale. 'Jesus.' He took a long pull on his beer. 'I didn't know.'

'Is that all you have to say?'

'I tried to call you,' he said. 'I came here, I looked everywhere for you. I finally found out you were in the hospital but that you were gonna be okay. I thought . . . I thought it was better if I didn't go to the hospital, if I waited until you got out.'

'Why? In case the police were watching?'

He flinched, and she knew she'd called that one right.

'Don't worry, I didn't tell them anything about you. I didn't tell anyone, except Charlie.' A surge of acid burned her throat, and she swallowed hard. 'And Gary.'

'You told Gary?'

'I had to. He caught me when I was trying to get out of town.'

'Shit. What did you tell him?'

'Oh, for fuck's sake. What you told me I should tell him. You know, how he should lay off me.'

'I'm sorry.'

'That's not good enough!' Daniel looked away. Drank more of his beer.

'Look at me, Danny,' she said. 'Look at me. I didn't ask for any of this. I talked to Charlie because I was desperate. He tried to help me, and he died. And you come in here with some *spy* toy, and then you just *sit* there, like, like . . . *Shit!*'

She'd moved the wrong way. Pain stabbed down her shoulder, her arm. It hurt to breathe.

'What's wrong?' He came and sat on the bed next to her, started to put a hand on her shoulder, stopped.

'I have two broken ribs and a broken arm, you asshole.'

'Jesus.' He chugged the rest of his beer, went to the fridge and grabbed another one. 'You could've stayed with me.'

'Oh, right. After you said you wanted to kill me.'

'Look, I was pissed off. I mean, how'd you think I was gonna feel? Come on, Gary was *paying* you to fuck me!'

'Like I had a choice? Like I could count on you?'

He sat down on the bed, next to her but not touching her, as though she were surrounded by some invisible barrier.

'You don't think I'm the one who did this, do you? Do you trust me now, at least?'

'Trust you? You must be joking.' She drank some of her beer. One beer with Vicodin, that wouldn't hurt, would it? 'But no, I don't think you did this. It's not how you operate.' Funny, how she was suddenly sure of that, if nothing else. 'I mean, the dump. Why the dump? It was hard to get up there. There were people who might have seen him. He could have just killed me on the street. Or anywhere. But it was making a point. Like the pig's head. You know? It was . . . '

Performance. That's what it was.

'Gary has a funny sense of humor. You said that. It's some kind of a game to him, isn't it? It's *fun*.'

Daniel nodded. Hung his head and studied his beer. 'He's a sick fuck,' he said.

'And you're . . . you're *what*? Who are you, Danny? A good guy? A spook? Some sleazy bus driver for drug lords?'

'The less you know, the better off you are,' he

said tightly. 'Look, I'll get you out of here. I've got an idea how to do it. But you have to play along.'

Was it better to play along with Daniel or trust Morales? And not just Morales but the system behind him as well. The corrupt cops. The suspect judges. The drug cartels, with their fingers in everything.

And the system behind Daniel? Did she even know what it was?

'All right,' she said.

It wasn't even the devil she knew. It was the devil she knew better.

They sat there for a while in silence.

'Is there anything I can get you?' he finally asked.

'No . . . Yes, this sling, this brace thing I'm wearing. I can't take it off by myself. And I hate this shirt.' The shirt Gary had brought her. 'I don't want to wear it.' Now she was crying. She couldn't seem to stop. 'Just help me get it off. And take it away. I don't want to see it.'

'Okay,' he said, a helpless note in his voice. 'Okay, don't worry. I'll do that.'

He helped her take off the sling and swathe, gently unwrapping the swathe, cradling her arm as he removed the sling. He guided her good arm out of the sleeve of the T-shirt, pulled the shirt over her head, and peeled it down her injured arm.

'Sorry,' he said when she winced from the pain of the movement.

'You can't help it.'

He was looking at her body now, staring and

then looking away, at the bruises, she figured, deep and purple on her ribs and arm, and on her hip, too, but he couldn't see that.

'There's a nightshirt in the dresser,' she said.

He nodded. Let out a short, hard breath. Then he wadded up Gary's T-shirt and threw it in the corner.

★ ★ ★

'There's a party I'm supposed to go to tomorrow. It's just up the coast. You'll come with me.'

'I'm not supposed to leave town. Morales told me.'

They lay in bed. He'd helped her with her nightshirt and the sling and swathe. Sweat gathered under its pads and straps. He'd taken off his shirt and lay there in his shorts. It was easier to talk that way, lying down.

'It's not far,' he said. 'Just in San Pancho. It's a little town past the north end of Banderas Bay.'

'How is that going to help? Going there?'

'I've got some business to do. But I can get a plane close by. I'll fly you back. To the States.'

She almost laughed. 'What kind of business?'

'It's complicated,' he muttered. 'Look, it's up to you. If you want to go, I'll take you.'

She thought about it. 'What about the police?'

'If they've got somebody watching, you're not going to look like you're running. We're just going to a party, that's all. And the cops here, they don't exactly have a lot of resources.'

'What about Gary?'

'Fuck Gary. He doesn't have anything to say about this.'

She was so drowsy — from the drugs, from the beer, from the pain in her head — that it was hard to think straight.

Was there another choice? She couldn't come up with one.

'What's everyone going to think, seeing me like this?'

'Don't worry about it.'

'They'll know,' she said. 'Everyone knows everything here.'

'You got mugged,' he told her, his face inches from hers, his features blurred by the dark. 'Robbed. But you're feeling better, and you wanted to go out, just to get your mind off what happened. Right? Can you sell that?'

'I guess.' He sounded like Gary, she thought.

'Try to sleep,' he said.

'You don't have to stay.' She wasn't sure if she even wanted him to stay.

'I'd better. You shouldn't be alone when you have a head injury. Didn't the doctors tell you that?'

She nodded. It's better that he's here, she told herself, and there was something comforting, she had to admit, about having him lying there within arm's reach.

'I'll get you out of this,' he said. 'I promise.'

34

He left early the next morning, before the sun had even risen. 'I'll be back to pick you up around four-thirty,' he said. 'I've got some stuff I have to deal with. Can you be ready?'

'I'll need some help getting dressed.'

'Oh.' He thought for a moment. 'I'll come at four. Does that give you enough time?'

'Sure.'

What did she have to do, other than dress? Not pack. She was leaving all these things behind.

After Daniel left, she managed to put on a pair of shorts and her Mephisto walking sandals (her cute Kenneth Cole flip-flops were lost somewhere up at the dump) and hobble downstairs for breakfast.

Forget a bra. That wasn't going to happen.

'Oh, Señora Mason, you look much better today!' Paloma exclaimed.

'Really?' Michelle doubted it. 'Thanks,' she added quickly. There was no point in saying what she really thought, not here, not now.

'Let me bring you some breakfast.'

Michelle sat at a table by the courtyard fountain. Drank a cup of coffee. Ate a couple pieces of toast and some fruit. Petted the calico cat when it came by looking for handouts.

She thought about writing Maggie another e-mail. Tell her what was going on. That she thought she'd be home soon but she really wasn't sure.

What was the point, though?

If I make it home, I make it, she thought. If I don't, what was the point of telling Maggie what had happened? How would that help anyone?

Would telling Maggie result in some kind of justice?

If I'm gone, what difference does it make? she thought.

Besides, if Maggie didn't know anything, maybe they'd leave her alone.

After that, Michelle took a Vicodin and went back upstairs to lie down.

*   *   *

'What should I wear? This?'

She showed Daniel the black dress she'd worn that night to the cocktail party downtown — the dress she'd bought with Gary's money.

'Yeah, that's fine.' He sounded distracted. 'Maybe bring along some shorts and a sweater or something. And your swimsuit, to make it look good. It's at the beach, and there's a pool. People'll be spending the night there, so no one's gonna wonder if you have some extra things.'

'So I can bring a toothbrush?' She tried to make it light. Why not? If she could joke about it, maybe it wasn't as bad as she feared.

'Sure.' He grinned. 'Hey, go to town — bring the floss.'

He helped her dress. She didn't want to look at herself in the mirror. If she saw how ridiculous she looked, how wounded, how *helpless* . . . she didn't think she'd be able to make herself leave the room.

'Ready?'

'Almost.' She had her tote bag, stuffed with a bathing suit, a pair of shorts, her favorite blouse, underwear, and the one sweater she'd brought, which so far she'd worn only once, on the plane from Los Angeles.

In the hobo she packed a lipstick, her Olympus E-3 and her point-and-shoot camera, a T-shirt, her passport, and the money that remained, about two thousand dollars.

As she stuffed it into an envelope from the resort hotel, she thought, If I'd just left it behind, maybe I would have gotten away. Maybe I would have made it to a bus going out of town. And maybe Charlie would still be alive.

There was nothing she could do about that now, except regret it.

* * *

Daniel had driven over in a different Jeep: older, considerably more battered than the tricked-out late model he'd driven before.

'New car?' Michelle asked.

'Mine's in the shop,' he muttered.

She wasn't sure she believed him. You're going to do something illegal, something dangerous, maybe you didn't want to do that in your own car.

'You okay? You're up for this, right?' he asked her.

'I'll manage.' She had to. For better or worse, she'd made her choice.

'We're heading into Nayarit now,' Daniel said as the road looped around the airport. 'Different time zone. It's an hour earlier here, just so you know.'

'Well, I'm not wearing a watch.'

They crossed over a broad, muddy river, continuing along the highway, passing great swaths of open land and jungle interspersed with parking lots and clusters of condominiums.

The highway swept close to the ocean, through a cluttered-looking town — 'That's Bucerías,' Daniel said. 'Nicer than it looks from the road. I've been thinking about moving up here. One of the best beaches around' — before it turned inland, into jungle-covered foothills.

'Are you going to tell me anything?' she finally asked.

Daniel sighed. 'Michelle, look . . . anything I tell you, you're not going to understand.'

'You know what? I'm not stupid.'

Calming breaths, she told herself. She was so angry. She felt choked with rage. 'Charlie told me some things. I didn't want to believe him. But I'm starting to.'

'I know you're upset about Charlie,' he began.

Her hand made a fist and struck the door, without her even thinking about it. 'Don't you say a fucking word about him!'

He didn't. He stared straight ahead and kept driving.

About ten minutes later, she saw orange cones, and then barrels, on the road. Ahead of those a couple of olive drab trucks — Humvees, maybe — with machine guns mounted on them. A half dozen men in fatigues, with weapons.

'Don't worry,' Daniel said. 'It's just an army checkpoint.'

They use the army, hadn't Charlie said that? One of the cartels. Or the army was helping one of them. She couldn't remember which.

Her heart started pounding.

'Calm down,' Daniel said. 'Don't act like you've got something to hide.'

He slowed and then stopped.

A soldier came up on either side of the Jeep.

'*¿Hablan español?*' the one on the driver's side asked.

Daniel nodded.

'*¿Tienen drogas o armas?*'

'No,' Daniel said, and then he rattled off something else that Michelle didn't understand, then gestured toward the backseat, and the soldier laughed.

She glanced over her shoulder. A golf bag filled with clubs.

The soldier on Michelle's side of the Jeep looked to be twenty years old, if that. He had thick eyebrows, a round face, and big, dark eyes, which he kept fixed on some point just above her head. She wanted to smile at him, but she didn't. He looked like a teenager, but he still carried a machine gun.

'Okay,' the soldier on Daniel's side of the car said. He lifted his hand in a wave.

Daniel touched his hand to his forehead in a half salute, and they drove off.

355

'Like I said, nothing to worry about. They're not after us.'

'So who *are* they after?'

He gave her a look. She couldn't tell if he was irritated or embarrassed behind his sunglasses. 'You heard him, didn't you? You understand that much.'

'Drugs and guns. And you're telling me you don't have any of those.'

His hands gripped the wheel. 'I told you it's complicated.'

'In the car? Are there drugs in this car?'

'No.'

'On the planes you're flying, then?'

'Let's talk about something else.'

'What does Gary want, Danny? After all the things he's done — after what he did to me — you can at least tell me that.'

For a long moment, he said nothing, just gripped the wheel and stared straight ahead.

She waited for him to say more.

'He wants me to keep doing my job,' he finally said.

'Which is what? Are you a smuggler, Danny? Do you smuggle drugs? Or guns? Or . . . ?'

'If you're not stupid, don't pretend like you don't know.'

She couldn't say anything at first. She hadn't wanted to be right.

'So it's true, what Charlie said? You're a spook? Smuggling drugs?'

'I'm an asset. Unofficial.' He sounded tired. 'I manage a supply chain. One particular pipeline. Make sure the vendors connect with the shippers and the goods and payments get where they need to go. Sometimes I handle specific deliveries. It depends. Lately I've mostly been ferrying cash. It's easier to launder money here in Mexico than it is in the States.'

Daddy's little bagman.

She thought about the conversation she'd had with Charlie. About the communist threat that didn't exist anymore. About the Contras . . . what had even happened to them?

'Why do you do it?'

'What kind of question is that?' He gave her one of his side-long grins. 'It's a job. They pay me.'

'You keep telling me you're not a bad guy. So tell me why. What's it all for? Tell me, I don't know, that it's to keep us all safe. You did it for your country. Whatever bullshit excuse you have. I want to hear it.'

'I don't have one anymore.' He shrugged. 'It used to be fun.'

'Fun?'

The word hit like a punch in the gut.

'Yeah. I did all kinds of stuff before this. Flew in and out of some interesting situations. Dropped in extraction teams and picked up people who needed saving, like a big fucking hero. Helped take out bad actors who were better off dead. No bullshit bureaucracy, we just did stuff. Good stuff. It was fun.'

He laughed. 'Problem is, you do this one thing that's not right so you can do the bigger thing that is. And all of a sudden, you're flying some poor asshole to a black-ops jail in fucking

Morocco so they can paste electrodes on his balls.'

Hearing this, she rolled her eyes.

'Okay, so you're a good guy and they steered you wrong, is that what you're saying? You're a victim here? Jesus, Danny. People are getting killed over this.'

'Most of them are in the game.'

She thought about all those stories she'd read, about the tens of thousands of people who had died here, in Mexico, casualties of the drug war.

People in the game. Drug lords and dealers and assassins.

Politicians. Reporters. Policemen. Kids.

People who weren't in the game at all.

'Like Charlie?'

He swallowed hard. Almost shuddered.

'That kind of thing . . . it's why I don't want to do it anymore,' he mumbled.

She let her head fall back against the car seat, winced from the pain the impact caused. She didn't know what to say. But there was something she still needed to ask.

'What about Gary?'

'He's a step up the chain from me. Not exactly an asset. Not exactly official. They keep it vague on purpose. It's not like everyone in the Company's involved. It's always been a little group, running their own game.'

'Well, that's a relief,' she said with a snort. 'So you're a . . . a supply-chain manager. What's *his* job? Human resources?'

'He handles problems. Guess he thought I might be turning into one.'

'What did you do?'

'Nothing. But he knew I wasn't happy. I made some noise about it. He thought maybe I was going bad.'

She thought about that, about what that could possibly mean in this situation, and gave up. 'Going bad?'

'Talking,' he said simply. 'Telling the truth. Naming names.'

'Why not just kill you?'

He gave her a look. 'That's pretty cold.'

'Well, shit, Danny, isn't that what these people do?'

'Not us. I mean, not like that. We're not — '

'You're not what? You're not criminals? You just take out bad actors?'

His hands gripped the wheel until his knuckles turned white. 'If I got to be a big enough problem, yeah, that could happen,' he said eventually. 'But he'd rather keep me working. I know the players. Know the ropes. I'm not that easy to replace. Some no-load like Bagger'd goon it up in no time.'

Clouds had started coming in from the coast. A few heavy drops of rain spit on the windshield, and then the sun came through again. She squinted against it, thinking that her head hurt, thinking that maybe he was right, that she couldn't understand. Or that she didn't want to.

'So are you?' she asked anyway. 'Going bad?'

He hesitated a long time. 'No. I don't think so. I thought about it. Tell the press, tell Congress, tell *somebody* . . . . Then I thought, who'd listen? Who'd care? A lot of them already know, and what could they even do about it? The people with the power to fix it mostly like things the way they are.'

'You still have plenty of excuses,' she said angrily. 'Not everyone's corrupt. There are people who try to do the right thing.'

'Yeah,' he said without heat. 'Hey, if you're looking for a hero, I'm not that guy. I'm too much of a chickenshit, I guess.'

She wasn't going to fill in the silence that followed. What could she say to that? Then she thought, When did I ever not just go along? When have I ever been brave?

'Me too,' she said.

She stared out the window, at the foothills shrouded in low-hanging clouds. 'Mostly I thought about quitting,' Daniel said after a while. 'But there's consequences to that too, you know? So I told myself I was getting my ducks in a row. Making sure I had insurance. Waiting for . . . I don't know what I was waiting for.'

'I don't understand,' Michelle said. 'I don't understand what Gary thought . . . what was the point of having me there? What did he think I could tell him, when I didn't understand what I was even looking for?'

'You were there, that was enough. Maybe you could tell him something useful. Maybe not. But you were there. And he could listen to us. Just to let me know that I can't trust anybody, that he's got his eye on me no matter what I do. He'd get a good laugh out of it later, you know? Come back to me, brag about how he set us up, make a few pussy jokes . . . I mean, why do dogs lick themselves, right?'

'Because they can?' She could hear the edge of hysteria in her voice, the rage again; she was shaking with it.

'Yeah. He could fuck with us, so he did. That's the kind of guy he is.'

'And what he did to me . . .'

'A warning. Like the pig's head. This is what happens when you don't play along.'

35

'You think you can keep it together?'

She nodded. There wasn't much choice.

'You got mugged,' he reminded her. 'You're feeling better now. You wanted to go someplace where you could relax. Somewhere quiet.'

'Okay,' she said.

They had driven off the main highway, on a series of local roads. She'd seen a little bit of the town, a combination of an old village with men in white straw hats riding horses on the streets and art galleries that looked transplanted from someplace like Santa Fe.

Now they were on a tiny lane that had been carved out of the jungle, narrow enough and so shaded by trees that it resembled a tunnel of green.

Ahead was a wrought-iron gate with a guard box, and a guard. No uniform, but built like a weightlifter.

'You don't have anything to worry about here,' Daniel said. 'It's just a party.'

The guard took in Daniel's face and nodded.

The gate rolled open.

'Whose party?'

He hesitated. 'His name is Curt Dellinger. He's a client.'

Dellinger. That sounded familiar, but she couldn't say why. 'A client?'

'I handle transportation for him sometimes,'

Daniel said, voice tight. 'That's all you need to know. Just stick to the story. Don't go off script. Okay?'

Great, Michelle thought. A client.

'No, it's not,' she said. 'You need to tell me why we're here. If you're doing some kind of business — '

'I just need to run something by him,' Daniel muttered. He turned to her now. 'The main thing you need to do is be cool. Show you can handle yourself. Can you do that?'

He was nervous, she realized, and in a way she hadn't seen before.

Maybe even scared.

'Yeah,' she said.

'Just stick to the story. Don't go off script. Okay?'

'I won't.'

They drove down a cobblestoned drive, then over to the left where several other cars were parked. There were a couple of valets there, or were they guards as well?

'Can you walk that far?' Daniel asked. 'I can pull up to the entrance and let you off.'

'I'm fine.' She wasn't really, but walking seemed like a good idea, testing herself, making sure she could move.

Daniel came around to the passenger side and opened the door.

'Let me help.' He offered her his arm. She grasped it with her good right hand, stepped out awkwardly, and he circled his arm beneath hers, around her back, to help her up.

She gasped, not wanting to, but it hurt and she

couldn't help it. 'I'm okay,' she said, to cut him off. She wasn't in the mood for his sympathy. 'Getting up and down's just a little hard.'

She leaned against the Jeep while he retrieved her cane.

They walked up the drive, toward the main house. It looked like a Malibu villa, Michelle thought, two stories, with white arches and a red-tiled roof. There were several outbuildings off to one side. One was obviously a garage. She couldn't tell about the others.

A Mexican woman in a white embroidered dress greeted them at the door. Smiling, she led them through a living room with a red-tiled floor. Leather couches and chairs, heavy wood polished to a warm glow, hand-woven rugs. Paintings on the wall, modern and some nineteenth century, she thought, of seascapes mostly.

Tasteful — and reeking of money.

The party guests were out on the terrace in the back, thirty or so people by Michelle's reckoning.

It was a large terrace, with descending layers, overlooking a garden and a pool, and beyond that the beach, the sand in striations of white, tan, and goldenbrown as it met the lapping waves. The beach was practically deserted, the water so clear, the sky so deeply blue that it hurt her eyes.

'Nice, huh?' Daniel said.

She nodded.

'Hang in there,' he said. 'Try to relax. That's all you have to do.'

They made their way to the terrace. As they approached, a tall, gray-haired man wearing khakis and an untucked Polo shirt excused himself from the conversation he was having and turned in their direction.

'Danny,' he said. 'Good to see you.' He had a long, lined face, a surprisingly soft voice with a certain clipped authority.

'Curt,' Daniel said. 'This is Michelle.'

He extended his hand to her. 'Pleasure to meet you.'

'Likewise.'

His hand was cool to the touch, and strong.

'Michelle's a friend of mine from Los Angeles,' Daniel said. He'd tensed up, she could tell, holding himself too still.

'Oh? On vacation?'

'Yes.' She forced a smile. 'This is a beautiful house.'

'Thank you. I don't spend nearly enough time in it.' He turned to Daniel. 'Danny, why don't you get your friend something to drink? Me, too, if you wouldn't mind.'

There were two waiters that she could see, circulating among the guests offering them drinks and appetizers; he didn't need Daniel to run and fetch them drinks. He was the boss, commanding his employee. There was no mistaking it.

'Sure. What can I get you?'

'Just a mineral water,' he said. 'How about you, Michelle? I have a really nice chardonnay, if you're interested.'

'That sounds great,' she said, wondering

— did he know what she liked to drink? Or was it just a guess? What the nice lady from Los Angeles would be expected to like?

'I'll be right back,' Daniel said. He rested his hand briefly on her forearm, the gesture of a conspirator, and headed inside.

Curt glanced at her sling, then back to her eyes. 'Did you have an accident?'

'Oh, it was . . . ' She swallowed, trying to push down the pulse in her throat. 'I got mugged.'

'I'm so sorry. That's terrible.'

'It's not as bad as it looks.'

'You know, I think I heard something about it. Something involving a policeman?'

How would he know that? She tried to remember whom she'd told, who would know. 'I . . . ' Her mouth had gone dry. 'I don't really know. It all happened so fast.'

'You look dizzy,' he said. 'Why don't we sit down while Danny rustles up those drinks?' He smiled. 'Take the chance to get better acquainted.'

They walked side by side farther onto the terrace, to a lower level that wrapped around the natural stone pool. There was a *palapa* there that overlooked the beach.

Curt took her hand and helped her sit. Her legs felt shaky.

'This is a wonderful country,' he said. 'But you do have to watch your step.'

'Bad things can happen anywhere,' she said faintly.

'Exactly.' He kept his eyes fixed on hers, a deliberate, uncomfortable scrutiny. 'Tell me a little about yourself.'

'Not much to tell. My marriage ended recently, so . . . ' She shrugged, forgetting what that would do to her shoulder, and winced.

Curt noticed. 'Oh, I'm sorry. You're all banged up, and here I am interrogating you.'

'That's all right.' She managed a smile. 'I wish I had something more interesting to say.'

'I have a confession to make.' He leaned forward, eyebrows lifted, making it a joke. 'I'm not very interesting either. I'm in finance. I have an investment firm, based out of Florida. Venture capital for start-ups mostly, and some real estate.'

Funny, she thought.

'My husband was in real-estate finance.'

'Ouch,' he said cheerfully. 'Bad time for it overall. Though I still have my fingers in a few things.' He gestured up the coast. 'That's one of our projects, right up there.'

Michelle looked to where he pointed. A large rectangle of bare, brown earth was cut into the jungle-covered bluffs, as if a giant brand had been pressed against the ground.

'Oh.'

'I know it doesn't look like much now, but it really is going to be special. Gated. Ocean views. Pool. Green technology. Solar paneling, recycled materials . . . '

'Hey.' Daniel had returned, a glass of wine and a sweating beer bottle between the fingers of one hand, a tall glass of sparking water with a wedge of lime in the other.

He gave the glass to Curt, then knelt down

367

and handed her the wine. 'You doing okay?'

'I'm fine. It's just great to be here, in a beautiful place like this. Thanks for having me,' she said to Curt.

'My pleasure.' He rose, swiped his forehead briefly with a handkerchief. 'Now that you're taken care of, I hope you can relax and enjoy the day.'

Michelle sipped her wine. It was, as Curt had indicated, excellent.

Daniel stared after him for a moment, then sat in the chair next to her. 'Good job,' he said.

She didn't ask, and he didn't offer. They sat for a while in silence, Daniel drinking his beer and snagging a couple of tiny tamales from a passing waiter.

'I'm going to go talk to some people,' he said. 'Eat something if you have a chance. It might be a while before we get anything else.'

'Okay,' she said.

After he left, a waiter came by with a fresh tray of hors d'oeuvres: crab taquitos and tuna ceviche. She took some and ate. She was sure the food was delicious, but she hardly tasted it. Another waiter came with a fresh glass of chardonnay. A few guests approached and introduced themselves — a banker, an official from the Mexican trade commission, an American who said he was in the oil business. Michelle smiled at them, thanked them for their expressions of sympathy and healing, made small talk. Like everything was normal.

She had the sense that she was watching herself from a small distance and realized she'd felt that way at parties for years.

Partway through the second glass of wine, her hip, her shoulder, her ribs — everything — started to throb with a dull intensity that was like a spreading headache. She needed to move, as much as that would hurt.

The beach looked so beautiful. She had a sudden impulse to go down there, to dig her toes in the golden sand.

She pushed herself to her feet, gasping a little as she gained her balance. Cane in one hand, glass of wine in the other, she limped around the dark flagstone pool toward the beach.

*   *   *

It wasn't like the beach in Puerto Vallarta. There were no vendors. A few sunbathers to the north. A couple from the party, arm in arm, strolling through ankle-deep surf.

Silence, except for the wash and crash of waves.

I almost died, she thought, staring at the waves, at the sun sinking into the horizon, melting the clouds around it into smears of pink and orange.

I could be dead tomorrow.

She kicked off her sandals. Dug her toes into the wet sand.

'Look who's here! And I thought you might be mad at me.'

36

'Did you come with Danny? Is he around?'

Emma swayed a bit, maintaining her grip on a half-full, oversize wineglass. She wore a gauze beach cover-up over a dark red bikini, her breasts barely restrained by the scalloped top.

'I . . . ' Michelle stood there, frozen. Why was Emma here? Was Oscar . . . ? She looked over her shoulder, flinching from the pain in her head.

'Why are you so nervous? There's private security for this beach. Like my father's going to allow any trouble.'

Father?

Michelle stared at Emma, who was studying her, her expression uncharacteristically concerned. 'What happened to you?'

'I . . . '

'Come on,' Emma said. 'Let's go sit down.' Now she giggled. 'And catch up.'

★   ★   ★

Emma led her to a little stone table on the terrace closest to the sand. Before she even sat, she waved at a waiter, held up her wineglass and two fingers.

Michelle carefully lowered herself into the chair. She felt like she'd had the breath knocked out of her — sucker-punched again.

'I usually hate these parties,' Emma was saying. 'Hardly anyone interesting ever comes, and of course Daddy doesn't like my friends.'

'Your father . . . your father's Curt?'

Emma snickered. 'Yeah. You didn't know?'

By now the waiter had arrived with fresh wine, whisking away Michelle's nearly full glass before she could formulate an objection. She couldn't think; it was like trying to see down a road obscured by fog.

'So what happened?' Emma asked.

'I . . . was mugged.' Stick to the story, she told herself; it's the only thing you can do. 'A couple of days ago.'

'Wow, that sucks.' Emma gulped her wine, and then she smiled, that studied sly look of hers, peering up through her eyelashes. 'I guess you won't want to go out with me for a while.'

The fog lifted, burned off by a rush of anger. 'Your boyfriend,' she said before she could stop herself. 'Oscar. Do you have any idea . . . ?'

'He's not my boyfriend anymore. We broke up. After he got what he wanted.' Emma pouted. 'Daddy was so mad at me. That's why I'm grounded.'

'Quit the little-girl act, Emma,' Michelle snapped. 'It's not funny.'

'I'd have to agree.'

Curt Dellinger stood there behind her, on the flagstone path that led down from the main house, trailed by Daniel, who looked as pale as he had the night she'd come home from the hospital, when she'd told him what had happened to her — and to Charlie.

'Busted,' Emma whispered gleefully.

'I didn't realize that you knew my daughter,' Curt said.

'We've met.'

'We went out the other night,' Emma said, giving Michelle's uninjured arm a squeeze. 'I took her to see a few sights. Off the beaten path.'

'It was an interesting evening,' Michelle said.

Daniel stepped forward. 'We'd better hit the road. It's getting late.'

'You sure you won't stay the night?' Curt asked. 'A couple of the bungalows are free. Some of those roads, after dark . . . they're tricky.'

'We still have a little light left,' Daniel said.

Michelle started to push herself to her feet with her cane. Curt stepped in, offered her his arm, and she clasped his hand, steadied herself, and stood.

The last rays of the sun lit Curt's face, bathing him in a pink-and-orange light. He looked like an advertisement for some preppy clothing company, she thought, like he should have a tennis racket under one arm, a Labrador by his feet.

The lines around his eyes crinkled as he smiled at her.

'Thank you for your hospitality,' she said.

'My pleasure.'

'Come back soon!' Emma called out, waving after them.

★ ★ ★

'Jesus, Danny. Why didn't you tell me that Emma is Curt's daughter?'

'Didn't think about it.' His eyes were focused on the dark road ahead, the road that led to the highway.

'Seriously? You didn't think that would be a good thing for me to know?'

'I didn't think it would come up. She'd rather be just about anyplace else than where he is. Only time I've seen the two of them together lately is when she needs him to write her a check.'

'Come on. She shows up at María's party, she makes sure I meet Oscar so he can find you, and her father is one of your *clients*?'

'Look, Michelle. Drop it. I'm telling you. In case you haven't figured it out, you are in a world of shit right now. I'm trying to fix it so you can go home and they'll leave you alone, and the best thing you can do is just forget about it.'

'You sound like Gary.'

He slammed his palm against the steering wheel. 'I am *nothing* like Gary.'

'Prove it,' she said. 'Just tell me something real. Or you can let me out by the side of the road and I will fucking *walk* home.'

For a moment she thought that he would. The Jeep slowed down. Fine, she thought. Fine. I have two thousand dollars. I have my passport. I'll get home by myself.

He heaved a huge sigh. 'Fuck,' he muttered. 'Emma likes stirring shit up,' he said. 'And she likes pissing him off. Maybe she's trying to make a play. Maybe she wants to show her daddy that she's got her own thing going on. Whatever. He wants what's best for him and his group, and he

373

likes it when things run smooth and he doesn't get embarrassed. Oscar and those guys, I don't know how they fit into that. Who's on top changes, and people get burned all the time.'

They'd made it to the highway. The Jeep picked up speed.

He turned to her now that the road was straight. 'There's some proverb. It's probably Chinese. It goes, you sit on the mountain to watch the tigers fight.'

He turned his eyes back to the road. 'What that means is, you let them eat each other. Instead of eating you.'

★ ★ ★

They continued south along the highway, back toward the city.

'Where are we going, or is that something else I don't need to know?'

'Town up in the mountains,' he said shortly. 'It'll take us a couple of hours.'

'So there's an airport?'

He snorted. 'Not exactly. Good airstrip, though.'

Great, Michelle thought. Could this get any sketchier? She could just picture dark men with mustaches and gold chains loading bales of pot . . . or would it be bricks of cocaine? Off of donkeys. Or Jeeps. Set to a Don Henley song. Wasn't there a movie like that, with Mel Gibson?

'And we'll fly, we'll fly where?'

'It's a little tricky,' he muttered. 'The plane's a

Caravan, and it only has about a nine-hundred-mile range, a little more with the extended tanks. But you can't land a jet on that strip, and there's no way I'm gonna risk going out of PVR.'

The Vallarta airport. 'Because of the police?' It only made sense, Michelle thought, that if she wasn't supposed to leave town, they'd watch for her at the airport.

Now he laughed. 'The police aren't a problem. There's a private aerodrome there that we use, and normally everything's taken care of. But with all the shit that's gone down, I'm not gonna chance it. If Gary's got a wild hair up his ass, it's better to just go around him.'

'In a . . . So this is a small plane we're taking?'

'Yeah, but they're awesome little birds,' he said, with real enthusiasm. 'Workhorses. You can practically land them in a ditch.'

Just great.

★ ★ ★

Bumpity-bumpity-bump.

'Hey, wake up. We're here.'

'I'm awake,' she said. She was, more or less. She'd been drifting in and out along the way, but her ribs and shoulder hurt too much to let her sleep soundly, and when she'd come closest to real sleep, she'd had a nightmare about not being able to move, about being tangled up in sheets.

She stretched as he opened the driver's door. The air had a crisp coolness to it that she hadn't felt since she'd left Los Angeles. The trees had a different scent, less weighted with fruit and flowers.

Daniel came around and opened her door. 'I'm going to start the preflight, so if you want to, you can wait in here, or outside, or in the plane — whatever you feel like. Let me know if you need a hand.'

'Okay.'

She swung her legs to the side and looked out the open car door. It was dark, but she could see the darker silhouettes of mountains ahead of her, surrounding a narrow valley. They'd parked in a dirt field, across from a whitewashed building about the size of a gas station food mart, dimmed to gray in the moonlight.

Michelle braced herself against the car seat and pushed herself to her feet. There was a small plane up ahead, on the far side of the lot. Daniel had unlocked the pilot-side door, hoisted himself up into the cockpit.

There was no one around. No one in the little building by the field. No gold-toothed smugglers with bales of pot or bricks of cocaine. On a hillside some distance away, she could make out the lights of some sort of long, low building, forming the rough profile of a roof and archways, and she thought she could hear a strain of music drifting down from it, too indistinct for her to note anything but a vague melody.

He was right, it was cool up here in the mountains. She shivered a little and grabbed her sweater out of the tote bag, threading her right arm into the sleeve and draping the left awkwardly across her back and over the sling.

She wished she could change, at least put on the shorts and shirt she'd brought, instead of having to wear the black dress. Maybe Daniel could help her before they took off.

She approached the plane. White with two-tone blue trim, 'Caravan' written in cursive script above a logo on the tail: a trident inside a circle.

There was a creak of metal, and a door on the side of the fuselage opened, and then Daniel lowered a ramp ladder strung on chains to the ground. 'Climb on up if you want,' he said. 'Seats in here are pretty comfortable.'

He came down the ladder carrying a folded stepstool. 'This strip's used mostly by sightseeing tours — Caravans fly in and out of here a couple of days a week. I flew this one in before I picked you up. Paid the guy who works here during the day some 'rental.'' He made finger quotes with his hands.

'Should I ask whose plane this is?'

'Nope.' He leaned the stepstool against the ramp. 'I'm going to get the stuff in the car.'

Well, it wasn't a tiny plane, Michelle thought, peering up the ramp. The running lights and cabin lights were on. There were a couple of padded bucket-type seats toward the cockpit and what looked like a larger cargo compartment aft.

'Pretty sweet, huh?' Daniel swung one sturdy-looking duffel into the plane, then another. 'I should just buy one of these and be a bush pilot.' He grinned. 'Fly medicine to war orphans, you know? Be one of the good guys.'

He headed back to the Jeep. Michelle

followed. Her tote bag and purse were still there, and she suddenly wanted to load them on the plane, to just get on with the next phase of the trip, wherever it was they were going.

'I'll take your stuff over for you.' He went to the rear of the Jeep, opened up the back hatch, and grabbed the bag of golf clubs.

'Need a hand?'

She didn't need to see him to know that it was Gary. Of course. He came around from the side of the building holding a flashlight, aiming it straight at her.

'Oh, if you could see your faces right now — classic!' he said. 'I wish I had a camera. But that's really more Michelle's thing. Isn't it, honey?'

'Gary, look,' Daniel began.

'You thought I wouldn't find out? You thought you could just pull strings and work around me? Now, what makes you think you can do that?'

There was a crunch of gravel behind them, the rough hum of an engine. A car.

'You go crawling to Curt Dellinger like he's gonna save your ass, like you've got some kind of high card you're holding over him.' Gary laughed. 'You think he gives a shit about you? Well, he doesn't. You know what he does care about? Problems. And that's what the two of you are.'

'We're not going to cause any problems,' Daniel said, staring at Gary's hands.

'Okay, here's the deal.' Gary stepped closer, and now Michelle could see, behind the glare of the big metal flashlight, that his other hand held a gun. Of course.

'We can't have people talking. Not that anybody's likely to believe anything you have to say, Michelle, but . . . it's the principle of the thing. It sets a bad example when people just say whatever shit they want to say and then they get away with it.

'And you know the way it works? You tell one person, and then it's just so much easier to tell somebody else. Isn't that right, Michelle? Because you told Danny, didn't you? Even after I told you not to say anything to anybody. You went ahead and talked. Didn't you?'

The engine behind them shut off. A car door creaked open.

'And then,' Gary said, stepping closer, coming right up to her, 'you told someone else. You told old Charlie, right? And look what happened.'

'Fuck you, Gary,' she said.

Daniel put a hand on her arm. 'No one is going to say anything else. Let's not make this complicated.'

'Believe me, I'm planning on keeping things simple.' Gary took a step back, out of Daniel's reach. 'I'm willing to give you a break, Danny, just this once. Because, frankly, you'd be a pain in the ass to replace right now. So I'm giving you a onetime opportunity here. You show me that you're loyal. You walk away from her, right now, and you do your job. That's all you have to do.'

'I've always done my job,' Daniel said, his voice tight. 'Always. You spun this whole bullshit paranoid fantasy in your head — you made this

379

whole thing happen, for nothing! You fucked up, Gary — you fucked up big time. So here's *my* offer: Let me take her home. You leave her alone, we'll forget about all this, and I'll do whatever you need me to do.'

She stood there helpless, listening to the two of them discuss her like she was some kind of package and the argument was about whom she belonged to and where they should send her.

'I don't think so.'

Gary glanced deliberately over their shoulders, at the car behind them. Michelle turned to look, since that seemed to be what he wanted.

The car. The one that had taken her to the dump. Leaning against it, the man, the big man with the mustache. The policeman. She was sure now.

'This isn't a negotiation. You stick with her and pay the consequences or you walk away right now.'

Daniel looked as well. 'Jesus. Come on, man. This isn't right. You can't . . . you can't do that.'

'She doesn't have to ride with him,' Gary said. 'He's just here to provide a little incentive.' He was close enough for her to see him smile. 'If Michelle's a good girl, she gets to ride with me.'

'Why don't you just fucking shoot me?' Michelle said. 'That's what you're going to do anyway.'

'Oh, sweetie, don't tempt me. Because it's definitely an option.' He turned to Daniel. 'But I'll tell you what: You show me you can behave, maybe I'll let her go. I like that deal better, now

380

that I think about it. Keeps you from getting any funny ideas once you're on your own, up in a plane somewhere.'

Daniel stood there, rigidly still, his hand beneath the strap of the golf bag, the bag resting on his shoulder, and for a moment she thought he'd risk it, that he'd go after Gary, that he was calculating the odds, the angles.

'So what do you say?' Gary asked.

Daniel slowly unshouldered the golf bag and propped it against the Jeep.

'Okay. What do you want me to do?'

Gary jerked a finger at the plane. 'Fly that back where it belongs.' He snorted. 'Jesus, you really thought you could just take it out from under my nose?'

Daniel nodded. 'I need to do the preflight first.' He turned to her. 'It'll be okay,' he said, his expression blank, and then he trotted off toward the plane.

So that's it, Michelle thought. He's not going to get me out of this. He's going to fly away and leave me here.

I'm not that guy, he'd said.

She stood there, feeling empty of anything other than rage.

'Here's what's going to happen, Michelle,' Gary was saying. 'I've got some acquaintances with a hacienda not too far from here. Out in the country. Nice and quiet.'

She could see Daniel over by the plane. He'd climbed up on the stepstool and was checking something under the nose.

'You'll stay there while we sort things out,' he

said. 'And we'll see what we can do about your attitude.'

'My attitude?'

'To start with, you really should be a little more polite to me.' He moved closer, and in a way she was glad he had his hands full. 'All things considering.'

Behind him she saw Daniel hop off the stepstool, walk toward them, lift a hand in the direction of the man by the car. 'Just need more light,' he called out.

'What is it, Gary?' she asked, and it felt good not to hide her contempt. 'Do you want to fuck me, is that it? But you, you're such a chickenshit you have to do it this way? With a gun?'

He laughed. 'You really are something, Michelle.'

'Or is it Danny you want to fuck? Is that why you wanted us to hook up? So you could hear all about it? Maybe listen in on your spy phone?'

Gary swung his flashlight, almost casually, cracking it against her broken arm, and she fell back against the side of the Jeep, gasping.

'That's enough,' he said. 'Now, be a good girl and maybe I won't make you ride in the trunk.'

Through a red haze, she saw Daniel coming up behind Gary.

'Hey, Gary — can I borrow your flashlight?'

Gary turned, and Daniel came out of a half crouch, launching himself at Gary, plowing the crown of his head into Gary's gut. They landed on the ground in front of her, rolling in the gravel, the flashlight spinning out of Gary's hand, and she couldn't see what was happening, just hear their animal grunts, running footsteps, and then gunshots, seeming to come from everywhere at once, one close enough to her head for her to feel the spit of copper. She dropped to the ground, landing on something. The golf bag. Her hand closed on the head of a club, a thick wedge of cold metal beneath her fingers. She yanked it out of the bag.

When she looked again, she saw Daniel straddling Gary, who lay on his back. Daniel held the gun, and he pointed it at Gary's head.

'You tell your friend,' Daniel said between gulping breaths. 'You tell him to get in his car and drive the fuck away.'

Gary lifted his hands. 'Okay. Okay. Guillermo!' he shouted. '*¡Súbete al coche — vete a Tres Cerros!*'

Daniel thrust the gun muzzle closer to Gary's face. 'He better not be coming back. Or calling any friends.'

'Don't worry. He won't do anything till I tell him to. Right, Guillermo?' he added loudly.

They waited. From behind the Jeep, she heard retreating footsteps. Then a car door slam, the engine start up, wheels crunch on gravel.

'That guy's such a pussy,' Gary muttered. 'Should've figured he'd be hiding behind a car. You gonna let me up now?'

'Thinking about it.' Daniel swayed a little.

'Hey, well, look here,' Gary said. 'You're bleeding. Now, how'd that happen?'

Michelle used the golf club to push herself to her feet. 'Danny?'

'I'm okay.'

383

As Daniel started to rise, Gary drove his knees into his calf, and Daniel fell hard to one side, and then Gary was up and kicking at his hand that still clutched the gun until Daniel's fingers finally opened and the gun skipped onto the dirt and gravel.

Gary took two quick steps and bent down to scoop it up.

Michelle raised the golf club with her good arm, braced with her bad, and slammed it as hard as she could against the base of Gary's skull.

'Fuck!'

His hands went to his head; he stumbled forward, regained his balance. Michelle swung again. This time the club caught him against his cheekbone, and she didn't care about the flare of pain down her arm, the stabbing in her ribs.

'Fuck you, Gary! *Fuck you!*'

She lifted the club over her head with both hands, brought it down on his neck, and he fell to his knees. 'Murdering cowardly cocksucking *asshole!*' She swung once more, against the side of his head, and then again, aiming for the same place.

He collapsed and was still.

She stood over him, breathing hard, the pain in her shoulder making her dizzy.

'Wow.'

Daniel had managed to sit up. Even in the dark, she could see the patch of black against the faded white of his shirt. Blood, soaking the shirt from the chest down to the ribs.

'Did you just take out Gary with a golf club?'

37

'I don't think it's too bad,' Daniel said.

'I can't even see it out here. Danny, we need to go to a doctor.'

'No.'

Gary moaned at their feet. Blood from his nose covered the lower half of his face like a mask.

'There's no exit wound, right? No bleeding out the back?'

'No, but . . . '

His hand hovered over his collarbone, near where the bleeding was. 'Probably from that other asshole's gun. Could've been worse.'

'You think you can fly a plane like this?'

'Come on, how many times have you driven drunk and made it home?' He tried to smile. 'Look, I don't think we have a better choice. I don't know whether you killed this fucker or if he's just going to have an even bigger hard-on for us when he wakes up. It's not good either way.'

Gary moaned again.

'What do we do with him?' Michelle asked.

Daniel shrugged. 'Leave him here.'

★ ★ ★

There was a first-aid kit on the plane. In the cabin light, Michelle could see the ragged purple edges of the wound, a hole about the size of a dime.

'Pour some water on it,' Daniel said. He sat in one of the leather passenger seats on the aisle. 'To irrigate it. Then alcohol. Just do it.'

She found a bottle of Evian stashed in the cabin's mini-fridge.

After that was done, she ripped open a package of sterile cotton per his instructions, pressed it into the wound, taped it down, and wrapped a roll of gauze over that, winding it under his arm and across his chest. Then an elastic bandage around his wrist, which was scuffed and swollen where Gary had kicked it. A couple of his fingers had puffed up like sausages.

'Okay,' he said. 'I think I'm good to go.'

'Danny, are you sure?'

'Close enough. I flew her over from PVR myself, all fueled up, checked from nose to tail, and assuming Gary didn't fuck with the plane, we're good.'

'Assuming . . . Should we assume that?'

He shrugged. 'He wanted me back in the fold, and he'd hate to waste a good bird. Anyway, I checked the big stuff. We're just gonna have to fly with it.'

They exited the plane one more time, to remove the chocks and cowl covers and tailstand, Daniel moving slowly and deliberately, at one point grabbing a wheel strut to steady himself.

Gary had rolled over onto his back, was muttering something Michelle couldn't make out. 'I guess he's not dead,' she said.

She crouched down unsteadily next to him.

Patted his shorts. Grabbed his wallet from the back pocket and then his BlackBerry from a clip on the waistband. Daniel gave her a hand up, and she stood. Dropped the BlackBerry on the ground. Stomped on it with the heel of her foot, again and again, feeling the plastic crack, grinding it into the dirt.

'We should take the clubs. Maybe do a quick wipe-down on the Jeep, at least get rid of your prints.'

'I can do that. Why don't you watch him?'

There was a bottle of Windex in the plane, and with that and a clean rag she wiped down the Jeep's doors and the steering wheel and the dashboard, and finally the rear hatch, while Daniel stood by Gary, gun in hand, swaying slightly. She thought he looked very pale, but in the darkness it was hard to tell for sure.

She managed to pick up the bag of clubs, staggering a little from the pain in her hip and ribs, and carried it over to the plane. Then she went back for the club she'd used on Gary. A wedge, she thought, recalling her brief flirtation with the sport.

For a moment she stood over Gary, staring down at him, resting the club on her good shoulder. He was conscious now, and when he saw her, he made a noise low in his throat and tried to sit up, then cried out and fell back, one hand clutching at his temple.

'Bitch,' he said. 'You bitch.'

She smiled at him. 'Don't tempt me, sweetie.'

* * *

'You wanna ride shotgun?'

'I guess.' She slid into the copilot's seat. The cockpit smelled of oil, leather, and hot wire. 'What do I need to do?'

'Nothing. Just relax.'

Right, she thought, looking at his pale face in the darkened cockpit, the bloodstained shirt, his swollen fingers fumbling on the switches and dials. 'What if you pass out?'

'That's not gonna happen.'

'What if it does?' she insisted. 'At least show me what to do.'

He hesitated, and then he nodded. 'Yeah, okay. Once we hit cruising altitude, I'll give you some flying lessons.' He grinned. 'It's fun. You'll pick it up in no time.'

She wasn't so sure about that. But she had nothing to lose from trying.

'What about Gary?'

'His car was on the other side of the building. I took his keys and his phone and the keys to the Jeep. Should slow him down for a while anyway.'

'But he'll come after us.'

'Probably.'

The engine started with a rumble and a whine increasing in pitch as the propeller on the nose began to swing counter-clockwise, then clockwise, joined by a lower buzz, growing louder as the plane taxied slowly from the field to the strip.

'Here we go,' Daniel said.

The plane bumped down the strip, picking up speed, the propeller now a blur, and she almost didn't notice when the wheels were no longer touching earth; they seemed to hover over the strip for a while and then suddenly rise into the night sky.

Now they were above the darkened mountains. She could see the lights of a small town nestled between the peaks, a little cluster of them, like a gathering of stars.

'It's beautiful,' she said.

'Next time I'll take you up during the day. We could follow the coast, like from L.A. to Seattle. It's amazing.'

He looked so pale, but maybe it was the light in the cockpit. Was there fresh blood on his shirt? She couldn't tell.

'Are you going to be okay, Danny?'

'I think so. If I can't hang, we'll stop. I promise. But I want to get across the border first, if we can.'

'Then what?'

'There's people who owe me favors,' Daniel said. 'And buddies of mine I don't mind owing. Maybe they don't have the juice that Gary does, but they've got some pull. Maybe it'll be enough.'

What if it isn't? was the obvious question to ask, but she didn't feel like asking it. She had the sudden notion that they could just fly like this forever, stopping now and then for fuel, taking off again, going where they wanted. That wasn't the way life really worked, and she knew that. But for now she would pretend it was.

We'll land where we land, she thought. And I'll take it from there.

Acknowledgments

One of the best things about being an author is that I get to work with a lot of great people. It's like finding one's tribe.

Many thanks to Dave Barbor, Kerry D'Agostino, Holly Frederick, Cathy Perifimos and all the great folks at Curtis Brown, especially my agent, Katherine Fausset — your support, creative insight and unfailing good humor are deeply appreciated. Besides, you like Drew Brees. This is important.

I feel so fortunate to have landed at Soho Press, where I get to work with passionate, talented and what can I say, really nice people. I don't know who I'd rather crash a party with than the Soho Criminals. Thank you, Bronwen Hruska for continuing the fine tradition of founding editor Laura Hruska and for adding your own vision and talent to a wonderful company. Thank you, editor Juliet Grames, for your editorial insight and for understanding that sometimes I need to be talked off a ledge. Thanks as well to Mark Doten, Michelle Rafferty, Kerrie Loyd, Ailen Lujo and Justin Hargett for your support and hard work. Thanks also to a group of Soho authors who unfailingly support each other and are just a blast to be around. Cara Black, who went out of her way to offer her friendship and advice, Tim Hallinan, the King of the Novel Café and the person I would always want to be on a panel with,

Leighton Gage, Henry Chang, James Benn, Stuart Neville, Lene Kaaberbol, Agnete Friis, Jassy Mackenzie — it's a pleasure to be your label mates.

Thank-you, David Shoemaker, for designing a cover that I'm thrilled has my name on it, and my amazing web designer/host Ryan McLaughlin, who has been such a pleasure to work with over the last few years, and to copy editor Maureen Sugden, for her incredibly thoughtful and detailed attention to my MS and for understanding way more about commas than I ever will.

I'm incredibly fortunate to also be published by HarperCollins UK — and I have had so much fun working with editor Jane Johnson, editor Emad Akhtar and the rest of the team there. Thanks for the blingin' gold foil! I hope to meet all of you in person some day soon, so we can settle once and for all where the 'rug' in 'rugby' comes from.

In my own life I'm fortunate to be surrounded by wonderful writers who have helped me immeasurably. Purgatory, Hellions, the Pit, the Fiction Writers Co-op, and of course, the Writing Wombats — all of you have been an unfailing source of cheer and support. Special thanks go out to beta readers Sherrie Super, Clovia Shaw, Sue Layborne, Jenn Nelson, Judi Fennell, Steve Prosapio, Christy Gerhart, Carol Galante and Gretchen McNeil. Other writers in my life whose support, e-mails and tweets have helped me on many a late night include Jenny Brown, Denise Dumars, Toni Dwiggins, David

Fitzgerald, Jennifer Hillier, Jennifer Hubbard, Elizabeth Loupas, Jan O'Hara, Pat Shaw, and Robin Spano.

Other friends and associates who have enriched my life, bought me booze and generally made me happy to be around, including: John Amussen and Andrea Bailey, Maryelizabeth Hart, Ben Lucas, Billy Brackenridge, Bill Galante, Richard Burger, Lisa Gollin, John Clair, Tess Amato, Jordan Foster, Ebbins Harris, Tommaso Fiacchino, Tony Mandracchia, Todd Tatum, Sarah McCarry, Jim Bickhart, Anne Fishbein, Vivian Archer and Joe Touch. I hope I haven't forgotten anyone, though I'm sure that I have. I would be nowhere without my friends and family, and I'm grateful every day that all of you are in my life.

The wonderful folks in Puerto Vallarta who helped me with research and generally made me feel welcome, including: Tom Williams, Chuchi TresPesos, Heidi Di, Katherine Hardin, Maureen Power Marugan, Christine Vincent, Doug Danielson and the PV Writers group.

I owe special thanks to: Brian Thomas, for house-sitting and making sure the felines were fed and happy. Mimi Freedman and Jon Hofferman, my Buffy night companions and videographers. Dana Fredsti and Bryn Greenwood, for their multiple reads, editorial assistance, and in Bryn's case, her ability to 'literary it up' when I was panicking about creating readers guides.

I'm saving the most important thanks for last.

There are two people who deserve special kudos: Pilar Perez, who introduced me to the city of Puerto Vallarta and without whose friendship this book never would have been written. And Nathan Bransford, my former agent, who would not let me get away with a single flabby sentence or lazy plot point. It's a working relationship that I will always treasure.

Finally, I would be remiss if I did not make this disclaimer: Puerto Vallarta is a beautiful, culturally vibrant city, with great restaurants, beaches and scenery, and I would not hesitate to vacation there any time. My main character's fictional bad luck should not be taken as a disincentive to visit this wonderful place.

We do hope that you have enjoyed reading this large print book.

Did you know that all of our titles are available for purchase?

We publish a wide range of high quality large print books including:
Romances, Mysteries, Classics
General Fiction
Non Fiction and Westerns

Special interest titles available in large print are:
The Little Oxford Dictionary
Music Book
Song Book
Hymn Book
Service Book

Also available from us courtesy of Oxford University Press:
Young Readers' Dictionary
(large print edition)
Young Readers' Thesaurus
(large print edition)

For further information or a free brochure, please contact us at:
Ulverscroft Large Print Books Ltd.,
The Green, Bradgate Road, Anstey,
Leicester, LE7 7FU, England.
Tel: (00 44) 0116 236 4325
Fax: (00 44) 0116 234 0205

Other titles published by
The House of Ulverscroft:

BLOOD LOSS

Alex Barclay

When a teenage girl is beaten and raped, in
the grounds of a derelict asylum, FBI agent
Ren Bryce is called in to assist. But she is
soon diverted to a missing persons case when
an eleven-year-old girl and her teenage
babysitter vanish without a trace from their
hotel room. Faced with conflicting evidence
and inconsistent witnesses, Ren works obses-
sively to unravel the dark family secrets at the
heart of the case, before it's too late . . .
Determined to uncover the truth, Ren's
behaviour becomes increasingly reckless.
Putting her own safety at risk, she enters a
world where innocent lives are ruined for
profit . . . and kidnap, rape and murder are
all part of the deal.

CROSSBONES YARD

Kate Rhodes

Ray and Marie Benson killed thirteen women before they were caught, tried and imprisoned. Five of their victims were never found. Six years later, psychologist Alice Quentin discovers a woman's body on the waste ground at Crossbones Yard. The wounds are horrifyingly similar to the Bensons' signature style. But who would want to copy their crimes? When Alice is called in to consult, her first instinct is to say no. She wants to focus on treating her patients, not analysing the mind of a murderer. But the body at Crossbones Yard is just the start, and the killer may already be closer than Alice knows.

STRANDED

Emily Barr

When her marriage breaks down, Esther Lomax needs to get away and hopes that Malaysia's unspoilt shores will provide some space and time alone. Sure enough, each day of her holiday finds Esther beginning to unwind and feel ready to face single motherhood. However, a day's boat trip takes a desperate turn when Esther and six other holidaymakers are deposited on an uninhabited island. Their guide, who had promised to pick them up in an hour's time, fails to return and the dreadful reality of the situation hits the group. With no means of getting back to the mainland and knowing nothing about each other, tensions erupt — and time is running out. Esther must ask herself the ultimate question: will she leave the island alive?

THE VANISHING POINT

Val McDermid

Stephanie Harker is travelling through the security gates at O'Hare airport, on her way to an idyllic holiday. Five-year-old Jimmy goes through the metal detector first. But then, stuck on the other side of security, she watches in panic and disbelief as a uniformed agent leads her boy away. The authorities, unaware of Jimmy's existence, become alerted by Stephanie's erratic behaviour. She finds herself brutally wrestled to the ground, and restrained — before she can finally inform them what has happened . . . and Jimmy is long gone. However, as Stephanie tells her story to the FBI, it's evident that this seemingly normal family is not what it seems. What is Jimmy's background? Why would someone abduct him? And, with time running out, how can Stephanie get him back?

ASSASSIN

Duncan Falconer

In Afghanistan, elite operative John Stratton leads a raid on a remote compound, leaving no survivors. Days later, in London, Stratton is contacted by an old friend in military intelligence with a curious message about being hunted by an assassin. When the officer vanishes, Stratton is drawn into a desperate race to secure a missing nuclear warhead that has been stolen from the Pakistan military. Against an unknown enemy, he begins a heart-stopping search for the bomb that will take him from a Taliban hideout, just a few miles outside Bagram Air Base, to the crowded streets of Manhattan.

LIVE BY NIGHT

Dennis Lehane

From small-time thief in 1920s Boston to one of America's most feared and respected gangsters, Joe Coughlin's rise to power is an epic journey beset by violence, double-crossing, drama and pain. And it is a journey into the soul of prohibition-era America . . .